FATAL THRONE

FATAL THRONE

THE WIVES OF HENRY VIII TELL ALL

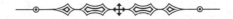

M. T. Anderson, Jennifer Donnelly,
Candace Fleming, Stephanie Hemphill,
Deborah Hopkinson, Linda Sue Park,
Lisa Ann Sandell

schwartz & wade books · new york

Text copyright © 2018 by M. T. Anderson, Jennifer Donnelly, Candace Fleming,
Stephanie Hemphill, Deborah Hopkinson, Linda Sue Park, Lisa Ann Sandell
Jacket art copyright © 2018 by Anna & Elena Balbusso
Interior illustrations © 2018 Jessica Roux

Visit us on the Web! GetUnderlined.com

Educators and librarians, for a variety of teaching tools, visit us at
RHTeachersLibrarians.com

Library of Congress Cataloging-in-Publication Data
Names: Anderson, M. T., author. | Donnelly, Jennifer, author. |
Fleming, Candace, author. | Hemphill, Stephanie, author. |
Hopkinson, Deborah, author. | Park, Linda Sue, author. | Sandell, Lisa Ann, author.
Title: Fatal throne : the wives of Henry VIII tell all / M. T. Anderson, Jennifer Donnelly,
Candace Fleming, Stephanie Hemphill, Deborah Hopkinson, Linda Sue Park, Lisa Ann Sandell.
Description: First edition. | New York : Schwartz & Wade Books, [2018] |
Summary: Seven award-winning young adult authors illuminate the lives of
Britain's King Henry VIII and his six wives from different viewpoints.
Identifiers: LCCN 2017024872 (print) | LCCN 2017038961 (ebook) |
ISBN 978-1-5247-1621-9 (ebook) | ISBN 978-1-5247-1619-6 (hardcover) |
ISBN 978-1-5247-1620-2 (library binding) | ISBN 978-0-525-64448-4 (intl. tr. pbk.)
Subjects: | CYAC: Henry VIII, King of England, 1491–1547—Fiction. |
Kings, queens, rulers, etc.—Fiction. | Courts and courtiers—Fiction. |
Great Britain—History—Henry VIII, 1509–1547—Fiction.
Classification: LCC PZ7.A54395 (ebook) | LCC PZ7.A54395 Fat 2018 (print) |
DDC [Fic]—dc23

The text of this book is set in 12.7-point Adobe Jenson Pro.
Interior design by Stephanie Moss

Printed in the United States of America
2 4 6 8 10 9 7 5 3 1
First Edition

CONTENTS

BEFORE YOU BEGIN

This book is about the six queens of Henry VIII.

We know much about Henry. In the centuries since his death, hundreds of books have been written about him.

Intelligent, charismatic, and handsome, the young Tudor king was loved and admired. He was brave, artistic, and athletic. He could debate theology, discourse on astronomy and medicine, compose music, joust, play tennis, and dance—all with grace and ease.

Henry ruled England from 1509 to 1547, at a time when his country was still emerging from the shadows of the late Middle Ages. Life was hard. Most people didn't live to see forty due to disease and the perils of childbirth. Women had few rights. Education was only for the privileged few; most of Henry's subjects could not read or write.

When Henry took the throne, the Renaissance had been flourishing in Europe for over a century, but England was only beginning to embrace its humanist ideals. Bold advances had been made in science and technology by thinkers such as Copernicus and da Vinci. Painters like Raphael and Titian, and writers like Dante, had introduced a new realism into the arts. Theologians such as Erasmus and Martin Luther were calling for reforms to the excesses of the Catholic Church, and Gutenberg's printing press was speeding the dissemination of their radical ideas.

Little would anyone have guessed in 1509 that Henry—a new, untested king—would eventually use those ideas to break with the past and set England on a course toward seismic political, economic, and social change.

Every king, no matter how powerful, faces threats to his rule, and Henry was no exception. He needed healthy, vigorous sons to strengthen his hold on the throne, but his first wife could not produce them. So he decided to get rid of her. The Pope, head of the Catholic Church, did not like that, so Henry got rid of him, too, and thrust Catholic England headlong into the Protestant Reformation.

We know much about Henry . . . but what of that discarded wife? And the five who followed her?

Too often, the six queens are seen only in their relationship to a forceful, mercurial king. Katharine of Aragon is the old battle-axe; Anne Boleyn, the seductress. Jane Seymour is the good wife; Anna of Cleves, the ugly frump. Catherine Howard is the giddy bubblehead; Kateryn Parr, the stoical matron.

But these women had lives of their own. They had dreams and hopes. Ideas. Opinions. Ambitions. They were fighters. Thinkers. Politicians. Strategists. They led troops into battle and hunted on horseback. They read, danced, intrigued, and sewed. They had children they loved. Pets they adored. They gave money to the poor and supported artists and scholars. They ate peacocks and swans, wore pearls in their hair and diamonds on their sleeves.

They defied expectations—Henry's, and our own.

My fellow writers and I have spent days, weeks, and months with their ghosts.

We've pored over books and essays. We've dug through papers and proclamations, read writs and acts, diaries and depositions.

We've stared at their portraits, trying to decipher their souls from their expressions. We've stood in the rooms they stood in. Ate in. Loved, argued, danced, and died in. We've followed them down paths they trod, gazed at the hills, valleys, and rivers they knew.

We've come to know the ghosts. We've asked them many questions.

And they've deigned to answer.

This book holds their stories.

The ghosts, in turn, forever hold pieces of our hearts.

A NOTE ABOUT SPELLING:

Several of the Tudor queens in this book have the same names. To avoid confusion, we have chosen alternate spellings in order to easily differentiate each queen from the others—as with Katharine of Aragon, Catherine Howard, and Kateryn Parr.

FATAL
THRONE

KATHARINE OF ARAGON

"Humble and Loyal"

24 JULY 1527

◇·◇

The world is still dark beyond my window, but I can make out the tall figure of my husband, King Henry VIII of England, in the stable yard below. Beside him stands his lover, the torchlight glowing on her smooth, young skin. They are readying to ride out. Just the two of them. Together.

I watch as he helps her up into her saddle, lifts her easily, holds her. For a moment, he cradles her little leather boot in his hand, caressing it tenderly, before making sure it is safe in the stirrup. My breath snags.

She laughs playfully, flirting, her eyes never leaving his as she places a hand on his upturned face.

I sink into a chair. "Madre de Dios, ayudadame," I whisper. Mother of God, help me.

My lady Maud Parr comes into the room. She looks startled to see me. "Your Grace, what are you doing up so early?" she asks.

"Sleep is impossible." I pick up my sewing, a shirt I am embroidering for Henry.

Maud sits across from me. "I must tell you something," she says.

I try very hard to listen. But the memory of Henry laughing with Anne, of him holding her in his arms, blots out everything else.

"Your Grace?" Maud says.

I blink. "Please, begin again."

I slip my hands inside the sleeves of my husband's shirt as she gathers herself to tell me about the letter Cardinal Wolsey has sent to His Holiness in Rome. In it the cardinal claims I was not a virgin when I married Henry. That I made love with his brother, Prince Arthur, when he was my husband, and that I lied about it. That I am lying about it still. That because of my treachery, my marriage to Henry is not a true union.

The cardinal is appealing to the Pope to declare Henry's and my eighteen years together illegal. He is entreating the Pope to grant the King permission to marry again.

Maud pauses before telling me the rest.

Perhaps, she wonders, the cardinal felt he needed to make a stronger case against me, because in the same letter he accuses me of being a sex-crazed woman who lured Henry into a forbidden marriage to satisfy my carnal pleasures.

Me!

And then—¡por Dios!—the cardinal tells His Holiness that my husband finds me too repulsive to sleep with because my sex organs are diseased. He says Henry has vowed never to use my body again; that it is too dangerous to his royal person; that lying with me will make the King sick.

I push the shirt's long sleeves up my arms and rub my face against its fine linen. Cardinal Wolsey is the King's closest advisor. He cannot have written such lies without my husband's consent.

How can Henry hate me so?

I remember our wedding night, the feel of his hands on my trembling skin; the hot, stinging pain of our first loving; the blissful relief of lying in his strong, steady arms, a true wife at last.

I pull my hands free of the shirt and lay it across my lap. I know Henry better than anyone else, certainly better than Anne Boleyn, for I have known him as a boy and a man; as a brother and a husband. Our destinies have been entwined almost since birth.

"I was betrothed in marriage to the Prince of Wales when I was but a child of three," I say.

"Indeed?" replies Maud.

I nod. "As Princess of Spain, I was a flesh-and-blood treaty, a breathing alliance between our two countries. And when I was fifteen I sailed to England to become his wife, and the future Queen."

Maud gets up and pours us both a small cup of wine. "I would have liked to have known you then, Your Grace."

"Oh, I was so young, and so sorry to leave my mother and my home.

But it was God's will that I go. I had unshakable confidence in Him—that He had favoured me and destined me for the greatest of things. I had no doubt that I would carry out my sacred obligation to fill the royal nursery with babies, most especially boys—heirs for the Tudor line." I pause. "It was la voluntad de Dios, *the will of God, you see."*

Maud nods with sympathy.

"But now the King has decided to rid himself of me. What can I do to stop him? Henry always gets what he wants. He takes it as his divine right."

I cover my eyes with my hand. "Oh, Maud, after all these years of marriage, is it truly God's will that it now be over?"

It is a question without answer.

In silence we drink our wine as the sun creeps slowly in through the windows, and my life unwinds before me like a spool of embroidery thread.

NOVEMBER 1501

I prayed to the Holy Mother for courage: "*Santa Madre, dadme coraje.*" Had I not prepared for this moment all my life? And yet, when my friend and lady-in-waiting María de Salinas left me standing alone in my wedding gown in the great hall of the Bishop's Palace, I felt like weeping.

Stop this! I told myself. Such behaviour will not do. A princess must preserve the dignity of her rank no matter what the cost. She must appear calm, with the peaceful composure of Christ Himself. Biting my trembling lip, I recalled my mother's advice: "Keep your chin up and smile, and no one will know you feel differently."

But, oh, it was so difficult! My new home, England, was such a strange place. I neither spoke the language nor understood the customs. I knew no one, not even *la familia* I was now part of—King

Henry VII, Queen Elizabeth, and their children, Arthur, Margaret, Henry, and Mary. I had been here but a fortnight and had met them but once, to finalize the details of my wedding.

My wedding! In just minutes, I would become the wife of a boy I barely knew: Prince Arthur, a thin, delicate fifteen-year-old who coughed often and tired easily. And who would one day be King.

I crossed myself and sent up a silent prayer. "*Santa Madre*, favour our marriage that we may fulfil your sacred purpose and—"

A boy's voice broke into my holy petitions. "I have arrived, Princess!" It was Arthur's younger brother, Prince Henry, come to escort me across the walkway into *la catedral*.

When he saw me, his mouth fell open with surprise.

I was dressed in the Spanish style, in layers of white satin that billowed out over the wide hoops beneath my skirt. On my head I wore a jewelled coronet from which an intricate lace veil edged in pearls and precious stones cascaded to my waist.

"You look pretty," Henry said in Latin, the one language we both understood.

Unlike his brother, the ten-year-old Henry had the appearance of a boy who embraced life. His handsome face was round and pink-cheeked, his hair gleamed reddish gold, and his blue eyes sparked with wit and mischief. Although he was six years my junior, the Prince stood as tall as I, and radiated life in a way Arthur did not.

I bowed my head at his compliment. "I am glad you think so."

"It makes no difference if I think you're pretty," he retorted. "You are meant to please Arthur." He looked suddenly sullen. "It is *his* wedding day."

"Someday you will have a wedding, too."

"I shan't have one as magnificent as this, with feasts and tourneys and pageants." He pouted. "I am only a second son."

"You are still a prince," I reminded him.

He said something in English before catching himself. "Will we always have to speak to you in Latin?"

I shook my head. "Already, I am learning my new language." I recited in stumbling English, "Good day . . . please . . . thank you."

He made a face. "That is not very good." He patted his velvet doublet. "Now, *I* am very clever at languages, much more clever than Arthur. I read French and Latin and English, and I am starting Greek. I am very musical, too—"

Trumpets blared.

Henry blinked as if he had forgotten our purpose. Then he offered his arm. "It is time."

We stepped from the *palacio.*

At the sight of us, a great roaring cheer from the crowds in the streets rose into the misty air.

"Huzzah for our Princess! Huzzah for our Prince Harry!"

Henry puffed out his chest.

But I suddenly felt weak. Clutching his arm tighter, and glad of its strength, I moved with him towards the cathedral. *Smile,* I told myself. *Keep your chin up and smile.*

The great church was packed, every possible space taken. People stood in the rood lofts and vaults; they perched on the wide sills beneath the windows; they pressed shoulder-to-shoulder against the tapestry-hung stone walls. Henry and I mounted the steps to the raised wooden walkway the King had ordered built along the entire length of the nave so that all might behold the marriage. As we slowly advanced, the congregation gaped and whispered. Before us an even higher platform had been built at the altar. Upon it stood eighteen robed and mitred bishops and abbots—the greatest men of the Church, come from all corners of the Tudor kingdom to sanctify this union between Spain and England.

Arthur waited there, watching us draw near. Reluctantly, Prince

Henry stepped back as his brother reached out and took my hand in his ice-cold one. His skin, in contrast with the white silk of his wedding suit, looked green-tinged, and a sheen of sweat glistened on his forehead.

We turned to face the altar. Prayers were intoned and blessings bestowed. Solemn vows were made.

"Wilt thou, Katharine, have this man to be thy wedded husband, to live together according to God's law in the holy estate of matrimony?"

"*Sí, acepto,*" I said. "I will."

Then Arthur slipped the heavy emerald ring onto my finger and I turned my mouth up for our first kiss.

His lips, like his hands, were frozen.

Church bells rang out.

We were *marido y mujer.* Man and wife.

We were alone. In the dark. In bed.

For the second time that day, I prayed to the Holy Mother for courage. "*Por favor, Santa Madre.*"

I knew what to do. My married sisters had whispered about it. Giggled. Isabella claimed it hurt no worse than twisting an ankle. And Juana declared it *paraso,* although how such an awkward and embarrassing act could be Paradise was beyond my understanding.

I looked at Arthur. He lay stiffly against the pillows, his arms pressed against his sides so as not to touch me. With his pale skin, he reminded me of the wax dolls I had played with as a child. Only moments ago, we had been publicly tucked into our marriage bed, our guests staring at the sight of us in our nightclothes. My skin still burned from the way in which Prince Henry's eyes—bright from too much wine—had raked over my bare arms and neck. The priests had said blessings over us and prayed for us to be "fruitful." Then Arthur and I were left alone. In the dark. In bed.

He coughed and turned to me. "I am not sure how to begin."

I closed my eyes in silent prayer.

Then, summoning my courage, I moved over to Arthur's side of the bed and boldly placed my hand on his chest. I could feel the sharp edges of his breastbone beneath his nightshirt, and the pounding of his heart.

"You may kiss me," I said.

His cold lips touched my cheek.

I forced a smile.

Encouraged, he pecked at my chin, my ear, my bare neck.

I tugged my nightgown upwards.

With a grunt of effort, Arthur rolled on top of me. He lay there, unmoving.

No, I thought, this was not the act Isabella had described—nor the one Juana had giggled about.

Then Arthur coughed. And coughed again. Wheezing, gasping for breath, he jerked upright. A paroxysm seized him. His shoulders heaved and a bright spot of blood dribbled down his chin. As I watched, another spot trembled on his lower lip for the briefest of moments before dropping onto my breast. Then he fell back onto his pillows.

I lay in the darkness and listened to his rasping breath. Twelve years of betrothal. The long journey to a strange country. Marriage to a boy I did not know. All had been for a single purpose, to join the royal blood of Spain and England as *Dios* intended. I could only accomplish this by bearing sons, and yet . . .

This is but one night, I reminded myself. *There will be hundreds, thousands more. There is plenty of time for me to fulfil my destiny.*

APRIL 1502

◇·◇

The priest lowered his head and prayed. "Heavenly Father, we humbly beseech Thee to have mercy on the soul of Thy servant Arthur, who hast on this second day of April departed this world. Take him, Lord, into Thy keeping."

"*Amen*," I said.

Shivering, I pulled my furs tighter around me. It was forever cold at Ludlow Castle, especially here in the chapel where Arthur's body lay upon the bier. Just weeks after our wedding, the King had commanded that we set off from London to distant, frozen Wales. *Por Dios*, but Ludlow Castle was a damp and draughty place. Arthur's weak lungs proved no match for the cold winds that buffeted the heavy, grey towers, or the foul rain that seeped in under the wooden doors.

I looked down at the shrouded body. No remedies—no leeches, nor oils, nor even the charred heart of a sparrow placed upon his chest—had kept my husband from taking his last, wheezing breath.

My husband, who had not been a true husband.

Although we had lived together for six months, I had spent but five nights in Arthur's bed. Each of those times, I had waited, hopeful and expectant. But Arthur never touched me. Instead, he slept fitfully, coughing and sweating despite the castle's winter chill.

I looked again upon my husband's body, and a sob caught in my throat. Yesterday, I had been the Princess of Wales and future Queen of England. Today, I was next to nothing. A dowager princess. A widow to be cast aside and forgotten.

Now young Henry would become Prince of Wales and eventually King.

And his wife, when he married, would be the next Queen of England.

I shook my head, disbelieving. Had I not been raised to be Princess of Wales and then Queen of England? It was my destiny. God's promise. But how could I fulfil that destiny if Arthur was no more?

Dropping to my knees, I stretched forwards and pressed my forehead to the cold stone floor. "*Santo Padre*, if You are testing me, then see! I prostrate myself before You. I beg for Your benevolence. I beg for Your blessing. I beg that Your will . . . and mine . . . be done."

AUGUST 1502

My mother sent instructions to Durham House—the manor to which I had been removed, isolated from court, after Arthur died. My ladies, she commanded, should begin packing immediately. A fleet of Spanish ships was on its way back from Flanders. It would pick me up at an English port. I was to be ready to board as soon as they dropped anchor.

I crumpled her letter. I knew God required that I resign myself and accept this new position in life He had given me. But, *O Dios*, was I truly to go home to Spain and live out my days in quiet widowhood?

And then . . . *un milagro*, a miracle, like the coming of spring after a cold, grey winter.

Arthur and Henry's father, the King of England, desired me to stay in his country. He desired a new marriage and a revived alliance with Spain. He desired, after all, the mingling of Aragon and Tudor blood.

No matter that Prince Henry was a child of eleven, all boasting and boyishness.

No matter that I was a sixteen-year-old woman, ripe for love.

You shall remain where you are, read my mother's next missive, *and you shall be married to the prince three years hence, when he is fourteen.*

"But how can this be?" asked my lady Agnes de Vanegas. We were walking in the garden when I told her the news. Her brow wrinkled. "It is a sin for a man to marry his brother's wife. *La Biblia* says so."

María leaned forwards, wearing a knowing look. "Not if the wife was not truly a wife. Not if she remained untouched."

Agnes covered her mouth in surprise.

"Already, His Holiness in Rome has granted us a dispensation," I told them.

At mention of the Pope, my ladies crossed themselves. As the infallible head of the Roman Catholic Church—the one true faith—only the Pope can dispense with any moral or legal obstacles to the *sacramento del matrimonio,* the sacrament of marriage. That is because he is God's mouthpiece on earth. The Lord speaks directly into his ear and the words come unchanged from his lips. If the Pope said Henry and I could marry, it was because God had said so. The Pope's dispensation made our union legal.

Legal beyond all question.

I shivered at the working of *Dios* in my life. He had whispered my name in the Pope's ear. He had made right what was wrong. Could I doubt any longer that I was indeed favoured by Him? Blessed by Him? Chosen by Him for the greatest of things?

I would once again be the Princess of Wales.

And the future Queen of England.

¡Un milagro!

SEPTEMBER 1502–APRIL 1509

It was weary work, the waiting. I reminded myself that I must remain constant and uncomplaining. But there were times when my patience faltered. *Dios, ¿cuánto más?* I asked. How much longer, Lord?

Seven years.

That was how long I waited while my closefisted father and

Henry's miserly one negotiated and renegotiated the terms of the marriage treaty. Blustering. Quibbling. Delaying. Year after year. They reached nothing but stalemate.

Isolated at Durham House, I spent much time in prayer.

"*Santa Madre*, I am growing older. I beg you to hasten my marriage."

"*Santa Madre*, forgive my impatience, but here I remain, twenty-three years old and still unwed."

"*Santa Madre*, I beg you. *Por favor*. Soften the old King's heart so that he allows Prince Henry to marry even without a signed treaty."

The King's heart did not soften. But on a rainy April morning, it stopped beating. The old Tudor King was dead. Prince Henry took the throne.

When I heard the news, I had my ladies wash my hair in water and wood ash, and launder my yellow damask gown.

Henry, I knew, would soon arrive.

MAY 1509

I was walking alone by the river, my head bowed in thought, when his page ran ahead to announce him.

"His Grace, King Henry."

And there he was, bounding towards me across the close-scythed grass, grinning like a little boy bursting with a secret. Yet he looked anything but boyish. His shapely calves bulged in their silk hose, and his shoulders were so broad they strained the seams of his doublet. A head taller than the rest of his men, he appeared older than his almost eighteen years.

"Kate!" he shouted.

I sank to the grass in a deep curtsey. "Your Grace, I am so sorry for the loss of—"

"Yes, yes." He waved aside my sympathy, and lifted me up. "Let us not stand on formality, dear Kate. Have we not known each other these many years?"

I knew not what to say. Indeed, I had not seen nor heard from Henry during most of my isolation. Still, gossip had found its way to Durham House even if the Prince had not. Thus I knew of his charm and wit, of his skill at jousting and tennis, his talent for playing and songwriting.

Henry took my hand in his. "Now that Father is dead, nobody shall tell me what to do. I am King. I make my own decisions."

Did I detect a shadow of that sullen boy who had escorted me to the cathedral on the day of my wedding to Arthur?

"I am sure your decisions are very wise, Your Grace," I replied.

"They *are* wise," he agreed. "And in regard to a wife, I have decided we shall be married immediately."

I could not speak for the joy that rose up inside me. Could it be at last? I sent up a prayer of gratitude. *Gracias, Santa Madre.*

"I have loved you in silence and from a distance all this time," he went on, "adored you from the moment we met." He twirled me around. "Rejoice, Kate! You will be Queen of England."

Already, I had decided upon my Queen's motto: "Humble and Loyal." Soon workmen would emblazon those words throughout the King's many residences, along with my personal badge, the pomegranate, the symbol of fertility.

But I told none of this to Henry. Rather, I blushed, knowing my eyes declared my unmistakable delight. I looked up into his handsome face. "You have made me very happy."

"And you shall make me happy, too," he replied. "You shall give me sons."

JUNE 1509

◇·◇

¡Gloria a Dios!

After years of waiting and praying, I was suddenly lifted up on the wings of cherubim and whisked to the palace at Greenwich, where Henry wedded me quickly and privately on a summer morning fragrant with roses.

That same evening he came to me long before it was dark. Grinning, eyes hungry, he wrapped me in his strong arms and tumbled me onto the bed. He buried his nose in my long hair.

"Henry!" His breath tickled my skin.

"I cannot stop myself," he said. "You smell heavenly, like lemons."

From the pocket of his robe he drew forth a strand of exquisite black pearls.

"A wedding gift," he said, "handed down through centuries of queens."

I shivered as he wound it about my neck. The pearls' smoothness felt delicious against my skin.

But not as delicious as Henry's kisses.

He moved closer, more slowly and sweetly now, until we lay together, our arms and legs intertwined.

"There is nothing to fear, my Kate," he said, running his lips along the lobe of my ear. "I am here. . . . I am your King . . . to love you forevermore."

Those kisses! Those caresses! As his hands and lips moved across my skin, I relaxed.

"*Paraso*," I whispered afterwards as I lay in the circle of his arms. My sister Juana had been right. I was a true wife at last. And it was Paradise.

Henry stroked my cheek. "I do love you, my darling Kate."

"And I you, Henry."

And I realized, to my surprise, that the words were true.

A fortnight later, Henry and I processed along a carpet of striped cloth beneath a golden canopy to Westminster Abbey. We walked slowly, solemnly, so that the cheering crowds might glimpse us. Oh, but we dazzled that day, Henry in his clothes of velvet and ermine, me in my purple velvet gown ablaze with jewels and my face glowing with joy.

It was our coronation day.

The Archbishop of Canterbury crowned Henry first, before the altar.

Then it was my turn. Bowing my head, I received the holy oil upon my forehead and upon my breast. The coronation ring was put upon my finger and *la corona* upon my head. I took the rod and sceptre in my hands, took my place upon my throne.

My heart swelled. At last I was a queen, a sacred and anointed queen, placed higher than mere mortals, chosen for His special blessings and granted divine grace. I had been tested, but I had prevailed. My destiny had at last been revealed.

This was God's plan for me. I doubted it not.

24 JULY 1527

The room is suffused with sunlight. But even its brightness cannot chase the memories back into their holes. I find myself remembering those first, carefree months with Henry. Oh, such joy! Our days were a whirl of feasting, dancing, masqueing, and hunting. And our nights . . . Heat spreads up my neck as I recall our eagerness for each other; the unexpected pleasures we found together.

I shake my head. "¡Idiota!" I cry. Pushing up from my chair, I throw Henry's unfinished shirt to the floor in devastating judgement upon myself. What's done is done.

But I cannot stop the memories.

JANUARY 1511

I rested against the pillows in the royal bed, exhausted but exultant. God had smiled on my marriage. Blessed me. Enabled me to fulfil my most sacred duty. In my arms lay my son. And he was perfection.

I traced the curve of his tiny ears with my finger, marvelled at the sweep of his eyelashes against his cheeks. He made a smacking sound with his sweet rosebud mouth. *Ay, mi precioso niño.* I would have to hand him to the wet nurse for his feeding soon. But not just yet. I wanted to hold him a moment longer.

Henry pushed his way impatiently into my bedchamber, disobeying the rules of confinement, and peered down at the swaddled infant in my arms. "God be praised, I have a son!" he crowed. His eyes blazed with triumph. "Do you not think he looks like me, Kate?"

"He does indeed have your red hair and blue eyes," I agreed. I did not remind him that I, too, had this colouring. I understood that this was the *King's* son.

"They are cheering you in the street," said Henry. "They cry, 'Long live Queen Katharine.' The people have taken you to their hearts."

I tore my eyes from my baby to smile at my husband. "As I have them," I replied.

"Of course, they cheer me as well," added Henry quickly. He shouted, "'Long live the noble King Henry!'"

The babe started and let out a cry.

Looking momentarily like a naughty child, Henry lowered his voice. Still, it trilled with excitement. "The people have already taken to calling the babe Prince Henry," he boasted. "They will accept no other name."

He waited for my agreement.

"Then it must be so," I said. "For there is no finer name."

"The people's wish is granted," he declared. "He shall be called after me—Henry the Ninth."

Henry began pacing around the room. "You must hurry and get well so you can be at my side for the grand celebrations I intend to hold in honour of our son's birth. There shall be feasts and dancing and a tournament—the greatest tournament England has ever seen. Hurry and heal, my dear Kate, so we may move on to Westminster and the rejoicings can begin."

"Nothing would bring me greater happiness," I replied. "But mustn't I stay with the Prince? He is still too delicate to attend such events."

Henry frowned. "The Prince shall stay behind, of course."

I hugged my baby closer. "We cannot leave him. He is too little. And he needs his mother."

"Well, I need my Queen," declared Henry. "Our subjects must see us, King and Queen in celebration together."

"But—"

Henry stamped his foot. His sudden vehemence startled me. "I will remind you that your duty—one of your *only* duties—is to be at my side for all state and court ceremonies. Besides . . ." He brightened. "How can there be a celebration in your honour if you are not there?"

I tried again. "My lord, I beg you to allow me to stay with our son. After our earlier sorrow, I—"

He held up his hand for silence. Henry did not want to be reminded of that other babe. The babe I had carried this time last year. The babe I had so miserably failed to bring living into this world.

"Let us not dwell upon unpleasantness, Kate," he commanded. "Not at this sweet moment. Today, you have at last given me the greatest of gifts. And in gratitude, I shall give you the greatest of celebrations." He smiled then. "Worry not, sweetheart. Our Prince will be left in the hands of the realm's finest nurses."

Just then my son cried lustily for his feeding. Striding back to the bed, Henry plucked him from my arms and handed him to the wet nurse, who stood in attendance beside the cradle.

"There, there, sweet princeling," the nurse cooed. She unlaced the bodice of her gown. "We shall have your tummy full in no time."

Henry turned to me. "You see? The finest of care."

Heaven help me, but I could not summon a smile.

FEBRUARY 1511

"Let us dance," said Henry. He held out his hand.

I was too tired to take it. Still weak from the birth, I had been whisked off to Westminster for weeks of celebratory jousts and feasts. No matter that I needed a bit more time to recover. Henry was restless and impatient. He longed to make merry.

Sadness, too, sapped my strength. I missed my little boy. It had taken courage to kiss him good-bye; to lay him in the arms of his lady nurse and walk away. I longed for him. Every moment of every day. Being separated from him was agony.

I dared not admit any of this to Henry. Not my weariness, nor my sadness. He would have been hurt if I had, and I did not want to cheat him of his joy. "I would rather watch *you* dance, my love," I said now. "Are you not the finest dancer at court?"

My answer pleased him. In a trice he was on the floor, whirling and capering and glancing time and again in my direction. Did I see him? Was I admiring him?

I could not help but smile.

Thomas Howard, Earl of Surrey, stepped onto the floor and caught Henry's arm. Henry stopped cavorting as the elderly nobleman whispered in his ear. His face went grey. Without excusing themselves, the two men hastened away.

What, I wondered, could be so urgent as to pull Henry from the festivities?

Within minutes, Surrey returned alone. "Your Grace," he said to me gravely, "the King desires to see you privately."

A sense of foreboding crept through my veins. Rising on legs that suddenly trembled, I crossed the great hall with him. Behind us, the musicians still played. The lords and ladies of the court still skipped and twirled. But it all felt aslant, out of tune.

Henry was waiting for me in the chapel. When I entered, he turned from the altar, tears streaming down his face. "Kate. Oh, Kate!"

I held up my hand. "No. Do not say it. I am not ready."

Henry came to me. He took my arm. "Our little babe," he choked out. Our son. He is dead."

"No."

"They tell me he caught a chill," said Henry, his voice cracking. "His tiny body was not strong enough to fight it."

I shook my head. "No! No! I left him brimming with health. Oh, Henry, I should never have left him. My boy . . . all alone . . . without his mother."

I fell to the floor, overwhelmed with grief. I sobbed and sobbed. *Santa Madre de Dios*, I was drowning in grief. I reached out a hand to Henry.

He did not take it.

I looked up.

His tear-filled eyes were upon me, hard and angry.

Even in my grief, I felt a flicker of fear.

Then it was gone, and Henry's expression softened. Dropping to his knees beside me, he wrapped me in his arms. I clung to him, my fists twisting in the fabric of his tear-soaked shirt.

I do not know how long we sat thus, but at last he spoke. "We are young yet, Kate. There will be more babes. You will see. There will be other sons."

I burst into fresh tears. I did not want other sons.

I wanted my baby.

24 JULY 1527

A verse from the Scriptures comes into my head: Those whom the Lord loves best suffer most.

A sob catches in my throat. I am most certainly one of God's best loved.

"Are you well, Your Grace?" Maud's quiet voice recalls me.

I have a sudden, urgent need for the warm darkness of the palace chapel; for the scent of melted wax and incense. "I shall go and pray," I say.

Maud stands, preparing to follow me.

"I shall go alone."

APRIL 1511

Our marriage turned as cold and dark as the English winter.

Henry withdrew to his apartments.

I withdrew to mine.

There was no comforting each other. We could barely be in the same room together. Henry detested my deep, keening grief. It sent him fleeing from me.

Every day I knelt with my rosary. "Why me, *Dios*? How have I displeased You? Why have You turned Your face from me?"

I knew Christendom was filled with great *milagros*. A statue of the Madonna begins to weep. Communion bread becomes human flesh. The marks of the Crucifixion appear on the wrists and feet of a simple farmer. So why could not my husband and I be blessed with the commonplace miracle of lasting love?

Dios did not enlighten me. I strained my ears, but I could not hear Him. As the weeks passed, I lost all sense of His presence. I lost my confidence in His will, and my joy in His blessing. I felt nothing but despair.

Winter turned to spring. The world thawed and greened. But still I grieved, cold and alone in my rooms.

And then . . . *¡un milagro!*

One morning, God in His grace returned. I knew this by the burning in my breast, the tingling in my limbs. In an instant, understanding found me.

It had pained Him to take my child, grieved Him to leave me alone in my sorrow. But this was not punishment for my sins. Rather, my trials had served His purpose. Like Job, who was left on the ash heap, I had been stripped of all I held dear. By suffering these trials, I had proven my faithfulness and demonstrated my wholehearted love for Him. My endurance had made me worthy.

Now, once again, He spoke my name. He called me to His service. His was a sacred plan, and I was part of it.

I lifted my tearstained face. "Your will be done."

MAY 1511–MAY 1513

Dios revealed His plan slowly, over months and years, through a string of faraway events that seemingly had little to do with my life.

French troops invaded Italy.

The Pope commanded them to leave.

The French refused.

His Holiness put his own papal troops in the field.

And one morning Henry burst into my apartments. "It is stunning news. The French and the Pope are at war!" He grabbed my hand. "Kate, I would ask for your advice."

For a moment I could not catch my breath. I squeezed my eyes shut as my heart rejoiced. *Gloria a Dios,* for His ways are truly wondrous!

The Lord had given me back my husband.

JULY 1527

I push open the chapel door, step into the darkness. No one else is here. Only the candles flickering in their glasses of red crystal provide any light. I move down the aisle, but halfway to the altar I stop. The circular space is so like my childhood chapel in Granada. Why have I never noticed this before?

My mind plays tricks. Suddenly, I am no longer at Greenwich Palace, but back in Spain, a seven-year-old sitting on a camp chair in my mother's army tent. She puts on her breastplate and picks up her sword. My mother is a queen, but she is also a warrior, equal to any man on the battlefield. "We are each of us soldiers for Christ, Catalina," she says, using my Spanish name, "born to fight for our faith and our throne; crusaders, defending our country from heretics. It is a holy war, and we must never falter."

I blink and I am ten, riding beside my battle-weary parents. Blood stains our path. Bodies bloat in the heat of the sun. "The cost of doing God's work is high," says my father. "Still, one must never flinch from bending to it."

I blink again and I am thirteen, holding my head high as I walk with my family up the winding path to the Alhambra. It has taken years of siege, but the fantastical palace with its white marble fountains and lush, fragrant gardens is finally ours. "Remember, Catalina, God pours out His blessings upon those who do His work," says my mother. "Dios es bueno. His abundance is great."

I rub my eyes and am returned to the present. A figure, robed and veiled, rises from behind the lectern. Moving like a mist, it glides along the aisle towards me.

I stumble backwards. "Santa Madre, help me."

MAY 1513

It was natural that Henry should come to me, the daughter of a fighting queen, raised on the battlefield. What did his ministers—those crusty, cautious lords—know about war?

"They claim a war with France will strain the Exchequer and leave England penniless," he told me. "They say our interests are best served by remaining on peaceful terms."

"Louis is an enemy of the Church," I replied, unable to keep my contempt for the French King out of my voice. "A heretic. A man who attacks His Holiness. Only you, Henry, can defeat France. Only you can defend the Pope and the Church." I paused before adding, "It will make you the greatest defender of the faith in all of Christendom."

Henry did not speak for a few seconds, then he cried, "By God, Kate, I will form an army, a great army, and march into Italy at the head of it. I will show those French cowards what Englishmen can do."

An idea formed in my mind.

"With you at the head of it, we are sure to be invincible," I said. "But need you travel all the way to Italy? Might you attack France instead?"

A slow smile spread across Henry's face. "That's it!" he burst out.

"We shall cross the spit of sea that separates us from France, start from Calais, and go on from there. Louis's attention will be diverted from Rome. He will be forced to fight a two-front war." He smacked his fist into his palm. "By Jove, he'll have no choice but to surrender to me."

"It is a brilliant strategy, my love."

"It is, is it not?" he agreed. I knew he was imagining his victorious return, laden with glory, *and* the coveted title "the Christian Monarch" bestowed by the grateful Pope. He whooped. "It will be a triumphant adventure!"

"It will be *una guerra santa*," I added. "A holy war."

We turned to preparations—mustering troops, buying horses, commanding blacksmiths to forge pikes, and ordering armour. One of Henry's churchmen—a heretofore unknown almoner named Thomas Wolsey—proved especially capable of organizing an army.

Thomas Wolsey.

I confess I did not like him. He was too fawning, too *zalamero*, too smooth. Still, I knew he shouldered the burdens of government for my husband, and I was grateful for it. Henry was not a King to toil over state business. He yawned through the Privy Council's meetings and grew impatient with the Lord High Treasurer's balance sheets. "Take care of it, Thomas," he would say. And Wolsey did, freeing Henry to hunt, or play tennis, or compose music on the virginals.

But now Henry had state business that thrilled him. He spent all his days with Wolsey, talking of nothing but weaponry and transport and provisions.

And he spent all his nights with me.

JUNE 1513

I bade farewell to my husband at Dover Castle. It was there on the strand, just before he set sail for France, that he called together his Council.

"I have prayed much over this matter," he told the assembled group, "and have decided upon the person who shall govern the land in my absence." He paused theatrically before turning to me. "Gentlemen of the Council, in my absence Her Grace, Queen Katharine, shall be your ruler."

A cheer rose.

Henry handed me the Great Seal of the Realm. "Take care of our country until I return, Kate," he said.

"You have my solemn oath."

He knelt before me for a blessing then, and I laid my hands upon his head. "Stay safe, my love," I whispered.

I felt no fear as I watched him go aboard his ship. I felt no sadness. I had been transformed! In a twinkling, *Dios* had elevated me above Princess of Wales, above Queen of England. He had raised me up to the very greatest of positions—ruler of all England.

Seated on my throne in my presence chamber, the room where I received the dozens of men who waited about to catch my attention, I read Henry's letters from France.

He was in high spirits as he detailed the excitement his army's arrival in Calais had generated. To celebrate their safe passage, a round of feasts and parades were arranged in his honour by the people of that city. "My new armour is roundly admired," he reported. "And many have declared me more handsome than King Louis."

Later, when his army invaded the town of Thérouanne, he wrote,

"The French cavalry fled before us like terrified mongrels." He added gleefully, "And I got to fire the cannon!"

I frowned. Still such a child, he needed to take his campaign more seriously. Clasping my hands, I sent up a silent prayer. "Deliver King Henry a great victory, *Santo Padre*, one that will make him the greatest monarch in Christendom."

AUGUST–SEPTEMBER 1513

But God did not will that Henry should win a great victory.

He willed that I should.

On a storm-lashed morning, a hundred thousand Scottish troops gathered on the muddy field at Edinburgh. They prepared to swarm across our northern border.

"With the King and his soldiers away, those Scottish rats smell an opportunity to attack!" exclaimed Thomas Howard, one of the few army men who had not gone to France.

"We must stand against them," I said quickly.

"But who will raise an army, Your Grace? Who will command it?"

I rose from my throne. "I will."

Dressed in cloth of gold, I galloped out into the country on a white horse, warning the people of the gathering danger. We needed men to drive back the horde of warring Scots. Who would fight? Who would come to England's aid?

Wherever I went, in towns and villages, the people flocked to see me. They bowed and touched the hem of my gown. They begged for my blessing.

"God smiles upon those who fight for their homes!" I shouted. "Does not English courage surpass all other nations?"

Cheering, they rallied to my banner—farmers and peasants, workers and tradesmen. They had not swords and armour, as did Henry's professional army. Instead, they came with pitchforks and scythes, choppers and billhooks. But their eyes shone with determination and purpose. Truly, they were soldiers of *Jesucristo* all.

"You shall lead some of these men north to attack the Scots at the border," I told Thomas Howard one morning in my presence chamber. I stood before a table spread out with maps. "I shall hold a line farther south."

"But, Your Grace . . . ," he began.

"I am the ruler defending my country," I replied. "I *will* ride out with my army."

This I did. Along the length of the line I galloped, my gold-and-crimson standard bearing my badge, the pomegranate, fluttering above my head so my men could recognize me and know I was with them. As I went, I shouted words to embolden them. "I urge you to victory. God is with you. It is His will that we do battle with the Scots. It is His will . . . and mine . . . that we defeat them!"

A fortnight later, a package from Thomas Howard arrived at my army tent. I opened it. Inside lay the bloodstained coat of King James IV of Scotland.

"The Scottish monarch is killed, his troops crushed at Flodden Field," wrote Howard.

¡Gloria a Dios! England was saved.

I clutched the bloody coat to my breast and danced about the room.

"Your Grace, calm yourself!" cried Maud.

"You must be careful," said María.

But I could not. Was I not the daughter of a warrior queen? I burst into a Spanish battle song remembered from childhood:

Los pendones están en el campo.
El rey debe levantarse de su alegre junta,
Y apartarse de la fiesta a pesar de que el vino se fluye,
Y tomar su espada y su escudo.

Banners are in the field.
The King must rise from his joyous board,
And turn from his feast e'er the wine be poured,
And take up his sword and his shield.

It was a pity the earl had not sent me James's head. What a prize
that would have made for Henry.

I almost laughed at the thought of how proud my husband would
be when he learned of my victory. Had I not guarded our kingdom?
Had I not defeated the Scots? Mine was a victory that would go down
in English history. *¡Santa Madre!* Surely God had never before lifted a
queen to such dizzying heights.

I laid my hand on my slightly rounded belly.

What I had kept secret—even from Henry, for I hoped to surprise him upon his return—was that I was again with child.

All the time I had been planning military strategy and riding out
to my troops, I had been carrying the Tudor heir.

This time I did laugh. I was a queen who could hold a kingdom
and carry a son. It was God's grace after sacrifice.

OCTOBER 1513

Autumn's breath chilled the land. In the garden below my window,
the once-lovely colours withered, and the trees, their branches bare,
stood like corpses.

One evening towards the middle of the month, I took to my bed early. My limbs cramped and I had a nagging ache in my back. Hours later, pain gnawed through my sleep. I pushed back the coverlet. Everything was wet. Wet with my blood.

"¡Por favor, Dios, no, no!" I cried weakly. It was not yet time. It was too soon.

Maud ran for the midwife while my ladies gathered helplessly about my bed.

He came in a rush, my small, frail son who had no life in him, and could not even take his first breath.

The midwife shrouded his limp, white body in a linen cloth. She moved towards the door.

"No," I said. "Give him to me."

My baby. I took in every bit of him—his fluff of golden-red hair, his pointy little chin so like his father's. He had blood on his head and I wiped it off, a motherly instinct to care for him even if he would never know my loving touch.

"Dormid, mi niño," I whispered. Sleep, my boy.

I had saved England for Henry, and lost him his son.

"The Lord gave, and the Lord hath taken away."

24 JULY 1527

It is not a memory.

It is not a trick of my imagination.

It is a woman dressed in a homespun robe of green, a wooden cross hanging from a leather cord around her neck.

"Fear not," she says. Stepping into the candlelight, she pulls back her hood.

She is plain of face, a common girl with sun-freckled skin. And yet . . .

her eyes! They glow with serenity and peace, like those of the saints por-
trayed in the altarpiece behind her. "Gloria a Dios," *I whisper. She can see*
into my soul. I know it.

She moves closer. "I bring you word from God in Heaven. He would
have you know, Catalina, that this is not the end."

She knows my childhood name, uses it with familiarity. I should be
angry at this unbidden intimacy. Instead, I am overcome with an urge to
fall on my knees.

She gazes at me as if she can see my thoughts. "Retiring from your
marriage will not serve His purpose. Did not God place you here at your
coronation? He asks that you live your life in the position that He ap-
pointed."

"How do you know this?"

She looks to the altar, as if seeking permission. Then she nods and
turns back to me. "Once I was but a simple servant-girl. Then one morn-
ing I fell into a deep trance. My master, in hopes I would be cured, carried
me to the church and laid me before the statue of the Blessed Virgin Mary.
For twelve days, I remained thus, neither eating nor drinking, the limbs of
my body stiff as cordwood. Only my lips moved, and from them tumbled
a river of words."

"And what spoke you?" I ask.

"Prophecies," she replies. "Predictions. God has blessed me with His
revelations. I am His messenger. And all that I say comes to pass."

OCTOBER 1513

◇·◇

I stood before the mirror. Despite the bright silk of my gown, I
looked far older than my twenty-seven years. I was pale and my face
was etched with weariness. I should have been abed, should still have
been recovering from the birth—and death—of our son. But Henry

was arriving from France today. He would expect me to be up and about.

I pinched my cheeks to give them a bit of colour. *He cannot be angry with me,* I reassured myself. *He must see that I had no other choice. I had to ride out. I had to rally the troops. Without his kingdom, what would Henry be?*

"Your Grace, the King has come," said Maud.

Forcing a smile, I went downstairs to the great hall to meet him.

"Ah, so here is my wife, the little warrior," he called out from his chair at the head table. He turned to his men. "Pray tell you hear echoes of her great acclaim?"

"Aye, Your Grace," came the reply.

"And all of England knows of *yours*," I said. "Welcome home, my love."

There was no mistaking the resentment I saw in his eyes as I leaned in to kiss him; no misinterpreting the brusque manner in which he helped me to my chair. As he tore into the meal, he was full of stories about towns captured and sieges won. Not once did he mention my victory at Flodden Field. When I rose to retire, he appeared relieved.

So I was surprised when he came to my bedchamber that night. I did not tell him that I was not yet completely healed, nor object when he pushed me onto the bed. There had to be another baby. But *Santa Madre*, I was so exhausted from my last labour. When he lay atop me, I thought my bones would splinter.

Once finished, he rolled to the far side of the bed and said into the darkness, "The child. It is a terrible disappointment for me."

A tear fell down my cheek. "It is a deep sorrow for us both."

He rolled over so he could look me in the eye. "You have been derelict in your most sacred duty, Kate," he hissed. Then he turned his back to me.

MAY 1514

And so my husband lost faith in me. No longer did he say to his ministers, "Let us ask the Queen about that," or "We must show this to Kate." It made no difference that I had won the greatest battle England had ever seen against the Scots.

It was Thomas Wolsey who had his ear now. Able, ambitious Wolsey. Daily his influence over the King grew.

"Wolsey adjusts his beliefs to fit the King's," María reported to me one morning as we walked in the gardens at Greenwich. "He reads correctly what the King wants and adapts to it. Anything the King desires, Wolsey gets for him."

Added Maud, "All can see his power increasing. When first he served at court, Wolsey did the King's bidding by saying, 'His Majesty shall do so and so.' But now he has commenced saying, 'We shall do so and so.'"

María leaned in conspiratorially. "There are many who claim Wolsey will soon be saying, 'I shall do so and so.'"

Santa Madre, where did that leave me?

Placing my hand on my belly, I silently prayed, "Let it be so, *Dios*." In my womb, the babe kicked. "Let it be so."

NOVEMBER 1514

Another child born into death.

Another Prince.

"My God, my God, why hast thou forsaken me?" Like *Jesucristo*, who cried out these words upon the cross, I whispered them as the midwife took my son's tiny body away.

My ladies huddled about my bed.

Por Dios, could I not grieve alone?

I pulled the coverlet over my face. My heart, shattered and sharp-edged, cut from inside.

Santa Madre, ¿por qué? I knew it was a sin to question His unsearchable ways, but I could not understand why He would wrench this babe from my womb. Why would He be so cruel?

Without removing the coverlet, I fumbled for María's hand. I did not want her to see my expression as I said brokenly, "Please, send for the King. I must tell him his baby is dead."

MAY 1515

———◇·◇———

Henry still visited my bed twice a week. But he no longer lingered afterwards. Rather, he performed his duties quickly, and without passion. I knew my body, sagging and shapeless from four pregnancies, no longer delighted him. In his eyes, I served but one purpose now. I was but a vessel, an instrument to produce his heir.

"Stay with me, Henry," I begged one night as he rose from my bed and pulled on his shirt. "Please, stay."

He looked at me with distaste. "I pray God we have conceived a male child this night," he said.

"I pray for nothing else, my husband."

"Yet your prayers go unanswered."

Silence stretched between us.

Henry picked up his robe. "God has turned His face from us," he finally said. "He is punishing us for marrying."

"No, Henry, it is not true."

"The proof lies before us, madam. Almost six years of marriage, sharing a bed, yet God has left us childless."

"We have had children," I argued. "Three children."

"All dead."

"That was God's will, Henry, not His punishment."

He knotted the tie of his robe and pulled his nightcap over his red hair. When finally he spoke, his voice sounded like a spoiled child's. "I should be blessed. I am the King of England. It is not right that I do not have a son." He shook his head. "It is not right."

JANUARY 1516

I could not nap. My back ached, and the great swell of my belly made breathing difficult despite the many pillows propped behind me. Clumsily, I swung my legs over the side of the bed.

"Your Grace?" said my lady Mary Norris.

"I feel like walking," I said.

Mary stood, preparing to go with me.

"I wish to go alone."

The last thing I wanted was to be in the centre of my giggling, gossiping ladies. I felt like an old woman among them.

Outside my apartments, I paused a moment deciding on a direction. It was too cold to stroll in the garden, and I did not want to walk towards the great hall, where I would surely meet people. Perhaps, I thought with sudden longing, Henry was in a generous mood today. Perhaps he would play cards with me. Turning, I moved towards his apartments.

The Gentlemen of the Chamber leapt to their feet and bowed low when I entered. "Your . . . Your Grace," stammered one of the men.

I approached Sir William Compton, who stood like a sentinel outside Henry's bedchamber door. "I would see His Majesty," I said to him.

Compton shook his head. "I am sorry, Your Grace, but the King is not to be disturbed. He is abed."

"Abed? In the afternoon?" Worry seized me. "Is my lord ill?"

I did not wait for an answer. Pushing past Compton, I flung open the door.

My husband lay naked on the great bed of state. And my lady Bessie Blount was with him, head thrown back, her golden hair tumbling about her bare shoulders.

I grasped the doorknob, feeling suddenly dizzy.

Henry turned. Our eyes met.

"Kate . . . ," he began.

I shook my head. What could he possibly say? How could I bear to hear it? I stumbled backwards, head ducked so Henry's men would not see the anguish and humiliation in my eyes. Then, gripping my belly, I heaved myself along the long gallery to my rooms and flung myself onto my bed.

How long had it been going on? Bessie had come into my service not long after Henry's return from France. With stunned clarity I realized she had been his mistress for years. Had I not seen him dancing with her most evenings, and riding out with her most mornings? Had I not seen the way he teased her and wrote her poems?

I had seen it, but I had refused to acknowledge it.

I longed to scream, threaten, pull out Henry's hair. But it was not possible. He was the King of England.

I recalled some advice my mother had given me long ago: "Remember, Catalina, your husband is free to take a hundred mistresses if he so desires. As King, that is his right. But he can take only one wife. No matter what he does, he is always your husband. And you are always his Queen."

"Always his Queen, but no longer his love," I whispered. And muffling my sobs in my pillows, I wept.

FEBRUARY 1516

I clenched my teeth to hold back my shouts of pain. A queen, my mother had taught me, never cries out in childbirth. And so I twisted and strained and gripped my ladies' hands, yet I made not a sound. There came an agonizing rending, followed by a warm rush from between my legs and then . . . *¡Gloria a Dios!* . . . a loud bawling cry.

I sobbed. "He lives?"

"The child is healthy, Your Grace!" exclaimed the midwife. "The child lives."

I wept with happiness. Freely. Openly. Before my ladies and the midwife and the wet nurse. At that glorious moment, I cared not a whit for queenly dignity. My son lived! He was healthy! He lived!

"Give him to me," I begged.

Maud and the midwife exchanged glances.

"*Her*," said Maud. "You have a beautiful little girl, Your Grace."

A girl? No! The babe was supposed to be a boy. A boy to be heir. A boy to return Henry's pleasure in our marriage. A boy to make him love me again.

I wept, but no longer from joy.

What would I tell the King?

Maud placed the babe in my arms. "Daughters are a special gift," she said, speaking from experience. Four years earlier she had been delivered of her own daughter, little Kateryn Parr, to whom I was godmother and who had been named in my honour. "You will see, Your Grace. There is a sacred bond between girls and their mothers."

In my arms, the infant snuffled against my breast, eager to feed. Not immediately gratified, she cried furiously, her face turning red and her little arms waving. I could not help but laugh. She looked so much like Henry.

A sudden happiness filled me.

This child was *un milagro*, the fruit of my prayers.

Yet again, the Lord had poured out His grace upon me.

I rubbed my cheek against my daughter's downy head.

"What will you name her, Your Grace?" asked Maud.

"Mary," I replied without hesitation, "after the Blessed Virgin, our most holy Mother of God, whose own name came from 'Miriam,' meaning 'bitterly wished-for child.'"

Henry took the birth of our daughter better than I expected. "She is healthy. That is what matters," he said, although his smile did not reach his eyes. "And if it is a daughter this time, by the grace of God, it will be a son next time."

MARCH 1516–NOVEMBER 1518

Next time . . . next time.

    Another boy.

    Another girl.

    Neither breathed.

    Seven children in all.

    Five boys, two girls.

    Six dead, one alive.

    This is how I numbered my pain.

FEBRUARY 1519

Gracias, Dios, for my little Mary. I poured all my love upon her. Love enough for seven children.

How I delighted to see her toddling and chattering, tripping over her skirts as she tried to curtsey, giggling and clapping her plump hands together. Surely there could not have been a more enchanting child in all England.

"Dance!" she commanded me one wintry morning.

Obligingly, I whirled my squealing daughter down the long gallery, then hugged her close before setting her back on her little feet.

"Dance!" Mary cried again.

"*Esperad, mi preciosa.* Your lady mother needs to catch her breath," I replied.

"Dance!" She stamped her foot. "Dance, dance, *dance!*"

How like her father she was. Her blue eyes flashed with anger, her tiny chin jutted out. And her voice! Although she was but a child of three, already she possessed an imperious voice, a voice that commanded authority, the voice . . . of a sovereign.

"God *has* answered my prayers," I whispered.

In that moment of divine insight, I knew the truth with soul-deep certainty.

O the depths of God's wisdom, how unsearchable His judgements and untraceable His ways.

I *had* fulfilled my sacred duty. I had given Henry an heir. Like the Virgin Mary herself, raised up by God to give birth to the King of Kings, I had been raised up to give birth to the next ruler of England.

"Mama, dance!"

Our little Mary, future Queen of England.

The Lord needed only convince Henry.

JULY 1527

"Have you a vision for me?" I ask the prophetess. I am filled with a sudden, solemn dread. "Are you here to foretell things that will come to pass?"

In response, her breath slows and the muscles of her face grow slack. Her eyes, fixed upon the altarpiece, take on a far-off expression.

I cross myself and step closer to receive His word.

MARCH 1519

It is a terrible thing when a woman need tell her husband that her courses no longer flow. It is doubly terrible when that husband is Henry, King of England. It took heart and courage to tell him the hard truth: My fertile life had ended earlier than expected. There would be no Prince for England.

At first, Henry said nothing. He just stood at my window, watching snowflakes swirl to the river below. When finally he turned to face me, his eyes were cold and narrowed, and his chin jutted out. "It is a cruel world for me, madam," he said.

"For me as well, my lord." I reached for his hand. "We tried our best, but we have failed."

"*We?* No, madam, I have not failed. It is *you* who have failed. You have failed in your most sacred duty."

I shook my head. "That is not true. I have given you a daughter— a healthy daughter, heiress to the throne."

"A girl."

"English law does not prohibit the crown from passing to a woman," I reminded him. "Why should your throne not go to our Princess Mary? Why should she not rule England as its Queen?"

"And have my country pass into the hands of her husband when she marries? I will not have it!"

"It is God's will," I told him.

"But it is *not mine!*"

JUNE 1519

Oh, *Santa Madre de Dios*, when the news—that cruel, cruel blow—arrived at court, I fled into our Heavenly Father's arms. From dawn to dusk I knelt in the quiet greyness of my private chapel. I prayed for Him to heal my heart. I prayed for Him to take away my anger. I prayed for the ability to accept and forgive. But above all, I prayed for understanding. "*Dios*, why do You torment me? Why give Bessie Blount a son—*Henry's* son—but not me? Why grace my husband's harlot with a healthy Tudor boy when I am no longer capable of doing the same? Is this Your plan? Is this Your punishment?"

Days later, Henry commanded the entire court, myself included, to attend the child's christening at the manor he had bought for his mistress. The taste of sadness and humiliation was strong in my mouth as I watched my husband standing proudly at the baptismal font, the red-haired newborn cradled in his arms. The babe looked so much like our own, departed Prince Henry. I blinked back tears.

"What is the name of this child?" asked the priest.

"Henry FitzRoy," declared my husband.

I could scarce believe it. I knew there was a streak of cruelty in Henry's nature, but how could he name this child Henry? And to heap on even more pain, he had given the babe the surname of FitzRoy, meaning "son of the King."

He turned and looked straight at me.

No one could have mistaken his thoughts: *See? I am not the problem. I can conceive a healthy son.*

JULY 1519–MARCH 1525

⬦·⬦

In his writings, Saint Augustine tells us to close the door to our consciousness and place ourselves in the presence of the Creator alone. "Speak not," the good saint writes, "lest it be for great necessity, or for great good." Is this not wise advice? And so time and again, I gripped tight to my courage. I held my tongue. And I spoke not about Bessie Blount and the vast allowance Henry settled upon her and the favour-seeking duke to whom he married her off.

I spoke not about Henry FitzRoy, who much resembled the King and was raised in the state of a great prince, with his own household and servants and men-at-arms. Henry even had the child brought to court, where he bestowed upon him a host of honours—the royal dukedoms of Richmond and Somerset, the Order of the Garter, the title Lord High Admiral.

I spoke not about this most public snub to the mother of the King's legitimate heir.

Nor did I speak about Jane Popincourt, or Elizabeth Carew, or Anne Hastings, or most recently Mary Boleyn. Henry singled her out just days after her arrival at court. *Por Dios*, I found her horsey laughter annoying.

Above all, I spoke not about the Boleyn girl's father, my steward, Sir Thomas Boleyn, who saw his daughter as a means to winning the King's favour. Thus he served her up to my husband as if she were a plump chicken plucked and ready for his pie.

No, I kept my peace.

Sometimes, silence best serves His purpose.

In those years, I appeared to the court as though made of stone, with no more feelings than the marble statues that stood in the garden. But love brimmed inside me. Love for my little Princess, my beloved

Mary. Being with her almost made me forget my pain at the absence of Henry's love.

Oh, but she was exquisite. Small and dainty as a goldfinch, she daily grew in grace and intellect—evidence of her pure royal blood.

I mothered her myself. Despite her having her own staff of the nursery—governesses and guardians, manservants, laundresses, maids—I was the constant guiding hand in Mary's upbringing. Who else could teach her all that a queen should know?

Court tongues, of course, wagged: "Queen Katharine acts as a commoner. She behaves like the wife of a sheep farmer; like a woman of market and midden."

I cared not. Mine was a holy duty. I was raising the future monarch of England.

And I delighted in it. I taught my daughter her prayers, helped her sew clothes for her dolls, gamboled about with her in the garden, sang with her, and trimmed her coppery curls. When she was four, I hired the finest dancing and riding instructors. When she was five, I commanded she receive her own chess set and her first hunting falcon. And when she turned seven, I took up the task of teaching her the crucial skills of reading, writing, and Latin. After our lessons, as a treat, we shut up the books and snuggled together on the couch while I told her stories of myself as a little girl in faraway Spain.

How I wished Henry took the same delight in our daughter. Certainly, there were occasional moments when he acted the part of devoted father. But he was not constant. He would ignore her for days, then swoop her up and carry her about, showing her off to the court and calling her his "dearest treasure." He expected her to squeal with pleasure, to kiss his cheek and smile prettily. And Mary did. Oh, she longed to please him! But she was anxious, too. She knew she did *not* please him, no matter how she tried.

"Did Father wish me to be a boy?" she asked me one winter's

morning just before her ninth year. "If I were a boy he would ride out with me and play games with me. He would stage mock fights with me as he does with Henry FitzRoy. He would shower me with titles and honours."

As she sobbed against me, my fury grew. How could Henry cause his own child such pain? But I could not use ill words against him. I could not criticize or reproach him. As his wife, I was required to preserve harmony and remain silent. I could do nothing.

I pulled Mary into my lap even though she was really too big. "No, no, *mi preciosa*. You must not think such things. You are perfectly made, God's holy creation, Princess of Wales, and one day, Queen of England."

JUNE 1525

One morning, to my surprise, Henry requested I join him for a dew bit, as he called his huntsman's early breakfast. Dressing quickly, I hastened to his privy chamber.

He was already chewing on a small loaf of bread when I arrived. Waving me into a chair, he reached for a wedge of cheese. "Ah, Kate," he said, his mouth full. "I have been thinking. I believe it is time we prepared Mary for queenship."

¡Gracias, Santa Madre! After all his insistence on a male heir, was it possible he finally accepted the idea of a woman on the throne? Was he finally content with Mary as his successor?

"Oh, Henry!" I exclaimed. "She will be the greatest of queens." I reached over and swept some crumbs from his shirt. "I will arrange for the best master in England to draw up an educational regimen. I will—"

He held up his hand to silence me. "I have chosen another course of action."

I did not like the cruel set of his mouth.

"While I refuse to bestow upon Mary the title of Princess of Wales, I shall give her the task of governing that principality." He drank from his goblet before adding, "I am sending her to Ludlow Castle."

"But she is only nine years old!" I cried. "And Ludlow Castle is so far away—a fortnight's travel. Henry, you cannot. She is but a child, a child who needs her mother."

"Do you want her to learn to rule? Do you want her to be Queen?"

"I do. You know I do. But this . . . this . . ." It took all my self-control to keep from bursting into tears. "You know the pain this separation will cost both her and me. Henry, please, do not do this."

"It has been decided."

"Then allow me to go with her," I begged.

"Your place is here, as my Queen," he replied coldly. "That is your duty."

He pushed back from the table. "You wanted Mary to be Queen, did you not? And so she shall learn to be one."

The sly expression on his face was easy to read: *You have not given me a son, and so I am taking away your daughter.*

AUGUST 1525

◇·◇

How could I bear her going? I stood outside the gates of Richmond Palace with Mary pressed against me, her head at my breast, her body fragile as a flower.

"When will I see you again, lady mother?" she cried.

"Oh, it will not be long," I said, forcing lightness into my voice.

Her arms tightened around my waist. "But I do not want to go. It is so far away. And I do not know how to govern."

"Oh, my darling!" How could I tell her that princesses must silence their wills, that their fates—though sometimes cruel—must always be accepted?

"Be brave," I whispered.

Henry stepped towards us. "So you are off," he said with smug satisfaction. He chucked her under the chin. "Do not look so grave, little Princess."

"I wish I did not have to go alone, Father."

"It is hard." Henry's voice deepened with false pity. "But sacrifice is required when ruling a kingdom."

Her lips trembled as he escorted her to the head of her royal procession and helped her onto her horse.

We stood and watched until the last of the royal train disappeared from sight.

"She will return for Christmas, will she not?" I asked, clutching at Henry's arm.

"Mary must learn to fend for herself. We must do nothing to interrupt her education." He smiled cruelly. "No, Kate, Mary shall be gone for years."

JULY 24, 1527

"*Thomas Wolsey,*" *the prophetess says. Her voice sounds deeper, different.*

I lean in. "*Yes? What of him?*"

"*He will be called to reckon for his sins, for the lies he tells His Holiness in Rome, for the blasphemies he wrote in his letter.*"

Oh, that letter! That horrid, horrid letter! My cheeks burn at the remembrance of how he dared suggest that Henry's and my marriage was not legal.

"*The Lord revengeth,*" *continues the prophetess.* "*Who can stand be-*

fore His wrath? His fury is poured out like fire, and rocks are thrown down by Him."

"Is this why you were sent?" I ask. "So that I would know of the cardinal's punishment?"

The prophetess stares unblinking for a heartbeat. Then she groans and her eyelids flutter. "The King . . . the King . . ."

APRIL 1527

I entered the chapel at Greenwich Palace to find my husband behind the lectern. At his side stood Thomas Wolsey. Over the years, the almoner had made the greatest leap any churchman could have made. Now he wore a cardinal's hat and bore the title of King's Chancellor. Henry had raised him up so high because he believed Wolsey could answer any question.

Opened before them was the Holy Bible. Wolsey pointed to a verse, and Henry read it silently, his lips forming the words. So absorbed were the men that neither noticed me until I had reached the altar.

The cardinal looked up. Obviously, it was a fattening job serving the King, for his red silken robes flashed, and he frowned at me over his protruding belly. "Your Grace, we had not expected you."

Why did the two look like stable dogs caught raiding the pantry?

"One's need for prayer is rarely scheduled, my lord cardinal," I replied.

He made a little bow. "A truer sentiment was never spoken, Your Grace."

He glanced at Henry, who quickly closed the Bible, saying, "I commend your piety, Kate." He clapped Wolsey on the shoulder. "Come, Thomas, let us disturb my wife's devotions no further."

As they passed down the aisle, I dropped to my knees and clasped my hands together. I was not praying, but puzzling. What had they been reading so intently? I waited for the chapel door to close behind them before moving to the lectern.

A ribbon of silver cloth still marked their page in the holy book. I crossed myself before opening it. "Make me worthy, *Santa Madre*."

So much beauty dwells between the covers of the Bible! The illuminated initials. The elaborately decorated margins. The miniature illustrations. But most breathtaking are the words of the Lord. These are written in Latin, which is the language God uses to speak to His Church. Only the most high—men of the Church and anointed sovereigns—can read God's language. The Holy Bible is so profound in its mysteries that the common man would be drowned.

Reverently, I turned to their marked page. It was in the Old Testament, the Book of Leviticus. My eyes scanned the Scripture until I came to chapter twenty, verse twenty-one: *And if a man shall take his brother's wife, it is an unclean thing; he hath uncovered his brother's nakedness; they shall be childless.*

"*Dios ten misericordia,*" I whispered. God have mercy.

MAY 1527

◇·◇

In the great hall at Richmond Palace, Henry danced hand in hand with my lady-in-waiting Anne Boleyn. Unlike the colouring of her fair, older sister, Mary—who had been my husband's mistress until just last year—Anne's eyes were very black and her dark hair very long. Tonight, she wore it interlaced with jewels and loose down her back.

No, I thought, *Anne is not as pretty as her sister. But she has a sense of style and a certain grace.*

She garnered attention. She was vivacious and witty; all eyes were upon her as she met my husband in the centre of the circle. They raised their hands and their fingers entwined. Anne laughed. So did Henry. His eyes, hungry and admiring, never left her face.

I knew that look.

It was time for my household to take its leave.

The music stopped when I stood. Reluctantly, but obediently, my ladies left their dancing and lined up behind me. All my ladies save Anne. She remained on the dance floor. Raising her narrow chin, she met my eye, then smiled, her teeth small and sharp as a kitten's. She did not look ashamed for disobeying. She did not look contrite. She looked defiant, and something else . . . victorious.

"She is not coming, Your Grace," said María.

My eyes went from Anne's face to my husband's flushed one. So she was his latest dalliance. Still, Henry would never allow such impudence; such an insult to the throne. I waited for him to command her obedience.

Instead, he remained at her side, his great hand wrapped around her tiny one.

The taste of humiliation was like iron in my mouth. Never had Henry shown me such public disrespect. Still, I would not expose my feelings. I was the Queen. No common girl would diminish that. Slowly, and with regal dignity, I turned and led my ladies from the hall.

Behind us, the music resumed.

"She does everything with him," María reported the next morning. "She eats with him, hunts with him, plays and sings with him." She made a face. "She even prays with him."

"Anne Boleyn is a beast," chimed in my lady Jane Seymour. Pale and mousey, Jane had come into my service two years earlier precisely because she lacked charm and beauty. Most assuredly, she would never catch my husband's eye.

Maud leaned forwards and raised her eyebrows meaningfully. "She does not do *everything* with him."

"Mistress Anne has bewitched him, besotted him!" Jane spat the words. "He will do anything to have her."

"And she requires much," added María. "She will not be like the others. She wants him to promise."

"Promise?" I said. "What could he promise?"

It was Maud, eyes flashing, who replied. "A throne, Your Grace. She will accept nothing less than your throne."

"Surely the King does not listen!" I exclaimed.

My ladies exchanged looks before Maud said, "Already the King has asked Cardinal Wolsey to investigate the possibility of divorce."

I held very still. I knew Henry no longer desired me. I knew he was bitter that I had not given him a male heir. But I could not fathom that he would try to set me aside. No matter the Scripture he had read in the chapel. No matter the gossip.

"The Pope gave us a dispensation," I said, more to myself than to my ladies.

"The King believes what Mistress Anne has told him," replied María. "That by marrying his brother's widow he has offended God. That he has been denied sons as punishment."

I was suddenly furious. What did a harlot like Mistress Anne know of God's will? "It matters not what she says," I snapped. "She is nothing but a commoner. He cannot marry her. He cannot give her a crown."

"They say he has already proposed to her," said María.

"And they say," added Maud, "that she has accepted."

23 JULY 1527

—◇·◇—

It was late, hours after the evening's merrymaking had ended, when Henry came to my apartments. "Kate, I have a grievous matter to discuss with you," he began. "It seems we have been living in mortal sin these many years."

"Who says this?" I asked, knowing exactly who.

"Learned men," he smoothly lied. "Men of the Church."

"They deceive you."

"It is written in the Holy Bible, Kate, in Leviticus." He forced a tear from his eye. "The truth has become so clear. Ours has been no true marriage because I unlawfully took my brother's wife. Oh, Kate, for all these years we have been living in sin."

I stared at him. Of course, none of this was a surprise to me. But to hear him say it aloud? *Santa Madre*, it was almost too much to bear.

"Our marriage *is* lawful," I managed to say. "The Pope declared it so."

"God's anger is there for all to see. Our sons are dead. We have no heir. That is our punishment."

"We *do* have an heir," I insisted. "We have Mary."

Henry's lips pursed, but then he went on as though he had not heard me. "My soul is in torment, Kate, and it breaks my heart to even say this to you." He dabbed at his eyes, pretending to be overcome by emotion. "But now . . . now I hear the voice of God speaking through me."

Now *you do*, I thought, *now that you have made promises to the Boleyn girl*.

"Kate, it is a terrible thing for us both, but we must separate. For the good of both our souls."

I wanted to scream that I knew all about his harlot. How dare he stand before me, playing the masque of a virtuous Christian King, and insult me? I was not a sinner. I was his true and lawful wife. I was his Queen, Katharine of England.

He rushed on, eager to have this unpleasantness behind him. "I would not want to put you through the embarrassment of a divorce. Your well-being is my deepest concern. Therefore, knowing your religious nature and your praiseworthy devotion to the Church, I have decided you should enter a convent. I know you will be contented there, passing your remaining days in peace."

Santa Madre, help me.

"That is, of course, after you formally renounce your marriage vows," he added.

Renounce my marriage vows? I could no more do that than I could choose to stop breathing.

Hot, angry tears spilled down my cheeks.

How dare he?

"All I ask is for your cooperation," he continued urgently. "Will you go to the convent, Kate? Will you?"

I refused to answer him. Instead, I fell to my knees and covered my face with my hands. "*¡Por favor!*" I cried. "*Santa Madre*, help me. Please, help me."

Henry lapsed into silence. At last, he cleared his throat. "That's right, Kate. Ask the Lord to bless and guide your thoughts. I am sure you will come to see that He and I know what is best for you."

He stood there but a moment longer. Then I heard the chamber door click shut. My husband was gone.

I remained on the floor until my knees ached and my back throbbed. Then I drew myself back into my chair and took a shaky breath. To renounce my vows and admit my marriage was illegal would make

Mary a bastard, no better than Henry's out-of-wedlock son. And I? I would be a harlot like Bessie Blount, like Anne Boleyn. Was this what God wanted of me?

I turned my face Heavenwards once more. *"Dios,* guide me accordingly, execute Your will in my life, reveal to me my purpose, O merciful saviour."

I picked up my needlework, a shirt I was embroidering for Henry. I felt so weary.

I rubbed the shirt's collar against my cheek.

My heart ached with sadness.

Outside my window it was still dark, but dawn was not far away.

Already someone stirred in the stable yard below.

I looked down.

24 JULY 1527

⬧·⬧

"The King . . ." *The prophetess is struggling, her facial muscles contorting, her eyes rolling back in her head.*

I take her arm to steady her. *"What about the King? What is it?"*

Her words, when at last they come, tumble out in a rush. *"God will call the King to obedience, demand that he cleave to his wife. But the King will turn his back on God's voice. He will abandon his true wife and England's true Queen to enter into a false marriage. To do so, he will usurp the Pope's power. He will form his own church, the Church of England, and he will make himself head of it."*

"No," *I manage to say.* *"Impossible."* *To overthrow the Pope was to overthrow God.*

"The King will sever the people of his kingdom from the true Church. He will make his subjects heretics, their souls—including his own— damned to the fires of Hell."

My legs cannot hold me. I sink into a pew. "It cannot be," I mutter.
"It cannot be."

"God is true, and He always speaks the truth."

I shake my head. "Can I not prevent this? What am I to do?"

"Resist," she says. "Resist though you be placed on trial and publicly
humiliated. Resist though you be cast aside and exiled. Resist though your
titles be stripped, your riches taken, your health destroyed, and your child
stolen from you. In the end, all that will remain will be your faith. Still you
must resist. Until your dying breath, you must shout out the truth. You
are the King's lawful wife and God's anointed Queen, sanctified by Him
through the Pope and the one true Catholic Church."

"And if I do all this?"

She gives a serene smile. "He will deliver unto you that which has been
promised since your childhood. The highest of things. Fulfilment of your
most sacred duty."

My heart is pounding. Blood rushes in my ears. "Mary will become
Queen?"

"I can only pass on what God has told me."

I turn away from her and kneel before the altar. Jesucristo in His suf-
fering looks down from His cross.

When I look back she is gone.

How long have I knelt here at the altar? My back has stiffened and my
knees ache. The pain assures me that I still live to serve the Lord. It seems
like years since I came to the chapel to beg Him for the return of Henry's
love. For a restoration of our marriage. For un milagro.

I know better now. I have buttoned my heart.

Now I pray for the strength and courage to withstand the trials God
has in store for me. It will be as He commands. I will not enter a nun-
nery. I will resist. I will do His work. Sometimes I will not understand.

Sometimes I will doubt. But I cannot be wrong. I cannot go wrong. This battle is God's battle, and I am His sacred soldier. I will know victory. If not today, then tomorrow. And one day, my daughter, God's true and rightful heir, will take her place upon the throne. My daughter, Mary, Queen of England.

Gloria a Dios.

HENRY VIII

Sir Loyal Heart

When I first saw her, I was a boy, just a child, and she seemed to me to contain everything I wanted from adulthood in the years to come. There was the savour of foreign nations in her strange clothing; the hint of secret wisdom in the way she watched us all; the reminder of a wider world of kings and armies in her opaque Spanish language (at first we could speak together only in Latin, meeting in some middle place foreign to both of us); the revelation of beauty and dignity in her serene walk; and lastly, in the conferences about her marriage with my brother, she gave me the first glimpse I had that friendship, and even love, are chits in games of power. Hands clasp, and then armies march. Lips meet, and scarlet cardinals of the Church come together in locked chambers. Nations move. Katharine had in her veins the blood of Castile and Aragon, the blood of kings, and our Tudor family's would mingle with theirs, and so we would make ourselves a dynasty to outlast the emperors of Rome.

Thus I gaped at her when I was a boy. I knew I was designed to be larger than the world, and when I was a child, I was already restless to take up the globe in my small hands. I saw my brother Arthur tasting the first fruits of power with Katharine at his side, and I mooned after her, as if she were adulthood itself. As a boy, I imagined that the kiss of this princess would impregnate me with sovereignty, the rule of the world.

But of course, though I was a bright child—quite extraordinary in many ways—brilliant even, by everyone's account—I did not yet understand the subtleties of power. I did not understand that Katharine herself was a pawn.

My father's interest in Katharine's marriage, first to Arthur, and then to me, waxed and waned depending on the politics of Spain. My father was a miser—a stringy-haired miser—and poor Katharine was left almost to starve as he decided whether she was useful to him and to our family. After my brother Arthur died (may Christ lead his weak, timid soul by hand to Heaven), Katharine and I became allies in that stingy court. We exchanged secret glances in the audience chamber as my father raged. This is when I came not simply to admire her, but to love her.

With my father's death, those grim years were over, and I grasped the throne with both hands. I announced to the world that it had been my father's desire that I marry Katharine. A few days after our coronation, I had my father's favourite ministers arrested, and so ended the regime of misers. After their execution, a pretty time of dancing began, and hunting, and all the pleasant sports of youth.

I had won what I had wanted. It was all mine.

Do not say that I did not love her. I did; I do. I was not "unkind" to her, as I hear some whisper. I always sought to celebrate her, to protect her.

I will always remember, for example, the joy I felt the night our first son was born—our heir so briefly in the world. The Queen's chambers had been closed to men for days, a secret place only for her ladies-in-waiting and the midwives. When a man brought me the news of the birth, however, I dashed immediately to her rooms and yanked aside the arras draped over the door—kicked the door open and rushed into the room of women, eager to embrace her and my boy and the world itself.

"God be praised!" I crowed. "I have a son!"

The people were cheering for us in the streets. We had an heir. England would be strong.

I could not believe Kate's beauty that night, though she was exhausted, and I could not accustom myself to the precious workmanship of our child (the chiselling of his lips, the volutes of his tiny ears). He looked exactly like his father: red hair, blue eyes. "How can I ever thank you for this greatest of gifts, Kate?" I asked her. "A son. An heir for England."

I lay half beside her, and we called him Henry, and then whispered—foolishly, for we did not know yet that our union was cursed—that he was our little Henry IX.

If that boy had not died—if she had given me more boys—all our lives would have felt as sweet as that moment, and in our love would have been the advance of nations.

After a few minutes of my Queen and me resting side by side, the nursemaids and midwives who had been scolding me this whole while to let Her Majesty and the little one sleep, brushed me towards the door. As soon as I stepped out of the apartments, I could not help myself, but darted back into the bedchamber to kiss her and our tiny Prince again.

I can barely think of it now without weeping.

That night, I strolled the agitated halls, unable to rest, joy was so thick in my veins. I could not sleep without release of ecstasy, so I called for a servant-girl named Polly whom I had several times found convenient, having seen a fine shaft of light illuminate her jaw in the stable yard, and we spent an hour in passionate embrace. As we did, giggling together, and as I felt the jubilation rushing through my limbs, I thought on my Queen wife, and my spending was a tribute to her.

"I am a maker of men," I whispered at the point of rapture.

"Funny, isn't it," said Polly, "that both the Queen and me have your flesh passing through us tonight?"

It was a coarse and repulsive jest, spoken with a knowing leer. As I have said, I always wish to protect poor Katharine. I was shocked.

"Polly," I said, "that is a disgusting thing to say. Do not speak that way of your Queen or compare yourself in any way to Her Blessed Majesty."

The girl looked confused. "But you and me, we're tricking her," she said. "You're lying to her. You're the one—"

I pushed the girl hard towards the edge of the bed. "I am *protecting* her. I will see no harm come to her." I grabbed Polly and squeezed her arm hard. "She will never hear of this. She will never know a minute's sadness."

I thrust the girl from me. She looked as if she might argue—as if I had not decreed her silence.

"She don't know that you have other women?"

"Compton," I called.

William Compton, Groom of the Stool, looked up. He was sitting near the bed, studying receipts by candlelight.

I ordered him to take Polly out, to dismiss her from her position, to send her into Cornwall or the north.

She wept, I think, but I explained that I could do worse; she needed to recognize my mercy.

When she was gone, it took me a long while to regain my poise and joy. She troubled me, which made no sense, for she was no one of importance, no one of my acquaintance. It was not until the monks sang compline that my thoughts were clear again, and my child's face floated above me as serene as the moon.

It is no good thinking of those things now. The years of—I will not call it failure, for it was not my failure—let us rather call it judgement. The years of God's judgement upon Katharine and me for wedding against His law. The small, dead mites, weakened by her womb.

I am a king and a maker of men. Kings run through my marrow and seek release. Make no mistake: If a physician could see my living veins, he would see them stuffed with royal homunculi hungry for rule, and the branches of my blood would appear to be a dynastic tree in miniature, waiting to burst forth and flower. So many nights, I can feel the unborn rampage.

But when my seed hit Katharine's morbid, chilly womb, my sons withered. So I've been told by several physicians—and I paid them enough to get to the truth of the matter.

Do not say it is her "fault." It is not her fault that she could not nurture my vivid seed. God's will was against us, and as time went on, she became a poor vessel for kings: damp and sad, no life in her limbs, always praying in frigid chapels.

Look at the history of our nation—of every nation—of old Rome itself: Where the succession of father and son is not clear, the whole country suffers. There are wars and revolutions. Think of the great Anarchy after the son of the first Henry drowned amidst the puking drunkards on the White Ship; for a generation, armies trooped back and forth across the kingdom and burned the fields; monarch fought monarch; a woman empress sought to become Queen of England, throwing everything into chaos; and there was no peace.

So the love between a king and queen is no dalliance. It is no pleasure. It is men's work. It is the route to power and safety for a whole realm.

For this reason, I knew that the best solution for the kingdom and for my beloved English people was to convince Katharine to put aside the crown. It was out of love and concern for her, too—for why should she suffer continual sorrow and sadness? Why should she spend her days frowning and worrying her rosary?

A nunnery was the perfect solution, though she would not agree. I could see her in comfortable rooms, well attended by noble nuns, sewing shirts for the poor. Writing letters to our Mary. Enjoying the warmth of the great hearth-fires in the winter and the cloister orchards in the summer. Perhaps she would acquire a monastery cat. Hidden away from the burdensome world, she would finally be at peace.

One woman cannot encompass me. I must spread my arms wider to embrace the whole globe; I only feel that I am myself when I am victorious and commanding whole nations, drinking in not merely the kisses of one set of lips, but the perfume of life itself.

Shortly after our daughter Mary was born to Katharine—with the promise still of future heirs, sons who could bear the weight of the kingdom on their shoulders—shortly thereafter, Cardinal Wolsey and I concluded a treaty among all the kings of Christendom. Wolsey worked the details; but it was largely my doing. I brought all nations together in a great truce of perpetual peace. Of course, you will say, it did not last long— peace can never be perpetual, where there is strength—but that is not my failure. It was the failure of the King of France and the Holy Roman Emperor, Katharine's own nephew. They could not keep from each other's throats. I brought them together, however, which was a great feat for the king of an island nation just growing into its full power.

And so I proposed to Francis I, the young, new King of France, that we meet in person to express our royal affection for each other, since our countries had so recently been at war. It was agreed we would come together for diverse festivities, jousts, and contests.

I can think of no happier time in my life than those splendid weeks on the shores of France.

When two kings of the greatest dignity meet, all must be planned well in advance so neither is seen to yield anything to the other—especially when they are two of the greatest monarchs of Europe, both young, both beloved by all people, both sportsmen, always eager for the prize. So we met on French shores—but on English ground, near the town of Calais, which I held as a foothold from the wars of our ancestors.

I ordered to be built there an enchanted palace of illusion, which rose up out of an empty field in mere days like the work of a magician—like the ones old Merlin had conjured up for his lady-love. Being cunningly made of insubstantial silks and soft canvases painted to look like marble and stone, it appeared in the twinkling of an eye—and it disappeared just as quickly a few weeks later when we were done with it, to the amazement of all. It took six thousand men to build, all at my command. It had turrets that looked out over the plains, and gilded carvings, and great windows of painted glass that glittered in the sunlight, and on its battlements stood statues of the most fearsome and famous warriors of old: Alexander the Great, King Arthur, King David, Julius Caesar, Charlemagne, Hector, and Hercules. Before the palace gate stood a fountain that spewed out wines, day and night. Under a statue of old, drunken Bacchus, god of liquor, it was written, "Whoever wishes, be of good cheer."

"Aha!" I said to Katharine as she saw the palace for the first time, with windows flashing and a light Cabernet spilling merrily from the fountain. "Won't the eyes of all guests be astonished?"

"It is magnificent, Henry," she agreed. "King Francis's hospitality will never equal yours."

I was delighted. "He will try and fail," I prophesied.

I led her through the palace by the hand, displaying all the rooms draped with costly silks and damasks. Her attention was caught by the statue of Hercules, who wore a lion skin of gold. He was wrapped in a banner that read, "In women and children there is little assurance."

She frowned. "That does not seem very courteous to the French Queen."

"That?" I said. "That! See, Kate, women are honoured here upon this field, but they are only guests. This is a place for man to meet with man and discuss the fate of the world. Not for women's talk of gossip, pretty dresses, and dainty toys."

I did not wish her to say something glum, so I pushed her playfully towards the bedchamber that had been prepared for her, and said, "Do not fear! Your elf-king Henry has summoned up a whole altar just for you alone, crowded with golden icons of the saints." At that, she smiled.

I pulled her to me and declared, "My Katharine, we are perhaps the greatest man and wife in all the world today."

She had petty fears: She said the King of France might betray me, and that he had invited me to this field only to catch me unaware with a greater force than mine. She was listening to the hen-clucks of the court, and I told her she should not meddle in the affairs of men.

When I went out to greet Francis, we met on terms of strict equality, each the mirror image of the other. Neither could arrive on the field before the other. I ordered a cannon fired from our camp to announce our readiness, and we heard an answering report from the encampment of the French. Then we issued forth, each court to meet the other at a green valley in the middle. Before me in parade went the gentlemen, squires, knights, and barons; with me rode the bishops, dukes, and earls, Wolsey by my side, and the Marquis of Dorset marching before me, carrying the great Sword of State in its sheath. We numbered in the thousands, but marched silently.

I had grown my beard out to match King Francis's. I had heard his was dark; mine was red as copper.

Latimer came riding up to me in haste. "My King and sovereign," he said. "I have been with the French army, and they are more in number than we are—double our number."

I did not fear them; I knew how Katharine would gloat if I showed fear, as if I'd taken her advice. I gave the order for us to march on.

I was dressed for royal victory in cloth of silver and damask ribbed with gold, studded with gems, and in a feathered black bonnet; no expense had been spared, and I had demanded over a thousand yards of velvet for my costumes. I recount these details of dress not to be womanish, but because my court must have presented such a beautiful spectacle to the people we passed—for there were thousands who had gathered to watch us ride out. They pushed and shoved at one another on the far side of a ditch while my retinue marched serenely on.

We came in sight of the French King and his retainers. At this moment, I saw that the Lord Admiral of France, riding in front of Francis, bore their Sword of State unsheathed and naked.

Wolsey was shocked. "They did not tell us their sword would be naked. I thought all swords should be sheathed."

"Show no surprise," I counselled him. "But I will not allow their sword to be unsheathed and mine to be sheathed. Both swords should be unsheathed."

"Agreed," said Wolsey, and he gave the command that the Marquis of Dorset should draw our Sword of State and carry it erect before me.

So we faced the French across the valley, King Francis's horde on one side, mine on the other. It was announced by heralds that everyone must be silent and completely still, upon pain of death. When all sound had ceased, when all the thousands were motionless, my cousin king and I rode down the valley towards each other.

We met for the first time upon that field, at its centre, where there stood a tent pavilion made of cloth of gold, heaped with Turkey carpets.

"My dear cousin," said the King of France. "I have travelled to see you because I wish so much to aid you however I can, given my tremendous might and all the realms that are mine."

I would not let this little boast go unanswered, and so I said, "Sir, neither your realms nor any other places of your power are the matter of my regard, but rather your steadfastness in keeping the promises we have made in our charters."

We embraced as cousins and declared our mutual love. I could see him taking account of me, as I took account of him, judging whether he would excel at the hunt, at hawking, at the joust, at the gaming table, at the architect's bench, in the diplomatic chamber. I had heard he was handsome, but he was not as handsome as I—his face a little too French, a real cheese-knife of a nose.

In the tent, we ate delicacies and discussed the important affairs of nations—especially the marriage between my little daughter, Mary, and his infant son, the Dauphin. (It is not my fault that that marriage never came to pass. The discussions were sound.)

And so began our week of feasts, bouts, tournaments, jousts, and contests of athletic pride upon the Field of Cloth of Gold. Never was more chivalry on display than at our meeting.

A pavilion was built so Francis and I could watch with our Queens, Katharine and Claude. We were young, sporting men, though, so we often went down, girded ourselves up, and cracked some skulls with the rest. We had agreed we would never meet in a contest against each other—for to do so would compromise the dignity of the loser. But still, we joined our subjects upon the field and delighted in the games.

I may say that I broke many more lances than Francis in the joust. And though we did not keep score, I am sure all the assembled must have noted my excellence in archery.

The more I watched the King of France, the more I knew we would agree on much and form a great alliance. Over the years, we would hunt together—not simply in the forests of my demesne, but across the fields and mountains of Europe. We were so alike.

I found he shared even my love of gemstones—and yet, this led us only to division, for he refused to admire, truly admire, the size, excellence, and clarity of my diamonds, my emeralds, my sapphires. He always told a tale of how he had a prettier one, a costlier one, back in Paris. At once, we felt like brothers—but as with brothers, I wanted to push him down in the dirt and make him cry to me for mercy.

One evening, we swapped women. Francis and his men made their way to my pavilion, where they dined with Katharine and her ladies-in-waiting. My men and I went to his encampment—a huge tent gilded with night stars and hung on a great mast—and I dined with his mother and Queen Claude. After our feast, my gentlemen and I slipped out and dressed for a masque in Russian garb and beards of gold wire, then went back in to charm the French ladies with our sweet talk and Moscow accents. We danced with them and together tasted plums and dates and sweet wines. When done, we bowed and left.

In the dark of night, halfway back to our encampment, we met Francis and his men going the other way, having just been served at my fairy castle with every delicacy that could be wrenched out of forests, parks, fields, salt seas, rivers, moats, and ponds. When I saw him, I wagged my beard of wires and cut a caper. I am fond of masque antics. He laughed, and in that moment, once again passing like mirror images, we felt, I believe, true friendship in our similarity. We embraced heartily and continued on.

Once he was gone in the darkness, however, I worried my leaping had been foolish. Some find masqueing infantile.

When I got back to our pavilion, I went to speak to Katharine.

"He enjoyed his feast?" I asked.

"He did. He is a charming man."

I looked quickly at her. "How charming is Francis?"

She sighed. "Oh, Henry," she said. "I must go to sleep."

"Did he like the monkeys with gold fur?"

"He was fairly in love with the monkeys. They stole the Lord Admiral's dagger and almost murdered someone with it. They flung ordure at the Bastard of Savoy."

"Do you know the time my groom spent brushing gold leaf into the fur of those monkeys? Did Francis appreciate that my royal touch had turned them gold? Like Midas's?"

"He wants the monkeys."

"He can't have the monkeys."

"I am worried the monkeys will sicken if they lick their own gilding."

"Did he dance with the ladies?"

"Henry."

"It is important that he enjoyed himself but took no liberties."

"Yes. He danced with us. He kissed all the ladies, too, except the ones he said were too old or ugly."

A man like myself—but too close for comfort.

And there are no ugly women in the English court.

One day, during the wrestling bouts, I could stand the rivalry no longer. Francis and I had been watching, while exchanging pleasant observations such as "Last week, when I entertained the Holy Roman Emperor . . ." and "In a letter the Pope recently sent to me, asking for advice . . ." I despise this kind of sparring—far beneath a king—and yet, when another is weak enough to do it, it would be wrong to allow myself to be conquered.

Breton and Cornish wrestlers were flipping each other on the reeds beneath us. I looked up from the sport to see Francis whispering to Katharine. The two of them paid no attention to the men writhing below. Katharine laughed.

It was a sight almost unseen. Katharine putting her hand before her mouth to hide her teeth—and laughing.

I stood and walked to the side of my rival. "We should wrestle, too," I said. "Down there."

The King of France was surprised. "The two of us?"

"Just us."

"Sir, we have agreed to undertake no contests against each other." He smiled, which seemed on its surface the smile of a friend, and yet dismissed me as an unworthy opponent—as if he were sorry for me, that I would stoop to challenging him; as if the need to challenge made me weaker.

"To turn down a contest of strength," I said, "is a great insult."

I moved closer, to tower above him; the body speaks its own challenge, one which demands more than words in response. Behind Francis, I could see Katharine dropping her eyes. She did not agree with me, and yet did not want to disagree.

Francis said smoothly, "Sir, it is against our agreed code, which our own heralds announced."

I answered, "Combat for glory is never against my code."

Francis looked displeased. "Let it be so, then. We will wrestle."

We came out before the court half naked. There was, strangely, no applause.

I faced off against him, and, as I will do when I wish to rush someone, filled my fancy with images of victory: the hunt, the stag finally bleeding, pawing at the ground in confusion as it dies and the dogs swarm around it; armed men bursting backwards as my lance unseats them; the aura of coronation. And I rushed the King of France.

So France wrestled England.

The arms straining—the legs shuddering—the solid self of the enemy finally upon me.

It does not matter who "won." The contest was, as I discovered, unfair, because wrestling was a specialty of that vain young man. Had we met in some sport I had trained in equally, there is little question who would have won. Yes—so—faith: He flipped me—and may have felt victory. I looked in his face and saw iron will as he held me down. There was something ugly and professional in his wrestling, not like a gentleman, but rather like those greasy vagabonds who travel from inn to inn, inviting locals to paid bouts in the stables. Unbecoming in a king.

And I lay there and vowed that someday I would seek out one of his women and bed her—bed her often, long, and hard—and so I did—and she said I was much more skilled at that pleasant wrestling than the God-damned King of France. Then he could not say that I was not man enough, when his own mistress lay heaving at my side, when I had stolen her from him. He could not know that she would one day bear my weight just as I, lying there on the Field of Cloth of Gold, bore his.

In that moment, trapped on the rug, I needed my Queen. I needed her to laugh off the contest and help me rise and save the moment. I needed Katharine to look at me with love.

But the sombre cow glared at me from the stands. I cannot forget the look in her eyes.

She looked down upon me as if she hated me for losing. (Not that I earned the defeat—Francis cheated, telling me nothing of his skill.) Or was it that her unforgiving eyes said that she found it pathetic I had even demanded the match?

She despised me. I am sure she despised me.

Just an hour later, she simpered over me. She hid that hatred. I would not see that look again for many years—until the time of the trial, when all the world was watching.

And during that trial, years later, I wondered: *Has she hated me all this time, since she saw me thrown at the Field of Cloth of Gold? Have I been deceived?*

Never mind. She is no longer mine. The pomegranate, cracked open, showed nothing but an empty husk, and so has been shied into the midden.

That night, after the wrestling, the King of France and I took our pleasure in my palace of illusions. I had to appear in public so I was not thought to be defeated.

We finished our feast and then passed down our scraps for the poor gathered outside the gates. When the time came for dancing, I found myself doing a brisk step with one of Queen Claude's maids of honour.

"Your Majesty," the girl asked, "did you enjoy your wrestling match today?"

I wondered whether she was being impertinent.

"We all have our skills," I said vaguely. "I have shattered many more lances than Francis."

She spoke English suddenly, to my surprise: "That rhymes in our own tongue," she said, and sang out, in translation, *more lances than Francis.* She lowered her head and giggled. She was, after all, but a girl.

I was displeased with the idiocy of this whole conversation.

"It must be difficult for a girl to enjoy and understand this great meeting," I said to her. "It is a serious business. The meeting of men."

"I think I understand it perfectly, Your Highness," she said. "Two weeks of men striding about, wagging their long poles in front of them, hoping someone notices. What else is men's business ever about?"

With that, we switched partners in the dance, and she was whirled away from me.

The next in the line, who moved in to take her place, was also a familiar of Queen Claude.

"You seem startled, Your Highness," she said. "Did your last partner say something amiss?"

"Who is she?" I asked. "She sounded English."

"She's the daughter of your ambassador, sir," answered the woman in my arms. "Her name is Anne Boleyn."

ANNE BOLEYN

"The Most Happy"

18 MAY 1536

◇•◇

The Tower of London
The Queen's Lodgings
A Few Hours Before Midnight

"She's locked herself in the closet," I hear my nurse, Mary Orchard, cry with alarm. She raps on the door. "Queen Anne, are you all right?"

I don't answer directly, but when she continues to knock I feel forced to say, "Yes, I'm fine, I just need to be alone to pray and prepare."

But that's not exactly true. I have prayed for many days now and am fully prepared to die. Indeed, I should have died this morning, but they delayed my execution to the afternoon. And now I am told it will happen early tomorrow. Being granted time when you are prepared to die is not a blessing. The mind wanders down paths perhaps best left unexplored. I find myself longing to explain how I ended up in this Tower to someone unprejudiced, someone far away, someone who doesn't know me. After weeks of captivity, I have finally found clarity. And now I wish to tell my story.

An empty chair rests in the corner of the small closet that I have used as a private chapel these past weeks. I imagine that the someone I seek sits upon it, eager to learn all that will be buried tomorrow.

I clear my throat. "Where to begin? Words hold such weight and consequence. I have not always been mindful of my tongue, and it has cost me. For if given the choice, people will believe the worst of you, not the best."

I hear rumbling outside the closet. It sounds as though my ladies press their ears against the door.

"Who is she talking to? Is someone in the room with her?" Lady Rochford asks.

"She's praying," Mrs. Orchard replies.

"No, she's not praying, because she's not speaking in Latin," Lady Rochford corrects her.

"Perhaps she talks with an angel?" young Caroline offers.

"Or a ghost?"

"Or perhaps she's losing her mind, before she loses her head," Lady Rochford says.

"Our poor Queen. Should we comfort her?" Mrs. Orchard asks.

"Let her be," my cousin Madge says with authority. "Queen Anne wishes to be alone. If she needs us she will call for us."

And there ends the debate.

Thank you, dear Madge.

I look back at the chair with a smile. "Where was I? Ah yes, people like to believe the worst of you. Indeed. Every story must have its villain, whether what is said to cast that villain is true or a torrent of lies. Truth is boring, after all, compared to rumour and lechery. And yet, were I quiet, without wit, and lacking all strength, could I have been cast as a bitch or a whore, a villain or a witch? I rather think not.

"I take comfort in the fact that God knows what is true and right, for He sees all. I shall die in peace because I have faith in this above all else.

"My downfall happened so fast. Not a month ago the King still insisted that the world acknowledge me as his Queen. And tomorrow I become the first English Queen to face the scaffold. Henry and I had been fighting, perhaps more fiercely than in the past, but a few weeks ago, I could never have imagined that I would become *la Reine sans tête*. The Queen without a head."

26 APRIL 1536

Greenwich Palace Gardens

"Down, Maman! Down! I walk," Elizabeth squeals, and wriggles in my arms.

"*Oui, ma petite rose*, but Maman wants to hold you in her arms today." I kiss my daughter's head of fire-red ringlets the exact same shade her father's was once. Now his hair is dappled with grey.

"*S'il te plaît?*" Elizabeth pleads with such sweetness that I have no choice but to acquiesce and let her go. She sprints away from me like a young foal after days of confinement. Several nursemaids chase the Princess in circles around the garden until they are quite out of breath. But their displeasure only delights her. For Elizabeth, everything's a game. She's so much her father already. Stubborn and playful. Charming and sly. And I pray that, above all else, she will be strong.

My dearest almoner, Matthew Parker, joins me on a bench in the centre of the garden. As we converse, Elizabeth dashes past us, blowing kisses and screaming, "Look, Maman!" every other minute, lest I forget she's here.

I hand Almoner Parker a gold locket with portraits of me and Henry inside. "It holds no great value, but when the Princess is older, will you give this to her?"

"Of course," Matthew says, somewhat perplexed. "But does Your Grace not wish to give it to the Princess herself?"

I shake my head. "I fear that may not be possible." Then, before he can dispute my premonition or offer words of comfort, I add, "Which brings me to the reason I summoned you here."

A sudden, violent crack of thunder shakes both sky and ground. From the look of the low, menacing clouds, it will be a nasty storm.

"Please forgive my directness, but I require from you a favour of some gravity." I take a deep breath.

"Should anything happen and I be sent away, as was Princess Dowager Katharine before me, I ask that you watch over Elizabeth. I need you to promise me that you will be her guardian, Almoner Parker. My daughter's father and the world may turn away, but I know if you are there for her, as you have been for me, then, and only then, can I be at peace. Promise me this, Matthew, please." Tears well up in my eyes.

Lightning branches above us, followed by another great smack of thunder. Elizabeth jumps into my arms. "Make it stop, Maman!" She burrows her little head against my chest and covers her ears with her hands, trying to block out what frightens her.

"*Ne pas avoir peur.* It's just a storm." I rock Elizabeth and kiss her head. "It will pass." I try not to look desperate as I await Almoner Parker's response.

He crosses himself. "I hope we will guide the Princess together, but I give you my word, Your Grace. I shall watch over and protect your daughter, always."

"*Merci,*" I say through tears. I could fall to my knees and kiss his feet, but that is not appropriate behaviour for a queen. I clutch his arm. "I will be forever in your debt." Rocking my baby, I add, "And please tell the Princess how dearly her mother loved her."

Almoner Parker nods.

"Take your leave now, that you might get ahead of the rain." I dismiss him as I rise with Elizabeth in my arms.

The Princess dabs at my eyes. "Maman, don't cry." She kisses my cheek. "Just a storm. It will pass."

I smile. "*Oui.*" Oh, *ma petite, je l'espère.* I really do hope so.

A second-story window on the east side of the castle stands open.

As I carry Elizabeth towards the palace, Henry leans out and unfurls his royal palm to feel whether the rain has begun.

Cradling Elizabeth, I call up to him, "Your Majesty!" The Princess and I wave, but I can see even at this distance that the mere sound of my voice causes Henry to wince.

"What do you want, woman?"

I smile, hoping that perhaps our daughter might bridge some peace between us. Lately when Henry isn't ignoring me, all we do is argue. And yet he asked that I accompany him on an extended trip to Calais in a few days, so he can't be completely without care for me. Perhaps being away from this miserable country will help. Perhaps a trip back to France, where our love caught flame, might spark Henry to visit my bed again. Unfortunately, I'm expected to bring that wretched Jane Seymour along as part of my entourage, so he will likely spend most of his time with his latest *amour*.

"Your daughter, the Princess Elizabeth, visits us today. Would you like her to come give her papa a kiss?"

"Did you think you would bring that child here and all would be forgiven, Anne?" Henry shakes his head.

There are many things I could say in response, but before I launch a retort, Elizabeth shouts merrily, "*Bonjour, Papa!*"

Henry spits out the window. "That girl is too much like her mother."

"She is your daughter and your heir!" I snap back at him.

"That little bitch of yours will never be my heir!" Henry screams, and slams his window.

Elizabeth begins to wail, but not before every servant within the palace has heard the awful exchange between Henry and me.

Without warning, the rain arrives in an angry downpour. I cover my little girl's head and run for shelter. "Your papa loves you,

Elizabeth. Always remember that no matter what he says, he loves you very much."

2 MAY 1536

---◇·◇---

From Greenwich Palace to the Tower of London

The call of a bird draws my focus from the tennis match. I look up, but see only sky. No one else stirs, so perhaps the sound was a figment of my imagination, one further sign that I'm losing control of all that surrounds me.

I feign interest in this game, even place a bet on my champion, yet ever since Henry's abrupt departure from the May Day tournament yesterday I can't shake the fear that something's terribly wrong. But I say this to no one, not even my cousin Madge.

Now I hear wings flap loudly overhead. In a wink of sun, I catch a flash of pointed feathers and hooked beak.

Sure as I am the Queen, a falcon hovers ten feet above me, midair. He eyes me as if he wishes to devour me, then swiftly takes his leave. I tap Lady Rochford, my brother's wife, on the shoulder. "Did you see that?" I ask.

She glances to the tennis court as if I mean to discuss something about the match. "See what, Your Grace?"

"*Le faucon.*"

Lady Rochford registers utter confusion.

"The falcon?" I repeat. "The bird on my royal crest."

Before I can explain further, a messenger presents himself. "By order of the King, Her Highness Queen Anne is summoned to present herself to his Privy Council chamber."

The tennis ball may still be volleying back and forth, but I feel all spectators' eyes on me. Henry must be very upset to humiliate me in this fashion. In the past he would never air our private squabbles in front of dignitaries. My foolish words of flirtation with Sir Henry Norris deserve reprimand and I wish that I had spoken not a one, but why does the King go to such lengths? I tried to make amends for this already. I will just have to argue my case with greater energy and devotion.

I stand up to follow the messenger, but my legs become heavy as granite, and I can't seem to move. From my neck to my toes, I feel that something is not right. And then I know what it is.

Mon temps est venu. My time has come.

The Privy Council chamber feels colder than a dungeon, even though the sun shines brightly through the windows and a fire blazes in the hearth. My uncle, the Duke of Norfolk, a man who has never been a friend to me; Sir William Fitzwilliam; and Sir William Paulet arise at my entrance, all with sombre faces.

My uncle delays a good minute before he begins. "Anne Boleyn, who rose so high, must you now fall so low? By your evil behaviour you have disgraced yourself and your family. And most grievously, you committed treachery and treason and dishonoured the King."

My uncle clears his throat. "Queen Anne, you are hereby formally accused of committing adultery with three men: Mark Smeaton, Sir Henry Norris, and another as yet unnamed."

"Pardon me?" I must have misheard him. "Did you say I stand accused of adultery?"

My uncle nods.

I stagger, confused for a second, before I turn hot as boiling oil. "These are ludicrous accusations! There is a grave difference between flirtatious banter and adultery, Duke Norfolk. You ought to be ashamed of yourself for giving credence to such nonsense."

My uncle shakes his finger at me. "Tut, tut, tut. Her Highness had best avoid adding perjury to the list of her offences against God and the King."

I would like to scream and knock my uncle to his knees. Instead, I look to the other men on the Royal Commission, Sir William Fitzwilliam and Sir William Paulet.

Fitzwilliam stares hazily out the window like a boy wishing to escape a tedious lecture. And Paulet, more statue than man, hasn't shifted since I entered the room.

"I am innocent. I protest these dubitable charges against me, and will bear no more abuse to my character." I indicate to my ladies that I intend to leave this chamber.

But the guards bar our exit.

"The charges are not dubitable. Witnesses have come forth," my uncle rebuts.

"They are lying. I am the King's true wife, and no other man has ever touched me!" I have inadvertently raised my voice. I gather my wits and breathe. "This must be a terrible misunderstanding. I will go to Windsor and speak to Henry. Someone has put forth wicked and false rumours."

William Paulet bows his head. "Do forgive me, Your Grace, but His Majesty was adamant in his refusal to speak with you."

"Might someone then petition the King on my behalf?" I find myself almost pleading.

All three men on the Royal Commission shake their heads.

"You are hereby under arrest and will be escorted by barge to the Tower of London as soon as the tide of the Thames turns down," my uncle proclaims, as if my guilt is already a foregone conclusion. Further argument is fruitless.

I force a smile at my ladies-in-waiting. "Well, it seems we are moving houses."

William Paulet looks at me with sympathetic eyes. "Your Grace can bring nothing and no one from your household. All will be provided."

My breath halts. "Might I see my brother before I depart? My father? My baby."

My uncle and Fitzwilliam shake their heads, and Paulet looks away.

I close my eyes. I am to be alone in the Tower without friends or family to comfort or counsel me. I try to hold fast to the brave and dauntless Anne, the one whom Henry fell in love with. I swallow hard. "If this be His Majesty's pleasure, I am ready, as ever, to obey."

In full daylight, not under the cover of darkness as is afforded most state prisoners, but so that the people may gape at me from the shore, I'm conducted up the Thames to the Tower of London—a Queen and a *prisoner*.

Three years ago, on a pleasant May afternoon not so unlike this one, Lord Thomas Cromwell orchestrated a very different trip up the Thames for me. I was on my way to be crowned Queen of England. The people flocked to these shores, if not to wholeheartedly laud me, to observe the great spectacle. Led by a golden dragon that breathed fire from its metal jaws, three hundred barges sailed in procession. The sky exploded with endless fireworks. Cannons tremored the land. So much pageantry, and all of it to proclaim, once and for all, that Henry had made me his Queen.

As we pass through the Court Gate of the Tower, cannon fire blasts and the barge rattles. The sound shatters me and I must grasp the side of the boat. Today, instead of celebrating my coronation, the cannon signals to the world that I shall be imprisoned.

Sir William Kingston, as Constable of the Tower, disembarks the barge ahead of me. When my feet touch ground, I feel queasy and unsteady and sink to my knees. I plead with the men who escorted me here, "God help me, I am not guilty of these accusations. I never sinned against the King. I am innocent!"

But they are unmoved. The lords commit me to the Lieutenant of the Tower.

I follow the constable and lieutenant through the Tower grounds, wrenching my neck to guess where my cell might be, and ask, "Sir William, shall I go to a dungeon now?"

Sir William is said to have been a formidable knight before age set in. And still his stare is intimidating. He shakes his head as my father used to when he corrected me. "No, madam. You shall go into the lodging you lay in at your coronation."

Once again I crumple to my knees. Then Henry must still care for me. He houses me as his Queen. The words spill out. "It is too good for me! *Jesu*, have mercy on me!" I wail and tremble, sloppy with tears. The foul-breathed liars who accuse me will be licking my boots or losing their heads, God help them! I break into sudden laughter, a laughter with teeth, a headless, heedless chortling.

For if the King still loves me, there is hope that he might pardon me. And then nothing else matters. Not this Tower prison or the false accusations against me. *Il y a de l'espoir.* There is hope, for the King has power over all.

3 MAY 1536

The Tower of London
The Queen's Lodgings

Spies. I'm surrounded by spies. Except for my childhood nurse, Mary Orchard, the five ladies who attend me in the Tower are enemies all—Lady Boleyn, my aunt and the wife of my father's younger

brother, who ought to stand beside me but instead is a staunch sup-
porter of the Lady Mary; Lady Anne Shelton, the mother of my favourite cousin, Madge, who never loved me, sometimes fears me, and
would rejoice to see my head on a stick; Mrs. Stonor, the wife of the
King's sergeant-at-arms, who serves only the King; Mrs. Coffin, the
wife of the Master of the Horse, who sleeps beside me on the pal-
let and says little but records in her mind everything I do or say for
Lord Cromwell; and Lady Kingston, the constable's wife, who makes
reports to him. They are all elder ladies and smell of dust mites and
disappointment. I question now whether the King has shown me any
favour at all, lodging me in these quarters.

No one has occupied these chambers since my coronation, and
they could yet use some airing out. Perhaps stuffed air suits a clois-
tered nun, but I am accustomed to palaces and gardens. Otherwise
the lodgings are as I remember them, quite luxurious and in the an-
tique style of my preference.

The spies and I gather in the large presence chamber. Even though
I wish to cry and curse my misfortune, I try to say little, in the hopes
that the ladies might reveal who is behind the treachery that has be-
fallen me.

"Lady Kingston, would you ask the constable if I might not see
my brother, George?"

The other attendants titter at my question, which elicits a very
scornful stare from Lady Kingston.

"You should make your requests directly to the constable," she
says sternly. "The ladies and I can provide you nothing."

"Then what, may I ask, is your purpose?"

Lady Kingston answers with a very wide smile. "To serve Your
Grace, of course."

Serve me to the wolves, perhaps.

Eventually, the other ladies become distracted with embroidery, and I'm able to sidle up to Mary Orchard and ask, "Why did they laugh when I mentioned my brother?"

"I beg your pardon, Your Grace, but the rumour is that George has been arrested and imprisoned in the Tower," Mary whispers.

I try not to gasp. "For what?"

"For"—Mary's eyes fall to the floor—"being with you in an improper and carnal way."

I turn red. My *brother* is the third man with whom I am accused of having been adulterous? I feel as if I might smash everything in the room. "Surely no one can believe—"

Lady Kingston interrupts. "What are you two whispering about? Mrs. Orchard, go busy yourself with the chamber pot." She looks at me. "Your Grace needs to prepare for dinner with the constable."

Except for its exquisite wainscot mantel etched with roses and the initials "H" and "A," the dining chamber of the Queen's lodgings is unremarkable. Across its long table sits Constable Kingston, with whom I am forced to take all my meals. At first I thought this loathsome, but today I'm eager to pull any information regarding my brother out of the man. But even with my clever tongue, Sir William is a brick.

I take a sip of wine. "I asked to have an audience with the King and was soundly denied. I asked to see my father and was told I could not seek his counsel. So now I enquire as to whether I might have a visit from my brother."

"You have been told, madam, that you are allowed no visitors while you are in the Tower," Sir William says sternly. He sniffs at his plate, clearly eager to dine.

"So Lord Cromwell will never visit me?"

"Well, perhaps he will."

"Please enquire as to whether the Lord Chancellor will visit me."

Sir William nods. "I will provide you the answer tomorrow."

"Thank you, I am much obliged."

Sir William tucks a napkin under his chin, picks up his knife, and prepares to settle into his meal. He assumes that our conversation is at a pause.

He must not often dine with women.

I wind the strand of pearls at my neck slowly around one finger. "If Lord Cromwell does not wish to visit me, would you enquire whether he knows anything further about the charges against me?"

The constable again nods, but with less patience.

"And does Lord Cromwell know if I shall be questioned and make a deposition? And if I shall give a deposition, who will question me?"

Another even less genial nod from Sir William.

"And has a trial date been set? And if a trial date has been set, then I presume the case against me must be recorded in some manner? And if a record has been made, can I not be told everyone who has been accused and arrested in regard to my case?"

Sir William looks dazed. I straighten the napkin in my lap. "Oh, and ask Lord Cromwell, if you please, that I enquire how fares the King? And Sir William, please do ask Lord Cromwell to pass on my good wishes and prayers for His Majesty." I smile at the constable.

Sir William stares at me. "Is that all, madam?"

"No, not *all*," I say. "Perhaps—"

Sir William interrupts. "Perhaps it would be best if Lord Cromwell paid you a visit, madam."

"If you think it best," I say. Before he takes his first bite I add, "I realize you may not frequently entertain royalty, but it is customary to address the Queen with formality."

Sir William must be starving, because he shoves an entire pig's foot into his mouth. "Yes, *madam*."

So already I am no longer the Queen to you! Well, *touché*, Constable. But Sir William must not realize that I can sword-fight with words, too, and far better than he.

"So, they have arrested my brother?" I ask him.

"I cannot say."

I scold him with a mischievous smile. "Are you not Constable of the Tower? How *incompetent* of you not to know the prisoners in your keeping." I swallow my first piece of meat.

"I *will* not say whether or not your brother is in the Tower," Sir William corrects himself.

"So then, George *is* a prisoner of yours. I ask you, sir, how am I to defend myself without knowing of what I am accused and who accuses me? I don't even know all of the men with whom I've committed adultery."

"I believe you know that well, madam." Lord Kingston smirks as he gnaws on a bone.

I pause.

"True." I nod.

Sir William abruptly stops eating and looks up at me, shocked that I would carelessly admit this.

My eyes enlarge. "For I have committed adultery with no one." Pleased with myself, I smile and lift my goblet.

"One man confessed," Sir William says.

My fist smashes the table. "That cannot be!" One might as well chop off one's own head. Unless the man was forced into confession. Lord Cromwell is a soulless dog and will go to any lengths, including torture, to get what he needs. "Shall I die without justice?"

Sir William replies, so earnest I want to wring his neck, "The poorest subject the King hath, hath justice."

If Sir William believes that, he is an abject fool.

Despite their claims, my hands are clean,
No guilt upon me ever seen,
Except my jealous heart doth mean
A wedge somehow was laid between
The King and his "Most Happy" Queen.

4 MAY 1536

The Tower of London
The Queen's Lodgings

When I closed my eyes last night, Elizabeth twirled among crimson rosebushes. In my dream, I picked her up and kissed her head, and for a heartbeat fled the confines of this Tower. We played together for several glorious minutes, and then the dream turned dark. *Ma petite* wandered into a garden maze. I called out, "Elizabeth!" and searched the maze to utter exhaustion, but I could not find her. I feared she was lost forever.

I woke up wet with tears, trembling. And yet I pray that this dream will visit me again, so we are together even if only for a moment.

The spies must have been told not to speak to me, so I can learn nothing further of the case being formed against me. They have been silent as spiders. But this afternoon I've decided we'll engage in a little needlework. We can fashion children's clothes for the poor out of some of my less ornate dresses. I pass out sewing baskets and some pieces of fabric and lining.

"I have figured out who is behind the false accusations and my imprisonment," I say as I choose my needle.

Lady Shelton moistens the end of her thread. "We'll not fall for that, Queen Anne. This is not a game of cards where you can bluff and trick us into revealing information."

I ignore her. "I prayed this morning and it all became very clear. I feel a fool for not seeing it before." I measure with my arm how much material I will need to construct a little girl's skirt. "For to prove that I was unfaithful with multiple men requires a masterful hand. And one man above all others has the ear of the King. Only Lord Cromwell could so quickly build a case against me. But not without assistance. Someone in my court must have fed him lies." I carefully cut my fabric in two. "Of course, I cannot yet be sure who betrayed me."

Lady Boleyn now laughs. "You always think yourself so clever, and yet no one is surprised that you are in the Tower. You've never been a victim, Queen Anne, only a viper. No one betrayed you. You betrayed yourself. You'll get no pity from me."

I lock eyes with my aunt. "I don't want your pity."

It's silent for several minutes as I baste running stiches down the hemline of my skirt. Then I say calmly, "Lady Boleyn is correct that my own actions led to my imprisonment."

"So you admit you were unfaithful to the King, lay with your brother, and wished for our dear sovereign's death?" the constable's wife asks.

"Of course I did none of those things." I shake my head. "But it is believed that I did, because of my past." I turn the fabric in my lap so I can backstitch and cover the seam. "It started long before Henry even knew I existed, when I left the French court and came back home to England in 1522. I was loath to marry the man to whom I was betrothed, James Butler, so I decided to choose my own husband, a husband I found worthy and pleasing. I worked to arrange my marriage to Henry Percy, and for this I was soundly whipped."

Lady Boleyn sighs as she snips away an errant stitch. "Oh, yes, I recall all of this."

"I had to be made an example." I untangle a knot in my thread and continue, "In Queen Katharine's court, I had become the arbiter of all that was *chic* and fetching. Whatever way I fixed my hair on Monday, on Tuesday all the ladies fashioned theirs that way. The men feared that because my style was imitated, I would be followed in regard to marriage arrangement as well. So the punishment for my 'brazen' behaviour had to be severe. They cast me out of the English court for several years—banished me to Hever Castle, my father's home in Kent."

"In my opinion you got off too easily," Lady Boleyn says as her basket falls onto the floor. Her awl rolls halfway across the room and pins scatter everywhere. Mrs. Coffin, whose chin, quite ironically, is shaped like that of a horse, immediately tidies up the mess. "You disgraced our family with that ridiculous Henry Percy affair," Lady Boleyn scoffs. "What woeful years those were for the family Boleyn. Your sister, Mary, was King Henry's mistress, and you were an upstart. It sickens me to remember all the dishonour you and your sister brought to us."

"Well, then you should remember that banishment was not my sole punishment. To further put me in my place, rumours were constructed—that I was a French snake with venom and fangs, not to be trusted. Devilish and grotesque, I had six fingers on one hand. Utter nonsense, but juicy and delicious gossip. . . ." I remove my gloves and hold up both hands. "As you can see, *seulement dix*."

This elicits laughter from Mary Orchard, Mrs. Stonor, and even Lady Shelton.

"Fine, but what has any of this to do with your being accused of adultery and locked in the Tower?" Lady Kingston asks.

"I think it will become clear," I say. "Where was I?"

"You had been banished from court," Mrs. Coffin reminds me. She does pay attention to my every word. And she also knits a fine pair of woollen stockings.

I smile at her. "Thank you. I was finally granted permission to return to court in the summer of 1525. And for whatever reason, perhaps because the rumours made me an intrigue, I found myself in the unenviable position of having the King's attention."

Mrs. Stonor stares at me as if I am an ungrateful child. "Most ladies at court would be thrilled to have the King's attention."

"King Henry had a wife his people loved." I rummage through my basket and find the perfect button to sew at the little skirt's waist. "I had been in enough courts to know that it never works out well for the mistress of the monarch. Katharine, the Queen I was bound to serve, would despise me. And selfishly, I wanted a husband with whom I could have legitimate children, not bastards.

"I tried everything I could to dissuade His Majesty," I continue. "Yet every action I took to escape his advances was misinterpreted. If I returned his gifts, people called me manipulative. If I ignored him, they said I tormented the King and toyed with his affections. If I spoke to him, I did so out of selfish ambition. Mean Anne Boleyn, the conniving *serpente française*. I had been back little more than six months when I felt forced to leave court a second time."

"I think you bend the truth," Lady Shelton says as she pricks and pounces a needlework pattern onto her embroidery. "You *chose* to return to Hever Castle—and a lady gets a reputation because she earns it."

I laugh. "I wish that were true! But sometimes, when the truth is not as dramatic as the rumour, it gets altered. And that's exactly what happened, God be my witness." I apply beeswax and thread my smaller finishing needle. "I admit it's a thrilling tale: The French whore slaps and insults people in Katharine's court. Evil Anne Boleyn tempts the King, flaunts herself in Queen Katharine's face, and acts in every manner vicious and cruel."

"If what people said about you was wrong," Lady Shelton sneers, "then why did you not correct them?"

"Dear Lady Shelton, who would have believed me? There's no use contradicting the story of record. My version's not nearly as amusing. Henry and his court prefer a good myth to a boring truth."

"Indeed." Lady Boleyn chuckles. I've never heard my aunt laugh when it wasn't with malice.

I drop my needle, then prick my finger retrieving it. "*Putain!*" It stings. The ladies look at me, horrified that I know such a word. "I will admit something of which I am very ashamed."

They all lean in, so close that I can smell their teeth.

I lower my voice. "While I returned home the second time, I caught the sweating sickness and nearly died. In my fevers, I often prayed that I would succumb to it, because I thought death a better fate than to sleep with the King."

Mrs. Stonor sets down her sewing abruptly. "That's a sin against not only His Majesty but God!"

I nod. "Yes. And when I recovered I felt dreadful for ever having thought it. I knew that Henry genuinely cared for me. If I could read you the letters we wrote each other that summer—so poetic and romantic! The truth was, we had fallen deeply in love. And I'm not ashamed of it."

"It was obvious to all that you had great passion for one another in those early years," Lady Boleyn admits. "But it was an immoral love and hurt Queen Katharine."

My face reddens, and my hands become fists. "Yes, there was Katharine. Even though she could bear no more children by then, and Henry could no longer bear Katharine, it is I, Anne Boleyn, who was blamed for everything. As if I caused all problems! As if Henry's need for a son were my invention!"

"You should have been content to be his mistress," Lady Shelton says simply. "But you are selfish and cruel. The King would have arranged a marriage for you after he tired of you, as he did for Bessie Blount."

I spool my unused thread, quickly at first, but then with less furore. "Yes, but that was not what the King wanted. He wanted a legitimate son. He already had a bastard, Henry FitzRoy. The idea to divorce Katharine, and the way in which to do it, came not from me."

"Whether or not it was your idea, His Majesty severed England from the Catholic Church in order to marry you, and our country has been shattered!" Lady Boleyn holds her needle as if she might take out her rage on the embroidery.

"You're wrong."

The ladies glare at me. It has been an undisputed fact that my marriage to Henry caused the break between him—along with all of England—and Rome. The people call me the Whore of All Christendom. The Concubine. The Evil Mistress!

I take a deep breath before I say, "Queen Katharine chose to sever the Church from England."

"Outrageous! How dare you say such a thing!" Lady Boleyn cries.

"Henry and the Pope asked Katharine many times to annul her marriage, and every time she refused. All she had to do was say their marriage was invalid and become the Princess Dowager, and England would have remained a Catholic nation. *She refused!* Katharine forced Henry to break with the Church. If he wanted to marry again and have a male heir, there was no other choice."

Lady Boleyn stamps her foot. "*You* should have refused."

"I should have refused King Henry the Eighth?" I cry, and it echoes through the chamber.

All the spiders cease stitching.

Lady Shelton stares at me a full minute before she twists her dull knife into my gut. "But after all that, you gave the King no male heir."

"True," I say. "I failed the King in many ways, but most of all, in that."

Quiet tears fall onto the little girl's skirt that covers my lap. Still unfinished, the skirt collects my pain like a napkin—soaks up everything untidy, that it might disappear and be forgotten.

> *I pray for the soul of my son,*
> *The heir I promised, the one*
> *To prove my place, then none*
> *Could doubt, could Queen Anne shun.*

5 MAY 1536

The Tower of London
The Queen's Lodgings

Lord Chancellor Cromwell always wears a look as if he smells something foul. Age has not been good to Thomas. Perhaps punishing people on the rack does that to a man, gnaws off anything beautiful or vibrant he once possessed, leaving him like pickings for the dogs. Thomas Cromwell helped seat me on the throne, and now he intends to snatch it out from under me.

He scuffles into my chambers and surveys the room. "Hardly a prison cell Your Grace is confined to."

I make no response.

"Sir William informs me that you have questions."

"Right to business, Lord Cromwell. You don't even wish to know how I fare?" I tease. "Well, I suppose you know that already, don't you?" I shake my head, then ask, "Might we be alone?"

"Very well." He waves his hand and dismisses my attendants before I even have time to adjust my gloves.

I can't decide if I should sit or remain standing. I elect to stand. "I know it is you, Lord Cromwell, who conspired to put me in the Tower." I pause for him to react, but he stares blankly at my headpiece instead of meeting my eyes.

"And I believe I know from whom you have support." I step closer to him. "I pity you, Thomas. Only a desperate man asks for help from his enemies."

"I'm certain I don't know what you mean, Your Grace," Lord Cromwell says without sarcasm. "But perhaps you should reserve your pity for yourself. It is you, not I, who is a prisoner."

I laugh. "Oh, you think you're not a prisoner?"

"Madam, I haven't time for this." He starts for the door.

I block his path. "I wonder why you must destroy me. Why not just send me away, as with Katharine?"

Lord Cromwell makes no answer. He taps his toe, impatient to leave.

But I have no intention of letting him go yet. I suspect that Katharine's daughter, Mary, and the Seymours are aiding Cromwell in his plot against me, and I want him to confirm it. "Why would the supporters of Lady Mary and Jane Seymour align with you?" I ask. "They know that it was you who turned Henry away from the Pope so he could marry me. They know you fought with vigour to destroy Katharine. Why would they ever forgive you for that?" I seek his eyes. "Is your shared hatred for me so intense that it alone binds you all?"

Lord Cromwell responds slowly. "Your Grace is in the Tower because of no conspiracy, but because of your vile and treasonous crimes against His Majesty."

I wag my finger in reprimand. "We both know that's not true."

"I did not want to believe that you could commit such crimes against our King," Lord Cromwell continues. "But I cannot argue with evidence. And now I expect that you and the men you took as lovers will be punished to the full extent of the law and put to death."

My fists would like to beat Lord Cromwell until he screams for mercy, but to show anger now would be weakness. "I do not doubt that, sir, for you are a soulless man. At first I wondered why you would destroy the lives of five innocent men, and not just mine. And then I realized that this scheme of yours works best if those who might defend me are implicated as well. I can only imagine what false evidence was presented to the King."

Our eyes meet. I widen my gaze with an aim to peer inside his skull. The man cannot handle more than ten seconds of direct scrutiny. He looks down, looks away.

"I can answer none of this." He tries to push past me.

I grab his arm and clench it as I would the mane of an unbroken horse. "*La faute est le vôtre!* All fault lies with you, Lord Cromwell! His Majesty is innocent in all of this, as are the noble men who stand accused beside me. I pray for you, Thomas. You, more than anyone else, require great redemption for your sins."

"Good day, madam," Lord Cromwell says, then wrestles free of my grasp and is gone. But he leaves behind a sour stench that lingers.

> *What vanity draws one to the crown,*
> *Round which vultures do abound?*
> *It's never safe, no truth be found,*
> *They vanquish love to knock me down.*

6 MAY 1536

◇·◇

The Tower of London
The Queen's Lodgings

All my thoughts today are of the King. I am flooded with memories of Henry and me. How could one who loved me so dearly allow me to be locked in the Tower? *Mon Henri, je ne comprends pas.*

When we were first married, the very sky above us proclaimed our love with thunderous applause. On that first trip to France together, our most successful trip to Calais when Francis, the King of France, publicly accepted me as your new Queen, violent storms held us weeks past our scheduled return to England. And that's when we became man and wife.

"Anne," you whispered as we strolled through the grounds of your French palace. You pulled me to your side. Rain fell in sheets like windows of glass. It soaked my hair and muddied my velvet gown. "Do you trust me?" I nodded and you covered my face with your hands and said, "Close your eyes; I will lead you."

I shut my eyes against the rain and took your hand. We walked for what must have been nearly a mile, over slippery moss and uneven rocks, but you held me securely.

I smelled the horses before we reached the stables. Under the cover of that meager wooden structure, we shook off our top layer of rain. The thunder of God's fierce whip cracked above us, followed by lightning like veins of fireworks. I trembled from the wet and the cold, and something deeper, too.

You wrapped a blanket, which had been hanging over one of the stalls, around my shoulders. "It's not elegant, but we are finally truly alone," you said.

I nodded and tried to stop my teeth from chattering. You slowly rubbed warmth into my hands and feet. We watched the storm in total silence.

Then you pulled from your pocket that exquisite rope of rare black pearls. I remembered immediately the same piece of jewellery having been on Katharine's chest. I knew exactly what you were giving me, the necklace passed down through centuries of English queens. "I want to see how it looks on you," you said.

I turned to the side so you could fasten it around my neck.

"No, Anne." You shook your head. "I want to see how it, alone, looks on the Queen."

And perhaps I should have hesitated, but I didn't. I could feel every part of my body completely at the same time, powerfully alive and alert. I felt as if I had swallowed the lightning. I wanted you more than I knew was possible. We had waited almost seven years. I nearly ripped off my dress.

Elizabeth may have been conceived not in the royal bed, but in a stable small and meek.

We had adjoining bedchambers in our house in Calais, yet there was always some attendant sniffing around us. But after the night of the black pearls, we found ways to sneak into each other's rooms. The stormy weather made for lots of time in bed. We feasted on each other like owls in a field of mice.

You were anxious to be married at the first sign that I might be pregnant. But I knew it was important that we say vows in England, not France. So as soon as our ship was safe at shore, we held our small, secret ceremony in a country church. We promised ourselves to each other until death do us part.

Little did I know that marriage to you would be more a parting of two lovers than a union. I believed that the love we shared was unique, transcendent. But eventually, I became just your second wife.

The first nine months, while I was pregnant with what we were certain was a son, you continued to shower me with love and affection. But I was no longer your playmate or confidante, no longer your equal. I became like a porcelain vase—precious, but weak.

You made clear to me my new position during the pheasant hunt in 1533.

Before dawn lit up the fields of Hampton Court, everything stood still. The day waited like a church bell to be rung. I fed my horse, Midas, three carrots for good luck, then advised the Master of the Horse how to adjust my saddle while I selected the perfect rifle. I was determined to be the one who killed the first pheasant, the victor, as I had been two years prior.

The Queen's stables lay on the far side of the palace, so when Midas and I trotted out to join you, most of your party was already assembled.

All talking ceased. You looked at me with horror. "Anne! What are you doing? Get down from that horse now!"

My cheeks flushed at the sternness in your voice. "But today is the pheasant hunt."

You quickly waved the others away so we could speak alone. Softer now, you helped me off Midas. "My dear, you cannot think you would come with us?"

"But we have always opened the season together, my love. I'm a better marksman than three-quarters of your men."

You smiled and patted the ever-growing bump beneath my gown. "The Queen has matters of far more importance now." Your next words were directed to my belly. "Hello, Prince of England! Tell your mother that she must think of you and your safety, not her own vain needs and rewards."

"That was not what I was—"

You kissed my forehead gently. "I know, my sweet. But do remember that the first role of the Queen is to be the mother of princes."

I nodded.

"I will see you at tonight's banquet." You mounted your horse as I turned Midas to return him to his stall.

You looked over your shoulder and called, "Wish me luck, wife! I intend to be the victor today!"

I tried to sound cheerful as I replied, "You will ever be the victor, dear Henry. The Prince and I send you luck and glory."

But after four pregnancies, I failed to provide you a son. I was no better than Katharine. I thought the roles of *amour* and wife were not so dissimilar, that a clever woman could be both at once. But for you a woman was either a mistress or a Queen. One you loved and flattered, the other you ordered about, expecting her to obey.

I don't want to believe that one who once loved me so much could be part of this, but I have never known the King to be anyone's fool. If I am in the Tower, you must want me here, Henry. *Je dis ça, je dis rien.* To say this is to state the obvious.

6 MAY 1536

Dear Henry,

I am at a loss for exactly what to say to you. I find myself in the most unlikely place, so much in your disfavour that I am a prisoner in the Tower. You request that I confess and thereby obtain my safety. But I don't know what Your Majesty desires me to confess.

I cannot profess a sin that I never even considered, let alone committed. You couldn't have a more loyal and loving wife. I could stand

before God and Your Majesty and assure you that I never faltered in
my duties. You chose me to be your Queen, which was more than I ever
deserved or desired. If Your Grace ever found me worthy, please don't
let the lies of my enemies persuade you that I am anything but your
dutiful wife. Don't let them tarnish my name or that of our daughter, the
Princess Elizabeth.

Put me on trial, but let me be judged by a jury who is not composed
only of my enemies. If the trial is open and fair, then justice will be
evident and my name will be cleared or my guilt proclaimed.

But if you have already decided that my fate is to die so that you
may find happiness elsewhere, I pray that God will pardon you and the
enemies who helped to construct my demise. Final judgement is with
God, and we all will soon enough stand before Him. I have no fear of
this, because I am innocent.

My only hope is that I alone will pay for this; that you will pardon
the innocent men accused alongside me. If you ever loved me, I beg Your
Majesty to grant this request. I pray that God keep you well and aid you
as you make your decisions. I write these words to you from my sad and
dreary prison cell.

> Your Most Loyal and Ever Faithful Wife,
> Anne Boleyn

9 MAY 1536

The Tower of London
The Queen's Lodgings

I have asked to see my almoner that I might take Communion and
make my confession, but Lord Cromwell denies me. Even the spiders
that spin about my chamber find this to be callous and unfair.

"Why would he not wish Queen Anne to confess to her almoner?" Mrs. Stonor asks Lady Kingston. "He could use a confession against the Queen at her trial."

Lady Kingston shrugs.

"Even lowly and common criminals are afforded the right to repent before their execution," Lady Boleyn says. "I shall petition Lord Cromwell on your behalf, Queen Anne."

"I would be grateful." I try to smile at my aunt, but it is a limp smile. I have not been able to eat or sleep much the past several days.

"You look poorly," Lady Shelton says with apparent concern.

"J'ai le cafard." My teeth feel like cannonballs. I struggle to speak. "It means I have the cockroach, that I have melancholia. I haven't felt this low since my miscarriage four months ago."

"You must pray, and ask the Lord for strength." Lady Boleyn takes my hand.

I am not used to such kindness from these women, and start to cry. "I have lost the words." I swipe at my eyes. "Have any of you had children come too soon?"

Every woman in the chamber nods.

"Then you understand how wretched it feels. And this last death for me was the most painful because I lost the King's son. I would not be here had our baby lived."

"The death of children hurts all mothers," Mrs. Stonor says. "But the death of the King's son is the greatest loss."

I pound the arms of my chair. "And yet there was one who attended me who delighted in that death. The Lady Jane Seymour."

"That cannot be true," Lady Shelton says.

"Oh, but it is," I say. "Never having been with child, she had no understanding of the emotions one feels when carrying a life within. That wench took up with my husband just after I became pregnant with my last baby. Whatever unkindness you all think I did to Katha-rine, I never was with Henry when she was still able to conceive. But Jane flaunted her affair with the King in my face. She and her best friend, Nan Cobham. And I could do nothing, for she had the favour of the King."

"But didn't you humiliate the girl?" Lady Shelton says. "I heard a story in which you put her to shame."

"You mean the time she blatantly defied me?" I wear anger now as I would a beloved hat. And it is much more fetching than sorrow. "I remember it well."

It was the summer of 1533, just after my coronation, when I was quite pregnant with Elizabeth. Every day my ladies and I collected items for the poor—scraps of materials, boots, leftover food from the kitchen, the ends of tapers, and coins from those more fortunate. In my court, I promoted charity, piety, and education among my atten-dants, not just embroidery and gossip. I kept an English Bible in my privy chamber and encouraged my ladies to read it. I believe firmly that a woman's mind is as capable as a man's, but it must be culti-vated lest it go fallow. Henry has always been an enlightened king, and he valued my discourse on many subjects, especially theology. So I would read Bible passages and discuss them with my ladies to clarify my thoughts before sharing them with the King.

One morning I asked my lady Jane Seymour to select a passage and read it aloud.

She looked at me blankly.

I waved my hand impatiently for her to "read any passage of your choice."

But not only did she fail to move from her chair, Jane turned away from me and sought out Nan Cobham, as if this woman commanded my court.

I shook my head and said to Lady Rochford, "Is the girl stupid or defiant?"

Lady Rochford shrugged, as perplexed by Jane's behaviour as I was. Quickly the room filled with whispers.

Jane saw that her behaviour was inappropriate and scurried up to the Bible. She flipped through several pages, but held each by the corner as if to touch the page might give her the sweating sickness.

I waited, but Lady Seymour spoke not a word.

I was now quite frustrated, and my tone became less kind. "*Vous avez un chat dans la gorge?*" It took a moment before I realized that no one, not even Lady Rochford, understood me. I translated, "Do you have a cat in your throat? Can't you speak?"

Still Jane said nothing, but her pale skin inflamed.

I leaned over to Lady Rochford and my cousin Madge and said, loudly enough that all my attendants could hear, "You don't suppose this girl cannot read? That I have a lady in my court of no education?"

Laughter erupted and Jane Seymour started to snivel like a child.

She pled to Nan Cobham, "I can't. An English Bible is against God's law."

"Stupid and vile creature, do you now dishonour the King and his religion?" I pointed my finger to my side and commanded, "Come here!"

Jane approached, even cowered before me, yet somehow maintained a judgemental eye.

I considered slapping her indignant cheek so she'd wear my handprint to dinner, but my dear baby Elizabeth kicked inside me for the first time. "Oh, how remarkable!" I cried with glee. "Feel that!" I placed Lady Rochford's hand on my womb.

"It must be a boy! Such a fearsome kick," my sister-in-law crowed, delighted.

"Lady Seymour," I ordered with a quick wave. "Leave my sight. And pray that I say nothing of your behaviour to His Majesty."

* * *

Lady Shelton shakes her head. "No, I speak of a different incident, one in which you ripped a necklace from Jane Seymour and then slapped her on the face."

"Oh, I happily admit to that," I say. "She deserved more than a slap. I tore that locket Henry gave her from around her neck so violently I injured my hand. That happened but a few months ago, soon after I lost my son. I was so miserable. I came to see the King, but he offered me no comfort. His only remark was 'I'll have no more sons by you!' So when Jane had the indecency to gloat in my privy chamber by twirling her locket, I snatched it from her throat and slapped her."

All the women look at one another, mortified.

"But I've met Jane Seymour. She is sweet and harmless," Lady Boleyn says. "And weak, as if one could crush her with a stare."

"Perhaps she appears harmless." I cross the room. "But to survive at court, one must be cunning. Beware the quiet ones, my mother always said. They are the greatest deceivers of all."

I press my hands against the window. A flock of blackbirds lifts off the lawn. I wish I could break through the glass and fly away with them. "I can admit when I have been outplayed with my own hand." I return my gaze to the women in the room. "Jane now unseats me in almost the identical manner in which I dethroned Katharine."

The bile rises in my throat. "The one difference being that Jane wants to take my head and the heads of five innocent men. She's not content to have only my jewellery, titles, sceptre, and crown."

"You are impossible, Queen Anne. The moment I start to feel sympathy for you," Lady Boleyn huffs, "you say things so utterly preposterous."

"I do, don't I?" I agree with a bitter laugh. "And I shall pay for them all."

POOR JANE SEYMOUR

It's a shame you've behaved so obscene.
I have wisdom could pass us between.
But I loathe you, will offer no keen
Advantage to Henry's next queen.

11 MAY 1536

The Tower of London
The Queen's Lodgings

By the King's merciful order, Lord Cromwell allows me to meet with my almoner, John Skip. It has been an immeasurable blessing to have John's guidance and comfort.

Reading this morning from the Book of Hours that Almoner Skip brought me, I found my mind wandering back to a time before Henry and I were married. We used to send each other secret love notes in a Book of Hours much like the one I cradle now. At the beginning of our romance, Henry and I found many ways to express our passion. We would sneak away on picnics and dance in secluded corners of the garden. We played cards until dawn just to be together. Henry would follow my trail of dropped handkerchiefs around the palace, then attack me with kisses.

I remember a certain afternoon when we were playing chess. I took out Henry's queen with my bishop and trapped his king. Anywhere he moved, my queen would now defeat him. I smiled and announced, "Checkmate."

Henry pushed away from the table. "Enough of chess." He yanked me out of my chair with great enthusiasm. "I have a surprise for you."

"I thought you had a meeting with your Privy Council this afternoon?"

"Posh, those things are so tedious. Lord Cromwell will manage without me. What did I make him Lord Chancellor for if not to attend to such matters so I might do as I please?" Henry gently kissed my neck, then whispered into my ear, "And it pleases me to spend the afternoon with you, my love, so fetch your cloak."

We raced on horseback through fields and forests, down dusty, deserted paths, until we reached Henry's newest palace at Hampton Court. Cardinal Wolsey, before his death, had spent years building himself this luxurious estate. Completed, it was grander than any palace the King possessed. When Henry first toured it, his eyes had flamed with jealousy. The cardinal immediately made a gift of the house to his sovereign and stifled his own discontent.

"You must see what I have done!" Henry boasted. "It will please you greatly, *ma chérie*." He dismissed all attendants and pushed open the ballroom door.

Every eave, every beam was etched with our entwined initials.

I gasped with delight. Henry squeezed my hand, then twirled me around the room in a lively gavotte. At the end of the dance he pulled me so close I could feel his heart beat against my chest. We kissed until we were breathless, our bodies aching to do more. Quickly he led me into his new privy chamber. A velvet jewellery box sat on the bed. He put his arms around my waist and guided me towards it. "Open it, my love."

Inside was the most beautiful sapphire necklace I had ever seen. "*C'est si belle. Merci, merci, mon amour.*"

Henry pushed aside the box. Before I could protest, he rolled on top of me, hard with desire.

"We cannot—"

Pressing a finger against my lips, he said, "I know. We will wait until you are Queen, and then I will fill you with sons." He kissed my neck, my breasts, and panted as he slid my hand inside his breeches. "But there are other ways to satisfy me."

When I hesitated, he whispered, "I will tell you what to do."

I was more than eager to obey.

What Henry taught me to do that day sustained him for seven years.

But how quickly things change.

Henry had always given up his mistress as soon as he could bed me again. But when I recovered from my last miscarriage, Henry kept Jane. Something had shifted in him. In his eyes I had become like a snake, poisonous and cursed by God. I lost my usefulness. I lost his heart. He showered Jane, not me, with gifts. I became a tempest of jealousy, and that pushed Henry even further away.

I raged and stamped my foot the last time I caught Jane curled around his feet.

"You are selfish and cruel to torment me like this, with her!" I yelled at the King as I kicked Jane's skirt.

"Remember to whom you speak!" Henry raised his voice so loud it echoed through the halls.

The wicked strumpet smiled at me.

"You would do well to act as did the one who came before you. She knew how to be Queen!" Henry thundered, then ordered his guards, "Take her out of my sight!"

I could not breathe to speak. But before the King's guards could drag me off, I stormed of my own will out of the room.

I probably should have accepted Jane; that might have spared Elizabeth the pain of what befalls me now. But then, Katharine knew how to be Queen and she ended up poorly, separated from her daughter, the Lady Mary, and dying destitute and alone.

But at least Katharine kept her head.

Henry wants always the rose and never the thorn. I thought he wanted it all, a partner of a more equal nature. But he does not. Or he does no longer.

Jane is now the King's tender rose petal, and I have become only that which stabs and causes him pain. But perhaps Henry forgets that a rose without thorns, a flower severed from the branch, smells sweet and looks pretty but withers fast.

My dear King, *pas d'amour existe sans douleur.* No love exists without pain.

12 MAY 1536

The Tower of London

THE TRIAL OF THE FOUR

The axes turned towards them, four men will pay,
All sentenced to die in five short days.
Their trials were doomed, not a chance had they.
When Henry said guilty, all jurors obeyed.

Mark Smeaton, I hope the devil will flay
You body and soul. No words can convey
My utter remorse for letting you play
Your music at court. I rue every day.

Dear Henry Norris, for you I shall pray.
The Groom of the Stool now cast away.
Loved so by Henry they had to belay
His servant and friend with claims you betray.

Good Francis Weston, your future is grey.
A fine partner in sport, a mate most gay,
Quite highly esteemed, so thus they portray
Their possible foe as lewd and risqué.

Will Brereton, you were there at Calais.
We've hunted together, but I must say
I know you least well. Perhaps you fell prey,
Opposed the wrong someone, got in the way.

My fate was sealed by the verdicts today.
But I'll beg of the King, let Anne alone pay,
And plead that these innocent men he stay.

13 MAY 1536

◇ · ◇

The Tower of London
The Queen's Lodgings

"She has been in the privy since before dawn," Mrs. Coffin complains. "And not for need of it."

"Queen Anne, come out, have some tea, and let us take off your nightgown and wash your face," Mary Orchard coos outside the door.

"I am going to die," I say. I swing open the privy door with great force, then collapse into the chair beside my bed.

All five ladies bustling around the bedchamber freeze.

"There is always hope of a reprieve," Lady Boleyn offers, but the slant in her eyes reveals what she truly thinks and what we all know: Henry will never stay my execution.

The room is warm; still I shiver. The accused men were found guilty and sentenced to die yesterday. My brother and I will suffer the same fate in two days.

"I searched my soul last night and discovered why it is God's will that I should die."

"Queen Anne, perhaps you should rest." Mrs. Orchard tries to brush back my hair.

I push her hands away. "I shall rest soon enough. You must understand this—in God's eyes I owe retribution, not for a crime I committed against the King, but for an injustice I did to another."

Lady Shelton, Lady Boleyn, and all my attendants surround me with cloths, a blanket, nourishment, and other items of comfort. But I want none of it.

"God is punishing me for my ill-treatment of the Lady Mary."

Mrs. Coffin's eyes widen. "Then the rumours are true. You tried to poison Princess Mary?"

"What? I did no such thing!"

Lady Shelton sets down the basin of water to cleanse my face, then separates from the rest of the group. "No, but what you did to Mary, the way you forced me to discipline her—poisoning the girl might have been kinder."

I feel as if something caged inside me breaks out of my chest. "I once said Mary will be my death, and I will be hers."

Lady Boleyn looks confused. "You cannot mean that Lady Mary is responsible for your death?"

I take a deep breath, then explain. "You all know that after I was crowned, Henry demanded that his subjects sign an oath which declared that he held supreme authority over both church and state in England, and that I was his only legitimate wife. Everyone either signed the oath or was hauled to the Tower. Lady Mary and Princess Dowager Katharine refused to sign it. However, unlike all others, they were not imprisoned. But their failure to do what Henry wanted infuriated him.

"He stormed around Westminster, so livid at Mary he punched his hand through the back of a chair. 'She is disrespectful, disobedient, and more stubborn than her mother!' he cried. 'She won't sign the oath? Then she will be *made* to understand her place!'"

Lady Kingston gasps.

I look down. "I hate to remember what happened next."

Elizabeth was only two months old when the King decided he would establish a household for her at Eltham. As my baby received titles, an estate, a livery, an inheritance, and a large staff, her half sister was stripped of all that makes one royal. Because of her shameful disobedience, Mary had nothing, and so was forced to live in Elizabeth's household. Henry sent me to Eltham and asked me to oversee the change in rank.

When I arrived, I was appalled. "Those draperies are dreadful," I said to Lady Shelton, whom I had chosen to be Elizabeth's governess. "Dour and Spanish. Have them changed to something cheerful for the Princess."

"Yes, Queen Anne," Lady Shelton said, and made careful notes of all my commands.

I ran my glove over the mantel and held up a finger of dust. "Not acceptable," I told her as I crossed to the window. "Where is the Lady Mary?"

Lady Shelton hesitated. "She complained that the smell of your perfume makes her ill."

"What? How dare she disrespect me! She will address me at once!" I cried.

With fear in her eyes, Lady Shelton explained, "Lady Mary has barricaded herself inside her bedchamber and refuses to come out until you leave."

I gritted my teeth and said, "She has, has she?"

I hoofed upstairs faster than a horse on fire. Lady Shelton trailed behind me.

I banged on the chamber door. "Mary!"

No reply.

"Mary, I know you are in there." I pounded harder. "The consequences will be dire if you do not answer your Queen!"

A muffled giggle and then Mary said, "No Queen is at Eltham today. And I have no obligation to speak to my father's mistress. The only Queen I will ever acknowledge is my mother."

"You dare to disgrace and defy your father?" I screamed. "I should rip out your insolent tongue!"

Mary laughed. "My father would never allow that."

"Let me in this minute!" I commanded. I repeatedly kicked Lady

Mary's door, almost demolishing it, before she finally released the lock. As I rushed towards her, she grinned.

I wanted to claw the smile off her face. I narrowed my eyes. "This chamber is too grand for the likes of you. You will serve the Princess Elizabeth and eat and sleep in the servants' quarters."

I turned to Lady Shelton. "No one shall call this bastard a lady until she learns respect."

Mary sniped back, "I respect those who *deserve* respect."

I exploded, "I should throw your proud Spanish blood into the sea!" and slapped her soundly across the face.

Mary gloated as if *she* had bested *me*.

So I hit the spoiled brat again. A large red bruise surfaced on her cheek.

The crease in Mary's forehead furrowed exactly as her father's does when he becomes enraged. She sneered at me. "Everyone hates you."

I ordered Lady Shelton, "Hold her in place," then drew back my arm and struck Mary with enough force to knock her to her knees.

Tears rolled out of her eyes, but still Mary did not cry out or recoil.

My palm stung as if I had burned it. I told Lady Shelton, "No food for the insolent bastard unless she wishes to apologize to me. She can repent or eat only her indignant words."

Lady Shelton nodded as a tear trickled down her cheek.

Elizabeth began to cry softly in a chamber below. A great need to cradle my baby welled up within me. I quickly abandoned Mary and followed my daughter's voice downstairs.

Mary ate nothing during the two days I remained at Eltham. She never spoke to me again.

"That's horrid," Mrs. Stonor says.

I inhale deeply. "Several times I offered to reconcile Mary with her father. In return, all I asked was that she recognize me as her Queen. But Mary refused to acknowledge me. I wanted to punish her. I deprived her of all comfort. I ordered Lady Shelton to lock Mary in her room and nail the windows shut when visitors came, so that no reports of her ill-treatment could be made."

Lady Shelton glowers at me with absolute loathing.

I use Mrs. Orchard as a crutch to help me rise. "I hate to remember all the vile things I did to a girl who chose to stand up for herself and her mother. I fear I have cursed Elizabeth to a similar fate. I pray that with the penance of my death, God will forgive me and spare my daughter."

Lady Shelton shakes her head. "There are not enough prayers in Heaven for that."

My lip trembles as I hold back tears.

Mrs. Orchard pats my shoulder. "Queen Anne, all children pay for the mistakes of their parents. And all parents make mistakes."

15 MAY 1536

—◇·◇—

The Tower of London
The King's Hall

Like a snake unfurling its long, venomous tongue, Lord Cromwell unrolls the list of charges for which I will be condemned. He looks at me, somewhat unnerved by my composure. Did he expect me to break down and weep? Did he imagine I would beg forgiveness for crimes I didn't commit? The man ought to know me better than that.

I am still unsure of what accusations I'll be asked to defend, nor have I been told what evidence will be used against me, but I am clear about the outcome of this trial. Nothing I do or say today will sway the jury of my peers. For they, as I, serve the King. I will be sentenced to death.

But that does not mean I must cower before my enemies.

Cromwell clears his wretched throat. He reads the paper without meeting my eyes. "'Queen Anne, who has been the wife of Henry the Eighth for three years and more, despising her marriage, entertaining malice against the King, and following daily her frail and carnal lust, did falsely and traitorously procure by base conversations and kisses, touching, and other infamous actions, the King's daily and familiar servants to be her adulterers and concubines.'"

A crowd of over two thousand has assembled to watch the Attorney General and Lord Cromwell present their case against me. They gasp at Cromwell's words, for the charges are designed to alarm.

Still I hold my head high. I have decided to think of this trial as just another royal event. It will likely be my final appearance as the Queen of England, and I intend to maintain grace and dignity. I chose my wardrobe carefully—a black velvet dress over a petticoat of scarlet damask and a small black cap with a white feather. My fashion has always been my armour. I suit up, and it makes me feel impenetrable.

Lord Cromwell continues, "'On the sixth of October 1533 at Westminster, and diverse days before and after, the Queen procured, by sweet words, kisses, touches, and otherwise, Henry Norris, Gentleman of the Privy Chamber, to violate her, and at Westminster on October twelfth, 1533, they had illicit intercourse at various times, both before and after, sometimes by his procurement, and sometimes by that of the Queen. Also the Queen on November second, 1535, and several times before and after, at Westminster, procured and incited her own natural brother, George Boleyn, Lord Rochford, Gentleman of the Privy Chamber, to violate her, alluring with her tongue in the said George's mouth, and the said George's tongue in hers, and also with kisses, presents, and jewels; whereby Lord Rochford, despising the commands of God, and all human laws, on November fifth, 1535, violated and carnally knew the said Queen, his own sister, at Westminster; which he also did on diverse other days before and after at the same place, sometimes by his own procurement and sometimes by the Queen's.'"

Someone in the crowd yells, "Filthy whore!" and then is echoed by many. Murmuring and spitting abound. My uncle, Lord Norfolk, who presides over this trial as the Lord High Steward and stands as proxy for the King, demands silence and order.

Lord Cromwell speaks more loudly, bolstered by the jeering spectators. "'Also, the Queen, on December third, 1533, and diverse days before and after . . .'" He recites a staggering list of my carnal crimes. December this, October then, names, dates, and locations bounce around the courtroom like tennis balls. "'At Westminster, William Brereton, at Hampton Court, Sir Francis Weston, at Westminster, Mark Smeaton . . .'"

I shake my head and prepare to enter my plea. But Thomas Cromwell, who clearly likes the sound of his own voice, isn't finished.

"'Lords Rochford, Norris, Brereton, Weston, and Smeaton, inflamed with love for the Queen, became very jealous of each other, and gave the Queen secret gifts and pledges while carrying on their illicit intercourse. And because the Queen could not endure any of them to converse with any other woman, she gave them great gifts to encourage them in their crimes.'"

He eyes me up and down with a look of contempt that might be dismantling if there were any truth in his words. "'And further, the said Queen and these other traitors conspired the death and destruction of the King. The Queen also said she would marry one of them as soon as the King died, and that she never loved the King in her heart. And thus, the Queen and the other traitors have committed treason in contempt of the Crown, and against the issue and heirs of the King.'"

The court roars and rumbles with such fervour it feels as if the ground might crack apart. Lord Cromwell almost smiles as he asks me, "How do you plead to these crimes?"

"Not guilty," I say with absolute resolve.

"Your plea is so entered," the Attorney General says, and gestures for the clerk to record it thus.

"Now we shall present the evidence against you," Lord Cromwell says. "On the first account with Henry Norris, a gentleman of the King's privy chamber, you stand accused of adultery on October sixth and twelfth, 1533, at Westminster, and we have sworn statements that—"

"October 1533?" I ask.

"Yes, that is what I said, madam."

"In October 1533 I was at Greenwich, not Westminster," I say. "It was not a month since the Princess Elizabeth was born."

"Perhaps you are mistaken about the date?" Thomas shuffles through some papers.

"I am not," I say firmly. "The birth of my first child was an eagerly anticipated event. I did not leave Greenwich for two months. And I entertained no visitors; I rarely saw even the King. Only the newborn Princess and my attendants. And I could most definitely not have had carnal relations on October twelfth, Lord Cromwell. It was but a month since I gave birth."

"Well, perhaps that date was miscopied in my papers, then. It matters not; what is important is the act of adultery you committed with Sir Henry Norris," Cromwell says as he readjusts his collar.

"I committed no adultery with Sir Henry Norris, then nor at any other time," I say. "And if the date does not matter, then why did you specify it? Perhaps the use of dates makes it appear as though you have a valid case against me, when in fact you do not, Lord Cromwell? May I ask, did Sir Henry confess to this?"

"Sir Henry was convicted of this crime and sentenced to die," Lord Cromwell says. "Whether he confessed is irrelevant."

"Indeed." I nod.

The crowd no longer screams "Filthy whore!" but sits quietly, listening to my every remark. Many heads shake in disbelief.

"As to the accusation of adultery with William Brereton on December—"

"I am not guilty of any of these accusations, Lord Cromwell, despite what your witnesses might have told you. I can directly dispute several other dates you mentioned, for either I was not at the palace you allege or I was in seclusion or I was miscarrying the King's child."

The crowd is dead silent. It appears the people of England, for once, are considering my side.

After I have caught Lord Cromwell five more times using an impossible date or location for my alleged adulterous act, the state rests its case. I am not allowed to present any defence beyond this.

My uncle as Lord High Steward calls on each member of the jury to announce his verdict. One by one, all twenty-six men say, "Guilty." The axe head turns towards me.

I sit unmoving, knowing that all eyes watch as the crown is removed from my head. Then my uncle strips me of every title ever bestowed upon me, and all my property. With each retraction, I feel as if he rips away pieces of my gown so that I'm left standing before the court in nothing but my shift.

As Lord High Steward, my uncle must read aloud my sentence. He took pleasure in arresting me less than a month ago, but now tears stream down his face. "Anne Boleyn, because you have offended our sovereign, the King, in committing treason against his person, the law of the realm is that you deserve death, either to be burned here on the Tower Green or to have your head smitten off, whichever the King prefers."

It's not that I had no expectation of receiving a death sentence. The four men accused with me were sentenced to die. And my brother, whose trial follows mine, will certainly be convicted and sentenced to die as well. But hearing my uncle read aloud that I will be burned alive or beheaded is something I couldn't entirely prepare for. My nurse, Mary, shrieks so loudly and dreadfully at the news that the Earl of Northumberland collapses and must be carried out of the hall.

Through all the chaos and shock, my eyes look to Heaven. And when the room settles enough for my voice to be heard, I address the judges and people. I try to maintain an even tone. "My lords, I won't say that your sentence is unjust. I believe you have reasons for what you have done, but they must be other than the offences laid against me in this court, because I am innocent of those. I've been a faithful wife to the King. I admit that I haven't always shown him the humility he deserved. I confess that I've been jealous and suspicious of him. And I wasn't wise enough to be discreet about it all the time. But God knows, I haven't sinned against the King in any other way. I don't say this because I hope to prolong my life. I have Christ's example of how to die, and I accept that that is now my fate. As for my brother and the others who are unjustly condemned, I would willingly suffer many deaths to save them. But if it so pleases the King, we will die together. Heaven holds for us endless peace and joy, and from there I will pray to God for the King and for you, my lords."

I don't know how the crowd or jury responds to my words. Because before I can lose courage or the balance required to walk with grace, I pick up my skirt and exit the hall.

What evident truths were found within
The trial of Anne and George Boleyn?

Hearsay and rumours of vague origin,
Vile perversions and myriad sin,
But positive proof of their crimes—
That was thin.

16 MAY 1536

The Tower of London
The Queen's Lodgings

His Excellency the Archbishop Thomas Cranmer enters my chambers. He looks uneasy at first, but then smiles with the warmth of one who has known me a long time. "How fare you, Anne?"

"As well as can be expected," I say. "Almoner Skip has been praying with me and preparing me these past days. And I feel ready to be with God."

His Excellency pats my hand. "That is good, child, very good. And I see that the King has returned to you this day your own ladies-in-waiting."

"Yes, he shows me great kindness in sending Madge, Lady Rochford, and young Caroline to be with me in my final days."

The archbishop indicates that I should be seated. "You were convicted yesterday and sentenced to die—stripped of your titles, your crown, and your property. But you are still married to the King."

I nod.

His Excellency rubs his chin. "As it stands, the line of succession gives your daughter, Elizabeth, primacy. For as long as your marriage remains valid, Elizabeth is Henry's one and only legitimate heir. Mary has been declared illegitimate, and Henry FitzRoy is a bastard.

Should the King have no more legitimate heirs, Elizabeth would sit on the throne when Henry dies."

I nod again, though I don't like where I think this is leading. "Elizabeth is a baby. I ache to leave her motherless, but knowing she shall have a place with the King eases my pain a great deal."

"I imagine it would," the archbishop agrees. "However, the King requests that your marriage be annulled." He opens his satchel. "I have brought some papers for you to sign to that end."

I clasp my hands together and try to remain calm. "Why would I want to annul my marriage and make my daughter a bastard?"

"Because the King bids you to do so!" His Excellency responds sternly. He softens his tone and pats my arm. "He could yet commute your sentence and send you to a nunnery." The next moment his voice explodes with terror. "Or he could have you burned on the Tower Green!"

I tremble. If I disobey Henry, he will surely take out his wrath on Elizabeth. But if I sign the papers, I make *ma petite* motherless *and* illegitimate, which is as good as orphaning her.

In this moment, I understand Katharine in a way I never have before. Above all else she had to do what was best for her child. And now I must do what will be best for mine.

"I will do as Henry asks, of course," I say, and begin to weep.

His Excellency hands me a quill. "This is right and good—for yourself, for your daughter, for your King, and for God. I will tell Henry how agreeable you have been, Anne."

I sign the papers, then fall to my knees. "Archbishop, please pray for and be kind to my Elizabeth."

"Of course," he assures me. But even though His Excellency gives me his word, he seems much more concerned with the papers before him. He gathers them and is quickly away.

And I am alone.

17 MAY 1536

The Tower of London
The Queen's Lodgings and Byward Tower

Five men, including my brother, George, will lose their heads early this morning. Following Sir William Kingston's orders, three guards drag me and my ladies to a different prison tower and force us to witness it.

A draught whistles through the Byward Tower as we stand silent at the window. We can hear nothing of the crowd or the men's speeches. After the axe falls, sometimes the head rolls in the sawdust; sometimes it just drops from the block like a clay brick. The executioner holds up each severed head for all to see before they cart the body away. My brother takes only one stroke of the axe, but Smeaton requires several blows before his head is smitten from his body. I try not to imagine the pain of that. By the fifth execution the whole platform is soaked red.

If this is to be my end, I know what it looks like now. If I am to be burned, that is another thing entirely.

Sir William Kingston enters my privy chamber smelling of sawdust, blood, and sweat . . . smelling of injustice. He has come from the men's executions on Tower Hill. "Madam, your execution has been set for tomorrow morning. You shall not suffer the flames, but the kinder death of beheading. The King has specially commissioned an expert executioner from Calais to sever your head in the French manner—by sword, not axe."

"The King is very merciful," I say.

Before Kingston leaves, I must know. "Did any of the men protest my innocence before they died?"

"All but the musician Smeaton. He confessed that he deserved to die," the constable answers.

"Well, then I shall soon see four men in Paradise. God have mercy on Mark Smeaton. I fear he has condemned his soul forever."

After the constable closes the chamber door behind him, Lady Rochford crumples at my feet. "Was it as awful as I imagine, to watch George, my dear husband—"

"You were right not to come, Jane." Madge pats her back and hands Lady Rochford some wine.

"I cannot bear to even think of it," she whimpers. She takes a large gulp from her cup. "I should have done more to save him. I tried to appeal to the King, but I failed. It's all my fault."

"No, Jane. You cannot blame yourself. My brother knew how devoted you were to him." I reach for her hand. "Your husband is with God now. And tomorrow I will join them."

Lady Rochford bites her lip to hold back tears, and my other ladies look almost as grim.

I clutch the hand of Caroline, who is but a girl of fifteen, my most recently appointed lady-in-waiting, and sweet as strawberry jam. One never heard an unkind word pass from her lips. "I have missed you all dearly," I say, forcing a smile. "It's been awful to be trapped here with the spies. So tell me what gossip goes around the court?"

"Are you sure you want to know, Queen Anne?" my cousin asks. "Much of it is about you."

"Nothing can be worse than what has already been said. So spare no detail. But to begin with, how fares the King?"

Madge raises her eyebrows. "Very well; some say *too* well. The King has been hunting, sporting with his friends, playing cards, in a very jovial mood around court."

I try not to look hurt. "And the Lady Jane Seymour?"

"She was removed from Westminster," Lady Rochford answers.

"And it is rumoured that every night the King visits her by boat. Some ballads have been composed about Jane and the King, not kind ones. People think it unseemly that you are in the Tower and Jane is pouncing on His Majesty."

I shake my head. "It makes me wonder if it wasn't Jane Seymour who gave testimony to Lord Cromwell for my arrest."

Madge responds immediately. "No, Your Grace. It wasn't her."

"You sound very assured, cousin. Why? Do you know who it was?"

"I feel confident about two ladies who spoke against you, but I can't be certain beyond that," Madge says.

"At my trial Lord Cromwell said *three* ladies in my household provided him with details that helped to condemn me," I remind them.

"Three?" Lady Rochford questions.

"Yes, three."

My sister-in-law quickly says, "Well, I know one was Nan Cobham."

I puff out my cheeks. "That woman has despised me ever since I arrived in court. I think she holds me accountable for every misdeed of the Boleyns. She hated my sister, Mary, as well. I should have known she would be eager to give false testimony against me. Who else?"

Madge hesitates. "It may seem unlikely, but the other informant is Lady Worcester."

"No, that's not possible," I say. "She is my dear friend. I was to be her child's godmother. I don't believe it."

Caroline speaks for the first time. "Did Your Grace not request that Lady Worcester attend you these last days? And yet she's not among us."

"But I assumed that was because she felt unwell with her pregnancy." I look around, pleading with my eyes for one of my ladies to say that I'm right.

"I'm sorry, Your Grace." Caroline rubs my hand.

"I feel as though I might faint."

Caroline finds a cloth and presses it to my forehead.

Lady Rochford slumps onto the floor and shakes with tears, despondent. "What will I do without George? Without you, Anne? What will happen to me?"

Madge shakes Lady Rochford with aggression. "What is wrong with you? Queen Anne faces execution and all you can think about is your own selfish interests? You should be ashamed."

"Don't be too hard on Lady Rochford," I say. "She has just lost her husband. In grief, many unlovely things slip from one's tongue. I will be with our Lord tomorrow. It is you, my ladies, who must remain *dans ce monde cruel.* I, too, worry what will become of you. And I pray for you all."

Caroline looks at me wistfully and asks, "Queen Anne, aren't you afraid to die?"

I shake my head. "No. I welcome death. It's a great relief to me. I have asked forgiveness for my sins and will be in Paradise. I only fear what will happen to my daughter when I'm gone."

"But you were convicted of crimes you didn't commit. How can you welcome your death?" Madge wonders.

"I didn't sin against the King, this is true, but I treated his daughter the Lady Mary with contempt. I convinced myself that to protect the interest of my own daughter, to protect Elizabeth's line of succession, the awful things I did to Mary were justified. But wickedness and malice are just that, and must be atoned for. I should have been kinder to her. Mary will never forgive me, and should not. God requires my death as penance to her."

Madge opens her mouth to say something further, but then closes it.

Caroline picks up her sewing. Lady Rochford kneels before the

Book of Hours. I seek a quill and parchment. Sunlight winks in and out of the room, dancing prisms around the floor. Ravens call one after another on the lawn. I wonder if Paradise will smell like the ink of this quill or like soot in the hearth or like the Greenwich garden in spring? Or perhaps Paradise will smell entirely new. I close my eyes, overcome with a memory of Greenwich roses newly bloomed, how they smell like dirt and soap and my sweet Elizabeth's hair. Elizabeth, *ma petite*, Maman's little rose, how I ache for you.

Jane, I assume, will be Henry's next Queen. I pray she treats the King's daughters with the kindness, fairness, and gentleness of a rose. Then she will be a far better Queen than I.

19 MAY 1536

◇ · ◇

**The Tower of London
The Queen's Lodgings
Just Before Dawn**

My cousin raps lightly on the closet door. "Sorry to disturb Your Grace, but the archbishop will arrive soon to hear your last confession."

"Has the night passed so quickly?"

"It's nearly dawn. Is there anything we can do for you, Queen Anne?" Madge asks.

"I need a few moments more, and then I will join you," I say.

I stopped speaking my thoughts aloud many hours ago. But whether audibly or in my head, I was talking to someone nonexistent and ephemeral—in truth, I told my story only to myself.

But how I wish it were otherwise.

How I wish that someone could have heard all this, and one day would share it with a particular little girl when she is ready. When she grows older. When she feels confused and afraid and alone. When she seeks the truth. When she misses her mother.

A soft light seeps under the door. The morning of my execution has broken. I feel weak-kneed and almost giddy.

Mon temps est enfin venu.

My time has finally come.

MY LAST SACRAMENT

As early-morning bells do toll
Let those who witness soon extol
I ate and drank and found console
And swore to God was faithful whole,
No carnal sins did I confess
For of such crimes I am guiltless.

19 MAY 1536

The Tower of London
From Queen's Lodgings to the Great Courtyard

It's odd, the Purgatory of these final hours. I've lost all sense of things. I can't describe the colour of the sky this morning or what flavours my jam. I no longer smell the damp earth or hear the birds sing outside the window. I have prepared myself so thoroughly to die it's as though I'm not here anymore. Yet I am.

Madge, Caroline, and my brother's widow pray beside me. However, the girls tend to cry more than they comfort. I suppose it's consoling to know they care so greatly that they mourn the loss of me already.

"Will you help to dress me one last time?" I point to the black robe lined in ermine with the simple white hood, and the scarlet kirtle to wear beneath it. I run my fingers through the soft fur. Royal ermine I wear to remind everyone that I will be the first Queen of England to lose her head. And red is the colour of martyrs. The neckline of my final piece of fashion drops low enough that I won't need to remove anything but my headpiece for the executioner. My last armour I've designed to aid in my destruction.

Madge blubbers as she adjusts the net covering my head. "Anne, you don't deserve to die. You cannot die!"

"I do deserve to die. I am prepared to die. And I will finally die today." I grasp her hands to stop her gushing about.

Now my brother's widow starts to wail. "No, no!"

I shake my head. "Ladies, please stop."

The girls muffle their sobs, but their faces hold the most sorrowful expressions.

I pat Lady Rochford's hand and smile. "Think of it this way: We ought to thank His Majesty. Henry just continues to advance me in my career. I began as merely a private gentlewoman, then he raised me to marchioness, and from a marchioness I became the Queen. And now, because I'm innocent of the crimes for which I'm sentenced, I shall die a martyr. Therefore, in Heaven I will become a saint. And there's nothing greater one can aspire to be. So, as always, the King proves ever kind and generous to me." I laugh at my cleverness.

Constable Kingston appears at the door, solemn as ever. "The hour approaches, madam. Make yourself ready."

I cross myself, kneel, and say a final prayer:

Ma petite, *I pray that I take all the bad parts of me and your father to the scaffold today, and leave for you, in you, only the good.*

Sir William clears his throat.

I nod at him and rise. "I am prepared, Sir William."

My ladies and I follow the constable one final time down the twisting staircase onto the Tower Green. Two hundred of the King's guard wait to escort me to the scaffold. I follow with my head held high. As the procession moves through the large twin towers of the Cold Harbour Gate, I see that a vast crowd has assembled in the Great Courtyard to watch me die.

If there's noise now, I don't hear it.

Whether there's rain or sun in this moment, I can't say.

But the scaffold, I see that vividly—a wooden structure draped in black, strewn with newly gathered straw. It sits only five feet off the ground, and several men stand upon it. But it holds no chopping block like the one for the five men who died before me. I will lose my head by the blade of a sword, not an axe. But where is the swordsman? No one brandishes a sword, and no one wears executioner's black.

Madge gently nudges me. "Queen Anne, don't forget to pass out your alms."

I nod at Madge and distribute my last coins to those in the crowd who look to need them most.

My purse emptied, the scaffold only ten feet ahead, a serenity washes over me. I feel as if I'm floating slightly above the ground.

Constable Kingston takes my arm and assists me up the scaffold's wooden steps. There are so many gathered to witness my death, more people than it looked like from a distance.

Before the constable releases me, I beg him kindly, "Sir William, I ask you humbly if I may speak to the people. I promise I have only good things to say."

Sir William nods without hesitation and I move to address the crowd, but first I ask one additional favour of the constable. "Will you please not signal for my death until I have finished?"

Kingston agrees. Now I take careful steps to the centre of the scaffold. My throat feels dry and scratchy and I wish for a drink.

"Good Christian people," I begin, but my voice sounds only half as loud as I need it to be, failing me in my last moment. I close my eyes, pray to Heaven, and try again. I repeat, more loudly this time, "Good Christian people."

The crowd falls hushed; not even a cough can be heard. I survey the faces before me. If my father's here, I can't readily see him. Perhaps he hasn't the strength to watch me die.

I know the words I want to say, but my voice quivers under the gravity of where I stand and what I face. "Good friends, I didn't come here to excuse or justify myself, for by the law I have been judged to die. So I come here to yield myself humbly to the will of the King, my lord." My voice becomes steadier. "And if ever in my life I offended the King's grace, surely with my death I will atone for it now. I don't blame my judges or any person or any thing, only the cruel law of the land. I beseech you all, good friends, to pray for the life of the King, my sovereign lord and yours, who is one of the best princes on the face of the earth, and who could not have treated me better. I submit now to death with good will, humbly asking pardon of all the world."

The crowd remains noiseless and still.

I look over at the constable and indicate that I am done. Then I address the men behind me, hoping to hurry things along. "Which of you is the executioner?"

Constable Kingston answers, "He will make himself known to you very soon." He hesitates before he says, "Madam, there is no hope for a pardon. You should confess now before it's too late."

"I have nothing to confess."

We hold each other's gaze for a few seconds.

Sir William nods. "I would think not. Then have your ladies prepare you."

Caroline removes my mantle of ermine.

"Please forgive me any harshness I ever showed to you," I say to my dear ladies. "You've been so good to me. Be good also to the next Queen and always faithful to the King. And try not to forget me," I say with a little less strength. "Pray for me."

I remove my headpiece, and Madge switches my net coif to a linen cap.

A man approaches me now. "I beg Your Grace's pardon, for I am ordered to do this duty."

"You have my pardon, sir, and be assured, the Lord's above as well." Then I ask, "What do I do now?"

The executioner points to the centre of the scaffold. "Please kneel and say your prayers."

I tremble so violently it's hard to walk straight.

As I drop to my knees in the straw, I have a vision of my head rolling off the scaffold. *La Reine sans tête*. The eyes on my decapitated head eerily maintain sight. They look, with panic, up to Heaven.

When will the sword come? I should have asked the man. I turn around to find the executioner. I can't see him. I don't know where he is! I look over to my ladies, who are bent in prayer. It's hard to breathe until I repeat, "*Jesu*, have mercy on me, *Jesu*, have mercy on me . . ."

I look above me and see sky, blue as a newborn's eye, gold winking through clouds of softest wool. "*Jesu*, have mercy—"

THE BALLAD OF ANNE BOLEYN

My time had come. My judgement read,
Condemned though innocent I pled.
More than crown knocked from my head,
So feared was I, they willed me dead.

And to my fall, how was I led?
No man but Henry shared Anne's bed.
I overstepped, and foes were bred.
Too quick my tongue, and hence I bled.

I prayed each day my sins to shed.
And learned to face death without dread.
Past Tower walls, saw light ahead
To dwell with God, my soul be fed.

Now that I'm gone, what shall be said
Of Anne Boleyn without a head?
Forget her fast, move on instead—
The falcon died, the phoenix weds.

HENRY VIII

The Lord God, Architect of all creation, simply spoke words in the vast emptiness and, with a few sentences, called this darkling world into being. At His word, the stormy wind arises or the sea is made calm.

In the same way, the King speaks, and lives are made or broken; palaces appear or are torn down.

In the month of May, a few days before the beheading, I rode with Thomas Cromwell to see one of the great monasteries sacked. I pointed at its splendid sanctuary, and the roof came off. At my command, men heaved the lead roofing up in rolls.

Now I was head of the English Church—no more foreign interference by the Pope—and it was entirely my right to dissolve the monasteries in my own kingdom and seize their property for the Crown. The Pope should never have defied my wishes, for now I took out my revenge on each and every shaved-headed English monk I kicked out and sent to pasture. My will cannot be bent or broken.

The monks watched their home torn to pieces in front of them as Cromwell showed me the tally of all the precious vessels of silver and gold, all of the livestock, all of the fields, orchards, and forests that became mine as this fallen house of God was emptied.

Cromwell was a man I relied upon: my principal secretary, Lord Privy Seal, Chancellor of the Exchequer—a man who had committed enough crimes in his youth to know how to be of use to kings. He knew how to make decisions like a man, and I trusted him in everything.

My bully-boy Cromwell displayed the accounts and I sat on my horse above him. Servants of the Crown were burning books and fraudulent holy artifacts. The leg of a local saint that stupid peasant-women kissed to cure . . . in faith, whatever rot besets peasant-women . . . It was clearly a dog-bone in a box. Cromwell's men threw it on the bonfire, along with the monks' straw mattresses.

The monks wailed as their dog-bone burned.

Cromwell yammered on about acreage, about the yield in rents, but my mind was not on the account of demolition and dissolution.

That May was a month of building.

The scaffolds. Five for her lovers: timber platforms to receive their blood, their heads. One for her. I knew she sat in her rooms in the Lieutenant's Tower, looking out the window day by day as they built her scaffold. She watched them raise the platform where she would soon take her final fall.

Once we built a palace wing together. We lay on a bed side by side—her dark hair unbound across her dimpled back—with plans spread around us. I asked her what she wanted for her apartments. She was always quick to see the practicalities, and spoke with the architects about all she needed. She chose all the queenly adornments. It was a game we played before we were married. Once we were wed, I was good as my word, and turned our plans to stone.

By my order, hundreds worked to build Anne's apartments. The walls would glitter with silver and gold, hung with Persian tapestries; her ceilings were mirrored. Her beds were draped with sarcenet and costly satins. The gates announced our love with her initial intertwined with mine, "A" and "H" in a lovers' knot. The masons and carpenters could not finish their work quickly enough for my Queen. I demanded that they work by night as well as day, by candle-light, however dim the chambers and half-built paths might be.

Once we stole there at the darkest hour to stand in the half-constructed courtyard. Our arms around each other, we listened to that black space building itself with chisel taps and the scrape of trowels.

She asked me in a whisper, the kitten, "Will it be beautiful?"

"It will, because it is yours. It is arriving out of the night like our future; like our heirs."

Outside her windows, I laid out a garden for her in the French manner with hedges that would grow into marvellous shapes as the years passed.

The French manner—she did everything in the French manner. Her hair, her gowns. Everything. With anyone.

Idiocy—idiocy! To think that slut could be a queen—I was so *deceived—so fond— so foolish.* How were my eyes not wrenched open by her sister, Mary, called in jest by King Francis the English Mare because so many men had ridden her—as he had, sidesaddle—as I did, too, for many months before I spied crafty Anne—Anne, who was taught Christ knows what lessons in the turrets and spires of Paris by the Devil knows what horde of men and snuffling boys. She was a master with me, and now I think of those gardens outside her windows and wonder whether she met the musician Smeaton there—Smeaton, a beggar dressed so poorly I once threw him some shirts—warbling to my wife, to the Queen of England, and then her whore's simper, ending with them rutting behind a topiary sphere.

I should have known better when I took her to the shores of France shortly before our marriage. I took her there so that King Francis would recognize Anne as my Queen—but then none of the women of his court would agree to receive her. Francis's own sister said she would not meet

with "the King of England's whore." It was suggested by the French ambassador that the most appropriate lady to greet Anne would be Francis's
own mistress, the Duchess of Vendôme.

I would not subject Anne to that indignity. She stayed at Calais; I went
ahead to visit Francis, and when my work was done, I returned to Anne,
and we dallied during the long rains. She wanted the Queen's jewels—the
jewels of my ancestors, of my dear Katharine—Anne wanted them all for
herself, for her perquisite.

And I—misled!—wanted what Anne had denied me for so many years.
Duped by her cunning, I felt sorry for her—my poor beloved (as I thought),
rejected by the royalty of France. I wanted to shield her from knowing the
disgrace she caused me.

So while we idled there in Calais and the rains fell, one day I hid a strand
of black pearls in my sleeve. I drew Anne out into a stable, which was the
only place we could find that was solitary. It was so cold, in faith, that I
chafed her hands to keep them warm, and then her feet. On touching the
intimacy of her toes, I couldn't wait any longer. I said to her that it was
time. . . . I took out the strand of pearls, which she must have known were
Katharine's before her. She eyed them with hunger like a chick squawking
for the worm.

Deluded, I didn't see that hunger, then. I saw only her joy. It is only in
memory that I have realized how quickly she grasped the strand, how desperate she was for it to be latched around her neck.

And then—I groan to think of that first dalliance, the pleasure and destruction.

It thundered overhead. God Himself gave me ample warning.

When the King of France finally visited our lodgings for a feast (without
any women in his train), I concocted a plan to force him to recognize my
future Queen. I held a disguising, and arranged for Francis to dance with
Anne, who was masked as a woodland spirit. He did not know her from her
step. When she finally drew off the mask and tossed its oak leaves aside,

teasing him, he was angry, but could not show it before the crowd. Then Anne tamed the King of France, asking questions about her old friends there, retelling rank gossip from when she was a girl. An hour later, he was laughing at her jests.

I should have known that nothing good would come of a woman the French themselves would not deign to greet.

They were laughing at me. I am sure they were laughing because I had invited a common whore into my bed. I paid her with a strand of pearls.

She was a brazen one: laughing openly at my clothes, laughing at the poems I wrote her, laughing at me with the others she bedded. Screeching at me like a Cheapside fishwife about my women, and all the while casting her eyes at other men.

When we were first in love, I was charmed by her bravery in speaking her mind to me—her frankness, as I thought it—her boldness. But as the year passed, I could hear only insult to me, a lack of the respect due a king. Hideous squawking from one who should bow to me always.

Then there was Thomas Cromwell, coming to me murmuring about her crimes. When he told me for the first time, Anne was out watching a dogfight in Greenwich Park. While she watched cur rip bitch, heard the baying and the jeers, I sat in silence, reading the depositions of her lovers. I hoped that it was not true.

Reading of all the abominations—with her brother —Christ have mercy. To curl side by side as babes in the cradle, and then squirm together on the bed of fornication . . . Unspeakable.

And Cromwell, who pried all this information out of her gallants through close questioning and the use of curious devices and instruments of pain—he now wishes to talk to me of acreage and rents.

"Quite profitable, as you can see, Your Majesty," he finished, and I was still seated on my horse by the pyre where books and a sainted leg bone burned.

She and I built a palace wing together; we decorated it for pleasure and the future; and now, she sits watching the scaffold being constructed; and at another palace, the limbs of disobedient heretics have been nailed above the gate. The whole world shall know the fury of a king, and what I build in my anger.

Cromwell tapped the list of items requisitioned from the monastery. "Good thing we didn't let Anne throw all this away—giving to beggars and poor widows who'd spend it all on drink."

I watched him crow about his Queen's defeat. He said, "The most absurd idea that whore ever had."

And then I began to pummel him. I was above, on my horse, so after the first few blows hit him, he bent down below the reach of my arm. Not, however, my boot—and I kicked him full in the side of the face. He fell to the ground, begging me for mercy.

"Don't speak of her," I warned him. "She will be dead soon enough."

"As you wish—as you wish, Your Majesty."

So he said. But he was unrepentant.

I took in his face, the bitter cleverness of it, and I growled, "If I ever found that someone—anyone—even you—had given me false information about her . . . false evidence . . . By God! By God! If I ever discovered that . . ."

I could not put the finish on my threat.

She must be guilty. There could be no question. I had loved her for her laughter, her impish laughter, and then she had laughed in my face, giggling in the dark while toying with paupers. In two days, she would be dead. In three, Jane, sweet Jane, would be my betrothed. Soothing Jane. Jane, who had no wiles, who had no French tricks, who wished only to help, to heal. To bear an heir. She would arrive for the first time at Hampton Court by barge, and I would take her to Anne's apartments, which would be hers, until I could build better.

Anne must have been guilty.

Thomas Cromwell stared up at me from the mud. The smoke from books of monkish lore blew over us.

He spoke apologies, mewled for mercy.

But we glared into each other's eyes like men who have ruined each other already, and who only wait to make the full disaster known.

JANE SEYMOUR

"Bound to Obey and Serve"

HAMPTON COURT

◇·◇

24 October 1537

There is blood. Blood everywhere. Blood on the sheets, blood between my legs. It is thick and red and sour.

There is blood on my hands, too.

WULFHALL

◇·◇

March 1525

They are sending me away.

"Lady Dormer absolutely refuses the match," Sir Francis Bryan's voice rings out, echoing down the hallway. "I did what I could, my lady. I am sorry."

Dinner had been cleared nearly an hour prior, and now I hide like the frightened lamb I am behind the heavy wooden door of an empty sleeping chamber. My mother and Sir Francis have remained in the hall of my ancestral home, to confer quite dramatically. I imagine my mother's ringed fingers turning her goblet around and around, making circles on the dark grain of the table.

My mother is silent. In the quiet space that follows Sir Francis's pronouncement, I swear I can hear her mind at work. "Can you find a place for Jane at court?" she finally says in response.

"My thoughts exactly," Sir Francis replies. "I am certain the Queen will have a spot in her household."

"You will go to court to serve as a maid of honour to Queen Katharine," my mother tells me later, her command ringing in my ears like the church bell's death knell. "Lady Dormer has succeeded in staving off the match between you and William."

"But, Mama—" My voice quavers as the humiliation of Lady Dormer's rejection and alarm at my fate sets in. I hate how weak I sound. How weak I always sound. Tears are quickly welling in my eyes, spilling out onto my cheeks. I always cry. I hate that, too. "Mama ... I shall be so very far from you. I don't want to go. I'm sorry Lady Dormer did not want me for her son. But please. Don't make me go."

Bess, my younger sister, squeezes my hand. I glance at her; I can feel the stricken look in my eyes. I have failed my family and, above all, myself. I did not love William, but I had hoped we might make a life together. Now, all hopes are dashed.

Bess's forehead wrinkles and she puts an arm around me. I am not comforted, for my mind is a chaos of hurt feelings and thoughts flying in all directions: I will never have a family of my own; I will never see my beloved sister again—how I shall miss her company. Instead, I will die alone—childless and unwed.

"Jane, you will go. It is the only option left. And moreover, it is up to you to return honour to our family. After the shame of this rejection, and your father's . . . misdeeds . . ." My mother's voice trails off.

Yes, my father's misdeeds indeed. Carrying on an affair with the wife of my eldest brother, Edward, all those years back—I was just a child then. He sullied what had been our family's respectability and nobility. My brothers' hopes of ever achieving any triumph at court were dashed. Not to mention Edward's life falling apart when he abandoned my two small nephews after he put out his wretched, disloyal wife. It was a terrible affair.

I have learned the character of men.

And now it seems a life of maidenhood and restoring our family's reputation has become my burden to bear.

"And when you are at court," my mother continues, "you shall carry yourself in the most dignified manner any courtier or royal family member has ever seen. You will carry the Seymour name back to glory." She leaves a brief, cool kiss on my cheek, then sweeps away.

I don't want to leave Wulfhall, out here in the west country, far from the drama and intrigue of court. I know what awaits me there. Lechery, secrets, and deception. I want nothing to do with it. And I certainly do not want to leave my beautiful home, the warmth of my mother's and sisters' company. Even my brothers' teasing.

I know exactly who I am: unwanted and undesirable Plain Jane, timid and meek as a mouse. How will I ever survive at court?

I bid farewell to the dusky red roses in my Young Lady Garden. I love how they climb wildly, tangling and tousling stems and thorns, petals of bloody sunset blanketing the ground. I love that there is no discernible order to this garden, planted who knows how long ago. No one in my family seems to know who the Young Lady for whom it is named is—or, for that matter, who the Old Lady is, after whom the other "Lady" garden is named. Oh, how I shall miss wandering through here, weaving my way between the rosebushes, inspecting the leaves for the telltale marks of insects or other sickness! This is my time, when I am free from the monotonous rhythm of needlework.

Still. It is what I know.

Bess skips outside and takes hold of my arm as I mournfully wind my way down the path. "I shall miss you something dreadfully," she says.

"And I shall miss you, my darling Bess," I say in return. "Do you think we shall see each other again?"

"Of course, my dearest one, we will," she says reassuringly. "And I am sure you shall be betrothed to someone far better than William Dormer in no time. A dashing knight, perhaps," she teases.

I smile back but feel far from confident.

"Bess, you know I wish you every happiness. Lots of bouncing babies and all that." I squeeze her arm and turn to embrace her. "Truly, I want you to be happy."

"Yes, well, we shall see what the future holds," she says dryly. "I'm a bit apprehensive, I must admit. Sir Anthony is very old!" We giggle and link arms again. "Jane, you will be fine at court. Just keep your eyes open and your thoughts to yourself. Find one friend who is true and trust no one else," she instructs. "Now I shall leave you to your rosebushes." She gives me one last embrace before ducking back inside the house.

I inhale the scent of my beautiful musk and Tudor roses one final time, gather my things, and enter the carriage to go east, to court.

The ride is bumpy and makes my joints, my bones, my head shudder and ache. The road, if you can call it that, is rutted and thick with the mud of late-summer rains. Twice the driver has had to jump out and nudge one of the wheels out of a sopping puddle. I don't mind the delays, though. They prolong the time till my arrival at court, and that is a good thing. Already, I miss the feel of Bess's warm embrace. Oh, what I wouldn't give to be back in our bed, whispering and giggling by the light of the candle's flame. But she is to be married, and I am to court. And so I have bade farewell to all that I have loved and known.

GREENWICH PALACE

◇·◇

July 1525

This nest of snakes is as treacherous and slippery as you might imagine. The women in Queen Katharine's court gossip and scheme without end. More than fifteen years have passed since King Henry and Queen Katharine married, and still the Queen has not born a male heir who can someday inherit the throne of England. These women whisper that she is barren now, and that the King is growing ever more impatient. He certainly barrels around the court looking restless, angry. They say that he will be seeking drastic measures sooner rather than later. Oh, the rumours swirl. The women giggle and hiss as new girls, one after another, try to catch Henry's attention.

We spend our days in the Queen's apartments, a series of chambers decorated with heavy tapestries of wool and silk, hangings of cloth of gold. It is all truly resplendent, unlike anything I have ever seen. There are about thirty of us maids of honour, but the Queen also has ladies-in-waiting, and of course the noblemen who oversee her household. All together, there are more than one hundred fifty people who come in and out.

In the evenings, we often gather in the great hall for dining and dancing and music. There are people everywhere. It seems as if the King allows all sorts of individuals to come to court—as long as one is well dressed or professes some magnificent business. There is much waiting and hanging about.

How the courtiers love to fight amongst themselves. They divide into ever-shifting factions that then manoeuvre against the others until the next division seems more powerful. It is a constant game of strategy, conflict, and quiet wars.

One maid of honour leads many of the others in their serpent games: Anne Boleyn, she is called. She is newly returned to court, and already leads. She is striking, with bright, birdlike features and dark, piercing eyes. She daren't taunt me too boldly to my face, as Queen Katharine strives to keep her household proper and genteel, but I so clearly do not fit in here. I know Anne and the other girls mock and laugh at me. My skin is too white, my chin too weak, my nose too big, my reputation too sullied after Lady Dormer refused my betrothal to William. My heritage too tarnished. Thus the scorn I bear. Plain Jane of the disgraced Seymour family.

Wulfhall has never seemed so far away.

Life here is an unending cascade of drudgery and sameness. Queen Katharine keeps us at our sewing, and reading the Bible, singing prayers. Except for the moments when King Henry appears. He is as handsome as I had always heard. Tall with bright, intelligent eyes and shining golden-red hair. He is so very *male*. I cannot help but marvel at the glamour of the royal couple.

Anne catches me staring. When the King and Queen exit the chamber, she turns to her hangers-on and with a spiteful glance at me, says, "It seems our poor Jane, here, has never seen a man before. She looks so goggle-eyed at the very sight of our King." They laugh and I feel my cheeks and the tips of my ears burn. I imagine I am as crimson as one of my Young Lady Garden roses.

"I have *brothers*, Mistress Boleyn," I say lamely. I lose my nerve and don't finish the thought: *Of course I have seen a man.*

Anne laughs once more, and I am certain I hear her hiss to her cronies, "Plain milkface Jane: No man will ever look back at her, either."

I want to crawl behind a tapestry and hide for the rest of my life. She knows exactly where to thrust her daggers.

"Jane?" It is Nan, my one friend here. "Are you all right?" I shake my head, tears welling in my eyes. "No, I suppose not after a display like that. Come on, let's go clean up, shall we?" She walks me from the room, to the basin where I can splash cool water on my face.

"Welcome to the serpents' nest," I mutter to myself.

One day, as I, alongside a bevy of maids of honour, am bent over a piece of needlework—we are assiduously sewing costumes for the coming masquerade—the King stamps into the Queen's presence chamber.

He is fuming. I overhear them argue as she airs her humiliation, the offence she takes not only at Henry's wandering hands and eyes, but also at the ennoblement of the King's bastard son, Henry Fitz-Roy, by his former mistress Bessie Blount. "Oh, how you shame me, my King!" Her shrill cry causes me to prick my finger. A single ruby drop of blood wells up at the site of the tiny hole. Every pair of eyes in the room is stuck fast to either the King or the Queen.

"You dare speak to me in such a way!" the King rages.

FitzRoy, who is but six years old, was brought to court and admitted to the Order of the Garter, with all sorts of honours and titles conferred upon him. Now he is to be raised as if he were the true son of the King and Queen. Poor Katharine, forced to bear the stain of dishonour. But I know that this is the way of men.

I never stopped to think of how my mother must have felt, all those years ago, when she learned my father had taken my own sister-in-law into his bed. I could think only of how broken my brother Edward seemed. How ferocious his anger was. But my mother, spurned so awfully, never once let her own grief or anger or humiliation show. She focused all her devastation on the rift between father and son—her son.

Now, however, I watch as the Queen's heart is trampled by her own husband, and I wonder what true feelings my mother must have hidden away. My heart aches for her. She seems at peace with my father, now that the rift is bound up. But I wonder . . . does the hurt that comes from knowing one has been mistreated and betrayed ever heal?

William and I were . . . friends. While I cannot say I was in love with him, nor can I say I was truly betrayed, I had hoped. I had placed my hope in the promise of a future—with him, with children, with family and the companionship and love that follow thereon. The disappointment I harbour is still keen, all these months later. But it is nothing compared to what my mother endured. To what Queen Katharine endures. My heart wells up with sorrow for her. My eyes well up, too. With the Queen's outburst, I let loose my own flood of tears. Oh, the embarrassment! Plain Jane indeed. And a witless, blubbering baby, too.

I glance up and catch Anne's eye. She smirks at me, then licks her lips and turns to watch the King. I note how he returns her gaze. Something passes between them. A flicker, a spark. Anne Boleyn also serves as a maid of honour to Queen Katharine, but there is a quality to her sly looks, her sleek beauty, that makes me uneasy. I think of a viper lying in wait.

Katharine weeps softly now. "I shall submit and have patience, my lord," she says.

King Henry's face is mottled purple and twisted with rage. I can see he wants to howl, to strike, but he keeps his voice low. "I shall speak with you later," he snarls.

When Nan sees me break into tears, she quickly pulls me to the far side of the Queen's chamber, presses me against the wall, and shields me with her body. Still, the King, in his fury, hears my snuffling and turns around, his eyes seeking out the source of the noise. When he spies me, he throws his hands into the air, disgust evident on his face, then hurries from the room.

Nan squeezes my hand gently and offers me a delicately embroidered handkerchief. I wipe my dripping nose. "You mustn't draw such attention to yourself, Jane," she whispers. I thank her, and thank God that there is one decent friend for me here at court.

I turn back to Anne and watch her dark eyes, thoughtful and sharp. If I didn't know better, I would think she is concocting a plan of some sort. I shall keep my distance from her and hope she leaves me alone. If I venture too close, I have no doubt she will strike and bite. She returns my gaze with a contemptuous one, narrows her eyes, as if to say, *Don't watch me too closely*, then spins away, a malicious half smile quirking her lips.

LONDON

◇ · ◇

March 1529

We sit in the Queen's chamber, sewing clothing for the poor and talking in hushed tones. Nan is beside me. We know that Katharine is no longer held in favour by the King. His attentions have turned to Anne Boleyn. Truly, he seems utterly transfixed by her. But Anne works no magic. Rather she understands what he wants of her and how to keep herself just beyond his reach.

She dances close to him when we gather in the great watching chamber at night, letting her fingers curl into the hair at the base of his neck. Then she sways her hips and dances away, and I think, *I could never do that.* I would never have the nerve. I see how he looks at her with such hunger. It makes my belly ache. Yet my heart aches for our Queen.

One evening, Anne coyly spins a golden bracelet around her wrist. "A gift from the King," she says to a gaggle of girls, casting her eyes about to see who is near, who is listening.

Queen Katharine's dearest friend and lady-in-waiting, María de Salinas, is close.

"He sent it to me with another love letter. He has sent so many letters, filled with so many silly romantic poems and other expressions of his love for me, I hardly know what to do with them." Anne's laugh is a cruel twinkling, like shattering crystal.

The other girls titter and look about, as though they do not want to catch trouble. But they are hooked. Anne's power is inimitable and seemingly without limit. She speaks as she likes, and keeps Henry on a hook, wriggling and no better than a fisherman's worm.

Nan turns to me and shakes her head, disgusted.

I whisper, "I cannot believe her brazenness. She truly knows no respect, has not a single care for the poor Queen. Anne is bound by oath to serve Queen Katharine, and yet she takes it upon herself to torment her daily." I cannot keep the heated anger from my voice.

"It is too sad, indeed," Nan agrees.

"Anne does not love Henry," I say. "The Queen is so true in her love for him. How can he not see it? How does Anne have him so transfixed?"

Suddenly, Anne is in front of me. She slaps my face and says imperiously, "How dare you speak so? You, little mouse, know nothing. And I will bid you to shut up."

I put my hand to my smarting cheek, tears welling in my eyes. I dare not say any more to her. Catching Anne's attention so was not wise. Not wise at all.

(QUEEN) ANNE'S COURT, LONDON

June 1535

How time marches on, trampling all of us, any of us—no matter our station—beneath her feet. Princess Mary, pitiable and prone to sickness and weak nerves, remains banished from court, isolated and alone. The poor thing is only nineteen. When I think of her, I cannot help but remember how my own family cast me out of Wulfhall so that I might work to raise them up. Pawns, all of us, it seems.

Meanwhile, her mother, Queen Katharine, lies dying, a drawn-out and, by all accounts, painful death, far away from London in cold, boggy Kimbolton. The whispered rumours that swirl through court say she continues to profess her eternal love for King Henry, despite his mistreatment of her. Oh, my lady Katharine is so good. Generous and kind, dignified and devout.

I recall how I hadn't wanted to leave Wulfhall, travel all the way to London. Those first weeks at court . . . months or years, even . . . the time blurs together in a haze like the fog hanging over the River Thames . . . I wept constantly from loneliness and fear. Yet, as the foreignness of it all has shifted into familiarity, I have found my way. Morningtime to noon, I am tucked away in the Queen's presence chamber, sewing—costumes for the balls and masquerades or clothing for the poor—and if I can deafen my ears to the whispers and gossip and plotting, I can almost find comfort in the quiet.

My mind wanders again to the welfare of Princess Mary. I wonder if she weeps, too, as she waits alone for news of her mother's demise, for the return of her father's embrace, for his forgiveness.

Now, she has been cast aside truly; the King has gone and married Anne Boleyn more than two years ago, and she's borne him a little girl. Elizabeth. She is a golden child, bouncing and giggling, the brightest light of her father's eyes. Her curls are the most perfect ringlets, her mouth a perfect rosebud. I have never seen a more beautiful child.

When my father occasioned to leave his sanctuary and come to court for the tournaments, he took the opportunity to grab my arm, his fingers digging in so that I was left with blue and violet bruising, and insist upon my taking the oath of service to Anne. I tried to argue against it, so disturbed I was by the way she comported herself in her treatment of Queen Katharine.

"Father, you cannot mean it," I said.

"Listen, daughter, and listen well," he said, his voice of steel. I glanced around his chamber, the dark wood-panelled walls seeming to close in on me. His breath reeked of onions and ale. "You will serve as an attendant to the new Queen, no matter how distasteful, detestable you find it—find her."

Edward stepped in then, to try to soften the blow. "Jane, you know Father is right. You must do what is best for our family, and that means doing as the King of England would have you do. Serve his new Queen-in-waiting. Not the one he has cast aside."

I couldn't help but stare at him, so surprised was I to hear Edward taking my father's side. I suppose time does mend wounds after all. Time, or perhaps, ambition. It seems my father and brother can agree on promoting the cause of the family. But where do honour, love come in? Edward's gaze was sympathetic but unwavering.

I bowed my head in supplication and said, "I will do this thing, brother." So now I attend Anne as a maid of honour. Imagine that: A once-maid-of-honour is now the Queen.

My friend Nan was married two years ago and left to live with her husband in the country. No one has filled her spot in my heart. Anne has amassed a large household, bigger than our first Queen's, but everyone is nervous and the genteel camaraderie that Queen Katharine once fostered amongst her ladies does not flourish any longer. Loneliness continues to plague me, but the heartaches of the last ten years have worn away, as the sea's ceaseless waves beat smooth the cliffs and rocks and sand.

Anne is not altogether unkind to the women who wait on her. She is a bit of an enigma. She still frightens me, especially when her temper flares, which it does often. And I know the latent cruelty that lingers beneath any façade of graciousness. I remember all too well her loudly whispered jibes. But then she also exhibits a seemingly boundless concern for the poor. She commands us to sew shirts and smocks for the widows and orphans. She gives more alms than Katharine did, and there is something angelic in all her charity work. But then Anne will fly into a fit of jealousy when Henry's lusty attention wanders, and she will do something spiteful, like steal all of poor Princess Mary's jewels or kick her fool. Once, though the Princess has been kept stowed away, out of sight, I even overheard her threatening to have Mary poisoned. Anne cherishes her own daughter, Elizabeth, who is a sweet little babe, coddling and stroking, spoiling and showering affection upon her.

Yet she infects the court—the whole kingdom, truly—with this new Reformist religion. She has broken with Rome entirely and bids her ladies to take up the English Bible she leaves about in her privy chamber. Ladies reading a Bible! The Holy Word. It is meant only for the men of the cloth to interpret, to explain, to teach and guide us. The heresy frightens me to the root of my very soul. She has poisoned everything.

I sit at my needlework, my shoulders aching slightly from remaining hunched over for too long without rising. I have been thinking about my faith. When I was a little girl, Father James, a priest my father hired to educate the boys, would sometimes give my sisters and me a lesson. He taught us to read and to say our prayers. I remember learning the letters of the alphabet. "A" for "apple," "B" for "boy," "C" for "Church." And in my mind the Church was the same as my faith. It was my safe harbour. Now Anne and the King have thrust everything into such turmoil. What happens to the folk who still believe in the Roman Church? Are we all doomed?

We are told to put away our love for Rome, to sever this deepest and most mystical of connections. But I find I cannot. I must keep these feelings a secret. Like so much else that goes unsaid in this new world.

I have watched Anne tease and tempt Henry, trading in secrets and enticement for almost ten years, and now here we are, arrived at this moment: hereticism and blasphemy unparalleled. I cannot countenance any of it, and I know my mother and father, and my brothers, feel the same.

But still, I watch and I listen, as I did in my first years at court, as I always have. And I see that the people of England are not happy at this turn of events. They loved Katharine; they hate Anne. Even the King's love for her seems, somehow, diminished. Tarnished. He looks tired.

I wonder if he regrets this marriage.

I wonder if he still loves her.

My sister, Bess, has written to me; she plans to arrive at Wulfhall later this summer. Having lost her husband last year, she has grown lonesome and wishes to be restored to the bosom of her family once again. By happy coincidence, I shall be travelling with Queen Anne and King Henry on their summer progress, which is, by and by, also due to arrive at Wulfhall. My heart soars at the prospect of being home again, of seeing my beloved sister.

WULFHALL

September 1535

I am home! Oh, how I rejoice. As we climb the stairs, I spy one of the older servants stumbling under the heavy burden he carries. I rush to his side and put a hand on his shoulder. "Are you all right?" I ask.

The old man nods, moving to gather some of the tumbled sacks. "Yes, miss. I am sorry."

I touch his arm and say, "Please, sir, you must be very tired. Let me gather these for you." I stoop down and begin to pick up the bundles until another servant comes and takes them from me.

I rise and straighten, then become uncomfortably aware of the train of people staring at me. For a moment I had forgotten where I was—or rather, I remembered too well that I was at home, but I'd forgotten I was here as a member of the royal court. Even the King is staring at me. I bow my head in shame.

Yet when I step inside, all the anxiety is shed, and I feel lighter, somehow. Bess has been awaiting my arrival in the chamber we used to share, and my feet could not feel sprightlier as I skip into the room to hug her.

"My darling Jane," she hums into my ear, "I am so very happy to see you."

"Oh, Bess, I have missed you terribly," I say.

"It goes hard at court, does it?" she says, her eyes knowing.

"Is it that evident?" I ask, a sad smile drawing my lips upwards, then down.

"I'm afraid so, sister," she says, taking my hand. "Come, tell me everything."

We huddle in our room, which we'd shared since we were wee babes, huddling beneath the coverlet on the bed where we slept and shared all our childhood secrets. I fall into my sister's sympathetic and familiar embrace as I tell her about the scandals and secrets, the wickedness and tension at court, and above all, how lonely I am there. "I shall never fit in; the secrets and lies and wicked behaviour just do not suit my temperament. Worse, I have grown older these last ten years, and now I am sure I shall never marry," I say with a sniffle. "I'm destined to remain alone, I know it."

And as she holds me, I feel my shoulders shudder, and all the crying I've suppressed these many years suddenly comes pouring out of me. I sob on and on. I'm helpless to stop, until I feel drained. Empty of tears, empty of sorrow, empty of everything.

"Oh, you must think me a terrible brat. I know you must be devastated, having just lost Sir Anthony," I whisper.

"Hush, Jane," Bess says, stroking my hair. "Don't say such a silly thing. I know you. I know your character, how kind you are. And I do not want you to lose heart: You can never tell what will happen next."

"But who will ever want me?" I say.

I don't cry anymore. Every last ounce of soul has been wrung from me.

Still . . . I'm lonely.

The royal party has overtaken the whole household, as one would expect. But in the evening, when I am used to walking about on my own, undisturbed, I find the proximity of so many bodies a nuisance. Before we are to go into the banquet hall for supper, I step outside into my beloved Young Lady Garden and breathe in the soft fragrance of roses.

"I am not so young anymore," I say aloud, a bitter chuckle escaping my throat. But I am so happy to see my beautiful red blossoms, as rich and bountiful as they were in my youth, I practically dance down the path. *Twenty-seven years old*, I think, *and what have I to show for it?* "Not a thing," I answer myself out loud.

Suddenly, I hear a quiet cough and I spin around, embarrassment already colouring my cheeks the same scarlet as the roses.

The King—he is here, sitting in my Young Lady Garden. He is looking at me with a strangely open and innocent expression on his face. He has such a morose look about him, so glum, the years seem to have fallen away, leaving a naïve young child where there was once a middle-aged man.

"Your Majesty," I whisper, sinking quickly into a deep curtsey.

"Ah, Mistress Seymour," he murmurs. I can feel his eyes sweep over me and I bow my head.

"May I be of service, Your Majesty?" I say softly, not daring to raise my eyes.

"Sweet Jane," he says. His voice is soft and maybe a little bit sad. "Perhaps you will sit beside me for a spell." He does not ask this of me; it is a command.

I sit next to him on the small bench. The smells of woodsmoke and wine roll off him. He touches his left leg—the old injury still troubles him, I suppose—and winces slightly.

"Are you quite all right, Your Majesty?" I ask him.

"I shall be," he answers grimly. After a pause, he says, "You are a good girl, kind and ever thinking of others, aren't you, Jane?"

I could almost feel sorry for him, he looks so lost. I know how desperately he wants to have a son to inherit his throne. I can only imagine how heavily it must weigh on him that he does not have this one thing. How could it not? I wonder what other burdens of kingship also trouble him. I wonder if he mourns the death of Sir Thomas More. I wonder if the break with Rome concerns him. I wonder if he misses his daughter Mary. I wonder if he is lonely.

So many lives ravaged by Anne.

"Mistress Jane?" he says again, interrupting my reverie.

I had quite forgotten the King had asked me a question. Keeping my gaze lowered to the ground, I angle my body slightly towards him. "I try to be, Your Majesty. I try to be kind and good in all ways."

"I am sure you do," he says. I steal a glance upwards and see a small smile lifting his lips. "You seem the loveliest and truest example of womanhood to me. I saw how you leapt to aid the old servant who dropped his parcels as we entered this house. I dare venture you did not intend to allow us such a clear window into your true nature. But there it was, and I was quite . . . moved by it." Henry sighs. "Compassion seems long absent from court these days."

I am at a loss for how to answer the King. He seems wistful and full of regret. But I have seen his own lack of compassion. Still, I must remember, it is wrong to judge what might be in the heart of another.

"I am sure we all strive to be humane, Your Majesty."

"I myself am not sure of that, Mistress Jane," he says.

"I suppose it is what I want to believe, so that I may continue to have faith in humanity. So that I can keep waking up in the morning and feeling that this daily mortal struggle is worthwhile." I speak more fervently than I am used to.

The King looks surprised. Likely, he did not expect so many words at once from me, or such a forceful delivery. "I do believe you are right, Jane." Now his expression turns admiring. "I think you are well and right to look for the good in people. I . . . used to do this. Perhaps you will be able to help set me back on this path?"

"I should like that, Your Majesty. However I may be of service," I reply.

Suddenly, Henry reaches for my hand. His touch delivers a very pleasant warmth that travels from my fingertips up my arm and straight to my belly. I could swear a butterfly dances in there. He holds my hand for a moment, brushing each of my fingers with his, running the pad of his thumb over my palm. I take this opportunity to study him; he is like a great golden bear, masculine and powerful. He straightens. "Would you do me the great honour of strolling with me?"

Henry rises from the bench, drawing me up beside him, then tucks my hand in the crook of his arm. The solidity of his thick arm, muscled from years of riding and jousting, and the close heat of his body fan the flame that is rising inside me. From the way he looks at me, I think Henry must feel it, too.

We set off down the path, and I reach with a free hand to graze the petals of a perfect rose. "I love this garden," I tell the King softly. "I have always thought of it as my own sort of sanctuary."

"What do you love about it?" he asks, his brow wrinkling with curiosity.

"The wildness, the way the roses have grown as they please. No one tames them. Yet they offer up their beauty and fragrance as gifts for the taking. When I was young I used to pretend that these Tudor roses loved me back," I say, smiling.

"Ah, an apt name for the species. Yes, there is something lovely about their wildness; yet, untamed as they may be, they stay within their bounds, offering their perfume as nurturance," he says with an answering grin. "Well, I think it quite fortunate that this is where we have met. So we shall always have another reason to love this garden well." He holds my gaze, before I blush and look down at the ground.

This is all so unreal. A laugh at the madness of it rises up in my throat and bursts forth before I even realize it. The King stops and looks at me, his eyes clearly showing his offence.

"Mistress Jane, is something I've said funny?" His voice has turned cold.

"Oh, Your Majesty, no—not at all. It is just that I am unable to believe this is truly happening. That you are here. With me. That we are in my garden, strolling together, talking as dear friends might do. The wonder of it just struck me. I am so sorry—I did not mean any disrespect, Your Majesty."

The King smiles warmly and says, "Ah, I understand. I am marvelling at it myself." He then begins to chatter about tomorrow's hunt, and my mind is set reeling. The King has asked me to stroll through the garden with him. He has conversed with me in what feels a sincere and intimate manner. *Me—Plain Jane?* What could this possibly mean?

I straighten and remind myself to act as a proper lady would.

"Your Majesty, would you allow me to ride out after the hunting party?" I ask, keeping my voice demure. "I should like to see you hunt."

Henry stops suddenly, surprised. "Why, of course. I would quite like that, too—I should like to see you upon a horse." Then his voice turns a bit sour. "I imagine the Queen shall ride out as well."

I glance at him quickly, admiring his golden-red hair, his tall stature. While he has grown portly with age, his eyes creased and rather smaller, he still cuts a handsome figure. He is still a lion. He catches my eye, any darkness the reminder of the Queen brought on now wiped clean away, and grins charmingly, then pats my hand. "Jane," he says, "I am enjoying our walk immensely. I hope that we can repeat this happy occasion once again, sometime very soon."

He continues to pull me along beside him, and as we wind our way between the rosebushes, my steps begin to feel lighter. My voice soft and full of cheer, I say, "Yes, Your Majesty, I am very much enjoying this stroll with you, too."

"Are you, now?" he says thoughtfully. "Perhaps we might meet again tomorrow."

"I would like that."

I wonder what he sees as he observes me. Plain Jane, who blends into the wall hangings? Or perhaps . . . a kindred spirit? I wonder if he could actually feel as lonely as I do. Perhaps I can be his saviour from his loneliness? And he could be mine.

WULFHALL

◇·◇

September 1535

At supper Henry sits at the head of our long dining table, while I am seated farther down. Anne has been seated even farther away, at the opposite end of the table. I cast my eyes about, wondering if anyone saw us come inside from the garden together, if anyone spotted him raising my hand to his lips. Could *she* have seen us? I am certain that no one could have witnessed the way my heart fluttered and danced inside my chest.

I feel safe; I do not think anyone particularly notices me, until I catch Thomas Cromwell, the King's highest advisor, watching me as he chews on the end of a chicken leg. He raises his goblet of wine to me, then pours the ruby liquid down his throat.

I swallow hard.

I glance once towards Henry when I feel him staring at me. I raise my eyes briefly to meet his, as though I'm drawn to him; then I drop my gaze again. I feel a small smile spring to my lips; I press my napkin there, but cannot wipe it away. My ears feel as though they are on fire. And a giddiness overtakes me.

Is this what love feels like?

The table is piled high with roasted mutton and venison, pheasant and capon, meat pies and a pig's stomach, and two peacocks, tail feathers fanned out over the platter. Wine and ale are flowing. As the meal goes on, this magnetism continues to connect me to Henry. My breath is racing with my heart, which could leap from my chest at any moment. But I do not want to act brazenly, I do not want to do anything that would scandalize my family.

If he grows weary of Anne, then I must not act like Anne. If he is taken with Plain Jane, well, then I must act like myself. *Who would have ever thought?*

After supper, my brother Thomas informs me that Master Cromwell did indeed notice that the King and I were strolling together in the garden. "He wishes to speak with you," Thomas says gravely.

"Surely he isn't interested in our Jane," I hear Edward saying incredulously as I re-enter the dining hall. My shoulders stoop a little bit. Is it so impossible to believe that someone could possibly find me desirable? Not even my favourite brother can conceive of it?

Nevertheless, here I am, sitting at the table, watching as the servants clean up, listening to my father and brothers and Master Cromwell discuss me as though I do not exist. They argue over the likelihood of the King's setting Anne aside, as he did Katharine. Even Sir Francis Bryan is here, encouraging them.

"Anne is a vulgar, obscene witch," my father spits. I marvel at his boldness and sheer defiance, remembering how he coerced me into taking the oath of service to her.

"Indeed, Lord Seymour," Master Cromwell says. "She has certainly bewitched our King." His lined, grey face turns thoughtful. He is rumoured to be a great brute, to have lived the life of a ruffian, but he has always struck me as one of the most intelligent and perceptive men I've ever encountered.

"But do you think we can . . . topple her?" Lord Bryan cuts in impatiently.

Master Cromwell folds his hands, lacing his fingers together. He sits back in his chair and lets loose a long sigh. "I think that the King grows tired of her . . . *ways*."

I wonder just what that means, but as my father and brothers glance at me, then shift uncomfortably in their seats, the tips of their ears reddening almost in unison, I can guess at the meaning. Her ways of making love, I suppose.

"Moreover, she has failed to produce a male heir," Cromwell continues. "I do believe there is a chance." He turns to me. "You, Jane, have caught his attention. Your modesty and virtue are what he needs now. You must not do anything to bring this into question." And here he glances at Edward. "Her virtue is intact, is it not?"

I want to fall through the floor, I could not possibly be more humiliated. I give the slightest nod of my head.

"Of course it is, sir," Edward answers sternly, looking at me askance.

I cannot bring myself to lift my gaze from the scarred oak of the tabletop. I trace the grains with my finger, over and over. Where I felt giddy and excited earlier, now I feel deflated, as they treat me like no more than a head of cattle, trampling this seed of something fragile and precious into dust.

"You must be modest, deferential, and submissive. You must be encouraging—but not overly so," Cromwell's voice intones. "You must keep your virtue intact, no matter what the King asks. If you do these things, if you are able to stay true to these instructions, I do think someday you could be Queen of England. But you must not reveal our plan to anyone. Not to your closest confidante, not to your dearest friend, not even to your sister."

"It is all right, Master Cromwell," I say quietly. I do my best to inject strength into my voice, not to let in a tremble. "I understand. And I will do these things. For the good of the King, for the good of England."

They look around the table at one another and grin proudly. I suppose I've performed well, then. They think they are so clever, these pompous men. I will do the things I have said I would, and I will marry, and I will bear children. And I will become the next Queen of England. But I will not do these things for power or spite. I will do them for love. And just maybe, I will succeed.

WULFHALL
◇·◇

September 1535

Henry has sent small tokens every day this week. Poems, a bowl of candied plums—never mind that he must have gotten them from my father's kitchens. And now a letter.

> *My dearest friend and mistress,*
>   *These few lines from thy entirely devoted servant are but a token of my true affection for thee. Hoping you will hold me commended to your favour and forever in your heart. For I do surrender myself unto you.*
>   *Your own loving servant and sovereign,*
>   *H.R.*

My hands tremble as I hold the paper, folding and unfolding it, bringing it close to my eyes to see the letters on the page. I cannot stop reading it, over and over again. Plain Jane has gotten a love letter. A true love letter. From the King of England. Henry loves me.

I know that I must bring the letter to my father. He and Master Cromwell read it quickly. Father makes as though to fold the letter and slip it into his pocket, but I hold out my hand. "Please," I say. "I should like to keep it. I will show it to no one."

He hesitates and looks questioningly at Cromwell.

"It is mine," I say pointedly. "Please."

Master Cromwell looks at me, cocking his head as though trying to get a clearer notion of who or what I am, as if I were some species of rare bird. I meet his eye, forcing myself to keep my spine straight, my gaze firm. Then he glances at my father and nods. "She may keep it."

His sharp scrutiny turns to land on me again. "But, Jane, remember to be a good girl. Keep the letter close. If the three of us know of the King's interest in you, others will know, too. If not now, then soon enough. There will be eyes on you at all times—unfriendly ones, at that. You seem to have a sensible head on your shoulders; keep watch for attempts at foul play. And remember: Queen Anne is capable of a great many things. A great many things not in the least bit savoury."

This is true, I know it well. But I cannot say that what my father and Cromwell and the other men are attempting is by any stretch *savoury*, either.

Yet there is something pure at the root of this. Love. I must hold on to that fact.

After the hunt this afternoon, I spy Henry dismounting his horse with some difficulty. Anne comes towards him, as if to offer help. He manages to swing his bad leg down, and roughly brushes her off. "Away from me, woman," he snaps. "Must you make me appear weak at every turn?" He turns and looks at me, his expression shifting and softening. He winks. I suck in a breath and stifle a laugh at his boldness.

Anne shrinks back, as if he has slapped her. Her face looks stricken. She turns to him. "My King, I would never—" She stops and watches him carefully, then follows his gaze. My breath hitches as her razor eyes find my own. She squints and her expression hardens. "I see," she says so softly I must read her lips to catch the meaning. "I see everything."

My heart skips a beat; my smile quickly falls away.

Once Henry has gone on his way, Anne comes towards me and grabs my wrist. Her fingernails dig into my skin, scratching and burrowing, as though she endeavours to tear my flesh from my bones. "Do you really believe, you little witch, that he will love you any differently from all the rest? Do you think you are so different from me? Do you think yourself better? Well, do not pretend. He will love you and tire of you just as he has done with the rest of us. Except, he made *me* his Queen. Do not presume to believe that he will treat a weak and ugly little milksop like you any better," she hisses. Her face twists, ugly, and her eyes sear into my own. "I know what he wants, as I know men. You know nothing!"

"I know that you have never loved him," I whisper, unable to meet her gaze.

"Fool!" she thunders. "You are a fool!" She whirls around and storms off after Henry.

LONDON

◇·◇

November 1535

Thomas and Edward have accompanied me back to court. They will take no chances, leaving this matter in my hands alone. But they needn't worry; all shall go according to their plan, and they will congratulate themselves, but I will know, it is because I love purely. This is my most precious secret.

At night, there is a great feast, with dancing and merrymaking afterwards. As throngs of courtiers ring the room, I spy Henry across the way. He stands there, surrounded by a doting crowd, and I can practically feel his blue eyes on me. I am having difficulty keeping myself from meeting his wolfish stare. But when I do meet his eyes, a twinge in my belly practically sends me rocking on my feet. It dances up and down the length of me and I can feel my heartbeat quicken. The moments seem to stretch out and out and out, and I am caught in the web of his stare, unable to focus on the chatter around me.

I am practically unaware of having drifted to a quiet corner, where at last I find myself alone. I cannot stop fidgeting, yet force myself to keep my gaze trained on the dancing slippers flitting across the floor in front of me. Then he is beside me. I feel him there, standing a hair's breadth too close, raising the hair along my arms. My cheeks burning, I look down at the floor, then up at him from beneath my lashes.

Appear chaste and virtuous in all you do, I imagine Cromwell and my father whispering in my ear.

"Your Majesty," I say softly.

"Mistress Jane," he replies, his voice husky. "You are enchanting, as ever. You send a thrill straight to my heart." Henry reaches for my hand and gently raises it to his lips, then drops a feather-light kiss on my fingers. Again my stomach turns slowly and warmth seems to travel from the spot where his lips met my hand straight through the core of me.

I know Henry flirts and I know I am far from the first. Still, I can't help but think, this is different. Precious and pure. Yet I know I mustn't let him sway me—I must resist his advances.

"Your Majesty," I murmur again, then drop my gaze.

"Jane," he repeats, his voice now a rumble that I feel all through my body. "I am in your thrall." He backs me deeper into the corner and presses against me.

"Your Majesty, I am so deeply flattered by my lord's attentions." I strive to keep my voice even and calm. I remember the men's instructions, again. "I could only wish for a husband to be so truly enthralled."

Henry backs away ever so slightly, a new look of admiration in his eye. "Yes, of course, my dearest," he says. "I should like to go for a stroll with you tomorrow, upon the noon hour. I shall summon you." He kisses my hand once more. "Let us enjoy the dancing for now. I'm afraid my leg renders me no more than an observer these days."

"I have always watched," I say, unsure of where the thought sprang from.

The King looks at me curiously. "Yes, Jane, I dare say I know this about you." He gives a small, funny smile, as though he is weighing this fact alongside another in his mind.

He takes my hand again and gives it a light squeeze. I lace my fingers through his and press back ever so slightly. It is even more surprising to consider how truly he has seen me, seen who I really am—how he knows me and still feels tenderly towards me. Once again hope fills my heart with joy.

GREENWICH PALACE
◇·◇

January 1536

Queen Katharine has died. My heart aches for her, but it breaks for Mary. The girl has taken so ill, with a terrible fever, we fear for her life as well. I tell Henry that he should write to her, allow her to come back to court. Henry wavers: At times he weeps for the loss of his first child, whom he once loved so dearly. But then he grows snappish and cruel, and reminds me of how she disobeys him, how she is a stubborn and selfish child, recalcitrant and, consequently, unwelcome. Mary, as I remember her, was always a sweet girl. Devout and unafraid to show off her intelligence. I admire her, even though she is seven years younger than I.

Sometimes it is hard to remember the coarse and quick-to-anger man and the tender one who showers gifts and sweets and loving words upon me are the same. I know his anxiety over not having a male heir troubles him deeply. But I am unable to understand why Mary could not inherit the throne. She is as learned as any man, thoughtful and wise. Whenever I think it is safe to broach the subject with Henry, I do. More often than not he changes the topic.

Now that I have learned of Mary's terrible illness, I feel it necessary to raise the question once more. "Please, Your Majesty, won't you make amends with your daughter? I know she loves you so," I tell him one night, as I stroll alongside him after supper.

He changes the topic to the next week's jousts, as though I did not ask. I sigh but link my arm through his, and do not mention Mary again. We have taken to sneaking away from the banquet hall for short periods, to walk through the gardens, much as we did that first night at Wulfhall.

* * *

Something terrible has happened. Henry has fallen from his horse during a jousting match. He has lost consciousness for nearly two hours. Everyone fears him dead. Cromwell keeps the knights calm as physicians bandage his wounded skull.

Mercifully, he awakens at last and the crowd around him begins to dispel. He looks all about, tearing the bandages from his head. "Cromwell!" he barks. Suddenly his gaze comes to rest on me, and it is as though a Heavenly hand clears a path between us. I fly to his side as soon as I can get past the ring of frightened dukes and lords.

He looks at me with twinkling eyes and winks. "You needn't worry for me, dearest." He takes up my hand and kisses it.

I heave such a sigh of relief in that moment. I curtsey and run inside, where I belong. Back in the Queen's chambers, I am greeted by stony silence. Admittedly, these last four months have not been easy, as I am still a member of the Queen's household. I believe she keeps me on so that she may hold me within her sharp gaze. She has not dared speak to me, although it seems everyone at court knows Henry fancies me, as he tires of her.

Later, after Queen Katharine's funeral, Henry calls me to him. He is sitting in the great hall, gnawing on a piece of meat. A platter piled high with candied fruits and nuts waits in front of him. When I come near, he grabs my wrist and pulls me down onto his lap. His arms encircle me and my body grows warm at his touch. He whispers in my ear that our time grows near. I squeeze his hand delicately but say nothing.

Suddenly, Anne stalks into the room, and when she sees us, she flies into a rage, her face growing stormy and dark as she howls, "You betray my heart!"

"Hush. Peace be, sweetheart. And all shall go well with thee." He tries to calm Anne, yet holds me in place. I shift uncomfortably, wishing I could run from the room. I am reminded, too, that she is carrying his child. If it is a boy, I dare not even think what will happen to me. Cast aside again. That's what.

Nothing will soothe Anne. Henry finally releases me, and I am allowed to flee. I hear her continuing to vent her fury, loud and shrill, before, I imagine, leaving in a whirl of black velvet.

That evening, Anne loses the baby. She wails from her bed, sticky with blood, "You have done this!" And I do not know if she is cursing Henry or me. "I have lost our boy!" she cries.

Henry enters her bedroom, and Anne resumes her furious shrieks, which I can hear through the walls from the outer room. "You have no one to blame but yourself!" she screams. "You have been so unkind to me!"

"Woman, you shall have no more boys by me," Henry shouts back at her. "None!"

I can't help but feel a flutter of hope. If he won't go to her bed, then I needn't worry.

"My King! Please! You have made this loss! You and that wench, Jane Seymour!"

The other maids of honour turn their stares on me from all around the presence chamber. I want to sink into the floor, but am rooted to the spot. The horror of the loss of Anne's child sickens me. So, too, do my own selfish thoughts of abandonment. Tears well in my eyes as the gravity of all that is happening comes clear.

"You and that wench have caused me too great distress. It goes so hard for me." Anne's voice is muffled now as her weeping grows louder. "Because the love I bear you is so much greater! My heart broke when I saw you loved another."

Henry has concealed his own anger within a quiet tone of contempt. "I shall speak with you again when you are feeling better." He spins and storms through the bedroom door, stamping past me without a glance, then out of the Queen's apartment.

Anne suddenly appears in the doorway, swaying, her hair wild and looking for all the world like some otherworldly demon. She looks straight at me and hisses, "I shall bear him another son, one whose legitimacy is not doubtful, like this one, for having been conceived during the life of the Princess Dowager." She sends me daggers with her eyes as she spits out these words.

A part of me flutters with fear. Could she be right?

But little does she know, the King is making other plans for her. Surely, Henry's and my love will win.

GREENWICH PALACE

◇·◇

February 1536

Henry prepares to leave for Shrovetide celebrations in London. He tells me it will be just for a few days, and then he will come back to me. "And," he says meaningfully, "by then, the wheels shall have been set in motion."

"My King," I tell him, "I wish only for your safe and speedy return." I twist around my finger the ring he gave me the week before; it bears Anne's initials set in rubies, but Cromwell assures me they shall have the rubies replaced to spell out my own initials. "But will these wheels carry us down the path to marriage?" I ask.

"Yes, sweetheart. The witch, the enchantress who has used the black arts to ensnare me, shall not impede us for much longer."

My heart skips a beat. Will he put Anne in a nunnery? Or lock her away in some godforsaken castle as he did Katharine? What will happen to her cherubic little daughter, I wonder. Will Elizabeth be packed off with her mother? A seed of pity takes root in my heart at the thought of her.

"Keep this token close to your heart and let it help you remember me tenderly," Henry says as he presses a small velvet-wrapped present into my hands.

"Your Majesty," I say, "you spoil me with too many presents." But I flash him a smile so he knows I am grateful. As I pull back the sumptuous cloth, a golden locket bearing a miniature portrait of the King nearly spills out. "It is so beautiful. I will treasure it and keep it close to my heart, always."

The King takes the chain from me, drapes it around my neck, then fastens the clasp. "You are divine," he says, kissing my hand. He lifts one hand to my chest, allowing a single finger to brush the locket, brush my neck. My breath hitches.

"Thank you, my lord." I close my eyes and pray for his speedy return. Who knows what awaits me in his absence?

Sure enough, early the next morning, as I am sitting hunched over my needlework, I cannot help but reach for the locket. I open it to gaze at my King's portrait.

I did not realize I was being observed.

"You dare!" Anne flies at me, shrieking and waving her arms. "You dare to flaunt one of the King's trinkets here, in front of me? You wicked little mouse! I shall trample you!

"I am powerful," she wails pathetically. "You are—you are *nothing*! I shall be rid of you, you wretched wench!" She runs at me and slaps me. Hard. Then she scratches my face, my shoulders, like some wild beast with claws, tearing at the necklace. She finally grabs hold of the chain and rips it from my neck, howling all the while. I am breathing heavily, horrified and shocked.

"You have no more power!" I shout at her, jumping up from my seat. "*You* are the wicked one! You never loved him! I love him truly!" I clamp my hand over my mouth, unable to believe the words that have just escaped.

"Get out of my sight," Anne snarls. "I do not want to see you again."

I run from the chamber and find my way out to the garden. I must think what to do next, for I shall not return to Anne's service.

When at last I locate my brothers, they bring me to their apartment and sit me down on a chaise.

"Here is a cup of water, sister," Thomas says, thrusting it before me. "Drink."

I take a sip and try to calm myself. I cannot stop my chest from heaving with breaths I can't catch.

"Where shall I go?" I ask. "What will become of me?"

"The King is at work to set Anne aside," Edward says, kneeling down to look straight into my eyes. "What will become of you? You will become the next Queen of England."

That afternoon, Sir Nicholas Carew appears, sent directly from London by Henry to deliver a token to me. "The King cannot bear to be parted from his dearest one," Sir Nicholas says. "He bade me bring you this." A purse filled with gold coins.

Oh, Lord, this I cannot accept. Something about taking money smacks of the unsavoury. Jewellery and trinkets, fine cloth and other presents have seemed so harmless.

I fall to my knees and kiss the letter Sir Nicholas has brought to me. "Please, Sir Nicholas," I begin, holding out the purse, "please beg the King on my behalf to consider that I am a prudent gentlewoman of good and honourable family. I am a woman without reproach, who has no greater treasure in this world than my honour, which I would not harm for a thousand deaths. If my Lord, the King, wishes to send a present of money to me, I pray him to do so when God might send me a husband to marry."

When Henry returns to Greenwich he shoves old Cromwell out of his apartments in the palace and lets Edward and my sister-in-law move into the suite of rooms so that I can stay with them. A secret gallery connects their rooms to Henry's, and now he can come to visit me without the eyes of so many upon us. Certainly this arrangement shall shield me from Anne's wrath. But it is isolating and lonesome, for my brother and sister-in-law go out during the daytime, and I am left alone to wait. And wait. And wait. For something to happen, for someone to come. It is terribly dull. And I am left with so much time to just . . . think.

Henry says he loves me. But surely it is not the same way he loved Anne. He loved her with a burning, ferocious passion. I think he loves me more quietly. But then, what does this love actually mean? Does he only think about what is *not* Anne-like? Does he only think about what is best for the kingdom? Does he only think about what is best for him? Someone obedient and submissive, too timid to make much trouble?

Or is it a wiser love?

Well, it seems there are those who will make trouble enough for us all. If not Anne, then there are plenty of others. I hear things, still, even at such a remove. I heard Edward talking about the rumblings throughout the land. The people are unhappy with Henry's move to empty out the abbeys and monasteries: the Reformist wickedness that Henry's divide with Rome has elicited.

I have felt myself so enthralled with this great romance, I have forgotten to worry for our eternal souls. I have neglected to think on this schism with our mother Church—how, under Anne's influence, Henry divided England—all of England—from Rome. Oh, the blasphemy. In the quiet, lonely moments when there is enough silence around me and inside me, I remember, and a sick feeling knots itself around my belly.

Moreover, I have caught wind that the people have started to mock me. I have heard the whispers of bawdy ballads, and I am ashamed. There is a pamphlet travelling about London bearing a lewd song deriding me, and while I have neither seen nor heard it, Henry saw fit to write and let me know of it. I chew on my nails as I pace the boundaries of this apartment. Does the whole of England hate me, I wonder?

All my life I have striven to be good. Virtuous, chaste, and devout. I do not know how to bear this stain of disgrace. And then I wonder, will my father and brothers, Master Cromwell, and myself—England—shall we all fall down into the dark depths of the underworld when everything is said and done, for following our blessed King into sin?

WULFHALL

◇·◇

April 1536

My dear friend and mistress,

The bearer of these few lines from thy entirely devoted servant will deliver into thy fair hands a token of my true affection for thee, praying you will keep it forever. Hoping shortly to receive you in these arms, I end for the present, your own loving servant and sovereign,

H.R.

"There is a case being built against Anne Boleyn!" My brother Thomas rushes into the house out of breath. He has been running. "I have heard it myself, straight from the old man's mouth," he says of Cromwell. "They will have a trial—she is to be charged with adultery and conspiracy to murder!" Thomas stops suddenly and his ears redden. "And, er, other things . . . ," he says, his voice trailing off. Edward looks up and nods brusquely.

Now my curiosity is piqued. What other things?

Then all that Thomas has recounted begins to register. "Conspiracy to murder?" I echo softly. "But that means . . ." I cannot finish the sentence. It means she will be put to death.

All this time, as I blithely went along with the plan to unseat Anne, I imagined she would be exiled to some cold, damp abbey to live out her days in silent solitude. I never once imagined . . . "Oh, no," I moan. I feel sick and wrap my arms around my middle. I swore an oath to serve Anne Boleyn, and now . . . now it seems I have been made a party to her execution. "No, no—"

Suddenly the hot sourness of bile rises up my throat. I run outside and vomit in the yard.

Bess has run out after me. "Darling," she says softly, handing me a cloth with which to wipe my mouth, "are you all right?"

"No," I say. And I burst into tears. I try to explain everything to her. She knew the King favoured me, but she did not know how we plotted—all of us, our father and brothers and Sir Francis—to overthrow the Queen. "I am now responsible for her death. How can that be?"

I sit down on a step leading into the house and hold my face in my hands. "I never imagined it would come to this. All this time, I thought Anne was horrible and had done such wretched things to Mary and Katharine, to the country, to everyone and everything around her, but I never thought she deserved death. What of her daughter? Oh, how can I ever live with this?"

I look up at Bess. Her blue eyes are sombre, and though she has thrown her arm around my shoulders, she does not meet my gaze.

"What did you think would happen?" she asks. "Truly, how could you have thought otherwise? If Anne were to live, she could reveal all of Henry's secrets. She could concoct further reasons to hold on to her position—a baby, a boy, perhaps, whether it was got by Henry or some other." Bess stops. "Don't you understand? It truly is the only way Henry can marry again."

"But . . . isn't this . . . murder?" I say. The sick feeling returns as the word "murder" takes form in my mouth.

"I don't pretend to know," Bess says. "Is it, when it is ordered by the King?"

I look out over the fields and rolling hills. All this land that once gave me such comfort, where everything seemed right and true—now it all looks wrong. "I do believe it is a sin. And I have sinned with them. I was vain and all too eager to drink in the attention. I craved the affections of the King. This makes me a sinner. But whatever happens next, I shall henceforth endeavour to be as good as God would want me to be."

"As a queen should be," Bess adds.

I look up at her sharply. "I can't—"

"Yes. Yes, you can," Bess says sternly. "At least do not let her death be in vain. Perhaps, once you are the Queen by Henry's side, we will be able to look forwards to some good."

I sigh and drop my head into my arms.

WULFHALL

◇·◇

May 1536

Anne is arrested and called to trial. I remain ensconced at Wulfhall, safe amongst my family, until Sir Nicholas Carew comes to fetch me. The King wishes me to take up residence temporarily in Sir Nicholas's house in Surrey. At least Edward and my parents may accompany me this time. I bid farewell to Bess, tears streaming down my face.

"Sister dearest, use your position. Use it well, and use it wisely," Bess says. She gives me a final hug.

"Bess, I know I have been selfish. Please forgive me, and remember me fondly," I say. "I love you."

"I love you, darling Jane. Be brave."

No one has ever told me to be brave before. But I shall.

My brothers ride regularly to London to witness the proceedings; they are eager for Anne's end. It makes me ill. I cannot eat, and I cannot sleep. I wait for news, my heart brimming with dread.

The King shall come calling tomorrow. I know he will expect to see me as I used to be, vibrant and of the living. Though I only want to pick at my food, I force myself to eat. Then I retire to my bedchamber and try to sleep.

Thoughts tumble through my head, however, and sleep will not come. I must find a way to make amends for this terrible crime. I shall endeavour to reunite the Princess Mary, who is the rightful heir to the throne, with her father. I shall endeavour to reunite Henry with Rome. I shall endeavour to do all I can for the sake of good.

*   *   *

"Darling Jane," Henry says, stroking my hand. We sit together in the parlour of Sir Nicholas's home. He is rather too close. "I cannot live without you. I cannot bear to be so far from you. Do come back to London."

I thought his touch would cause me revulsion. But while the pleasure I used to find in his caresses has gone, I am relieved that I do not recoil from him.

"As you wish, my lord," I say softly, eyes to the ground.

"Jane, are you all right?" Henry asks worriedly.

I look up at him, surprised. "I—" I stop myself. I do not think he would like to hear of my inner struggles, my sense of horror at what awaits Anne and the men accused with her. I force a small smile to my lips and say, "Yes, my lord. I am quite well, thank you. You are so kind to ask."

"You are my very heart," Henry says grandly. "Of course I ask."

I allow him to kiss my hand, then wait for him to rise. But he doesn't. He stays in place.

"Jane," he says, "are you troubled by something, by the unfolding of events?" He looks at me carefully.

This is a test, I think. And I must pass it if I hope to achieve anything. If I hope to spare Anne a meaningless death.

"I am only troubled by how all these matters upset you, my lord," I answer. "I wish only to aid and serve you in whatever way I may."

"You already do, my sweetest. But I know these are troubling times. Have faith, my darling; it is your essential kindness and compassion that wed you to my heart. I know you are strong enough to weather any upset. We shall navigate these times and troubles together." Henry takes up my hand once more and holds it to his chest.

Perhaps our love can be as it was once more. Someday. "Yes, let us navigate them together," I intone, tightening my grip on his hand.

LONDON

◇·◇

May 1536

We have been granted dispensation by Archbishop Cranmer to marry. And tomorrow Anne Boleyn goes to her death. I prepare my wedding clothes as Anne prepares her speech before the executioner's sword shall take away her words.

And when Anne draws her final breaths, Henry announces our betrothal to his Privy Council.

After, Henry stays with me through the evening; we don't speak much. Henry dons a white robe to mark his state of mourning, and we have supper together. He is placid, introspective, and I am grateful for the quiet.

When we have finished eating, he takes his barge back to Hampton Court. My family and I shall join him there in the morning for our betrothal. Before he leaves, Henry comes to me and gathers both my hands in his.

"My darling Jane, I love you. We shall be married!" he proclaims jovially. Then he turns before I can even respond, and is rowed swiftly away, the lanterns swinging gaily from his barge.

The next morning, our betrothal ceremony is brief, with only my family in attendance, and when it ends I bid Henry farewell. My parents and I shall remove to Wulfhall, to await my wedding day.

When I am home, I try not to think about what reflections and prayers must have run through Anne's head as she waited for the executioner's blade to bite her neck. I try not to wonder if she blames me from wherever she is—Heaven or Hell, I know not. I try not to think about her blood on my hands. But it is impossible to keep these thoughts from my mind. And every time I remember to stop them, I cry. Then pull myself up and ply my mind with new questions and ideas.

I do try to think of what my emblem as Queen might be. Anne's was a falcon, which—while I do not want to speak ill of the dead—seems rather fitting, a swift and cunning carnivore that preys upon smaller birds.

For me, something different. The phoenix rising from the ashes. This shall be my badge. I will be born anew when I become Queen, and all the bad deeds, the selfishness and foolishness, will be burned away, and from those ashes, I shall rise, ready to bring more light and more love into this sometimes benighted world.

May 30, Whitehall Palace

Henry and I both arrived here yesterday. And truly, I was so happy to see him. He looked, for the first time in many years, at peace. Today, we married.

The ceremony was a marvel. It was held in the Queen's Closet and my whole family was in attendance. I wore a sumptuous gown trimmed in ermine—never have I seen such finery. A great train of ladies followed after me, as we walked in procession, and though Henry looked older and fatter, he was still dashing in his way. Above all, he looked happy. The glow of joy on his face, I think, suffused mine, too. Yellow-golden flames of a thousand candles cast a glow about the hall, and I think even my overly pale skin must have appeared luminous in that light. Bess walked just behind me and she squeezed my hand before I met the King. I turned to look at her, and her eyes shone with joy. As the bishop spoke, I felt my heart racing as though it would fly from my chest. This was it. The moment I had waited for all my days.

Then I was enthroned in the Queen's chair in the great hall under my own canopy of estate.

Life is truly beginning. I shall have my family and babies and all I ever wanted. I shall bring this King and his kingdom to peace; this is my mission.

None of it seems quite real. I am holding court; so many gentle-persons have come to pay respects. I do not believe I have ever spoken to so many people. I do not believe I have ever felt so many eyes upon me at once.

Henry presents me with a golden cup, designed by Hans Holbein and engraved with our initials entwined in a love-knot. It is beautiful. Master Holbein has also engraved on the cup my motto, working it flawlessly into the design: "Bound to Obey and Serve."

After the festivities and endless feasting wind down, Henry rises from his seat, offering his hand to me. "And now, the wedding night!" guests shout.

If the floor would swallow me in this instant, I would feel no re-gret. Humiliation sends a fiery warmth over my face; I am sure my cheeks are as red as cherries. Henry waves his free hand and calls on his subjects to hush. "Can you not see, my virtuous and beautiful wife is too chaste for you lot?" he cries gleefully. Then he whisks me from the hall.

Henry is gentle as he undresses and strokes me, telling me softly how beautiful I am, how innocent. And I do feel these things. But mostly I am scared.

A grown woman should know about the marriage bed, but I have never been touched so by a man. And while my sister explained the rudiments, somehow, the knowing from her telling does not seem quite the same as knowing from doing.

But Henry guides me tenderly, with loving words, and our first night together as man and wife is surprisingly sweet. The magnetic attraction I once felt for him has faded, but there is an underlying affection.

As we lie in bed together, my legs wrapped around his good, right leg, my head resting on his chest, I run my fingers up and down his arm slowly. He sighs contentedly and kisses me softly on the lips. "This is as a marriage should be," he says.

"Is it, my lord?" I ask.

"Do you not feel it, sweetheart?"

I look up at him and smile. "You know, I think I do."

We journey by barge to Greenwich, where we spend our honeymoon, a blissful week, during which we talk of small and happy things; how we will celebrate Christmas, what we shall name our son, when he comes. Henry boasts to all who will listen that we shall have a son by next year. I am anxious; I know how much it means to him. And I know what has happened to the women who came before me who failed to give him this one thing his heart so desires. And of course, I want a baby, someone to cherish and love with all my heart. A baby I shall teach to be kind and just and true. So that when he becomes King, he shall rule like a lion. Like a phoenix rising from the ashes. And I shall reunite Henry with Mary; she deserves this kindness. And the little baby I hope to have someday—he should know his sister. And Elizabeth, Anne's daughter, too. We are all God's creatures.

WINDSOR CASTLE

◇·◇

October 1537

I know my subjects say I am distant and cold. But I feel just as strongly as I did before I ascended the throne. Now, though, the question of whom to trust is ever more present. I talk to Princess Mary most of all. I have succeeded in reuniting her with her father. And Henry was so happy, when Mary submitted to him, to assume once again the role of loving father. She is very grateful and remains at court, constantly by my side.

Christmas 1536 brought such joy to our household, as Henry summoned Mary to court. Oh, how full of love and happiness was their reunion. I have done one good thing, I think. One very good thing.

And even gladder are we, now that I am with child. Nothing in the world could bring either the King or myself greater joy than the prospect of a new babe.

All I want to do is eat quail, and Henry indulges me. He is so jovial, every little wish or want I have, he is only too happy to grant.

This autumn, after a terrible labour, I bring my son into the world. Edward. Three days and nights, the labour pains go on and on and on, until I am certain my body will simply break. Still, my darling Prince seems content to stay inside my womb. The waves of pain creep up on me with all the stealth of a bear, throbbing and thrashing and causing me to scream until my throat goes raw; then they tiptoe away as quickly as they came.

I am ravaged, splitting apart, it seems. I do not think I can possibly endure. Then, finally, wrapped in a great ribbon of blood, my most beloved, perfect little boy bursts into the world.

Silence. My heart stops, my chest heaves. Three days. Three nights. And there is only silence. Anna, the maid who has dutifully wiped my brow with cool, wet cloths, looks at me, her face ashen.

Then.

A mewling cry fills my sore and exhausted body with relief and joy such as I have never known. He lives!

I shall love you forever, I think as I hold my beautiful baby boy in my arms, stroking his soft golden-red hair, so like his father's. But all of a sudden a blinding wave of pain takes hold of me. The nurse grabs the baby away, and a wet cloth is brought for my forehead. Henry comes to see us, and he is overjoyed. He snatches our boy from the nurse's arms and dances around the room with him.

"Edward!" he cries, beaming with pride and unadulterated happiness. My own heart swells at the sight of my two Princes, until another spear of pain stabs my belly. I fall back into the pillows and stifle the soft cry at my lips.

Edward's christening is to be held two weeks hence. I try to help with the planning and preparations from my bed, but I cannot seem to gain my strength back. Terrible waves of pain grip me at regular intervals. And when they ease, I just want to sleep. I am not well, but I cannot miss this celebration. I cannot miss one moment with my son. Yet something is not right. I am not well, I know it.

HAMPTON COURT

<hr>

24 October 1537

I am so thirsty. A single droplet of water would suffice. No, this isn't true. I could drink the River Thames for want of a drop of water. "Please," I murmur, unable to find the strength to speak above a whisper. This fever now steals my voice. My mind, too, for in the nighttime, when the chills and pain overtake me, I feel I am somewhere else, long ago. Perhaps in the gardens of my childhood home, my precious Young Lady Garden. I'm not quite sure where real and unreal begin and end. The pain begins as a sudden throb in my womb, then radiates throughout my body, and I cannot stop shivering.

I will never see my darling boy again. This I know. And when that thought enters my mind, I know I've fully returned to what is real and true. I sinned against Anne Boleyn, and now it is my turn to die. I tried to make up for what we did with better deeds. To no avail.

The pain in my belly becomes a blinding flash in my head, in my heart. My baby. He is lost to me. My king, my husband is lost to me. All is lost to me. My heart shatters.

Henry has come. He lies beside me and holds my hand, strokes my hair. But he is horrified by my sickness. Still he stays, and tells me sweet things, promising I shall recover and see our Prince grow to be a strong young man. Our Prince. I am the one who gave the King a boy, the heir for whom he has so longed all these years. I did this. I did. I, Plain Jane. I filled this household with love again, with hope and a future. I did. I, Plain Jane.

The chills engulf me once more. Then darkness.

HENRY VIII

Sweet Jane. Jane. Sweet Jane.

How could she leave me, and so soon, amidst such triumph? The mystery of the mortal body . . . How, when I am holding your flesh so tight, can the soul escape it?

My arms should clench your spirit in its place. Don't go.

You have given me a son. A golden son.

So stay, stay, and we shall be for all time together.

"Bound to Obey and Serve." So she did obey and serve—but there was no law binding Jane to do so. The only monarch dictating her meekness and service was her own gentle and compassionate heart.

I took no notice of her—she was quiet as a mouse—until I once saw her gather up packages for a household servant. This kindness was so like her, as I learned.

The court is hard. The world is hard. I have enemies all around me. Factions move buzzing past me in the audience chamber. I try to steer the realm between Popery and the lies of the German worm Luther, and to do so, I must condemn many to burn. And Anne—whose playful laugh became a hexen cackle in my ears—she and her faction deceived me.

Ambassadors scratch out secret letters in ciphers, and they are joined by traitors who smile at me in the Privy Chambers. I have received many heartless knocks in this world, and some have unhorsed me. My closest men betray me. Whom, then, could I trust?

I could trust sweet Jane, who served and obeyed.

I had to undress her on our wedding night and guide her in love; but my love for her started months earlier, when she once undressed me with kind, quick fingers: by which I mean simply that she unwound my garter where it chafed the ulcers on my leg. She drew down the stockings which were stuck to the flesh with old blood and sticky humours. Taking cloths, she washed my wounds.

I admired the way she did not gag at the wounds, but instead asked with care, "This is from the joust, Your Majesty? I have heard that your horse fell upon you."

I informed her, "I have been pierced by no lance and cut by no sword. These ulcers erupt daily without any wound to cause them. They have grown worse since the fall at the joust, but . . ."

"Then what?" she asked, bewildered.

"They are a trial from God."

"It seems unfair."

"My blood is so hot, so full of its own royal virility, that it bursts forth from the skin. It needs no wound for excuse."

"These ulcers must make it hard to ride, Your Majesty. You should rest yourself."

"Sweet Jane," I said. "Sweet, simple Jane. I am a sporting man. I still must ride." I grimaced as she washed the sores. "Imagine another man who could walk and ride with such ulcers. You cannot. Another man could not bear them. Imagine another man who could bear to have physicians lance his ulcers with hot pokers. You cannot. No other man could bear the pain."

She smelled the pot of salve I had given her. "What is this, that you wish me to spread?"

"It is a plaster of my own devising. I have studied many medicines and arrived at this one as the best. A man must be able to heal himself. It is a subtle mixture: white lead, ground pearls . . ." I winced as she spread it on my leg—but still, she had a gentle touch that knew pain and comfort.

"Your Highness . . . Your poor Highness."

"Not poor. Far from it. Even wounded, I do what other men cannot when they are whole." Through gritted teeth, I insisted, "This leg is not a weakness, therefore, but a proof of strength. A new victory every day over pain."

She agreed, and thereafter, she would smile with pride at my stoical strength when she saw me lowered onto my horse with a crane—for after a certain time, I had to be lifted by an engine—a temporary measure until my health improves. (Consider instead that harridan Anne, who could not stop herself from gagging at the smell of my ulcers when they appeared.)

That moment when she unwound the garter from my leg—a ribbon embroidered with my motto, "Evil to him who thinks evil"—that was the undressing that caused me to love her.

She would be my refuge. The embrace of warm darkness and sweet understanding after the harsh trumpets and alarms of court. Someone I could trust, after all this time. Someone who knew how to take me into her arms, though I was so much larger than she (a bear embraced by a mouse!), and let me lie there, peacefully.

I cannot believe that she is gone. So short a time.

I once said that kings ran in my blood. Now her blood is on the sheets. My blood fought off its own corruption. And yet, in this beautiful boy she birthed, my blood lives on.

I held him tight, when I was done holding her. She grew colder. He was warm.

I admit no defeat when I say: That night, and for many nights after, I cried.

ANNA OF CLEVES

"God Send Me Wel to Kepe"

7 JULY 1557

Chelsea Manor

There is a vulture in my room.

He perches by my window.

Is he one of Henry's men?

They all look like dark-winged scavengers.

It's the long black robes they wear, with ruffs about the neck.

It's their eyes, too. So bright. So shrewd. Alert to every weakness.

It's the way they circle their victims. Then bide their time in the safety of the high branches as the wounds leak blood.

Wherever they lead, Death follows.

This one waits and watches.

Trying to lead Death to me.

"Lady Anna, can you hear me?"

Like a drowning woman, I struggle out of the black depths towards the surface. Gasping. Writhing. Clutching at my sheets.

"You cried out, my lady. Are you in pain?"

I force my eyelids up. And regret it.

The sun's rays, slanting in through my windows, are like shards of glass in my eyes. And the pain in my belly . . . God in Heaven, the pain.

"She needs more medicine. Alice, bring the bottle."

I press the heels of my hands to my eyes. Take a breath. Try again. My vision clears and I see that which I thought a vulture is no such thing, only my physician, Edmonds, in his gown and cap.

"Here is a draught to ease your suffering," he says.

He helps me sit up. Takes hold of my chin. Presses the cup to my lips.

I turn away. I don't want it. It is syrup of poppy and puts me in a deathlike sleep, one filled with ghosts.

But then the pain comes again, and though I appeal to Our Saviour, His mother, and all the saints to release me from this agony, it only grows stronger. There is a keening in the room, a rising wail. With a shock, I realize it's coming from me.

"Madam, *please . . .*"

It is Edmonds, still at the ready with his vile drink. I submit. I have no choice.

In anything, it seems.

Ever.

What woman does?

I sleep. And dream. And find myself in Rochester once again, at the Bishop's Palace.

Where I was doomed.

Where I was saved.

It is New Year's Day, 1540, and I am twenty-four, not the old woman of forty-one I am now. I am standing in the great hall. Courtiers attend me. There is a loud, echoing boom as the doors are thrown open. Four men walk through them, ghosts all.

The first is Cromwell, Henry's chief minister and the one who arranged our marriage.

His head has been severed from his neck. He holds it in his hands. The bloodless lips move. "Anna of Cleves!" they bellow. "I went to the block because of you! Every cow in the byre, every pig in the sty, knows how to make the beast with two backs. Could you not learn?"

Gardiner joins him, dirt from the grave on his black bishop's gown. He barks questions that would shame a bawd. "Are you a virgin? Did the King penetrate you with his privy member? Was there blood on the sheets?"

Norfolk appears, a tattered, clacking corpse. His lips have rotted away, yet still he shouts. "A slack belly? Sagging dugs? To the block with her!"

And lastly Henry himself. He has pig's eyes and fingers like sausages and is as fat as three men. He wears a coat of velvet and a codpiece the size of a dinner plate. The sores on his leg ooze pus through his stocking. He smells like a midden.

He kisses me. Just as he did when first we met. This time, though, I do not wipe the kiss off.

"I loved, Anna! Oh, how I loved. As no man ever had," he cries brokenly. "My love was as warm as the sun, as deep as the sea. I thought it would last forever, but you destroyed it."

He weeps then, heaving great, blubbering sobs. Bright tears fall from his eyes. They turn to diamonds and bounce off the floor.

Despite the stink, I kiss him, too. More tenderly than ever I did when I was his wife.

"You loved, Henry, yes," I whisper. "Thank God in Heaven you never loved me."

I wake hours later. Or is it days?

The pain is still with me but bearable now.

Edmonds is with me, too. He is talking of poultices with Alice. She is the gardener's girl, and lately my nurse. Lettie, my maid, cannot abide blood.

Edmonds casts my horoscope. Applies leeches, black and wriggling, to my distended belly. Dips his finger in a bowl of my urine. Sniffs it. Tastes it. Frowns. Alice watches his every move.

I suspect much of this is for show and would like to send the old fraud packing, but the cancer in my womb gnaws like a wolf and his elixirs are all that stand between me and torment.

Edmonds pokes and prods, scribbles and frowns, then hands

Alice a bottle. He instructs her how to administer it and takes his leave, promising to return on the morrow.

I am fond of Alice. She is an honest girl with a nimble mind. Clean. A good worker. Shy, because of the large red birthmark that mars her face. The village boys taunt her about it. Her father worries no man will have her.

One of the kitchen girls brings chamomile tea. As Alice pours me a cup, a little red beetle with black spots lands on her hand. Lady-cows, the English call them.

"They are good luck," I say. "I make a wish when one lands on me. Did you? What was it?"

As soon as the words leave my mouth, I regret them. A flush creeps up the girl's neck. It reddens the parts of her face not covered by the birthmark.

"I dare not say, my lady."

My heart hurts for her. "Ah, child. I *know*. You wish to be beautiful. What girl of sixteen does not?"

An awkward nod, a miserable shrug—those are her answers. She walks to the window and shakes the beetle off.

I see her downcast eyes, the sag in her shoulders, and the old anger rises in me again. I am skin over bones, as weak as water, yet I sit up in my bed, for she must hear me.

"Do not wish for beauty, Alice. Wish for cleverness instead. Wish for a strong back and a strong will. They will do you more good than red lips and dimples."

She looks at me as if I am mad.

"Beauty is naught but a commodity," I tell her. "There is no beautiful girl in the world who does not have a father, uncle, or brother scheming to profit from her looks. The Duke of Norfolk was one such. That old whoremonger pushed three of his nieces on the

King—Mary Boleyn, Anne Boleyn, and Catherine Howard. They did not do so well out of the bargain, but he certainly did."

Alice's eyes grow round. There are not many who would dare to call a duke of England, even a dead one, a whoremonger. But living in England does not make one English. I am German still, and do not make a pavane of my words.

"Have you heard of Jeanne d'Albret?" I ask her. "She was a beauty, a French princess. At the age of twelve, she was to be married to my brother, the Duke of Cleves. She refused and was beaten and had to be carried to the altar." I give her a conspirator's smile. "Had you met my brother, you would not blame her."

Alice giggles behind her hand.

"It goes even harder for poor girls," I say. "You learn to outrun the village boys and dodge the busy hands of your master. Perhaps you make a marriage and think yourself lucky. Then you learn that your husband gambles or wenches. You object. He breaks your nose. The magistrate shrugs."

The talking makes my throat rasp. I reach for my cup. Alice helps me drink from it.

"Be glad of your plainness, for I will tell you a secret," I say as she takes the cup away. "Plain girls can prosper. We can make our lives our own. We can go about our business without so many lewd words. Without so many slobberings and gropings and hands up our skirts."

Alice shakes her head. "You are being kind, my lady. Girls such as myself can never prosper."

"I am *not* being kind, child," I say indignantly. "I know whereof I speak. Henry the King thought me ugly. He told me so."

"The King said this to you?" Alice asks, aghast.

"That, and all the other things men say when they wish to shame a woman. That I was old. Stubborn. Dull. Stupid. Fat. That I smelled.

Henry said it to me, to his friends, to his courtiers. I think the whole country knew of his complaints."

"How did you bear it, my lady? The shame of it?"

I know the poor girl asks not for me, but for herself.

"I could bear it because I knew the truth, child," I say. "There was one of us in that marriage who was old, fat, and smelly, and it wasn't me."

"The King was cruel to speak thus," Alice says, but in a low voice. As if Henry, dead these past ten years, might somehow hear her.

"He was, yes," I say. "But I think mostly he was afraid."

Alice is sceptical. "Kings are afraid of nothing," she says.

"This King was afraid. I know it, for I'm the one who made him so. I made a mistake, child, a grave one."

"What was it?"

"I made my face a mirror when it should've been a mask, and what the King saw there terrified him. He hated me for it, and never, ever forgave me."

Alice's curious grey eyes tell me that she wishes to know more, but the talking has exhausted me. I close my eyes and sink back into my pillows. I will rest for a moment; then I will tell her. But when I open my eyes again, hours have passed. It's dark in my bedchamber and I am hungry.

Moonlight, slanting in through the windows, illuminates a sleeping Alice. She lies next to my bed in a wooden trundle. She must've had her father bring it to my room. The thought touches me.

It grieves me that I never had a daughter. I love Mary and Elizabeth, but they are nothing like me. Alice is. She is practical. Capable. A girl made for the country, not the court.

I do not want to wake her. I will get my own supper. I can do it. The pain is down to a dull gnawing.

I swing my legs out of bed, slide my feet into my slippers, and leave the room quietly. Alice will scold if she sees me up, and for a small, slight girl, she is fierce.

I know something is not right the moment I step into the hallway. It has become wider. And longer. Like a gallery. Scores of costly portraits line the walls.

"It is the poppy. Only the poppy," I tell myself.

Faces stare back at me. Henry's. Cromwell's. Norfolk's. Surrey's. They are all gone now, but so vivid and true in their frames, they look as if they will draw breath and speak.

There is only one who could paint thus, only one who could forever fix his subject's soul to canvas—Holbein.

He sits in the middle of the hall, painting. Black blisters, marks of the plague that killed him, mar his broad, bearded face. It is hard to look at him.

I walk up to his easel and peer at his canvas. It's my betrothal portrait he's working on. Back in 1539, Henry sent him to Cleves to take my likeness so he could see what I looked like before he offered marriage.

"I wish I had painted you in a blue dress, Anna. Blue suits you," Holbein says.

"I wish you had not painted me at all. That portrait was the cause of all my trouble. You made me pretty, but I am not."

Holbein had posed me looking directly at the viewer in order to hide my long nose and pointed chin. He made my skin paler than it was and left out my smallpox scars.

"Cromwell slipped a bag of coins into my hand before I left for Cleves," Holbein explains. " 'The portrait must be pretty,' he told me. 'Whether the lady is or not.' "

"You could have refused the bribe," I venture. "You could have painted me as you saw me."

Holbein snorts laughter. "Only fools refused Cromwell. He wanted the marriage very much."

"Far more than I did," I murmur, still staring at the girl I never was. "To Henry, how I looked was all that mattered. Not who I was."

After I had sat for Holbein, I'd asked my mother why Henry got to see a picture of me but I did not get to see one of him.

"You don't need to. It matters only that you please your husband, not that he pleases you," she'd replied.

"But what if I don't love him?" I'd asked.

She'd given me a scathing look. "Love is for milkmaids, Anna. Royal marriages are for making more royalty. The man must like the look of the woman for that to happen. Otherwise, the bread doesn't rise."

"And the woman? What if she doesn't like the look of the man?"

"Then she can close her eyes while he does his business and do her accounts in her head."

I knew what business she meant. I'd seen dogs mounting bitches and rams tupping ewes. There always seemed to be a good deal of kicking and biting involved, but it would not be like that between a man and a woman. It would be like the pretty songs the troubadours sang. That is what I believed.

Memories of my wedding night, long submerged, rise and bob on the surface of my mind now like bloated corpses. I want no part of them.

Angrily, I turn on Holbein. "Why do you keep painting this portrait? The business is over and done!"

His eyes meet mine. "Because time grows short, Anna. You must settle your debts."

I am taken aback by his presumptuousness. "I *have* settled my debts! Do you think I do not know that I am dying?"

He mutely resumes his work.

"Holbein, answer me!" I demand.

I tug at his jacket, but still he makes no reply. Furious, I smack his easel, trying to topple it, but only manage to hurt my hand.

The throbbing brings me back to my senses. I step back and see that I am pummelling a linen chest.

I must eat something. Food will chase the ghosts away, I think as I shuffle to the kitchen.

My manor's halls are easily traversed, even in the dark, but the stairs are a different matter. The stepping motion wakes the shadow-child growing in my womb. I double over, gritting my teeth. When the spasm finally eases, I continue to the kitchen.

Delicious scents greet me. Yeasty dough rising for tomorrow's loaves, smoked ham, strawberries, and other things I cannot keep down. I light a candle, rummage through the larder, and emerge with a bowl of custard. The cancer has so disordered my insides, my diet is now that of a weanling's.

I take my meal at the wooden worktable. The custard is thick and nourishing, rich with eggs from my hens and cream from my cows.

I am enjoying this simple fare when I hear something: the rustle of silk. Soft, sliding footsteps.

And then I feel something. A cold breath on my neck.

I was wrong about the custard. Wrong about the ghosts.

One of them is right behind me.

Slowly, I turn around.

"Boo!" a woman shouts at me.

Her face is covered with livid red pustules. She's wearing a ragged shroud. My heart nearly bursts from fright.

"Ha! Scared you!" she crows.

"Go away, phantom, *please,*" I beg, covering my eyes.

"Anna-Maus, don't you know me?"

There was only one person in the world who called me by that name.

"Greta?" I whisper, lowering my hands.

"Look at you! White as milk!" she says, laughing. "Ha! So funny!"

"Yes, well, the dead do terrify the living. Especially when they look like you," I say, still trembling, but irritated now, too. Greta always was one for stupid pranks.

"Smallpox," she says, grimacing. "Awful, isn't it?"

"I remember. My mother wrote to tell me of your death. I cried for weeks."

Greta was the daughter of a Cleves baron, and my close friend ever since we were tiny. She gave me my nickname, she said, because I looked like a little mouse, always peeking out from my mother's skirts. She accompanied me to London and returned home a few months after I was married. How I missed her.

"You still love sweets, I see," she says, nodding at my custard. "You could never get enough apple cake. Do you remember when your mother caught us filching slices? My backside ached for a week. God in Heaven, but she was strict. I don't think a day went by that one of you four children didn't get a whipping. She loved you best. Sibby was vain. Mali was soft. Wilhelm was a pisspot. But you were clever, like her."

Greta is chattering away as if we'd never parted, as if she weren't dead and ghastly to behold. But I cannot bear seeing my beloved friend so ravaged, and tears well in my eyes.

"Why do you come, Greta? Why do you haunt me?" I ask her.

She grows sombre. "Because there is a thing left undone."

Her words trouble me. They echo Holbein's. "What thing?" I ask, anxious to know. "I have settled my affairs. I have . . ."

But my words trail off as Greta transforms from a corpse into the beautiful young woman she once was, and the kitchen falls away like a painted stage set, and I find myself in the courtyard of my family's castle in Düsseldorf, capital city of the Duchy of Berg.

I look down and see that my nightclothes are gone. I'm wearing a velvet gown now, and underneath it a fine woollen kirtle. A fur-lined cloak hangs from my shoulders. Gold chains and a jewelled pendant lie heavy against my chest. God only knows how my mother procured them. My family is not wealthy, but a good impression must still be made.

I remember this place, this day, so well. I am twenty-four, and leaving to marry Henry. I tell myself that this, too, is only a poppy-dream, but my heart swells with happiness to see my homeland again.

It is November. Early snow falls like sugar through a sieve. It dusts the castle's turrets and towers, eddies over the cobblestones. The smell of woodsmoke hangs in the air.

Greta is standing next to me. "Hurry, Maus, *go*," she tells me. "If good-byes are to be said, they must be said quickly."

I start with an endless line of German nobles. Some I've known since I was a child, others I've never met. They bow and curtsey. Wish me godspeed. Some press sweets into my hands, or good-luck charms. I want so much to make them proud of me.

I linger too long with them, dreading the thought of saying good-bye to my mother and sisters because I fear I will never see them again. And to my brother, Wilhelm, because there is always the possibility, however slight, that I will.

I curtsey to him first, as I must. He is not only my brother but also my lord, the Duke of Jülich-Cleves-Berg—though that is a mouthful and most call him simply Duke of Cleves. He rules our father's ancestral lands—Cleves and Mark, as well as our mother's—Jülich and Berg. He is a strutting rooster of a man who loves to pick fights. He battled over toys with me when we were children. Now he battles over Guelders with Spain.

Wilhelm smiles as I rise. He embraces me and kisses my cheek. It's all for show. As he holds me close, he whispers to me in an assassin's voice.

"Do not disgrace Cleves, Anna. Do not fail in your duties. And do not think you can come back here if you do. I will banish you to some draughty castle, after I beat you silly. Remember how lucky you are that I made this match for you, for you are no spring rose. Remember, too, that Henry may be a powerful king, but he is also a man, and like all men, he requires only two things of a woman: that she keep her legs open and her mouth shut."

"Good-bye, Wilhelm," I say, hoping the crowd will think it is only the cold that reddens my cheeks.

I bid my sisters farewell next—lovely Sibylle, the eldest, who married Johann Friedrich of Saxony, and Amalia, the youngest, who is not yet betrothed.

Mali cries and makes me promise to send her something pretty from England. Sibby kisses me stiffly. She still has not recovered from the fact that I made a better match than she did when she is so much prettier.

Then comes my mother. I curtsey to her, then falter. My shaking legs will not allow me to rise.

"Get up, Anna," she commands.

How can I? How can I stand and walk away? I have only memories of my father, who died a few months ago. But even when he was alive, it was my mother who was my sun.

When I was a child, I was always at her elbow, and she was everywhere all at once. She is still this way. Up before dawn, not abed until midnight. Her days are spent receiving nobles, hearing complaints, and hosting banquets, as a duchess must, but she also corresponds with our ambassadors, mixes medicines, and pokes in the soup pot.

No one can match her pace or live up to her expectations. It is she who runs the castles, the duchies, our lives. Wilhelm only thinks he does.

"Up, child. *Now.*" There is a warning note in her voice, one I know well. I master my emotion and rise.

She takes my hands in hers. "Give the English king many fine sons and daughters. Obey him in all you do. Bring honour to your brother and your country. . . ."

I see the same things in her eyes now that I've always seen when she looks at me. Pride. Worry. Love. And disapproval. Over my needle-work. My hair. My fondness for pretty gowns. We girls received more slaps from her than kisses. More black looks than smiles. But it was she who picked out our Christmas presents, who told us fairy tales at bedtime, who taught us how to choose the best plums for jam. I love her and fear her. I can't stand to leave her, but I can't bear to stay. I can't breathe without her, yet she suffocates me.

"Above all, Anna, remember what I've always told you: Life deals the cards—"

"—but it is up to us how we play them," I finish.

I remember the first time she said this to me. How could I forget? I was small, and playing Landsknecht with Wilhelm. We bet walnuts instead of coins. After he won for the third time in a row, I burst into tears and ran to my mother, sobbing that he got all the lucky cards and I got none.

What I wanted was sympathy and soft words. What I got was a slap. My mother took me by the ear and marched me straight back to the nursery.

"You will sit back down with your brother, Anna, and resume the game," she scolded. "You will not get up again until you win. Life deals the cards, but it is up to us how we play them. The sooner you learn that, the better off you'll be."

Wilhelm was allowed to get up for supper. To get a drink. To relieve himself. I was not. It took me five hours. I was hungry. Tired. I wet myself and had to sit in it. But just before nightfall, I beat him. I *won*.

"Of all the things I taught you, that is the most important," my mother says now. "Never forget it."

I nod. It's all I can do.

My mother pulls me into her arms. My fingers dig into her back. I can't let go.

As always, it is she who does what needs to be done. "It's time," she says, releasing me.

"Come, Anna! The carriage is ready!" Greta calls. I hear excitement in her voice and it pulls at me.

"Go now, child," my mother says.

I tell myself I will see her again. I *will*. And then I turn away before she can glimpse my tears, and hurry to Greta. A chariot has been prepared—a small, fleet carriage covered in cloth of gold. We are to ride out of Düsseldorf and through the lowlands to Calais. From there, we will sail across the channel to England.

A servant hands me up. I settle myself next to Greta. Mother Lowe, supervisor of my German ladies and a fierce old battle-axe, is with us, too, to ensure good behaviour.

My retinue is over two hundred sixty people, with almost as many horses. All along the line, drivers shout to the grooms. The horses stamp and snort and shake their bells. Cheers go up. A whip cracks and the outriders set off. The chariot lurches forwards and picks up speed. Faces pass by in a blur. I look back, desperate for a last glimpse of my mother.

I spot her. The rest have rushed forwards to send me off. She stands back, alone. Her face is resolute, but her cheeks are wet, and I know then that I will never see her again.

An instant later, we are out of the keep. The castle disappears behind us, and then Düsseldorf's narrow streets, its market square, the tower of Saint Lambertus, the Rhine. I grip the side of the chariot with one hand to steady myself. Everything I've ever known is falling away.

Greta takes my other hand. "No looking back," she says. "From now on, only forwards."

And then, as quickly as it came, the vision fades and I am back in my kitchen.

"Do you remember that day?" Greta asks me.

"I do," I say.

"What do you remember most? The crowds in the towns we passed through, cheering and waving? The handsome outriders, so dashing in their uniforms?"

"No, not those things."

"What, then?"

I try to tell her, but emotion wells up inside me and I cannot speak.

I remember facing forwards in the chariot, as Greta said I must. Away from my past, towards my future. I remember that the snow stopped and the skies lightened.

I remember pressing a hand to my chest to feel my heart.

It was beating so hard.

It was breaking.

It was singing.

Alice calls for me, but I cannot answer.

I am made of pain.

My bones and vitals, my skin, fingernails, each strand of my hair. I taste pain. See it. Hear it.

I am curled up on the stairs, unable to move. The wolf woke while I was in the kitchen and tore into my belly. I tried to return to my bedchamber, but my legs gave way.

Blood from my womb has soaked through the rags between my legs, through my nightclothes. It pools underneath me. Am I to meet my doom here on the cold stone steps?

Womb. Doom. Funny how they rhyme in English.

One's body is one's fate. A woman is nothing, only a vessel. Hollow. Empty. Useless. Until a man fills her up and she brings forth sons.

That is what we are told. But it is not what I know.

For all but six months of my life, I had no man. But I never felt empty. I never felt useless.

My womb was never full, no; but my head was. I had so many thoughts and ideas, they made me dizzy. Ideas for the laying out of gardens and the making of cheese. The keeping of bees and raising of sheep.

My heart was full, too. I loved my mother and Sibby and Mali. Greta, too. I loved the Princesses Mary and Elizabeth. Little Edward. Horses and cows. Music and honey and apple trees.

I was a woman alone, yet never lonely. I was enough for myself. Nay, more than enough; I was a feast.

Had Henry known, I would surely have gone to the block.

To be happy without him was the highest of treasons.

"Oh, dear God. Oh, Mother Mary."

I feel Alice's hands cup my face. There is fear in her voice.

"My lady, what has happened? Speak to me, *please!*"

"I was hungry . . . did not want to disturb you . . ."

"It is much more disturbing to find you thus!" she cries.

My maid Lettie comes. She screams. Her noise brings the cook, the scullery girl, two milkmaids, and Rafe, the boy who turns the spit.

"We must get her to her bedchamber! Help me lift her to her feet!" Lettie shouts.

Alice turns on her like a vixen defending a kit. "Do not *touch* her," she warns. "Rafe, fetch my father, and then the physician. Jane, Betsy, bring hot water to Lady Anna's bedchamber."

As the servants mammer and fret, Alice takes my hands and whispers soothing words. A moment later, John the gardener rushes in.

"She is too weak to stand, Father," Alice says. "Can you carry her?"

"God's wounds, how can there be so much blood and she still be alive?" John says softly.

He lifts me easily and carries me upstairs. Alice spreads several old sheets over the bed. He places me on it. Jane and Betsy have already brought the water.

Alice ushers everyone out, then doses me with pennyroyal to stanch the bleeding. After I have swallowed that, she feeds me poppy syrup. Then she attends to the mess. The sodden dressing is thrown into a basin. My clothing follows it. I am washed, every inch of me, and a new dressing is applied.

Finally, I am put into fresh nightclothes and propped up in my bed. Little by little, the poppy pushes the wolf back into its den. I close my eyes, exhausted, as Alice replaces the bloodied sheets with fresh ones and tucks soft blankets around me.

"Take the pillows away, child," I say. "I wish to sleep."

"No, my lady."

My eyes open wide. "No? *No?*"

I am more than at Death's door, I have one foot over his threshold, but even so, I bristle at being told *No* by my own servant.

"You must not sleep," Alice says anxiously. "You have lost a great deal of blood, and I fear if you close your eyes, you will not open them again. Tell me the rest of the story."

"*What* story?" I snap. I am so weary I would give this manor, and everything in it, for five minutes' rest.

"The one about you and King Henry. You said you made your face a mirror when it should have been a mask. What happened, my lady?"

I shake my head.

"You will *not* sleep," Alice vows. "If I have to fetch pot lids from the kitchen and crash them together, I shall."

I narrow my eyes at her. "Threats now? You are a proper little termagant, mistress. I shall not forget this."

She ignores my dire tone. "You made your face a mirror, when it should have been—" she prompts.

"—a mask," I say.

The merciless girl keeps prodding. "Why a mask, my lady? Were you at court? Was it a masquerade?"

I rasp out a bitter laugh. "When is court *not* a masquerade?"

"A young princess, a mighty king, mirrors and masks . . . it sounds like a fairy tale," Alice says.

"It was. A very dark one."

Alice makes a face. "I do not like the dark ones. They tell of monsters."

"Yes, they do, child. But they also tell how to beat them."

I sit forwards, possessed of new strength. To my amazement, I want to talk. I want to tell the story.

Alice sits down in the chair by my bed. Her gaze settles on me. She is intelligent, this girl. Not easily swayed or upset. She would make a good physician. A good lawyer or magistrate or mayor or a thousand other things she'll never be.

"You said the King was afraid," she says sceptically.

A smile twitches at my mouth. "You do not believe me."

"You are but a woman, my lady. How could you make a king afraid?"

I look at Alice, but instead of seeing her, I see myself. Eager. Anxious. Hopeful of a handsome prince. It was seventeen years ago. How is that possible? How can the moments of a life last forever, while the years go by in a heartbeat?

"It happened on a winter's day, at the Bishop's Palace in Rochester," I begin. "I'd been travelling for weeks through Germany and the Low Countries on my way to London. It was the most exciting thing that had ever happened to me. Wherever I stopped—Antwerp, Bruges, Dunkirk—trumpeters played and bonfires blazed. I was given sweetmeats, jewels, gold. My voice was hoarse from talking, my cheeks ached from smiling. I was overwhelmed, but I remembered my mother telling me to bring honour to Cleves, and no matter how tired I was, or how much of a struggle it was to understand the English, and to make myself understood to them, I was always cheerful and gracious."

Alice leans forwards, her elbows on her knees.

"When I reached the port of Calais, the celebrations there dwarfed everything that had come before. Though Calais bordered France, Henry controlled it, and in entering it, I was entering England. He wished my first sight of his realm to be spectacular, and it was. His Lord Admiral, with many other nobles, rode out to meet me. They were accompanied by yeomen in blue and crimson and mariners in Bruges satin. Throngs of people lined the road. There were so many guns firing and cannon going off, I could barely see a foot in front of me for the smoke."

Alice's eyes are shining. "This is a good fairy tale, my lady!" she exclaims.

"I have not done telling it," I say ominously. "Henry sent fifty ships to collect us, festooned with banners. They made one of the loveliest sights I've ever seen. There were two days of feasts and jousts, but then, when we were to set sail, foul weather delayed us. It wasn't until after Christmas that we finally made our crossing. After a rest in Dover, we rode on in a storm and arrived at Rochester on New Year's Eve. We were to spend two nights there, then continue to London."

"Why, there is no darkness to this tale at all!" Alice says happily.

"I could barely sleep that night, thinking how the morning would bring not only a new year—1540—but a new life. I should have been so happy that night, but I wasn't."

Alice's smile fades. "Why not?"

I pause, remembering the enormous bed I'd tossed and turned in. The wind howling around the palace. The hail beating at the windows.

"I was exhausted from travelling. I'd caught a cold. Worst of all, I was homesick," I tell her. "I dared not say so, though. It would have been an awkward way for a guest to behave, and I was awkward enough already."

"What do you mean?" asks Alice.

"Have you ever attended a feast or revel and there's a girl in the corner in an ugly dress who can't seem to say or do the right thing no matter how hard she tries?"

Alice lowers her eyes. "I have. That girl is usually me."

"She was me, too," I say. "To begin, my clothes were all wrong. The English ladies followed French fashions. Their necklines were square and low; their bodices cut close. My gowns had high necklines, puffed sleeves, and such wide skirts that I looked like a beer barrel in them."

Alice tries to smother her giggles. I tell her not to bother.

"My jewels were pretty," I continue, "but not as pretty as those of the Lord Admiral's wife. The English ladies' headpieces were sleek and elegant; mine made me look like a spaniel. No one said anything to me, but I caught the glances and the smirks. When you can't speak the language, your eyes make up for your ears. And as bad as my clothing was, it wasn't the worst of my problems."

"What was?" asks Alice.

"My lack of accomplishments. The English ladies danced and sang. They played instruments and told jokes. They knew French and Latin. They were swans and I a clumsy duck. I'd never been taught to sing or play music. In Cleves, having such skills marked a woman as frivolous. I could read and write, but only German. Wilhelm was the one who received an education."

"What did you do, my lady?" Alice asks.

"I consoled myself by imagining my prince," I say. "I hoped he would be kind and handsome. People said he was tall, with a fine head of auburn hair and well-turned legs. I also distracted myself with entertainments. There was a bull-baiting on New Year's Day. I watched it from a window in the great hall, though I did not like it. I thought it cowardly and cruel to set dogs on a bull. In the midst of all the noise and blood, the doors to the hall banged open and half a dozen men came in. They'd been riding; their cloaks and boots were muddy.

"One of them, an old man who was heavy and lame, bowed to me and told me he had a present from the King. Then he kissed me. His breath was foul, the kiss revolting. I wiped it off with my hand and pushed him away, shocked. How dare he! I was the King's betrothed, not some harlot in a bawdy house.

"I sought my German ladies. '*Wer ist dieser verrückte Mann?*' I asked them. Who is this crazy man? They looked as alarmed as I felt. The English ladies were averting their eyes, as if they'd just witnessed a terrible accident.

"The old man took a faltering step back, a stricken expression on his face. *Good*, I thought. *That will teach you to keep your hands to yourself.* He left the room. His friends followed him. I turned my attention back to the bull-baiting. A few minutes later, the man returned. Only now he was wearing a coat of purple velvet. Trumpeters were playing a fanfare. Courtiers were bowing and curtseying. I looked left and right, utterly bewildered. I had no idea what was happening. Greta was the one who figured it out.

"'*Es ist Henry, der König!*' she whispered.

"I was stunned. *Henry the King? This smelly lunatic? It can't be*, I thought.

"'*Der König, Anna! Sie müssen vor ihm knicksen!*' Greta hissed at me.

"I dropped into a curtsey and stayed there, grateful to have a few seconds to collect myself. I knew my marriage was about alliances, not love, but I was horrified. All I could think was *This shuffling old man will be my husband.*

"By the time Henry raised me from my curtsey, my heart was hidden. He welcomed me, then led me to a private chamber. I told him, with the help of an interpreter, how happy I was to be in his magnificent realm. I said his prank was very clever, hoping to smooth any rough waters, but it was too late. Henry smiled, but his eyes were cold. He bade me good night and withdrew. Later, I learned that he had been so impatient to meet me, he decided not to wait in London for my arrival, but to travel to Rochester in disguise to play a lover's trick and surprise me. He was certain I would recognize him as my betrothed, because of the true love I was bound to feel for him."

Alice giggles again.

"Have you ever heard such nonsense?" I ask her. "And it came not from some moony little scullery girl, but the King of England! Who was nearly fifty and had been married thrice before, and had killed his first wife by cruel treatment and sent the second to the scaffold.

One thing I have noticed, child, is that tyrants are the grandest romantics. They can burn a heretic alive one day, compose a love sonnet the next."

Alice is still smiling. But I feel only sadness as I recall the aftermath.

"I didn't understand anything. Not the language, or the customs, or Henry. I was unprepared for the ways of the English court. No one told me that Henry liked such pranks, or that he might play one on me," I say. "If they had, how different my life might have been. Henry saw himself as young and virile still, and his courtiers knew to cast their faces into masks of admiration to preserve the illusion. But I did not. My face was the looking-glass that showed Henry to himself not as he would be, but as he was."

For a moment, I see Henry again. Standing there in that muddy cloak. Old. Broken. Mortal. And for the first time, knowing it.

"To this day, I am sorry for it. Sorry for him," I say softly.

"Sorry for *him*, my lady?" says Alice, incredulous.

I nod. "Henry needed love like no one I have ever known. And his greatest romance was with himself. It survived heartbreak and betrayal. Outlasted injury, illness, treason, and death. It survived everything and everyone, Alice. Everyone but me."

"Did you have a pretty wedding gown?" Alice asks, determined to keep me talking.

She moves to the window and watches anxiously for the physician.

"You are relentless, child. Can you not just let me die?"

"No."

I heave a sigh. "It *was* a pretty gown," I tell her. "It was made of cloth of gold, embroidered with pearls. I wore jewels at my neck and waist and a gold coronet. My hair was blond then, not grey, and it cascaded down my back. Henry wore crimson and cloth of gold. The sleeves of his coat were slashed and tied with diamonds as big as hazelnuts."

"Diamonds on his *sleeves?*" Alice echoes.

I nod.

"How many diamonds, my lady? Four to a sleeve? Five?"

"Dozens. Too many to count."

Alice turns to me, dumbstruck. She cannot imagine such wealth.

"What was the ceremony like, my lady?" she asks, when she finds her voice.

"Delayed," I reply wryly. "Two days before the wedding, Henry's councillors suddenly became concerned about a betrothal contract between myself and Francis, heir to the Duchy of Lorraine, that had been undertaken when we were children. My German ambassadors assured the English that the contract had been dissolved, but they'd neglected to bring the paperwork from Cleves to prove it."

"What happened?"

"The English were reluctant to press ahead with the wedding, but my ambassadors were adamant that the proper documents could be swiftly fetched from Cleves, and they offered themselves as hostages against the outcome. I was told to sign a paper declaring I was free to marry, and the wedding proceeded. At the time, I thought the delay was due to officials being officious, but I was wrong. Henry was behind it. He was looking for a way out of the marriage."

"But he didn't find one," Alice says.

"No, he did not. Count Overstein, a German noble, walked me to the altar. Archbishop Cranmer performed the ceremony. Henry presented me with a gold ring engraved with the words 'God send me wel to kepe.' Afterwards, there was a feast. The whole time, I told myself all would be well. Our first meeting had been a disaster, but I thought if I tried hard, I could be a good queen to Henry."

"And were you, my lady?" asks Alice. "I should think so. You are a good mistress to me."

I smile at that. "I did my best," I say. "When I became Queen, I was given my own apartments, my own chamberlain and attendants. I liked having my own household. I liked having work to do, things to manage. I tried to win the love of my servants, and the common people, with kind words and good works. I tried to win Henry's love, too. I studied English diligently. Played the card games he liked. I had my dresses remade in the French style that he favoured."

"Did the King do any remaking?" Alice asks, peering out of the window again.

"Not a bit. He was the tailor, Alice. And we, the court, were his cloth. He shaped us to fit his fancy."

"Being Queen sounds exhausting," Alice says.

"It was," I say. "There is no privacy and little quiet. The only time you are alone is at prayer. Which is why so many queens are pious. I never complained, though. My conduct was exemplary. Everyone said as much. The French and Spanish ambassadors. Henry's courtiers. Henry himself said my conduct was well and seemly. But it didn't matter. The damage was done."

I think back to our first night together, as man and wife.

"Yes, I was a good queen. In most things, but not all," I say.

And then I stop speaking.

Because this is a memory for myself alone.

The servants undress us. Give us wine. Put us to bed.

There are carvings on the headboard. Of a man wearing an enormous codpiece, a woman with downcast eyes, plump little cherubs. Our initials, "H" and "A," are painted in the centre.

I am awkward. Scared. But determined, too. This is how children are made, and I must make some.

"Give the King many sons, Anna," my sister Sibylle had told me, "and many daughters, too. Sons make wars, and daughters prevent them."

That is what I'm doing here, isn't it? In bed with an old man who doesn't like me? Joining England and Cleves. Preventing France and Spain from attacking my old home, and my new one.

I see Henry's belly jiggling inside his nightgown as he gets into bed. Veins, raised and gnarled, wind around his calves. I glimpse the dressing on his ulcerated leg, freshly changed but already wet with pus.

He drains his goblet and places it on the bedside table. Then he flops back against the pillows, takes a deep breath, and blows it out again.

"I suppose we should get down to business," he says, rolling onto his side. "I need a bull calf from my new German cow."

I try to smile. I don't understand all his words, but I know "cow" because it sounds like its German counterpart, *Kuh*.

He unties the strings at the neck of my gown. *Will he kiss me?* I wonder. *Will he say something tender?*

Wordlessly, he snakes his hand inside my gown and gropes my breast, hefting it as if it were a ham at a market stall. Then he lifts the hem of my gown and heaves himself on top of me.

I can barely breathe while he makes his attempt, so great is his weight, but not breathing is no bad thing. His breath has not improved, and the smell from his festering leg makes my stomach twist. There is a great deal of heaving and grunting, but nothing more.

"Call yourself a woman? Help me, you cold fish," he mutters, grabbing my hand and placing it on his member. I squeeze it. Perhaps a bit too hard. "Ouch! That *hurts!*" he yelps. "God's blood! Are you trying to pull it off?"

Another attempt. His hands are on me again, rougher now. But the bread does not rise. The sausage does not swell. I bite the inside of my cheek so hard that it bleeds.

Henry cannot do what he must. He swears. Rolls onto his back. Groans. "This is *your* fault," he says. "Dugs like a sow, and the belly to match."

Sow. *Sau.*

Hot, angry tears roll down my cheeks and soak the pillow.

I am not a cow, a sow, a fish, or any such animal, I tell him silently.

I am not my breasts, my belly, my legs, or that which lies between them.

I am my head and my heart. All that I know, all that I love, everything I hope for.

I am the blue waters of the Rhine, sparkling in the sun.

I am ripe pears in a basket. Fresh nutmeg. The smell of Christmas.

I am swallows soaring over wheat fields.

I am the hymns the choristers sing. The rise and fall of an old German lullaby.

"*Ich bin all diese Dinge. Diese Dinge und so viele mehr,*" I say. I am these things. All these things and so many more.

Henry can't understand me. I don't even know if he hears me. He's half asleep.

He rolls over. Farts loudly. And starts to snore.

"My lady, what's wrong? You're so pale. Are you bleeding again?"

A worried Alice is leaning over me, peering at my face.

"I'm fine," I say, waving her concern away.

"You looked as if you were in pain."

"I was. It passed." As most hurts do, given time.

"The physician will be here soon. I know it," Alice says anxiously. She sits down again. "You said you were a good queen in most things, but not all. I do not believe that. You are good at everything you put your hand to. How could you have failed the King?"

"I did not amuse him, child. Henry was not afraid of much, but he was terrified of boredom. His courtiers were run ragged devising entertainments for him. Hunting. Jousting. Racing. Masqueing. Hawking. Dicing. We were so different, Henry and I. He liked theology. I liked cheese. He liked witty words and jests. I liked to sew." I pause, then add: "And of course there was Catherine Howard."

"His fifth Queen," Alice says.

"Indeed. She became a lady-in-waiting to me through the influence of Norfolk, her uncle. And in no time, the King's eye fell upon her—just as Norfolk hoped. Catherine was everything I was not—pretty, a flirt, full of fun and mischief. She was an enchantress who could make an aging man appear young and lusty again, if only to himself. And Norfolk, the clever bawd, set her price high. Catherine would be Queen—nothing less—or Henry could not have her."

I am interrupted by the sound of hoofbeats carrying in through the windows. I am glad, for the ache has begun again. "That will be Edmonds on that fine grey gelding of his," I say. "And it sounds as if Rafe is ahead of him on my little chestnut mare."

In a flash, Alice is back at the window. Then she is gone, out of the door and down the stairs, to hurry Edmonds along.

"I was so naïve. Such a fool," I whisper to the empty room.

I had no idea what Norfolk was planning. I thought Henry would take Catherine to bed, not to wife. After all, I was his wife. We had been lawfully married before God, and what God joined together, no man could put asunder.

But I forgot who God was.

In England, God was Henry.

*   *   *

Moments later, Edmonds is at my bedside. As he examines me, Alice tells him all that has transpired. The lines in his forehead deepen as he listens.

"You did well to give pennyroyal in the amount you did, Alice. It stopped the bleeding," he says. "You have saved your mistress's life."

"Shall I pay her extra for that or dismiss her?" I grumble.

Edmonds ignores me. "I only wish my apprentices had your good judgement," he tells Alice. "One's a fool, the other's a rogue."

Alice's face glows like a torch at his praise. What a strange girl she is. She actually enjoys this foul business.

"I'm going to prescribe a stronger medicine for the pain. It contains poppy as before, but mixed with mandrake," Edmonds says.

Alice nods. "Shall I send Rafe to the apothecary?"

"It will take too long. We shall make it up, you and I."

Edmonds pulls one nasty thing after another out of his bag—powdered worm, white lead, the dried excrement of a newborn, toad's gall, a vial of cowpox scabs—until he finds what he's after.

Alice caresses the sinister mess as another girl might stroke a lover's face. She shies from nothing—not blood, nor pain, nor Edmonds's bag of horrors.

By the time the two of them have finished their concoction, the wolf has returned. I cannot endure another bout of agony and tell them to give me a good dose. Alice carefully measures out the correct amount and helps me drink it.

Seconds later, my head begins to whirl. This new elixir is much stronger than the last. I lie back in my bed, helpless.

Black seas wash over me, wind-whipped and storm-driven.

I go under. Sink down through the dark waters.

And swim with the drowned.

* * *

Cromwell sits in a chair on the other side of my bedchamber. He holds his head in his lap as if it were a small dog.

"Can you not put it atop your neck?" I ask him. "It's disconcerting to address your crotch."

"Had you addressed your husband's crotch, my head would still be atop my neck," he says archly, but he complies with my request, holding it in place with his hands.

"Blame yourself," I retort. "You are the one who brought the match about. You should have left me in Cleves."

He glares. A frosty silence descends. I break it, for I am angry with him. Still.

"You are late, Thomas, by seventeen years. I sent for you after I became Queen, hoping for your help with the difficulties in my marriage. You ignored me then, but you come now?"

"What you asked of me was dangerous. I knew what those difficulties were, you see."

"How?" I demand.

"Henry. He told me that you so repulsed him he could not bring himself to make children with you, and did not even try."

I flinch at that.

"My spies, however, told me a different story—that Henry did try, but failed," Cromwell continues. "They listened at your bedroom door. Eavesdropped on conversations you had with your German ladies. Pawed through your dirty bedsheets looking for stains. I knew you would tell me the same, and to even *whisper* that the King was impotent was treasonous. Had anyone overheard us, we could well have been sent to the Tower, so I stayed away."

I laugh mirthlessly. "And how did that decision play out? Not well, I would say, since you ended up in the Tower anyway."

As I speak, I notice the hacked flesh about his neck and shoulders. It is a gruesome sight. "Does it hurt?" I ask, softening towards him.

"Not anymore," he replies. "It did at the time. The executioner was a bungler. It took him five tries."

My anger fades and sadness takes its place as I remember this brilliant, fearsome man striding the halls of Henry's palaces, his black robes billowing behind him. It was Cromwell who threw the Pope out of England and gave the English a Bible they could read. It was Cromwell who dissolved the monasteries and convents, sold off their lands and treasures, and made his master rich.

His power was second only to Henry's, and courtiers parted like the sea before him, smiling and simpering and hating his guts. He was a threat to them. They were the old order, and he was something dangerous and new—a self-made man, a blacksmith's boy who forged himself into an earl.

"You did not deserve such a terrible death, Thomas. I am sorry for it," I tell him.

His bright, busy eyes look up at me from under his black brows. "Was Henry?"

"At the time, no," I say. "He played cards with Norfolk and Surrey a few days afterwards, and every time he was dealt a knave he called it a Cromwell."

"I'm sure Norfolk laughed the loudest," Cromwell says.

"But not longest. He lost favour, too. Henry changed after your death. He suffered bouts of melancholy. Once I brought him jam made with plums from my orchard. He ate it from the pot, then put his head in my lap and wept. He cursed Norfolk. Said the old rogue cost him the most loyal advisor he'd ever had."

"Did he?" Cromwell asks. His lips curve into a smile. "I am pleased to know it. Would that one could preserve the best moments of a life—the kindnesses, the laughter—as one does plums in a jam."

"Thomas ..." I say. There is something I've always wanted to ask him.

"Yes?"

"How did you not see Death coming? You, who saw every move long before it was made."

He laughs. "But I did see it coming. Always. Everywhere. Death is never far from those whom the King favours. What I did not see coming was the Howard girl."

"You might have sidestepped your fate had you chosen someone other than me for Henry," I tell him. "Someone beautiful. Christina of Denmark, perhaps. Or Mary of Guise."

"I tried, but they were unwilling. They'd seen how Henry's first three wives had fared. Christina told my envoy that if she had two heads, she would place one at Henry's disposal," Cromwell recounts, chuckling. "That girl could afford to make cheeky statements. She had a powerful aunt, Mary of Hungary, who was determined to keep her from a bad match."

"And I had no such. Only a brother determined to sell me to the highest bidder," I say ruefully.

"Wilhelm was playing chess, as we all were, and you were the pawn," Cromwell says. "The move to unite England and Cleves was a clever one, if I say so myself. Wilhelm was an appealing ally. He was a Reformist, but not a Lutheran—Henry loathed Lutherans—but he had strong ties to many of Germany's powerful Lutheran nobles. They would come to Henry's aid if France or Spain attacked him, and Henry would help Cleves if Wilhelm's battle over Guelders turned into a war."

"People said that you could not have cared less about Henry or England, and that you pushed for the alliance with Cleves only to further the Protestant cause," I tell him. "They said you were secretly a Lutheran yourself and kept heretical books."

He gives me a dark look. "People being *Norfolk*," he retorts. "I doubt many would have listened to his nonsense, had my work not unravelled so quickly. France's alliance with Spain soon soured, which meant that Cleves's friendship was no longer as important to England. You were a disaster . . ."

"Why, thank you."

". . . and then there was Catherine Howard. Henry's lust for her was the lever Norfolk needed to topple me and grab power for himself. He and his Catholic allies had me arrested on charges of treason and heresy for promoting your marriage and the new religion."

"What a shock it was when you were sent to the Tower," I say. "We all thought Henry would release you. No one believed he would kill you."

"Least of all me," he says, with a bitter laugh.

There is another thing that has always puzzled me. "You had valuable currencies, Thomas—gold and secrets. Why did you not use them to fight harder for your life?"

Cromwell gazes out of the window for some time. "I was tired," he finally says.

His words spark an image in my mind, of the bull-baiting at Rochester. I remember how the bull's sides heaved from fending off his attackers, how blood ran down the animal's torn face.

I remember how a mastiff, powerful and vicious, sank its teeth into the bull's haunch. The bull stumbled and went down. He was not beaten, not quite, yet he would not get up. He bellowed once, most piteously, then lowered his mighty head. An instant later, the dogs closed in.

"For over a decade I served Henry," Cromwell says. "No one was more devoted to him. From dawn to dusk, there were people in my chambers wanting favours, advancement, positions in the King's household. And Henry himself . . . my God. He smashed the world apart, all to bed Anne Boleyn. Then he tossed the broken pieces at my feet and commanded me to glue them together again."

His voice is heavy, so full of heartbreak, that my own heart hurts for him.

"I had little to live for," he continued. "My wife and daughters were dead, taken by sweating sickness. My son was safe, protected by his marriage to Jane Seymour's sister. There is peace in death, Anna, and I welcomed it."

I understand him well. "I would welcome Death, too, but he will not come. Why not, Thomas? Why does he send you instead?"

"Because there is a thing left undone."

This thing undone that the ghosts speak of is the key to my release, I am sure of it. "What is it?" I ask, desperate to know. "Tell me!"

He does not answer. Instead, he gazes at my chamber door. I know it is useless to resist. I rise from my bed, and he from his chair. We step through the doorway, one after the other, and find ourselves in Greenwich Palace.

The Queen's apartments, my apartments, are exactly as they were in the winter of 1540. My ladies are there, exactly as they were— sewing, laughing, gossiping. Even my chair is where it was, close by the fire. It is empty.

"No. I do not wish to visit this place," I say.

But Cromwell isn't listening.

Snow is falling. It is bitterly cold. I enter the scene, stepping back into my past like an actor stepping onto a stage. Cromwell watches from the doorway.

A shirt I was embroidering for Henry lies in a basket by my chair. I sit down and pick it up. As I start to stitch, the voices of my ladies carry to me. Jane Rochford's. Eleanor Manners's. Catherine Howard's. Sound behaves strangely in this room. Though they whisper, I can hear some of what they say: *She dances like an ox . . . cannot even play the lute . . . will never please the King . . .*

Oh, how I prefer the honest violence of men, who will bash in another man's skull and be done, to the thousand shallow cuts of women's malice.

I am not only embarrassed by their words, but frightened. I am married three months now, and still a virgin. Henry comes to my bed, but only to keep tongues from wagging. We pass our nights chastely. I am supposed to provide him with sons. What will happen to me if I do not?

"Give him sweet kisses. Tell him he is handsome. Say he is your heart's desire," Greta advised when I told her of my trials. I'd tried these things, but Henry had only winced and rolled over.

My sewing is interrupted by a noise at the door. I hear male voices. Shouted greetings. Laughter. It is Henry, come to visit his Queen and her ladies. Like a great warship he surges into the room, with lesser vessels bobbing in his wake. He is dressed in green velvet. Pearls and diamonds decorate his hat.

I curtsey as he approaches. He bids me stand, asks if I am well. He smiles at me, but his eyes dart about the room like flies, hovering over the faces of my ladies, until they light on Catherine Howard's.

I see how his gaze crawls over her body. So does everyone else.

Greta glances at me as Henry walks over to Catherine. "He will quickly tire of the girl. She is naught but a prating fool," she whispers. "Do not worry. There is not much to see in her."

But there is. And I see it.

It is not her pert round breasts straining under her too-tight bodice that I see. It is not her tiny waist, her pretty face, or her fetching smile.

In young Catherine Howard, I see my doom.

The scene changes and I find myself standing at a window in Richmond Palace. Cromwell looks on from a dusky corner.

It is still 1540, but summer now. I have been Henry's wife for six months and things have only grown worse between us.

We argue over much: my coronation, which never seems to happen; my household, which has too many Englishwomen in it for my liking and too many Germans for his; his children. I believe Edward should have the attentions of a stepmother; Henry does not. I believe that motherless Mary and Elizabeth should spend more time with their father; Henry does not. What Henry does believe is that I've grown wilful and stubborn. *My new Queen has the disposition of a mule and the face to match,* he muttered after one such disagreement.

He has sent me away from Greenwich to Richmond. For my own good, my chamberlain told me. Plague has broken out in London, and the King, ever mindful of my safety, wants me far from contagion.

But I know there is no plague.

I also know that Henry sent Katharine of Aragon to Richmond when he wished to divorce her. I know that Catherine Howard has left my household to live with her ailing grandmother, and that Henry, who loathes sick people, visits the old woman to enquire after her health. Wearing satin, perfume, and a fancy hat.

I look out of the window. Below me, Henry's men are crossing the courtyard, their heads bowed against the summer rain.

"The vultures are on the wing," I whisper.

Stephen Gardiner leads them. He is Bishop of Winchester, and a lawyer—one who worked to obtain Henry's divorce from Katharine.

Richard Rich is with him. He is a lawyer, too, but one who does not so much follow the law as invent it. It was he who declared it lawful for Henry to confiscate Katharine's possessions.

Charles Brandon, Duke of Suffolk, is amongst them. He is Henry's close friend, and the man who humiliated Katharine by dismissing her household after Henry married Anne Boleyn.

These men will do anything Henry asks. They have turned on

cardinals, chancellors, nobles, and queens. Their presence here fills me with dread. They come when I am alone, when my ambassador and protector, Karl Harst, is at court. Why? What do they want?

The men are ushered into my presence. Their greeting is courteous, their bearing sombre.

Gardiner talks. Rich translates his words into German for me. He explains that there is to be an official enquiry into my and Henry's marriage. Troubling questions have arisen. Parliament wishes them to be addressed.

For a few seconds, I cannot breathe. This is not Parliament's doing; it is Henry's, I know it. He wishes to put me aside and needs justification, however flimsy, to do it. Greta was wrong. He has not tired of Catherine Howard. On the contrary, he means to marry her.

Dread blossoms into fear and threatens to overwhelm me. I strangle the dark bloom. No matter what, I must keep my head. For if I do not, I will surely lose it.

"You say questions have arisen. What questions?" I ask calmly.

Rich clears his throat. "Questions regarding your betrothal contract with Francis of Lorraine," he replies. "A certain document, recently obtained from Germany, casts doubt upon its dissolution."

"The King and I were wedded months ago, according to the laws of God and man. And now you come to tell me that the paperwork is not in order?"

Gardiner's eyes narrow. He was not expecting questions, only compliance. He and Rich confer, then Rich speaks again. "We understand, Your Grace, that you are a woman and as such not able to comprehend the thorny complexities of the law. I shall attempt to clarify the issues."

"They are perfectly clear," I counter. "I was betrothed to Francis when I was a child, but the contract was revoked. You know this. Everyone does. I signed a document before the wedding attesting to the fact."

"Yes, Your Grace, but a *new* document has come to light."

"Where is this document?" I demand. "It is my right to see it."

Rich feigns regret. "I'm afraid that's not possible. It must be examined by the court."

"When does the court convene? Surely there is time for me to see it beforehand?"

I expect him to say next month.

"Tomorrow morning."

"T-tomorrow?" I stammer, stunned by the speed with which they've struck. "But I must send a messenger to my brother. He will not be pleased by these events. And I—I require time to obtain lawyers of my own."

"I'm afraid there will be no messengers. The King has barred all travel out of England until this matter is concluded."

I am terrified now. It's all I can do to keep my composure.

"Your Grace," Rich continues, "surely you see the necessity of the enquiry. If the King's marriage is not legitimate, neither are any children it might produce. The King, eager to comply with God's will and the dictates of his conscience, has granted his consent to the enquiry. He will accept the findings of the court, whatever they may be, and wishes you to do the same."

"And if I do not?"

Rich smiles tightly. "The King has admitted that he himself, from the start of your marriage, was troubled by the very same issue that now worries Parliament. So worried was he that he refrained from consummating the marriage." He pauses. "The court will hear statements from the King and various witnesses. Other examinations could be conducted, too . . . if need be."

He does not make plain his ugly meaning, but he doesn't need to. I understand it. I will be examined to confirm that I am still a virgin.

They watch for my reaction to their threat. They are enjoying this. The idea of me on my back, the King's doctors poking and prodding. I am scalded by embarrassment and cannot speak.

Gardiner leans in close to Rich. "The King said she would be difficult," he murmurs.

I understand those English words, for they are simple ones. I hear frustration in Gardiner's voice—and something under it: fear. It puzzles me. Why would *he* be afraid? I watch him trade worried glances with the others, and in that moment, I know.

It took Henry nine long years to bring about a divorce from Katharine of Aragon so that he could marry Anne Boleyn. He wants his pretty Catherine Howard and he wants her now. He is old and failing and has but one son. He cannot wait. He cannot afford another rebellious woman.

Gardiner talks on. Rich translates in his bad German. Suffolk casts black looks at me. The dreary English rain drums against the windowpanes.

But I hear none of it. I am listening to another voice. One inside my head. Inside my heart. My mother's voice.

Life deals the cards, but it is up to us how we play them.

I lift my chin. For the moment, I am still their Queen and they must heed me. "Go back to Henry," I say, "and tell him . . ."

"Yes, Your Grace?" Rich says, hoping he has scared me into submission, hoping he has won.

But he has not, not yet. I hold some cards of value: resistance, defiance, courage. Will they be enough?

I take a deep breath. "Tell him I do *not* consent."

A servant closes the door behind the men and I collapse into a chair, my bravery gone.

What have I done?

I imagine my head cut off and lying on the scaffold floor.

If it lands this way, I will see my own body. Slumped sideways like a sack of meal.

If it lands that way, I will see the crowd, or the sky, or the executioner's shoes.

Some say the head lives for several seconds. The eyes blink. The lips move.

Still, it is a better death than hanging. It can take several long minutes to die from the rope, all the while swinging and kicking and shitting your skirts.

Henry is known to burn people, too. Or have them drawn and quartered, the executioner carving out their innards while kitchen girls gawp and picknose boys jeer.

These images fill my brain.

Henry hounded Katharine of Aragon to death. He murdered Anne Boleyn.

These things he did to women he loved.

What will he do to one he does not?

"The hardest thing about a bluff is not making it, but waiting it out. Wondering what cards your opponent holds," Cromwell muses. He circles the chair in which I sit, his long robes rustling. "And wait you did, Anna. *What will the court decide? What will Henry do?* Riders could come at any moment, ordering you back to Cleves or to the Tower. You didn't know which, did you?"

"*You* did," I say. "You were in the Tower when the hearing was held. You gave a written account stating that Henry believed I was not his lawful wife. You wrote that it grieved him to think he would never give his realm more heirs."

"Henry wanted support for his case. I thought by giving it I might save my life. And yours. I was half right," he says wryly.

Fury flares in me now, as it did then. "Even my own ladies testified on Henry's behalf," I say hotly. "Lady Rochford stated that after I was married, they'd told me they hoped I'd soon be with child, and I'd replied that I was not. Lady Manners had wondered how this could be and had asked me if I was still a virgin. I'd said of course not, because the King kissed me good night and slept next to me in bed. 'Madam, there must be more than this, or it will be long ere we have a Duke of York!' she'd exclaimed. From this exchange the court concluded that I was innocent of how children were made, which proved that Henry had not consummated our marriage."

Cromwell chuckles. "Lady Rochford was seen wearing a new ruby ring after the hearing. Norfolk paid her well for *that* story," he observes.

"Story indeed," I fume. "In the early days of my marriage I could hardly string together three words of English, much less describe my nightly relations with Henry. The hearing was a farce. Why was I not allowed to testify? To speak for myself?"

"These were delicate matters. I'm sure the King didn't want to discomfort you," Cromwell replies, his tongue firmly in his cheek.

I roll my eyes. "What Henry didn't want was for me to tell the court that I'd shattered his illusions. That I made him feel broken and old."

"Can you blame him, Anna?" Cromwell asks. "What is a king without illusion? The illusion of limitless wealth? Of absolute power? Illusion is all that keeps his people in check and his enemies at bay. Wives disappoint. Sons die. Allies become foes. Illusion is a king's only true friend."

"Ah, Thomas, I see why Henry wept for you," I say, moved by his devotion. "You were the only one who understood him. You should have outlived him."

Cromwell shakes his head. "I died at the right time," he says. "Henry was in decline. His first Queens were dead. Many of his old friends, too. The great pageants, the masques and hunts, the jousts that went on for days, they were no more. The Henry who had once been—our handsome, laughing Prince—was gone. The man who'd taken his place was a limping old melancholic, and it broke my heart to look upon him. Henry was our sun. How cold our world grew as he faded."

Voices carry from the hall, interrupting us.

"The vultures return," I say, eyeing the doorway as Henry's men walk through it.

"At least Henry didn't make you wait long," Cromwell says, stepping back into the shadows. "The whole business was over and done in a matter of days."

I rise from my chair. My heart is pounding. These ruthless men hold my life in their hands.

They greet me. Rich is again amongst them. He enters into a long-winded account of court proceedings. I listen impassively, all the while silently shouting at him to come to the point. After what seems like an eternity, he tells me that the court has carefully examined the agreement made on my behalf with Francis of Lorraine and found that it was, in fact, a marriage contract, not a mere betrothal promise.

My heart lurches. My legs turn to sand. What does this mean for me? Somehow, I manage to keep myself upright.

Rich finishes by telling me that in the eyes of the law, and God, I am Francis's wife, and have been these many years. Henry has accepted the court's ruling, he says, and wishes for a divorce.

I am the wife of a man I've never even met. I would laugh out loud at the absurdity of it if I weren't so scared.

Rich and his companions wait for my reaction to Henry's wish, but I will not give them one. Not yet. I am still playing my hand, and like all good players, I betray nothing.

After a moment, Rich speaks again. He tells me the King is prepared to make me a generous settlement—*if* I cooperate. He lays out Henry's terms, and as he does, my head spins so violently, I must steady myself against a table.

Henry will not send me to the Tower or the scaffold. Instead, he will make me his sister.

I shall remain one of the highest-ranking ladies in the land. Only a new Queen, should there be one, and the King's daughters will come before me.

Henry is giving me money, land, manor houses.

He is giving me Hever Castle.

Bletchingley Palace.

Richmond Palace.

Sweet God in Heaven, I am rich.

I can keep my servants. My clothing. My jewels.

I can stay in England. I don't have to go home and face Wilhelm's wrath.

The future my brother chose for me fades like the morning mist. A new one emerges, one I could never have imagined.

My marriage is ended.

My life begins.

I am free.

I am *free*.

Cromwell smiles.

"You were a pawn, Anna of Cleves, but you played like a queen," he says. "You survived us all. Who would have thought it?"

He is fading before my eyes. He is leaving.

"Take me with you, Thomas," I beg. "Why must I stay here with ghosts and the hard memories they bring?"

"Memory is a high palace containing many rooms. Some of the doors we rush to open; others we lock forever," he says. "Death dwells in this palace, Anna. Keep opening doors and you will find him."

He kisses me, his cold lips like the winter wind against my cheek. And then he is gone.

Determined to die, I open another door. My face falls as I see who is in the room.

"*You* are not Death," I say reproachfully.

"Sorry to disappoint you," Holbein says.

He glances up at me from his easel. His eyes linger on my face. "I wish I'd painted you after your divorce," he says. "I could have made good money exhibiting such a painting. You were like an elephant—"

"I beg your pardon!"

"—or a zebra. A coconut. A pineapple. You were an oddity."

"Are these your compliments? I would hate to hear your insults."

"You were that rarest of creatures—a divorced woman. You were happy, and your happiness made you beautiful."

"I *was* happy," I say, remembering my first days of freedom. "Too happy. My God, how I spent money. On jewels. Books. Nutmegs. Vanilla beans. Pear trees."

Holbein's eyes glint with mischief. "Do you know what Marillac said about you?"

I shake my head.

He affects the French ambassador's accent. "'She is as joyous as ever, and wears new dresses every day; which argues either prudent dissimulation or stupid forgetfulness of what should so closely touch her heart.'"

We both laugh.

"Foolish Henry," Holbein sighs. "You were a young, healthy

woman, Anna. I'd wager a purse full of gold that you would have given him the fine, strapping sons he wanted had he kept you as his wife."

"Perhaps," I say.

But I doubt it. Henry always said it was my ugliness that made him incapable of fathering children with me, but no babies were made with the pretty Queens who followed me, either. I was tempted, many times, to remark upon this to Henry, but held my tongue. Beauty is blameless and so are kings.

"What are you painting now?" I ask, eager to change the subject. "Do not tell me you are still working on my betrothal portrait."

"No. I am working on a new portrait for you," he says.

"*For* me?" I echo, puzzled. "Do you mean *of* me?"

He shakes his head. "*For* you. To settle your debts. You must settle your debts, Anna. The bad done to us, we must forgive. The good, we owe to the next man."

"Again you talk of debts?" I say, my good humour darkening. "*What* debts, Holbein? Speak plainly!" I am so frustrated with him, I am shouting. "My bills are paid! My will is complete! My best jewel will go to Queen Mary. My second-best to Elizabeth. My servants have all been found new positions . . ."

I stalk up to his easel as I harangue him, and peer at the canvas, and my words fall away.

The portrait is of a girl. She is wearing the plain clothing of a servant. Her hair is covered by a simple linen cap. There is a birthmark on her face.

"Time grows short, Anna. Settle your debts," Holbein warns.

And then he is gone and I am back in my bedchamber and dawn is breaking.

Its pale light steals in through the windows, summoning me out of the darkness.

*   *   *

"Hush, my lady, do not upset yourself," a voice croons. "You have been dreaming. There is no Cromwell here. No Holbein. Just me."

It is Alice. She is sitting on the edge of my bed, a worried expression on her face. She takes my hand in hers.

"It's all right. I am here."

"Yes," I say. "You are here, Alice."

And then I start to weep. For myself. For Henry. For his dead Queens. His doomed son. For Cromwell. For Greta. For apple cake and snow and horses. The Rhine and the Thames. For rain-soaked days and black-robed men. For the dark fairy tale that is life.

"More poppy," says another voice. It belongs to Edmonds.

Alice rises to fetch it, and at that instant, as I watch this good, clever girl, I know.

I know why I have not yet died. Why the ghosts have come. Why Holbein made a portrait of her. I know the thing I've left undone.

"Alice!" I say. So loudly that both she and Edmonds jump. "Fetch some hot milk. I am chilly."

I am not really, but I need her to leave the room.

"That is not a good idea. Milk taxes the digestion," says Edmonds.

I wipe my eyes. Sit up in my bed. "What will it do?" I ask. "Kill me?"

Alice looks to him. "Sir?" she says uncertainly.

Edmonds sighs. "Fetch it, child, before she fetches it herself."

I wait until the door closes behind her, then I pounce. "You must take her on. She must become your apprentice."

"Take whom on?"

"Alice! Who do you think, the cat?"

Edmonds regards me closely. "You have had too much poppy, madam."

"She is capable. A good worker."

"She is also a girl."

"You said yourself that your two apprentices were useless. Alice is clever. She would be a great help to you."

Edmonds strokes his beard. "There is much truth in what you say. But her father is a gardener. He cannot afford the apprentice fee."

"No, he cannot," I say, hope leaping inside me. "But I can."

"A girl apprenticed to a physician . . ."

"I will double the fee."

"Why do you wish it? How would it benefit her?" Edmonds asks. "She will never become a physician. Medicine is for men."

"How will it benefit her?" I echo, an edge to my voice. "By allowing her to use her gifts. By giving her pride in work well done. What is her alternative? Who will marry her? What shall she do? Dig furrows at her father's side? A mind as sharp as hers, wasted on turnips. I cannot bear it."

He gives me a long look. "This wish to do good deeds . . . it is a common deathbed urge. But one person cannot change the world, my lady."

I groan with frustration. Fresh tears prick my eyes. Tears of anger.

I think of Henry. He was one man. A second son not meant to rule. The King of a small island only, yet he changed the world. I think of his daughter Mary, who proves every day that a woman can occupy a throne. I think of Cromwell and Luther, and how they stole God from Rome.

"Oh, Edmonds, you fool, can't you see?" I say, with all the passion left in me. "By changing a life, just one life, you *can* change the world. It is the only way anyone ever has."

15 JULY 1557

There is a vulture in my room.

He perches by my window.

I cannot see his face, but soon I will.

He will fold his dark wings over me.

He will carry me away.

I am almost ready to go.

Almost, but not quite.

Up in the high palace, my mother is weeping.

She storms and rages. Tears at her hair.

She died thus, driven insane by war and the loss of her ancestral lands.

Wilhelm fought Spain over Guelders. Spain won and took not only Guelders but the Duchy of Jülich, part of my mother's dowry. She mourned the loss deeply and died soon after, heartbroken.

"Anna? My child, is that you?" she asks.

I embrace her. "Mother, why do you rage so?"

"The doings of men have driven me mad. Everyone told me I must accept what I cannot change. But I wished to change what I cannot accept, and that is where the trouble starts."

"Do not grieve. I will join you soon. We will go back to Cleves and make a plum tart."

But nothing I say can soothe her. She shakes me off. Marches back and forth. Weeps. Then shouts, "How could I have raised such a stupid, stupid son?"

"Mother, do not cry over Wilhelm," I plead, taking her cold hands in mine. "He is not worth it."

"Ah, Anna," she says sorrowfully. "You think I'm crying because I had such a foolish son and everyone knew it. But I'm not. I'm crying because I had such a clever daughter and no one did."

Morning has broken. The summer sun streams into my room.

By some miracle, the ravening cancer slumbers.

Edmonds has gone home. He has left me plenty of medicine, but I shall not be needing it.

"I wish to walk out this morning," I announce as Alice enters my room.

"But Dr. Edmonds says—"

"Fie on him. Help me dress."

Alice sighs unhappily. "Yes, my lady."

Though it is July, she makes sure I am warmly attired. A woollen kirtle goes over my linen shift, and a gown over that. I am winded after these exertions but marshal my resources.

Alice puts a blanket and two pillows in a large basket. She tucks her sewing in, too. Then she offers me her arm. We make our way out of the manor, through the gardens, to my fields.

The beauty of midsummer takes my breath away. The sky, so blindingly blue. The lark singing her heart out. Roses of every hue tumbling over stone walls.

I have been busy these past few days. I have added lines to my will.

As I walk, words I spoke to Holbein come back to me.

How I looked was all that mattered. Not who I was.

Who Alice *is* will matter. I have made sure of it.

Her fee has been paid. Edmonds will take her on. She does not know yet. He will tell her after I am gone. I have left her a good sum of money as well.

This girl will not spend her life digging turnips. She can make her own plans, command her own future. She will belong to herself.

Henry freed me and I have freed her. That was the debt to be settled. Maybe one day, Alice will help set a girl free, too. Maybe one day, the world will change so radically that girls will not need freeing.

Maybe.

I have seen my priest as well as my lawyer.

"Confess your sins," the priest told me. "Forgive those who have sinned against you so that you may find forgiveness."

On such a summer morning, it is easy to forgive. With the sun on my face, I forgive England its autumn fogs, its bitter winters, its dreary, sodden springs. I forgive my brother for bartering me like a sack of flour. My mother for packing all the wrong clothes.

And Henry. I even forgive Henry.

As I reach the edge of a barley field, the hem of my skirts heavy with dew, I see not vultures now, but a flock of crows holding a noisy parliament amongst the furrows. I walk on. Past fields of wheat and rye. Past my apple trees. To my destination—the grassy banks of my trout pond.

Alice spreads the blanket out and eases me down onto it. She puts the pillows behind me. I close my eyes and lift my face to the sun. She pesters me for more of my story.

"There is no more. You have it all. I lived happily ever after," I say.

"There is no such thing, my lady."

"No?" I say, smiling. "We shall see, child. We shall see."

I gather the last bits of my strength and open my eyes. I look at Alice. Her head is bent over her needlework. I gaze at the pond and see Henry's dead Queens walking along its edge. They beckon.

"Soon, soon. Wait for me," I whisper.

And then I turn to Alice.

"I have one last story," I say. "Another fairy tale. We Germans love our fairy tales."

"I would like to hear it," she says, "monsters or no."

"Good. I shall tell it. And then I shall sleep."

Once upon a time, there were six Queens who married the same King, one after the other.

The first was a beauty, with red hair, blue eyes, and ivory skin. She gave the King a child, but it was a girl. So he banished the Queen and took her child from her.

The second, whose beauty was as dark as her soul, also gave the King a daughter. And for this, he cut off her head.

The third, as mild as milk, gave the King a precious son, and oh, how he loved her for it. But the womb that gave life to the boy stole life from the mother. She died of childbed fever.

The fourth Queen . . . ah, the fourth Queen. The King called her ugly and put her aside.

The fifth Queen was young and the fairest of them all. Her eyes sparkled. Her laughter was music. The King adored her, but she loved another. So he cut off her head, too.

The sixth Queen was learned and the King did not like it. He would've cut off her head, but she begged his forgiveness for being clever and he let her live. Years later, childbed fever took her, too.

They are dead now, those beautiful Queens, all dead. And the King is dead. All his men, too. And the precious son for whom he remade the world.

But the ugly Queen?

Ah, *she* lived, child.

She lived.

HENRY VIII

How Cromwell thought to match his King with that German sow is beyond me.

I have often been called the handsomest prince in Christendom, admired for the turn of my leg and the beauty of my face. Perhaps a few years have passed, but they have only added authority to my stance and dignity. How dare Cromwell deceive me and send into my bedchamber a dismal, stale girl, a cheese-jowled Teutonic frump who couldn't even join in the pleasant jest of masquerading?

When she first landed on English shores I believed (from Holbein's false portrait) she was a beauty—but still, I was not eager to meet her. Sweet Jane's death haunted me. I was sunk in a seemly gloom. I was always afraid for the infant Edward's health, and ordered all the walls and linens in his chambers washed twice a day until they reeked of vinegar. The sight of him reminded me always of his mother.

And yet it reminded me of my duty, too. I must ensure that there is a line of heirs. Each of my royal sons has been struck down, save Edward. Each has been sapped of strength by the wombs that carried them, vessels either weak or wicked.

My people expect a sturdy line to spring from me.

And so Cromwell arranged this new alliance, and I prepared to meet Anna of Cleves. I thought from her portrait she would be beautiful—a young, cooing, merry little thing.

And the thought was awful. I was exhausted and sorrowful. I had no desire to entertain a mere girl.

I am, however, always thinking first of the ladies, and I wished her to feel welcome in her new homeland. I resolved to put a happy face on it. The night before I was to meet her, New Year's Eve, I sat in a feasting-hall before a fire with my Gentlemen of the Privy Chamber and drank hot Yuletide hippocras until the world seemed to blush again. I drank to steel myself. At first I drank in rage. Then, as the liquor rings on the table ran together and blotted out the memory of Jane, in faith, I drank in a state of fierce joy.

We all were loud and rowdy.

"Come, now, Your Majesty," said one of the men. "Bed this Hessian and make a Duke of York for us."

"I shall build the finest Duke of York," I promised.

They all cheered.

I looked carefully at them, and wondered whether they spurred me on because they feared I grew too old, too infirm, too sleepy. Of course, my age matters not a bean. I am young in the mind, young in the loins, and I could not have them doubt me.

So I exclaimed: "Boys! How about this: To her tonight! Yes? We'll visit her now, boys! Why should I wait?"

Cromwell said, "She is not expecting you, Your Majesty, until tomorrow."

"I am King of England. Isn't that right? King of England?"

"Your Majesty, we are to meet her at Greenwich."

"But we shall go now. Heh? See? Come, my lads. Let's gallop down to Rochester and spring a surprise. Let's show this German beauty we are still frisky, despite the grey hairs!"

It was quickly arranged: We ordered our masqueing gear from a recent disguising, put on visors and wigs, and set out in a drunken rout, after a few of the younger pips, who couldn't hold their hippocras, vomited over the battlements.

We laughed as we rode through the chilly night, and it was a game like the ones I had played in my youth. We passed the frozen villages, the dark towns where my subjects huddled in sleep. I leaned close to my steed and spurred it on. I saw before me the girl's face Holbein had painted, but as she would look when we began our antics: laughing, thrilled to see the King of England play a prank upon her—*a wonderful man,* she will think, *a monarch who is still merry. Is this,* she will think with awed delight, *my new husband?*

She is a young thing. She will like jests.

And so we reached her lodgings, where the crowd enjoyed a bull-baiting. In the crush of the contest (the bull bellowing as the dogs assaulted it), my boys pressed people backwards to make room for me to dismount. I could barely contain my anticipation as they levered me off my horse.

Up the stairs we ran in our disguising, and charged through the door, chanting, "Mugga mugga mugga mugga," like barbarian monsters come for kisses. The English ladies knew who we were at a glance, and were delighted by our play.

Her face: so sombre. My bride and I stared, each upon the other. I was the older one, not she—I was the one who was bereaved—I was the one who should be sombre. When I kissed her, she did not understand the jest, did not squeal. Her cheek smeared beneath my lips.

I cannot abide people who can't laugh.

She was one of those dreary people who find no thrill in life. Who could wed such a person?

There in that moment, with the bull screaming outside, too weak to hold off the dogs, I knew the marriage would not work. I should have to be rid of her soon.

How Cromwell could have thought to pair us is a mystery to me.

I should not speak ill of her, for now she is my sister. Strange to say, now that she is not my consort, I find her pleasant to be with. I want nothing from her. She wants nothing more from me. It is restful to know a woman who is of no use to one whatsoever.

Our conversations: dogs, their habits, their tricks. Cuisine, its cooking. The palaces I build, where, as I show her plans, she even smiles sometimes at their whimsy.

Sometimes I wonder about her smile, which did not appear in Holbein's complacent portrait.

It is the smile of a victor.

CATHERINE HOWARD

"No Other Will Than His"

FEBRUARY 1542

A solid wooden block, about knee-high. The two guards who have brought it up the stairs to my rooms are grunting and puffing—it must be very heavy. They heave it onto the floor and leave.

I walk around it once, looking at it from all sides. Then I touch the top—gingerly, at first. I don't know why; it's not as if it can hurt me.

The top has been sanded very smooth. There will be no splinters when I kneel down, turn my head, and place my cheek upon it.

Splinters. Such a small thing. But I *have* to think about the small things, all the time.

Because if I don't, I'll start screaming and never stop.

SUMMER AND FALL 1539

Sixteen. I'm sixteen now, as grown as I'm going to get.

I'm not tall and willowy like Margaret, or dark and fulsome like Bess. I used to wish I were, but then I found out that some men are drawn to girls who are petite and have auburn hair, and enjoy dancing and a good laugh. Men like Henry Manox, the music teacher at Chesworth House.

Along with the other girls who are wards of the Dowager Duchess of Norfolk, I have lessons in reading and writing, sewing, dancing, religion, and music. There are usually around a dozen of us, the number changing as younger girls arrive and older ones leave to marry. The Dowager keeps two households, Chesworth in Sussex and Lambeth Palace in London; we travel between them as it suits her.

Manox taught me how to play the clavichord.

He also taught me how to kiss.

But I wasn't long with Manox, because then I met Francis Dereham, a courtier at Lambeth. Stars afar, what Francis hasn't taught me isn't worth knowing. When I'm with him, I can't get enough of him; when I'm not with him, I can't stop thinking about him. Sweet torture!

He and a few of his friends bribed young Mary, the chambermaid, for the key to our dormitory. They visit two or three times a week, late at night. The evenings start out with laughter and wine, or with games, or riddles and stories. But no matter how they begin, they always end the same way: with Francis in my bed, the two of us kissing as no one in the world has ever kissed before.

The first time, he lay with me in his doublet and hose, but it didn't take long before we were completely naked. In such a frenzy for each other, we were incautious, and then I panicked waiting for my monthly blood. I cried to him that I mustn't get with child, for if I do, the Dowager might turn me out. Francis soothed me and stroked my hair, and then showed me the ways of love without that worry.

What he has taught me above all else is to feel utterly free in bed.

"My little Cat," he often says, "the bed is an island, a world of its own."

"Meow," I always reply. A silly joke, but one that makes us laugh.

Francis says that as long as we're both willing, we can try anything without pause or shame. Such freedom from the restraints of being a woman outside the sheets! He has taken to calling me "wife," and has asked me to call him "husband." And I do, of course—I'll do anything to please him.

One fine autumn day, I can't bear to wait for night, so I arrange to meet him in the forenoon. Lambeth Palace is so large that there are lots of private corners. I stand with my back to the wall under the east wing stairs as Francis kisses my neck and my breasts. I can feel the heat of my blood, my pulse surging in every hidden part of me; it's more than marvellous. My skirts are raised so he can stroke me deeply, while I bring him satisfaction with my hand.

Then I straighten my skirts and hair, and take a few breaths so my colour might calm a bit. Francis glances around to make sure that the corridors are empty, and gives me a last long kiss before he leaves.

"You mustn't look back at me," he says.

"But why not?"

"There is an old story, that looking back brought bad fortune to two lovers. Resist the temptation, my darling Cat. It will make our love all the stronger."

"Tell me the story, meow."

So he tells me about Orpheus and Eurydice, and how Orpheus walked out of Hades with his true love behind him, and he'd been told not to look back, but then he worried because he couldn't hear her, so he took one little peek, and that ruined everything. She got snatched back into Hades. Such a sad story, and now it gives me a thrill not to look back at him when he leaves, thinking of those poor doomed lovers.

A fortnight later, we're pressed together under the same stairwell when I'm stunned by a blow to my head.

"Lady Catherine!" thunders the Dowager. "How do you dare!" She strikes me again with her fan, as I shriek and try to dodge her blows.

Next she turns her fury on Francis. "Base, impertinent scoundrel! You would menace *a Howard girl*? Fie, fie!"

She beats him on his head and shoulders until he finally escapes. "Gather your things," she shouts after him, "and make it your heart's desire that I not lay eyes on you again."

I can hardly see, I'm crying so hard. The Dowager relents a little and softens her voice. "He is the son of a yeoman, Catherine. Not a drop of noble blood. You are not a child any longer—you must know that he isn't a suitable match."

"I don't care," I say, heaving with great, ugly sobs. "I love him."

She ignores me. "I shall say nothing of this to the Duke. Be certain you give me no cause to regret this kindness."

Francis and I see each other once more before he leaves. He tells me that he's planning to go to Ireland.

"Ireland! But when will I see you again?"

We lie in bed, my head on his shoulder. "Dear wife, you know it is not uncommon for a man to depart from his beloved for months, or even years," he says, "and return with the love between them all the stronger."

"How will I bear it?"

"I should think this will cheer you." He reaches for his doublet on the floor, then holds out a leather purse bulging with coins. "One hundred pounds, near all my worldly goods save what I must have for Ireland. Keep it for me, and if I should not return, it is yours forever."

"If you should not return!" I cry. "How can I, now that you pair it with such a thought?"

In the end he persuades me, and I take the little purse, wetting it with my tears. After such distress, our lovemaking is hot and keen, and I want it never to end.

A girl in the throes of first love. How is it that such honest passion could years later be transformed into treason and evil and death?

DECEMBER 1539

I wish he wouldn't look at me like that.

My uncle, the Duke of Norfolk, is looking me over as if I'm a—a cow, or a firkin of butter. Or a codfish. With only the one thought in his mind: *What use can I get of her?*

I wonder if he looked at Queen Anne the same way. Poor Anne. She was my first cousin, God rest her soul; he was her uncle, too.

This time, though, there's a good reason for his shrewd sneer. "She may have two new dresses," he says to the Dowager.

New dresses, because I am to be at court.

At court!

The King's new bride has arrived from the Continent. He wants her to learn English, so he dismissed most of her German-speaking attendants. *Hundreds* of girls and women vied for places to serve her, and my uncle the Duke has secured a position—*for me.*

It's the best of all dreams! I was very young the last time I moved to a new household, but I remember it too well. I can see that poor wee eight-year-old girl standing in the entry hall of Chesworth House. Small for her age and looking even smaller in that vast hall, so frightened and sad, her mother dead, her father feckless, she and her siblings farmed out all over England to whomever would take them in.

Even so, I was by nature cheerful and lively. I soon made my place among the girls by devising bits of mischief—like the time I stole the chambermaid's cap and tied it onto one of the Dowager's dogs. I still laugh to think of it! The household has been a happy enough place for me, except when I'm forced to listen to the Duke and the Dowager complain about my father being the worst of the Howards. Measles and cankers, if I have to hear about it one more time . . .

No matter, no matter now. What matters is *I will be moving to court.*

"New dresses look ill with old hoods," the Dowager says.

My uncle frowns. What a sour face he has, like a dried apple full of bad gas.

"Would you have it said that your niece is not well suited to attend the Queen?" she says. I'm glad she doesn't look at me; if she did, I might burst out laughing at how she's goading him.

He waves impatiently and leaves.

Which means yes, that I may have hoods as well as dresses, because "no" would have been a loud and nasty harangue.

I clasp my hands and turn to her. "I can never thank the good Dowager enough," I say, then shower her with praise and more thanks. It was the Duke who secured the place at court, but it was the Dowager who chose *me* for the position, from among the many girl cousins and relatives.

"And, madam, if I may, I look well in green. Might one of the dresses be of green silk?"

Two new dresses and two new hoods! I grew up in castoffs, for my father never sent the Dowager anything more than my keep, and often, as she liked to remind me, not even that. A new ribbon, once or twice, but a new dress? Never.

For one dress, kirtle and skirt in palest green satin the colour of new leaves, with sleeves a deeper green. For the other, a skirt of burnished-copper damask over a kirtle of cream, the copper a match to the auburn of my hair. When I first donned the green one and looked in the glass, I could hardly believe it was me!

My hoods are trimmed with ribbon and French lace. The Duke won't let me have pearls on them, the old barnacle. He said maybe I can have them later, once I've pleased the Queen and earned her trust.

Joan says I'll be the only girl at court without pearls. She sleeps two beds over in the dormitory and is mostly my friend. Now she's jealous and says snippety things, so I'm not sorry that she's leaving soon to be married. But I *am* sorry we'll be parting on bad terms because I've known her ever since I first came to the Dowager's household. I hope one day we'll make up. The hard part about that is, both people have to be of the mind to make up *at the same time*, and it doesn't always happen that way.

I'm too busy to worry about it much. And best of all, I'm too busy to miss Francis. Being fitted for my dresses; learning the dances most favoured at court; horseback riding and archery added to my lessons—the King likes the ladies to ride out and sport on occasion. Such fun and excitement!

But of course there are boring and tedious duties as well. I spend hours in the Dowager's presence chamber so she can tutor me on the ways of the court. Curtseys and modesty to my betters. Firmness without cruelty to the servants. Above all, I'm supposed to observe the Queen every moment and learn to predict her needs so that she'll like me, and depend on me above all the other maids.

"Catherine, you know why the Duke has gone to such pains to garner you a place at court?"

"So that I might have the honour of serving my Queen?"

I think it's a good answer, so I'm startled when she cuffs my ear. I let out a mewl like a sick kitten.

"Witless girl!" the Dowager scolds. "You are at court on behalf of the entire Howard family. You must never forget for a single moment that you serve the Queen *as a means of serving the Duke*! He requires two simple things. You are to keep your eyes and ears open for any news that might be of interest to him. And you are to make a good marriage with a courtier, one who has His Majesty's favour, so as to strengthen our family's ties to the King."

Make a good marriage? I feel a twinge in my heart over Francis. But I've had no word from him since he left, and who knows how long he'll be away? I once thought I couldn't live without him. And he'll always be the first man I ever loved.

But I've learned that I *can* live without him, and I can even be happy. Now my mind fills with visions of handsome young men, kind and courtly, sporting and brave … a fine dancer … someone who makes me laugh …

If the Duke wants me to make a suitable marriage, it seems that I can have some good fun along the way!

JANUARY 1540

The great hall is lit by what must be a thousand candles to celebrate His Majesty's wedding to Anna of Cleves. Everywhere I look, I see silks and jewels, furs and pearls, silver and gold. Goblets of wine, trays of sweets, tapestries and draperies, banners and tassels: It's impossible to see everything at once, but that doesn't stop me trying.

On a dais at one end of the hall, His Majesty and the new Queen are sitting on chairs of velvet and gold. Snipes and snails, isn't he big! I've heard talk that he's grown stout; now I see for myself that he's very broad indeed. But he's a tall man, and his clothes fit him beautifully, and he is *King*, after all—it wouldn't seem right if he were thin and feeble.

The new Queen is tall, too, and strong-boned. If I stood beside her, I'm sure I would barely reach her chin. She's wearing a gown draped with chains, in the German style. In truth, she isn't very pretty—all the ladies have said so—but there's something about her, a kind of grace. Maybe it's the way she holds her head. I try to do the same, my neck straight but my chin down so I won't seem haughty. . . .

In my lovely green dress, I am every bit the maid of honour: Who would ever guess that I was once barely more than a foundling?

I thought on this before my arrival here at the hall. I thought that if I keep my head lowered and skulk around like a beaten dog, people are *more* likely to notice, not less. The trick is to get them to notice something else—and I know how.

Dancing! I love it so! I think it must be because of the music, which seems to enter my ears and go straight to my blood, and makes it impossible for me to stay still. The worst part about learning to become a proper lady is having to sit and wait for what seems like *days* at a time, embroidering or folding linen the best part of the day—fah!

But dancing is much in fashion at court, and I've loved it since I was a child. I love learning even the most complicated patterns—I practise them on my own if no one else will practise with me. *One-two, step and turn, one-two, dip or bow* ... Counting steps, turning crisply, keeping time with the music, dancing is a delight for both my mind and my body. What fun during a pavane or galliard to glance up at a gentleman's face and then away, and know that he's admiring me, all without missing a step or losing the beat. The Dowager told me that the Duke himself once remarked on the charm of my dancing. Imagine!

"Ladies, will you dance?"

Three courtiers stand before us. I glance quickly at Lady Dorothy and Lady Margaret, then nod demurely.

We curtsey and are led onto the floor. The music begins: a lively galliard, my favourite dance, and I simply can't help laughing in delight.

One-two-three-four, hop! One-two-three-four, hop!

The sweeps and slide-steps take me past the dais. I'm breathless and laughing when, in the middle of a turn, I see His Majesty looking at me.

No, surely not at *me*. I glance over my shoulder, but I don't see anyone in particular, and then I look back again and this time there's no doubt—it *is* me he's looking at, his eyes bright, and a smile on his fat royal face!

Should I smile back at him, is that too bold? But if I don't smile, will he think I'm rude? I don't know what to do—and he's *still* looking at me—*one-two*-don't forget the hop—and it's so awkward to pretend I don't notice, I can't ignore him, I have to do *something*.

I open my eyes wide and nod at His Majesty, a *tiny* nod, with my mouth in a not-quite smile.

The dance finishes. I curtsey to my partner. I don't look at His Majesty again, yet I'm sure to remember this all my life—the night my dancing pleased the King!

The very next day, I'm surprised when the Dowager comes to visit. She wants to walk with me, so we take a turn around the maids' chambers.

"Catherine," she says, her voice low in my ear, "the Duke has news. The King has ordered that the Privy Council find a way to annul the union."

"What union?" I ask.

"Ssst," the Dowager hisses. "The Cleves woman, of course."

"But what can you mean; they've only just married!"

She pinches my arm as we walk. "Would that you were not as witless as you are young," she scolds. "Listen, and hark: The King is markedly displeased with the new Queen, he likes her not a farthing. He has ordered Cromwell and the rest of the Council to find a way out of the marriage. The Duke says that the King intends to take him another wife, *and that he asked about you.*"

I stop and stare at her. "Asked—asked . . . ," I stammer, "who— surely not—"

"Yes, yes. He spied you dancing last night, and thought you charming."

"But—but how can you know this?"

"At court, everyone knows someone," she says. "It was all over-heard by one of my own men in attendance to the Duke for the cel-ebrations. Now the Duke thinks to put you in the way of the King."

I feel faint; my knees wobble. The Dowager leads me to a bench, where I gulp air like a dying fish.

"Madam," I say weakly, "I have only just arrived here. I—I don't mean—might it be that the good Duke is mistaken? The Queen's attendants are mostly new to court; perhaps His Majesty is asking after all of us."

The Dowager looks at me thoughtfully. "There is sense in that," she says, "and it would not do to act the fool and throw yourself at him. Continue as you have, then, until we know if the marriage will sunder or not. But you must be ready to receive the King's favour should it fall to you."

The King's favour . . .

Everything is happening too fast. It's madness enough that I've gotten my first real dresses—and am now at court—and got to attend His Majesty's wedding—but *this*—oh, this!

FEBRUARY 1540

I sit at a dressing table with a mirror in front of me. Lady Rochford, of the Queen's privy chamber, brushes my hair. As she arranges my cap and hood, she speaks quietly.

"The Bishop has invited you to Winchester Palace tonight, *at the King's request.* Likely, His Majesty will bid you to his side for a time."

Lady Rochford has been at court through the reigns of three Queens. She earned the King's gratitude by testifying at the trial of my cousin, Queen Anne, so the Dowager told me that I must take care to remain in her good graces. It seems odd to me: I should be cordial to her even though she testified *against* my cousin? But the Dowager pinched my arm when I asked about it, and scolded that my place was not to question, but to obey.

Now I look at Lady Rochford's reflection, my eyes wide. I'm supposed to sit beside the King, and speak to him? I half rise from my seat in alarm.

"Whatever will I say?"

She pushes me gently back down. "It is said that he is charmed by the gaiety of your youth. Do not try to be other than you are. He does not seek cleverness or worldliness. Rather it is your sprightly nature that would cheer him."

The evening ahead is suddenly terrifying. I can't—I simply *must not* displease the King. It might mean ruin for my whole family.

The worst of the Howards, that's what they call me and mine. And yet . . .

I look at the reflection in the mirror, a face so solemn and scaredy. *How far you've come,* I say to her silently. *You arrived at the Dowager's alone and bereft, but then Manox wanted you, and Francis loved you, and the Duke and Dowager chose you for court. Here is another challenge. Courage!*

I lift my chin. The girl in the mirror nods.

"Come. Sit."

The King beckons me from a dais at the head of the hall. A large chair holds him. No, not a chair, a *bench*—one that two men and a woman of normal size could fit in, and His Majesty fills the whole thing himself.

Winchester Palace is of course not nearly as grand as His Majesty's Whitehall. But the great hall does have the loveliest rose window. I wish I could see it during the daylight hours, with the sunshine streaming through. If I were to stand on the brightest spot of colour on the floor, I think it would make quite a pretty picture.

To His Majesty's right sits our host, the Bishop Gardiner. A chair is brought for me, placed at an angle so the King can see me easily. Dinner is finished; now courtiers bring trays holding goblets of wine and plates of sweetmeats. I see sugared almonds, my favourite, but I don't dare take one. I might look unseemly, chewing and swallowing in front of His Majesty.

"How do you find court, Lady Catherine?" the King asks.

"Very well, Your Majesty."

"What most pleases you about it?"

A frightening moment—is there a wrong answer?

Then I recall Lady Rochford's advice to be myself. *Fine, then. So what does myself like most about court?*

To my surprise, the answer comes easily.

"So many lovely things, to choose among them is an effortful task," I say. "But if I am forced to choose, I would say the music."

"Yes?"

The King seems pleased by my response. But he's waiting: I'm supposed to say something more.

"Your Majesty, never have I heard music such as at court. It—it seems to fill not just my ears but the whole of my being to my very toes, so that they begin to tap without my bidding."

The King laughs heartily and turns to the Bishop. "She has a true feeling for music!" he exclaims. "Let us have some, then!"

The Bishop speaks to a courtier, and with a clap of hands, musicians are summoned. Lute and recorder, not a grand ensemble as at Whitehall, but still very nice, the lute sweet underneath, the recorder melody a little sad. The King asks for songs written by one of his favourite composers, Mr. Cornysh.

While the music plays, I ponder what to say when we start talking again. His Majesty is grand and glorious and not like other men, for he is King of All England. But he's blood and bone, too, and in that way, he *is* like other men, so I think of what I know about them.

Henry Manox and Francis Dereham enjoyed instructing me—Manox at the clavichord and kissing, Francis at lovemaking. They liked holding forth on subjects they thought they were good at. I'm guessing that His Majesty might be the same? He's an accomplished musician: Everyone at court knows that he composes songs himself and can play several instruments. So off I go!

"Your Majesty, may I be so bold as to ask a question of you?"

"You may ask whatever you wish, Lady Catherine."

"I know a little of the clavichord, but that is all. Is there an instrument you prefer above others?"

The King looks very pleased. He starts talking about different instruments—lute, harp, recorder, clavichord. . . . It seems that he loves music as much as I love dancing, and this is a delight to me.

At last he asks what sort of music I like best, and I reply at once. "Oh! Music for dancing, Your Majesty."

He laughs again, and this time I join in. What I said wasn't really very funny, so I'm not sure why he's laughing, but *I'm* laughing because I'm nearly giddy with relief. The Bishop is looking on us kindly, and Lady Rochford is nodding at me, and then the King kisses my hand and holds it in his for a moment, actually for quite a few moments, so it seems I've done what I was supposed to do, even if I'm still not quite sure what it was.

MARCH–MAY 1540

◇•◇

Through the winter and spring, I go to Winchester Palace two or three evenings every week. Lady Rochford and I are always the only ones invited from the Queen's household. It's an odd bit of codfish, being the Queen's dutiful maid of honour during the day, and then keeping His Majesty company in the evening. I'm always reminding myself never to speak of the Queen when I'm with the King, and the other way round—I get quite dizzy thinking about it.

The parties are small affairs, attended by a few dozen courtiers and ladies considered trustworthy by His Majesty and the Bishop. They're not nearly as gay as the gatherings of the full court, but I don't mind: The King almost always calls for dancing. He does this because he knows I love it, which is so very dear of him.

His Majesty doesn't dance himself because his leg hurts too much; Lady Rochford says it's from ulcers that won't heal. But the ladies who've been at court for years say he was a truly fine dancer when he was younger. Now he loves to watch *me* dance.

"So small and quick, you're like a wren or a robin," he says, "and during the more lively turns, you seem to fairly fly."

He often bids that I should be partnered with Mr. Thomas Culpeper, Gentleman of the Privy Chamber. A distant cousin to me on my mother's side, Mr. Culpeper has been favoured by the King since he was a small boy. He's so much taller than I am that when we dance the volta, he lifts me high in the air.

We laugh, and the King claps his hands and laughs with us.

Oh, His Majesty's eyes do sparkle when he sees me! He laughs a lot at the things I say. Really and truly, our conversations are quite the nicest I've ever had. But I won't say that to the Dowager or anyone else at court because it might sound disrespectful of His Majesty, which isn't what I mean at all. It's hard to explain, but I think His Majesty likes the me who is the Catherine me, not the niece of the Duke of Norfolk of the Howard clan me. Fah, what a mouthful.

I keep wondering what will happen when the Queen finds out. I ask the Dowager, who says that the Queen is too afraid of the King to ever confront me. Perhaps—but what if she does? It seems I'm not to worry about that puddle until I step in it.

Anyway, the Dowager is pleased with me. But my uncle the Duke is a pickle of a puzzle. Sometimes he's almost jolly, kissing me on the mouth and vowing that I'm the most prized flower of the family. Other times he questions me fiercely, asking me to recall the King's exact words and how many times he smiled at me.

The Duke talks endlessly about how the Howard family has to lead the battle to guard the true faith. He mutters about the Great Bible, and says that anyone who even looks into it might burn in Hell. I don't understand that, because if God is Almighty and knows everything, then surely he knows English as well as Latin, so why should a Bible in English be such a dreadful thing? But I mustn't say such nonsense—I mustn't even think it. I don't want to burn in Hell.

I listen as well as I can until it's just too tedious, then I pretend to listen, keeping my eyes on his face while my thoughts stray into the wherever.

The worst of those meetings with the Duke and the Dowager are when they discuss whether I should become the King's mistress. The Duke says that I should remain in the King's favour *without* bedding him. The Dowager says that I mustn't seduce His Majesty, but that if he asks to bed me, I should comply.

It's mortifying to hear them talk about me like this.

"You would, at least, be the only one so serving him at the moment," the Dowager declares, "and that is no small thing."

Everyone at court knows that the King claims his marriage to Queen Anna isn't a true marriage because they've never made love. I puzzle over that—how can a man and a woman newly married share a bed, yet not have any fun in it?

For once I'm in agreement with the Duke. I don't want to become the King's mistress. I've seen how easily a mistress is cast off, and many of them never marry. But of course what I want doesn't matter.

Then I can't help wondering . . . *What would it be like, to lie beneath such an enormous man?*

*　*　*

I take the box from the page, then give him a smile and a small copper coin. I lift the lid and see that there's no note, so I call out to ask him who sent the box, but he's already gone.

The other maids and ladies circle me as I hold up the gift. "Oh!" I say.

"Oh! Oh!" We sound like a flock of starlings, and I'm the loudest because the gift is such a wonder! It's a velvet hood, the most beautiful one I've ever seen. The band is edged with *pearls*, too many to count, and the hood itself with gold and stones. The very latest style, with two fine combs to hold the band in my hair—I won't have to use pins, the troublesome things, which never stay in place and are forever pricking me.

"Whoever could have sent you such a gift?" Lady Dorothy asks.

I draw in my breath, my thoughts suddenly tangled: The Queen is sitting not five paces away. Her English is still not very good, but how much does she understand? *I can't—I mustn't—*

"I'm sure I don't know," I mumble.

"But surely you can guess?"

"Yes, guess, Catherine!"

"You must have some notion!"

I blush and put my hand to my forehead to give me time to think. "It might be—I wonder if—"

I'm starting to panic. Is the Queen looking at me suspiciously? Can she see the sweat on my forehead, my neck?

Then Lady Rochford is at my side. "How can she know, with neither note nor word?" she says in a scolding voice. "Lady Catherine, it seems that you have an admirer of both means and discernment. When you learn who he is, you must promise to enlighten us."

"Oh, yes!" I practically screech in relief. "Of course I will!"

And at last the attention returns to the hood itself, and it passes from hand to hand for everyone to admire. I don't look at Lady Rochford, but I think she can sense my thanks.

I wear the hood on my next visit to Winchester Palace.

"My lady Catherine, how well you are looking," His Majesty greets me smilingly, seated on the dais in the great hall as usual.

I flush at his compliment. As I rise from my curtsey, I turn my head slowly so he can see his gift from all sides.

A chair is brought for me, but before I sit, he beckons me towards him, then speaks so only I can hear.

"With the hood comes a request," he says.

I draw in my breath. *He's going to ask me to be his mistress. And I will say yes because I have to, for the sake of my family, and I mustn't think for even a single second what will happen to me when he casts me aside.*

"Whatever you will, Your Majesty," I murmur.

"Sweet girl," he says. He leans closer still. "I request ... your patience."

"My patience?" I'm so surprised that my voice squeaks.

"I have made my plans, and they will be realized. It is taking more time than I would like, but I promise you that the prize will be worth the wait. Can you do that for me, dear Catherine? Can you wait, and trust in your King?"

"Oh, Your Majesty!" I exclaim. "There is no one I trust more. If you bid me wait, I will, and will be glad of it."

"A rose," he whispers, and touches my cheek. "Like a single perfect rose you are."

And now I know that His Majesty is himself waiting.

Thunder and wonder! The King of England is waiting—*for me!*

JUNE–JULY 1540

◇·◇

More gifts: Embroidered brocade for a new dress. A gilded box, carved with birds and flowers and hearts, and lined in velvet. A pomander ball: a whole Spanish orange, studded with hundreds of rarest cloves from the Moluccas. It scents the corner of the chamber where I sleep, my bedding, my linen shifts, my hose.

And then, a length of quilted sarcenet! That most precious silk, light as a butterfly's wing, layered and padded, enough for two full sleeves. Lady Rochford says I mustn't have it made up, not yet, it would make people suspicious, because no one has ever heard of a mere maid having sarcenet sleeves. I feel as if I can't blink, or even take a full breath. Because if I do, I'll wake from the STRANGEST DREAM EVER DREAMT.

The court has been all buzz and hum with gossip and scandal. It's impossible to tell what's true and what's not, and sometimes I think no one even cares so long as it's exciting. Most shocking of all: the arrest of the Earl of Essex, Thomas Cromwell.

I can't believe it! Cromwell has always been the King's favourite advisor. Just weeks ago, His Majesty bestowed on him the earldom, with all its lands and holdings—and now he's mouldering in the Tower. Cromwell is the one who commissioned the Great Bible, which means he's against the true Catholic faith, which makes him an enemy of the Howards. The Duke is so pleased about Cromwell's arrest, it's as if his face has almost remembered how to smile.

As for the King's attentions to me—they're no longer a secret, but not yet public, either. People stare when I pass, and whisper afterwards. It's rather thrilling to be the subject of so much attention, but at the same time, I don't like the whispering, I always wonder what's being said.

A few days after Cromwell's arrest, we're listening to a harp player in the Queen's apartments. She's obviously not amused, and dismisses him after only a song or two. When she rises from her seat, I curtsey along with the other ladies. She walks a few steps—and stops before me.

"Lady Catherine," she says.

Instantly my face flushes. I stay in my curtsey, keeping my head down and silently cursing the Dowager. I knew this moment would come—why did she not prepare me with what to say or do?

"Your Highness," I murmur.

"Look at me."

Slowly, I straighten my knees. Slower still, I raise my head, terrified of what I will see on her face: anger, hatred, bitterness . . .

But when I finally force myself to meet her gaze, I see none of those things. Instead, she is studying me keenly, with an expression of—of what, I'm not sure.

The whole room seems to be holding its breath. The moment lasts an eternity.

"So young," she says at last, and shakes her head.

With a final look, she sweeps past me and out of the room.

I can feel all eyes on me. Every stare feels like a pin, pricking me mercilessly. I turn and walk away. It takes every bit of my strength not to run.

As I reach the safety of the empty corridor, I all but collapse against the wall. I'm panting, sweating, my heart pounding. The entire brief but agonizing episode runs through my mind again—and I realize that the look in the Queen's eyes was one of *pity*.

Indignation makes me straighten my spine, and I hold my head high. *I'm* the one the King loves now. Why in the world should she pity me? It's jealousy, that's what it is. If she weren't the Queen, I'd say she was a jealous old cow.

*   *   *

The Queen leaves to go to Richmond. Her Lord Steward says that there's plague in London, and she's being moved to safeguard her health. I can hardly remain in her court now, so I'm summoned back to Lambeth Palace, supposedly to care for the ailing Dowager, who isn't ailing at all.

I learn soon enough that there's no plague—it's just an excuse. After the Queen's departure, it takes only a few days for the King's marriage to be annulled by the Church. Then the annulment is confirmed by Parliament, and the former Queen Anna of Cleves is declared the King's sister.

A sister? How can a wife become a sister? I get a clout on the ear from the Dowager, but I don't think it's wrong that I asked. The Dowager says there's no need for me to understand. When someone says "You wouldn't understand," what they really mean is "We don't want you to know." Besides, I understand one thing well enough: The King no longer has a Queen.

Blink. Pinch. Blink again.

I run from the Dowager's apartments back to my room—I have my own room at Lambeth now; I don't have to sleep in the dormitory anymore, not since I became the King's favourite—and I throw myself on the bed. I bury my head deep in the pillows, and then let loose a shriek—the loudest and longest I can manage. I'm not crying, but I shriek and scream over and over, flinging away the pillows, pummelling the mattress with my fists, and everyone comes running. The Dowager at least understands—she shoos them all away and leaves me alone, shutting the door firmly.

Finally my voice gives out, and I lie there, limp as an empty silk glove. I'm not sure what I'm feeling, my mind is in such a whirl, but I know why I screamed: What else is a girl supposed to do when she learns she's going to be Queen of All England?

* * *

It's not fair: They expect me to act like a woman with the King, but they treat me like a child. I see this clearly when I'm instructed to choose a retinue. First, there's the wonder: *I* am to have attendants! Then the excitement—whom should I choose? I know it's not very Christian of me, but I feel a little mean gladness that some of the great ladies who never thought me good enough are now fluttering and twittering around me.

I want to pick the girls and women I like best, those who are good-natured and love to laugh; or are kind and gentle; or dependable and discreet. But it turns out that I don't actually get to choose at all. My uncle and the Dowager do the choosing for me. My attendants are to be ladies from families who practise the true religion, or have other-wise allied themselves with the Duke.

The Dowager will herself be one of my Great Ladies. Lady Roch-ford has served in the privy chambers of Queen Jane *and* Queen Anna, and she will remain in mine. Lady Nan Herbert, at court through the reigns of all four of His Majesty's Queens, is some years older than me, and I don't know her well, but she's said to be sharp-eyed and wise. A few other ladies are quickly chosen, and the Dowager says I'll be able to add more attendants later. But for now, there's no time to bring up anyone not already at court.

Along with the Duke and the Dowager, I travel with my retinue to Oatlands. It's a lovely palace west of London, on a rise overlook-ing the countryside. My ladies and I are given an entire wing of fine rooms. Then the King and a few of his trusted courtiers arrive, in-cluding His Majesty's chaplain, the Bishop Bonner.

And in small, quiet haste, I am married to the King of England.

In the midst of all the bustle, a thought I've been avoiding disturbs my joy. I can't forget . . . that I am His Majesty's *fifth* Queen.

None of the other four met with good fortune. My ponderings go back and forth like a ball being played at tennis.

No good comes of becoming his wife.

—But there can't be bad fortune for five *wives in a row!*

Why should I be any different?

—I am different! I'll be so good to him, I'll do everything I can to be a perfect wife and Queen!

Surely all the others said the exact same thing.

—But the way he looks at me—with such light in his eyes! That can't be feigned. He loves me, truly he does!

And I make sure that this thought is my last on the subject, always.

I sit up in the bed. It's the grandest bed I've ever seen, fancy carvings and drapes of real silk. Lady Rochford told me that Oatlands Palace was acquired by the King for Anna of Cleves. They never joined as man and wife, so it pleases me to think that I'll be the first Queen to make love to the King in this bed.

Three of my ladies flutter around me. One brushes my hair, long and loose; another adjusts my shift; a third folds back the linen sheet just so. A knock at the door: They arrange themselves in a neat line and curtsey deeply as the King enters with his gentlemen.

The ladies depart, Nan giving me a last reassuring glance.

His Majesty stands with his back to the bed as his courtiers undress him. I look down at the coverlet, at my hands, at the ends of my hair. . . . If we were alone, I might have looked at him, but with his attendants in the room, I feel abashed. None of them look at me, but I can feel them all wanting to.

There's a pretty silk ribbon at the neck of my shift. Nervously, I untie it, then start to tie it again.

Suddenly the whole bed jerks and lurches, and I'm bounced nearly onto the floor!

The King is so large that he can't get into the bed unaided. While

I was busy with the ribbon, his courtiers lifted and heaved him, and when he landed, my weight was simply no match for his.

His gentlemen turn and settle him; I'm jolted and bounced still more, and I can't help laughing as I clutch at the drapes to keep from falling out of the bed.

An abrupt silence.

I swallow my next laugh. Have I erred by laughing? Will His Majesty think I'm mocking him?

Then he speaks. "If it makes her laugh, you shall do it again."

So his courtiers raise him up and set him down and bounce me again, and our first night as husband and wife begins in laughter.

His gentlemen dismissed, the King takes a moment to speak with me. We sit in bed, pillows at our backs, the sheet pulled up chastely.

"My darling Catherine, it grieves me that our wedding had to be so small an affair. I would that it were the grandest ever."

I look at him in surprise, touched by his words. It's true that I sometimes imagined a splendid wedding—and then would chastise myself sternly. The mere fact of marrying the King ought to suffice for any girl.

"Your Majesty has not known me long enough to know me so well," I say.

He smiles. "All girls dream of their weddings, surely," he says. "But hear me out: There will be talk of you, not only at court but in London, in all of England, even, I dare say, on the Continent. I wished to spare you that, for at least a while. We will tarry here at Oatlands, and I will show you Hampton, and I will take time to be quietly with my lovely bride before I must share her with the world." A pause. "Do you find me selfish in that?"

"Your Majesty—"

"Henry. When we are abed, I bid you call me by my name."

Henry. I say it first silently, to see how it feels on my tongue, and—odd notion—I think of my first taste of a fig not long ago: strange, but not unpleasant.

"Henry," I say aloud but cautiously. Then, "Henry," more boldly.

He laughs. I love making him laugh.

"Henry, I will answer your question by telling you what I have chosen as my motto."

My motto was the source of much discussion with the Duke. Everyone at court knows that Queen Jane was the King's best-beloved wife, so the Duke suggested that I model my motto after hers, which was "Bound to obey and serve." He favoured "Sworn to honour and serve," but I thought this was much too similar. I did want to emulate her modesty, but couldn't I do it in my own way?

Then I thought of how men like to hear themselves spoken of as much as they like to hear themselves speak. And so I got the notion to put the King himself into my motto. None of the other Queens' mottoes mention him; I'm the first Queen to do it.

"Your motto!" he exclaims.

"Yes." Now I sit up a little straighter, as I imagine a Queen should, and I lift my chin and clear my throat.

"*No other will than his,*" I say.

"No other will . . ." he echoes.

I look at his face, and I see an expression of great tenderness.

"I could not have better chosen," he says, "Catherine, my rose, my rose."

Earlier in the day, Lady Rochford whispered to me, "He will need a deal of assistance."

I looked at her in puzzlement.

"To achieve"—she glanced around to make sure no one else was listening—"*the act of love.*"

I was very glad she told me—now I knew what to expect. I felt as perhaps the gentlemen do before a joust: Hearken to the challenge!

I know the ways of love. That's not bragging, it's honesty. For the first time since the King began wooing me, all doubt and pause vanish from my thoughts. *I can do this, and do it well.*

The King has near fifty years in age. His leg pains him terribly, and it's clearly a trouble for him to move around in bed. So I decide to move for both of us.

I start by untying my shift and slipping it off, not wanting to get it twisted or tangled. My dear King's eyes widen with lust at my nakedness. I lean over and kiss his forehead, his right eye and then his left, his left cheek, then his right. Already his hands have found my naked breasts, and he pants with pleasure.

I rub my chin on his beard and laugh at its rough tickle. He chuckles, but only briefly.

"Catherine, sweet," he pleads.

I pull off the sheet. He's wearing a fine linen bedshirt, fastened across his enormous belly with three sets of laces. I undo the first set and kiss the flesh of his chest.

The second set, untied at his belly. A longer, slower kiss, and a moan from my King.

The third set untied, I begin kissing and licking and sucking, and he moans louder. I keep on for what feels like forever—this is what Lady Rochford meant—and at last I decide that it's the right time. I quickly straddle him—as best I can, what a stretch, he's so very wide!

He grips my waist. I raise and lower myself, riding him with my thighs and buttocks, twice, thrice, and bring him to a triumphal finish: His groan at the end is as big as he is.

I'm quite winded, so I tumble to the side; it's like falling off a—a bear, or something. I look at His Majesty—no, at Henry. He's clearly in that luscious haze of afterness, but he manages a weary smile before his eyes close.

He's snoring before I get my shift back on.

AUGUST–DECEMBER 1540

The gifts I receive from His Majesty in honour of our marriage! My Lord Chamberlain can hardly tally them fast enough. Wonder and thunder, His Majesty gives me *four* estates. One belonged to his former Lord Privy Seal, Thomas Cromwell. My uncle gloats that Cromwell was executed on my wedding day, and that his head is the finest gift of all. I don't say anything, but after the Duke leaves, I rush to my stool chamber, my stomach heaving. I didn't know about this before, and am sickened to think that my happiest day should be so tainted.

But I do my best to put it out of my mind. It's not hard: All I have to do is think of that girl, the tiny sad waif who grew up with no true home of her own—and now owns lands and castles and holdings and more.

The King sends a flood of other gifts to my chambers. Jewels, dresses, furs. Clocks and music boxes. A splendid book bound in gold and studded with precious gems, on a chain to circle my waist. It's very beautiful, but—I'm sorry to say—heavy and awkward to wear. It bangs against my leg and leaves a bruise.

The Dowager and Lady Rochford tell me again and again that I have to show great appreciation for His Majesty's generosity. If a dress arrives, I'm always supposed to wear it the next time I see him. This means that I wear a new dress almost every day, sometimes even twice in a day!

It's a dreadful bore spending so many hours being clothed and unclothed and reclothed. Some of the dresses and hoods are darling, and I can't wear them again because of all the others that keep arriving. Worse yet, there are whispers at court of my greed and fickleness: that I demand a new dress every day, that I refuse to wear a dress more than once. Lies and liars—I'm helpless against such cruel gossip. My sole comfort is to remind myself that the only person at court who really matters is the King.

With him, I am succeeding beyond the Duke's largest hopes.

It is, for His Majesty, an autumn of bliss. He's so delighted by our nights that he seems to feel a renewed joy for the passions of his youth, feasting and music and the hunt. We travel from palace to palace, Windsor, Hampton, Greenwich, wherever His Majesty thinks we'll be best amused. When I'm at his side, he embraces and kisses and caresses me no matter who else is there. Bishops, ambassadors, advisors—I can't help blushing, even though they're all dried-up old tortoises.

At the holidays, the King presents me with more jewels, including a rope of *two hundred* pearls, each as big as the end of my thumb. As I admire it, I see looks passing among some of my ladies.

"What? What is it?" I ask.

"Nothing, Your Highness," says Lady Eleanor, her face a mask.

I give her and the others what I think of as my Queen stare. It's a patient-but-stern look, but I'm not very good at it yet.

Fortunately, Lady Lucy is as eager as a puppy, and answers quickly. "We were wondering, Your Highness, which other Queens have worn those pearls."

My happiness is abruptly snuffed. I look at the pearls with dismay.

But Lady Nan speaks. "I have seen His Majesty with every Queen," she says, "and never has he shown such fondness as he does for our Queen Catherine." She takes the pearls from me and drapes them around my neck. "That makes these pearls different, though they be the same."

I'm so grateful to her. Now I can wear the pearls, and love wearing them. Later I give her silk for a new dress, in blue, for she likes blue best and it suits her well.

JANUARY–MAY 1541

I don't know what it means to be Queen.

Actually, I haven't been crowned yet. There hasn't been a coronation—the Duke curses regularly over that—but the King says it's a bad time for an extravagant ceremony, he doesn't want to spend so much money. And he doesn't want to interrupt the enjoyment of our days together. I'm Queen *Consort*, and when I give birth to a son, that's when I'll become the crowned Queen.

The Duke keeps reminding me that my main task is to please the King in bed and get with child. But there must be more to being Queen. The King rules the people. The Queen cares for them. That's how Lady Nan put it to me, and I like thinking of it this way.

The Queen usually hears petitions and pleas from the people, but the Duke and Dowager say I'm too young for this. My Lord Chamberlain and his courtiers take over the task. I told the Duke that I want to hear at least some of the petitions—how am I going to learn, otherwise? But the crusty old barnacle said no. So I have to look for other ways to be useful. I want to be thought of as a good Queen, beloved by the people.

At court I learn that the Lady Margaret Pole is imprisoned in the Tower. I don't quite understand the twisted history behind her imprisonment, but what I do know is this: She's a *very* old woman, near to seventy years, and the Tower in winter is a bitter misery.

I speak to my King.

"Your Majesty, I seek your permission for an act of charity."

"Why should you, my Queen? Surely it is a matter for your almoner."

"No, for I fear it might not please you if you should hear of it from others, so I would tell you myself. I have two woollen cloaks, one with fur, and some gloves and some other warm things, and I would have them given to the Lady Margaret Pole, for she suffers dreadfully with cold in the Tower."

"What! You would succour my enemy?"

"Your Majesty, how can she be a threat to you—she's shrivelled and withered and as dried up as—as an old raisin!"

He laughs at that, and I take heart and plunge on. "Besides, such a kindness would show that you are merciful even to your enemies, a power wielded by only the wisest of rulers."

That last was said to me by my lady Nan when I asked for her advice.

I see the King's face grow thoughtful now. "I do not care for you to trouble yourself over politics," he says. "But true enough that it would not serve well to have the people feel pity or sympathy for any of the Poles."

I look at him pleadingly, and lean towards him and let my breast brush his arm as if by accident. He laughs again, not a bit fooled, then kisses the top of my head. "Do as you will, my sweet rose," he says.

I thank him with kisses, delighting in my success. And as the weeks go by, I make more requests, on behalf of three prisoners. All of them are freed, including the well-known and well-loved poet Sir Thomas Wyatt, a longtime friend of the Howard family. The court is so pleased with his release that both His Majesty and I receive much praise, me for interceding, the King for his mercy.

Yet I have to admit that there are times when being Queen is a bit of a bother. Before I married the King, I received a letter from Joan Bulmer, who grew up with me as one of the Dowager's charges. She was in great dismay, unhappy in her marriage, and she begged me to find her a place at court.

I tell the Dowager about her plight, and we arrange for Joan to become one of my chamberers. I'm happy to be able to help an old friend. Her appointment is followed by pleas from more of the girls I once knew, Margaret and Kate and Alice. All are given places in my household.

After that, the Dowager comes to me with a request. "An acquaintance of ours desires a position at court," she says.

"Yet another?" I say, with a sigh, wondering who this time.

"You will of course remember him—Mr. Francis Dereham, of late returned from Ireland."

My mouth and eyes widen in astonishment. "Mr.—Mr. Dereham! Oh, but surely—" I gasp and stammer.

His Majesty has never asked me about my past, about other lovers. My lovemaking shows plainly that I'm not a virgin, but it seems to be his preference to pretend that I never existed for any man but himself. If Mr. Dereham boasts of bedding me, that might well enrage the King, and I don't know how many times the Duke has told me that I must never, ever anger him.

"How do you say?" the Dowager asks.

I gulp in a breath. "I—I'm surprised, for I recall the circumstances under which Mr. Dereham departed from your employ. He was not . . . in your favour then."

She narrows her eyes and shakes her head. "Must everything be explained to you as to a child?" she whispers fiercely. "That is precisely why he must be given a position—in exchange for his silence."

Snipes! I see the reason for her thinking, but I still wish I could banish Dereham to a post half a world away.

He is to be assigned a position as my secretary.

When Mr. Dereham takes up his appointment, I ask for a private audience. He greets me with a correct bow. It's been more than two years since we last met. I'm startled to find that I'm moved to see him again. I welcome him to my court and wish him well. Then I gather my courage and look at him solemnly.

"Mr. Dereham, I would have you take heed what words you speak here at court," I say.

"Your Grace, I am honoured by my appointment," he replies. "I expect that your household will be a most happy place for me, and so long as it is, you need never fear."

His voice is smooth, but there's a sharp look in his eyes. I understand him perfectly. He bows again and leaves.

I feel as if I've brought an adder into my nest.

It's been months, and I'm *still* not pregnant.

I can't understand it. But my worry is nothing compared to the Duke's. He's so upset about it that he forces me to tell him everything about my nights with the King.

"He completes the act, you are certain?" the Duke asks, for the hundredth time.

I can't hold my tongue any longer. "Sir! If you doubt my word, I would invite you to witness for yourself—but I must first ask of my husband his permission!"

The Duke splutters in anger but makes no other response. From then on, he doesn't badger me quite so relentlessly.

Besides this unhappiness, the King's leg has gotten much worse. The pain puts him in a dreadful mood. Nothing I do or say can relieve him. At first he's peevish, then cross, and then angry. I know he's not really angry at *me*; still, it hurts my feelings when he growls and snaps.

But mostly I'm just worried about him. One evening I go to visit him in his privy chamber. Lord Brandon, the Duke of Suffolk and a member of the King's Privy Council, stops me in the hall.

"Your Highness," he says as he bows his head and dips his knee. "I am sorry, but His Majesty is unable to see you."

I blink in surprise and glance behind me at my ladies. "But what can you mean?" I ask.

"He requested that I convey his regrets." His voice is kind, but he hasn't answered the question.

A chill stiffens my neck. *Did Henry really say that? How can I be sure? What if he needs me, and Lord Brandon is trying to stop me seeing him? But why would he do that?*

This is what being at court does to you: I'm starting to hear things that haven't been said, and see things that might not be there.

Lady Rochford steps forwards to whisper in my ear. "Tell him you will return tomorrow. Be gracious."

"Be gracious"—when I want to flounce past him and accidentally tread on his foot . . . But Lady Rochford has told me that Lord Brandon is in great favour with the King just now, which is why I must take care. I don't know how she knows all these things, but she does.

I incline my head a little. "Thank you, Lord Brandon. I will return this time tomorrow. Will you please tell His Majesty that my thoughts are with him always, and that I wish him a good night?"

"I will, Your Highness."

He bows. I turn and go back to my rooms.

Day after day, His Majesty refuses to let me into his chambers. I get so worried that I can't sleep. How can I please the King and get with child if he won't even see me?

My ladies scurry about like clever mice, collecting bits of news.

"It's his leg," Lady Nan reports. "The ulcers have putrefied. It is not just the pain, but the terrible smell, Your Highness. He does not wish you to see him in this way."

"But I'm his wife," I say in distress. "If I can't help at a time like this, it makes me feel worse than useless!"

In desperation, I summon the King's favourite courtier, Mr. Thomas Culpeper. Upon his arrival, I notice my maids and ladies fluffing and primping; his considerable good looks have not escaped their notice.

Nor mine.

"Your Grace," he says, and bows most prettily.

"Mr. Culpeper. Will you tell me please how His Majesty does today?"

He looks around quickly, and I sense that he doesn't want to spread news of the King's ill health. I nod at my ladies and wave my hand for them to leave us.

Once we're alone, I speak firmly. "Mr. Culpeper, I am the Queen Consort. I should know of His Majesty's state, and I give you my word that what you say is between us only."

He still seems uneasy, but finally says, "I would speak of things that are—not very pleasant, Your Grace."

"You may speak plainly. I must know how he does."

"The wound on His Majesty's leg was blocked. It went black, and was grave indeed. The doctors were forced to lance it."

I feel myself grow faint, and have to grip the arms of my chair.

"Your Grace?" He leaps forwards in alarm and steadies me with a hand on my shoulder. I draw a breath, which brings me back to myself. Then I sit up straighter and shrug my shoulder a little, to signal that he should remove his hand.

He does, and steps back. "His Majesty has been in terrible pain, but the wound is draining now," he says. "He will be feeling better soon."

I thank him and ask him to return in the morning.

My poor darling Henry—once so fine and fit, the most beauteous ruler in all Europe.

Snipes and snails, I'm in such a muddle. Worried about His Majesty's health, terrified that maybe he doesn't care for me anymore, wondering when I'll get to see him again. And something else.

Something that has to do with Mr. Dereham. At court I've met a lot of gentlemen, born and raised to nobility, and now I see Mr. Dereham quite differently than when I was a girl. He's holding our past as a kind of ransom. Really, he's no gentleman.

But he has also stirred up memories of our time together, and made me realize that I'm not completely happy in my marriage.

In bed with the King, it's always about *his* satisfaction. My own doesn't seem to matter a fart or a farthing. I *never* feel what I felt when Mr. Dereham was my Francis—the breathlessness, the urgency, the wild desire.

I realize now that I miss those things, and not just a little. I miss them desperately.

On the tenth day of my not seeing the King, Thomas Culpeper visits me again at my request.

"His Majesty is feeling much better now," Mr. Culpeper says. "He requests your company this evening."

Are his eyes twinkling? Of course he knows what it means for the King to request my presence: He's one of the men who hoists His Majesty into the bed. If his eyes *are* twinkling, it's quite the cheek. I stare at him for a moment.

A pause. A breath. A stroke of silence that lasts a little too long.

Or is it only my imagination? Mr. Culpeper leaves me wondering.

That night, I work hard to please His Majesty. It's no simple trick to be gentle and tender because of his leg, while at the same time arousing him and using every wile and skill to bring him to finish. Then he falls asleep immediately, without a word or a caress or even tenderness. I remind myself that he's been ill, but it doesn't help.

I lie awake long into the night, him wheezing and snorting through his fatty jowls, me crying silently.

Back to my rooms in the morning. I'm almost finished dressing when Lady Rochford dismisses the maids and takes up the hairbrush herself.

"He is here," she says in a near-whisper.

"His Majesty?" I say with a start.

"No, not His Majesty." Her voice drops even lower. "Mr. Culpeper."

Her face is a complete blank, but I'm not fooled. She's on the hunt for secrets, which she hoards like jewels. Now I remember that she was in the room yesterday when Mr. Culpeper and I were talking.

Her gaze rests on my reflection in the glass. "Please tell him I no longer have need of his visits," I say.

"Your Grace?"

I look down at my lap. I should cut her off now, right this instant, before the conversation goes any further.

But I know what she's thinking.

"I would that the King lives longer than any man ever lived," she says. "Even so, he being so much older than you, it is not treason to expect that you will one day be a widow. You would best be prepared against the day, and certain alliances are more valuable than others, worth your trouble to cultivate now."

I close my eyes.

Whether or not I give birth to an heir, as a widowed Queen I will need a champion at court—someone to protect my interests once the King is gone. Lady Rochford is intimating that a member of the powerful Culpeper family would be suitable for the role.

She is telling me to take Thomas Culpeper as a lover.

"I would know nothing of which you speak," I say, making my voice as stern as I can. "It vexes me to repeat myself: Please see that he is dismissed."

And at last she leaves me.

I stare at my reflection, seeing the doubt in my eyes.

I don't want him for a lover, I don't! It's impossible—I mustn't think of it, not even for a second.

And from that very moment, I can think of nothing else.

JUNE–SEPTEMBER 1541

The court will travel north towards York tomorrow, for the King's progress. A spectacle, wherever we go. Hundreds will march in uniform and unison, archers with their bows drawn, banners and horses, glitter and pomp and huge crowds cheering.

But tonight, Thomas Culpeper will come to my privy chamber.

Lady Rochford has made the arrangements. Because of tomorrow's early departure, the King will not want my company this evening. I feign preparing for sleep, my hair loose around my shoulders. Lady Rochford dismisses the other ladies and maids. After they're in bed, a knock sounds. She opens the door, then slips out and stays in the next room, alone.

My plan is to speak with him, to propose that if I become a widow—without wishing for the King's death, for that would be treason!—we might have an understanding. We have to meet alone, for if we're overheard, someone might misinterpret our words; it could sound as if we're plotting against the King.

I'll say what I have to say, and then dismiss him. It will take only a few moments.

He comes into the room and bows. "Your Grace."

Candlelight flickers. His shadow dances on the wall behind him. He's not as tall as the King, but his physique is straight and strong, so unlike His Majesty's heaving tottering bulk.

I've prepared my words carefully. I open my mouth—and nothing comes out.

I stare at him as if I've never seen him before.

He's so handsome. His eyes, his lips . . .

I don't know how long I'm standing there—a moment? an hour?—before I realize that he's staring at me, too. Somehow we've moved until he's within reach. He raises his hand to touch my hair, and I close my eyes.

I'm already gasping. For a desperate moment, I'm sane enough to realize my madness, and I try to take a step back, to push him away. . . . How is it that I step *forwards* and pull him towards me instead?

He holds my face in his hands.

"Please." I can barely whisper, choked by my desire.

He lowers his head and kisses me gently, almost hesitantly. At the first touch of his lips, I'm like a starving beast—I surge against him so hard that he nearly loses his balance. He backs into my dressing table and leans on it, and I step between his legs, my hands clutching at his shoulders, my mouth on his in a frenzy that I can't control. Then he grasps my hair and pulls my head back and kisses the hollow at my throat, groaning with urgency. His lips move up the length of my neck and find my mouth again.

If the ground beneath my feet split—if there were suddenly an abyss beneath me, I wouldn't be able to tear myself away from him.

I'd fall to my death with my tongue seeking his.

In Lincoln.

In Pontefract.

In York.

We find back stairs and back doors, deserted galleries, forgotten closets. We meet for a single kiss, or for entire nights of passion. The danger of being discovered sharpens the keenness of our lovemaking.

I can't keep from him. I'm helpless, my desire a fever, raging, burning. This isn't the same as what I felt with Francis Dereham. That was a girl's first awakening, new and green and tender. The girl has grown into a woman who knows what she wants and needs. For all the enjoyment my girl-self felt, she could never have dreamt the ravishment I know now.

In a hidden alcove at York Castle, I bury my mouth in his shoulder to stifle my cries. Our bodies are fused with such heat and fervour, it's as if we're one being, and on finishing, we fall away from each other, nearly senseless.

"Zounds!" Thomas laughs ruefully as he peers at the bright beads of scarlet on his shoulder.

"Oh, no!" I've bitten him—hard—and never even knew it! I kiss the wound and lick away the blood, and then he kisses me again.

But despite the wildness of our rapture, I *never* allow him to finish inside me. *Not once.* For that would be treason of the worst kind against the King, to get with child and not know who fathered it.

I insist on this with Thomas, no matter how he pleads, and because I'm so steadfast, I convince myself that I'm fulfilling my duty of loyalty to His Majesty.

Who suspects nothing. As always, I dine with him, and sit with him in the evenings, and go to his bed whenever he asks. I'm still his rose, and I make sure that I'm always light and gay with him, to disguise my true state.

For though I want Thomas with a craving like an illness, I do love the King, my Henry. Truly I do!

OCTOBER–NOVEMBER 1541

◇·◇

We tarry in York for weeks, waiting for His Majesty's nephew, James, King of Scotland. James never arrives, which puts His Majesty in a terrible mood.

When we get back to London, I'm relieved to learn that we'll go to Hampton Court in November. The King loves that palace, smaller and warmer and more inviting than many of the others, and it's my favourite, too. I hope we'll stay to celebrate the holidays there.

One night shortly after our arrival at Hampton, Lady Rochford makes what are by now the usual preparations for a visit from Thomas. The other ladies are dismissed, and she herself will stand guard. If the evening grows too long for her, she'll wake either Joan or Kate to take her place.

I twist my hair and pin it in place, for I plan to unpin it and let it tumble free at the right moment, as part of our lovemaking. Lady Rochford is preparing the bed. I turn from the mirror to speak to her.

"Why do you do it?" I ask. I've been wondering about her for some time now.

"What?" She pretends not to know what I mean.

"Why do you help me and Mr. Culpeper?"

She risks almost as much as we do, if anyone ever finds out. I think I know the answer. She collects gossip the way a magpie collects shiny things. Having more news or knowledge than anyone else makes her feel special. Or powerful, maybe. Or both.

I wonder if she'll admit this.

A pillow in her hands, she stops what she's doing and looks at me. I'm stunned to see her face—sunken in lines of pain and shadows of sadness.

"You must know, Your Grace, that everyone believes me a traitor since—since the death of Queen Anne," she says. "I would like to have married again, but no one would have me. No one will ever have me. My only life is here at court."

She places the pillow on the bed and pulls its slip free of wrinkles. "What would become of me if I were to be turned out? It cannot happen. I must do all I can to ensure my place here. You, Your Grace, being so very young—you are my best chance. If I should serve you well, you will one day become Dowager Queen, and keep me in your household for the rest of my days."

A moment's pause. I nod. "And so I shall," I say.

We might be fools, both of us. But I'm absolutely certain that we're telling each other the truth at that moment—the truth as we believe it.

Thomas knocks then, and she leaves us.

The first snow falls at Hampton—only a few flakes, not enough to whiten the ground. But the air is crisp and clear, and those tiny bits of icy lace seem to promise a festive holiday season.

My ladies and maids are merry. We're in my presence chamber learning a dance. The Spanish ambassador has a new courtier who brought with him the latest dances popular at the court in Aragon and Castile. This one is called a canary.

It's my favourite kind of dance, with lots of lively, intricate steps. Lady Lucy was first to learn it and is trying to teach the rest of us. *One-and-two, hop clap! One-and-two, skip clap!*—we're all laughing at our bumblings and mistimed claps.

Then Lady Nan rushes into the room. "Your Grace!"

One look at her face, and I stop giggling. She looks truly alarmed! I take a step towards her.

"Nan, what is it?"

She glances over her shoulder, and before she can speak, two of the King's guards burst in without knocking. Their faces are like stone. One comes forwards while the other stays at the door.

The air in the room changes, tightens.

What is this?

"Good morning, sirs," I say. "We did not expect you—we have been dancing."

"It is no time for dancing," says the nearer guard. "We have come at the behest of His Majesty. You are to remain here in your rooms at his pleasure, until such time as he deems."

"Remain here—what can you mean?" I ask. "I am shortly to dine with His Majesty. I will speak to him of this."

I hurry to my dressing chamber to arrange my hair and my hood, slightly askew. Then I make for the door.

The guard will not let me pass. My confusion flickers into the beginnings of fear.

"I would see the King," I say. I'm trembling, but I give him my best Queen stare.

"My orders are to detain you here."

"I am sure you have misunderstood your orders!" My fear makes me shrill.

Thomas. Could the King have found out about Thomas? It must be—what else could it be?

Panic rises in my gorge. I whirl around and catch sight of Lady Rochford, who gives me a look so quick I might have imagined it.

She cries out and staggers towards the guard at the door, then goes into a swoon so he has to catch her before she falls. A ruse! It gives me the chance to throw open the door and rush from the room.

I run.

I know where His Majesty will be. It's time for him to hear Mass, as he always does, in the small chapel next to his apartments.

"Henry!" I shriek.

—*enry enry enry* echoes in the cold stone corridor.

My skirts swirl around my feet; I grab the fabric with one hand so I can run faster. I have to see him! I have to tell him that I love him!

"Henry! Henry, my lord and King!"

Behind me I hear the pounding of boots on the stone floor. I'm gasping, I can't breathe, I can hardly see.

"HENRY!"

I trip on the trailing edge of my skirt and nearly fall. The guards reach me and grab my arms, one on either side. They lift me off my feet. I writhe and twist, kick and scream.

"No, no! I must see him! I must see the King!"

They begin dragging me back towards my chambers.

"You cannot! I am the Queen! You must— HENRY! HENRY!"

My ladies are already at work.

Lady Rochford tends to me in bed. Lady Nan goes and returns. When I am recovered enough to sit up, she tells me what she's learned.

"A letter," she says, "left for the King in his pew at chapel."

"What of this letter?" I whisper.

"Its sender is unknown. It tells of a woman named Mary Hall, who knew you as a ward of the Dowager."

When I was a ward . . . Another life, another world.

"But I don't know this Mary Hall!"

"It tells, too, of her brother, a man called John Lascelles," Nan says, her brow knit in thought. "Hall would be her married name, then. You may have known her as Mary Lascelles."

"Mary Lascelles?"

Mary, the chambermaid! Who slept in the dormitory with us— who gave the key to Francis and the other young men—but it makes no sense. I've had nothing to do with her for years. She can't possibly know anything.

I start to cry again, my distress and confusion blotting out all thought.

For two days I'm so worried that my whole body aches. I don't sleep for a single second—I lie in bed with my eyes wide, my jaw sore from gritting and grinding my teeth. I send message after message to the King, with no reply.

Finally, on the third day, I get word that Bishop Cranmer will be coming to see me. He's a Reformist, in favour of the Great Bible, so he's already against my family. And me.

Oh, why can't it be Bishop Gardiner instead?

My ladies dress me carefully, in a gown of grey silk. It's modestly cut but has black sarcenet sleeves. It says that I'm sober, not frivolous— and that *I'm still Queen*. I decide to enter my presence chamber *after* the Bishop is admitted. It's a small thing—I won't make him wait, I don't want to anger him—but it will be another reminder of who I am.

He arrives in the forenoon. He doesn't bow, just tilts his head, more a twitch than a bow, as if his neck pains him. Then he nods without smiling.

Now I know for certain that this isn't a friendly visit.

"If you wish, Queen Catherine, you may choose one of your ladies to remain in the room. However, she may not speak."

I look immediately to Lady Nan. The others leave the chamber. The Bishop's man brings him a chair. We sit, and I lace my fingers in my lap.

He begins. "Do you know Mary Hall, *née* Lascelles?"

"Yes. She served the Dowager during my years as a ward."

"Do you know Master Henry Manox?"

"Yes." I tighten my fingers against each other. "He—he was the music teacher at Chesworth. And Lambeth."

"Mary Hall sends word through her brother, John Lascelles, that Manox was your lover."

"No!"

"You deny it?"

"He was never my lover! We kissed a few times, that is all."

"You are certain? Mary Hall alleges more than kissing."

I look away from him.

"Well? Was it more than kissing?"

I clear my throat. "There may have been—a time or two when I—when he touched—when he put his hand beneath my shift." I find strength in the truth. "But no more than that. He was not my lover. I was barely more than a child."

He blinks at that, and I feel I've won a small victory. But his next question makes my spine stiffen with worry.

"Do you know Francis Dereham?"

"Y-yes."

"In what way?"

"He—he was a courtier. For the Dowager."

"And he was your lover."

My thoughts are suddenly like snakes, hissing, slithering, poisonous. Yes, he was my lover, but is that a crime? It was long before I even met the King. Is Francis Dereham the reason I'm locked in my rooms?

"He—" I look at the Bishop in confusion.

"And you brought him here to court, to continue your liaison?"

"No!" I shout. Now I'm not confused at all, and I want him to know it. "Mr. Dereham came to court at the behest of the Dowager—I've hardly spoken to him since his arrival!"

He presses his lips together for a moment before he speaks again. "You should know, Queen Catherine, that we have spoken to Dereham at—at some considerable length. He has made a full and frank confession. From you we are merely seeking confirmation of what is already known."

At some considerable length. His meaning is clear: Francis Dereham confessed after being tortured.

"We were—yes." My voice drops to a whisper. "We were once lovers. *A very long time ago.*"

"Were you also husband and wife?"

I jerk my head up. "No!"

"Dereham says otherwise."

"We were never married!"

The Bishop stares at me sternly. "Queen Catherine, are you aware that if a man and a woman promise themselves in marriage and commit acts of fornication, they are considered married under the law, even if no priest be present?"

My heart beats in a wild panic. If it can be proved that I was married before, with a husband still alive and well, it would mean that I had no right to marry the King. Hiding a marriage from His Majesty—this must be the crime I'm accused of!

"Dereham says that you were promised to wed, and that he bedded you many times. He also says that before he went abroad, he left with you the whole of his life's savings. With whom would a man do that, save his wife?"

I remember Francis asking me to call him husband, and him calling me wife. I thought it was nothing but a lover's game.

"No, I swear to you, we were *not married!*"

"You were! You were espoused under the law, and you continued your liaison when he came to court!"

"No!" I'm on my feet now, my fists clenched in frustration. "If he says it, he lies! I will allow that I lay with him, but there was no marriage!"

"He gave you money, he married you—"

"No! He was not my husband. I was not his wife!"

I don't know how many hours we spend at this. Again and again, the Bishop accuses me of a prior marriage contract. Again and again, I deny it. The sun is nearly gone from the sky, and he hasn't stopped asking the same question.

I'm weeping now, in a state of exhausted despair. "No, no, no! I must speak to my King! Please tell him—tell him I beg him to see me. I have married no man but him, he is my only husband!"

I fall to my knees before the Bishop. I kiss the hem of his robe, sobbing so hard that I almost make myself sick. Lady Nan can bear it no longer. She rushes to my side as the Bishop and his man finally leave.

Lady Nan talks to everyone she knows, coming back to my rooms with shreds and scraps of whispers. The first day after the Bishop's visit, she learns that the Privy Council has issued a new law making it a treasonous crime for a consort not to tell the King about prior relationships.

"But there was no such law when I married the King! How can they do so?"

I rage against the unfairness, but in truth I'm not angry—I'm afraid. Someone wants to make very sure that I'm found guilty of a crime. It has to be the Duke's enemies: the Reformists, who want England to have its own church, not one led by the Pope. If they can topple me, the Duke and the rest of the family and the religious conservatives will come crashing down with me.

I realize then that in a way, it's not really about me. It's about men wanting to be as close to the King as they can, men wanting power. To them, I'm like a piece on a game board, to be moved as it suits them.

It makes me feel helpless—and furious at the unfairness. All this has come about because I danced at the King's wedding to Anna of Cleves. . . .

Nan learns more the next day. "John Lascelles is a Reformist," she says.

Small comfort that I guessed correctly.

Lady Nan goes on. "If the Bishop comes to question you again, you must claim mistakenness. That you were indeed contracted to marry Dereham."

"But it's not true!"

"Listen, Your Grace. Believe it if you can, the Bishop was trying to help you find your way out. If a marriage contract existed, then your marriage to the King was not legal. If it was not legal, then you were never married to him. If you were never married to him, then there was no crime committed to the marriage."

I'm so confused I can hardly think. I thought that a prior marriage would count against me, but Lady Nan is saying the opposite! Now I'm worried that I may have lost my chance.

"Lady Nan, we must get the Bishop to come back! I'll do as you say, I'll confess to a prior marriage, if only he'll let me speak to the King."

I know this about my Henry: He can be swayed if spoken to in just the right way. I'll beg his forgiveness and swear my love—he loves me, I know he does, and if I can see him and talk to him and . . . and make him laugh, this will all be just a dreadful mistake.

". . . with a prior marriage, you would no more be Queen, but nor would you be a—a criminal."

Lost in my thoughts, I haven't heard all of what Nan is saying.

"Not Queen?" I shake my head violently. "But that would be a terrible disgrace! Not just for me, but for my family. The scandal—"

She grips my hands. Her expression is more than serious—she looks terrified.

"Your Grace," she says urgently, "you must understand the nature of the charges against you. It is not a question of scandal—it's a matter of saving yourself."

Saving myself?

I stare, my mouth open in shock. *Surely she doesn't mean—it's not possible—*

During the endless, sleepless hours of the past few nights, I imagined being cast out of Henry's life. I imagined having to return to Chesworth House, stripped of my lands and holdings, first humiliated and then shunned by everyone at court. I imagined the same for all the Howards, and how they would hate me forever, for failing them.

But never once did I imagine what Lady Nan is implying now: that my fate is to be the same as that of my cousin Anne Boleyn.

I start shaking from head to toe, my teeth chattering so wildly that I nearly bite through my tongue. My knees give way, and Nan catches me as I fall.

My head aches constantly. I eat little and sleep less. The news worsens each day: The King has left Hampton Court without a word, without even a message of farewell.

On hearing this, I tear at my clothes, howling, and my ladies must force me to take a sleeping powder.

Almost every member of the Howard clan has been imprisoned, including the Duke himself. Only the Dowager was spared: When the guards went to take her, they found her abed, ill from agitation, and left her there out of sympathy for her advanced age.

Then I learn that Thomas Culpeper has been arrested. Francis Dereham named him, while being tortured a second time.

If Francis knew, then others did. Probably many others: Far easier to ask who *didn't* know than who did. How could I ever have been so clodpated, to imagine the affair a secret?

I send Lady Nan to Whitehall. She spends two days there finding out what she can.

"What news?" I demand on her return. She has come to my privy chamber; most mornings now, I don't seem to have the strength to even get dressed. "Did you see my King?"

"Only in passing, Your Grace."

"Tell me."

Nan hesitates. "He—he does not look well, Queen Catherine."

"Ill, do you mean? Is it his leg?"

"No. I do not mean sickness. His face, his bearing . . . he looks most downcast, Your Grace. Even heartbroken." A pause. "It is said that he raged first, when told of the—the latest charges."

The latest charges: my affair with Thomas.

"He swore he would kill you both himself, and demanded a sword. But then he broke down and wept, and the Council were all chagrined."

I want to tear out my heart. I've cuckolded the King. Not only that, but with his favourite courtier—a stab to his back and then a cruel and terrible twist of the knife.

But it was a crime of recklessness, not treason; I've betrayed the man, not the throne. I will be sentenced to die as a traitor, when in truth I'm only a fool.

If I could see the King, and tell him this, and beg his mercy!

The Bishop comes again. Lady Nan heard that he was moved by my emotion during our first meeting, but when I begin crying this time, it is no deliberate act. I can hardly speak for gasping as I try to tell him that I was mistaken—that I was indeed married to Francis Dereham.

If he pitied me before, there is no sign of it now. I should have known better than to hope: He has survived decades at court by means of unswerving loyalty to the King. My tears mean less than nothing to him, compared to Henry's desires.

He says that Thomas Culpeper has confessed everything, even to declaring that he would marry me once the King was dead. Under the law, this is treason: Just wishing the King dead is considered a crime equal to the act itself.

Joan Bulmer and Kate Tilney and Lady Rochford have been arrested and admitted their roles in aiding my relations with Thomas. Their confessions and his are all the evidence required. I will not stand trial. The Privy Council will seek a Bill of Attainder with Parliament—a pronouncement of my guilt without the necessity of a trial.

"You will be taken to the convent at Syon to await the passing of the bill," the Bishop says.

He has prepared for me a full and frank confession, which pronounces all my crimes against King and country. It states that I duped the King into a false marriage, and then conspired with others who wished for his death. I haven't done any of those things, but the Bishop swears to me that signing the confession is my only chance at mercy.

I sign in a fog of numbness. I can't feel the quill in my hand, and when I'm done, I can't even read my own name.

The Bishop's departure is followed almost immediately by the arrival of Lord Thomas Seymour.

"Jewels, furs, dresses, and hoods," he says coldly to my ladies.

He has come to confiscate all my queenly things.

It took just six months for His Majesty to make me his Queen.

It has taken only six *days* for him to unmake me.

DECEMBER 1541–JANUARY 1542

◇·◇

Now it is I myself, my body, to be taken away, to the convent at Syon. My body alone, for my soul wanders lost and alone in a land of terror, and I can't do a thing for it. As I leave Hampton, I'm escorted through the great hall, past the wooden screen at its entrance. I catch a glimpse of one of its carvings: an "A" and an "H" entwined in a lovers' knot. All those carvings were ordered removed after my cousin Anne's death, but this one was missed.

As I look at it; the "A" seems to twist and writhe and transform, snakelike, into a "C."

At Syon I'm given three rooms. Lady Nan is allowed to stay with me, along with three other attendants and a staff of servants. I have a fire at all times, and am given ample blankets and cloaks, a few even of fur. I am still being accorded at least some of the respect due to a Queen.

My days here are mostly quiet. I cry a lot. My ladies often cry with me. What a miserable sight we are.

The hours are so very empty, with nothing to distract me except for the occasional word that reaches us from court. Lady Nan wonders if there might be some sympathy for me, because of the sudden change of the law, and the Bill of Attainder, and because I'm so young. But I know she says this only to comfort me, for unlike Queen Katharine or Queen Anne or even Anna of Cleves, I have no champion at court. My uncle the Duke made too many enemies: There's no one to plead for mercy for me.

Lady Rochford, imprisoned in the Tower, has gone mad. The law used to say that no insane person could be put to death. So that law, too, has been changed to the reverse, and she's been sentenced to die. How convenient to be able to change the law whenever you feel like it.

One day I ask Lady Nan for news from court, as I do nearly every day.

"None, Your Grace."

But she answers too quickly, and doesn't look at me.

Then I remember the date. It is the tenth of December: the day that Francis and Thomas are to be executed. As a gentleman, Thomas will be allowed a merciful death by beheading. But Francis, a commoner, faces being hanged, drawn, and quartered.

I wake in the night screaming. I was dreaming of his agony, and of my own horror in knowing my affection to be a vile, poisonous thing: They are both dead because I loved them—Francis, because I did not know any better; Thomas, because I should have.

FEBRUARY 1542

I am no longer Queen Consort. The title has been taken from me by the Privy Council and Parliament. Still, my ladies dress me as a Queen, in black velvet. I want to leave Syon as a good Queen would, with sober dignity.

But when the guards come to take me to the Tower, something inside me shatters into pieces so sharp that I feel my insides bleeding. I shriek in pain, and struggle and flail and kick and fight with more strength than I knew I had. Finally they are forced to pick me up by my arms and legs and carry me down to the boat. I wish I could laugh at what a ludicrous sight it must be.

The boat is not an open barge, but covered, so no one will see me as it travels up the Thames. The Lord Privy Seal and some members of the Council ride in a boat in front of mine, with Lord Brandon and his soldiers behind.

My ladies comfort me as best they can, and I am calmer now for their sakes. After some time, the boat heaves and shudders, and I realize that we're passing under a bridge.

London Bridge.

I close my eyes, and swallow, and swallow again to keep from retching.

The spikes of London Bridge hold the impaled heads of executed prisoners. The bloodied heads of Thomas and Francis are there now.

I hear Francis's words in my head, telling me not to look back. I can't see outside, but I close my eyes anyway. Tears trickle out from under my eyelids, hot on my cheeks, stone cold by the time they reach my chin.

My stay in the Tower will be a short one. I make arrangements to leave what remains of my wardrobe to my faithful attendants. I wish I had something else to give them, rather than clothes full of grief and bitterness. Only a few short days ago, I was Queen of All England. . . .

The warden comes to tell me what will happen in two days. He describes the yard, and the platform, and the wooden block.

"Might I see it?" I ask.

He looks at me in puzzlement. "See what, madam?"

Madam. Not "Your Highness." Don't think I don't notice.

"The block," I say. "Could it be brought to me?"

His confusion changes to astonishment. "You wish to have the block *here?*"

No one has ever asked this before, despite the countless numbers of condemned prisoners who've been held in the Tower. The next day, two soldiers lug the solid, weighty block up the stairs. They put it on the floor in the middle of the room. I ask them to leave me for a few moments.

As I walk around it, I realize that I was wrong at Hampton Court. My fate is *not* to be quite the same as Anne Boleyn's. Her death was by sword. Mine will be by axe. She didn't put her head on this block—I'll be the first Queen ever to do that.

I remember how distressed I was leaving Syon, and I'm absolutely determined that it won't happen again. There will be people watching, and how I comport myself will be my last act on this earth.

I picture the yard and the platform in the chill clouded dawn. I imagine myself there. I practise approaching the block and kneeling. Gracefully, regally, for I was indeed once a Queen—a Queen truly beloved by her King.

One-two, one-two, step and kneel . . .

What would I do, if I could have a day or even an hour of my life again? I think about this a lot, and decide on three things.

I would make my King laugh, and hear him call me his rose.

I would forgive someone his or her sins, whether against me or against those I love.

I would dance.

HENRY VIII

I am so alone.

Teeming crowds fill the apartments of my palaces. They all plot against me. The women laugh, the men scheme. Those I do not hate, I still can't trust.

I may smile, sitting in state, but only to conceal my sorrows and to keep watch over ministers who wish me dead. I feel no joy. I, King of the English, suffer more than any other man on this island.

Curse her to Hell. I will not say her name. The Church teaches the ingenuity of devils. Where she lies now in their fiery realm, headless and screaming, may they find torments for her severed flesh as fine and keen as the pleasures she offered her lovers. Rods heated in flame. Screws dripping with blood. Hooks to rend.

This is all that can give me pleasure when my own body is wracked by its pains. My head aches like an awl hammered into my temple and eye. My legs shred themselves like the stigmata of the saints—wounds that arise from nowhere and pierce with pain. The royal blood runs freely, but not at my bidding. Ancient injuries twinge. I cannot stand or sit or lie down without suffering. The only thing that soothes me is the hope that in Hell, the same is happening to her.

I need aid to move. Once I was a shining prince; now I am stranded in a body bloated like an island kingdom, hot with distempers and assaulted by its own corruption.

I am alone, all alone in this world, and surrounded by the unsteady sea.

KATERYN PARR

"To Be Useful in All I Do"

THE ENDLESS MAZE OF DEATH

Summer 1546

It is the hand of the Lord that can and will bring me out
of the endless maze of death.
—Kateryn Parr, *The Lamentation of a Sinner,* 1547

No one can help me now.

I stand before this gleaming wooden door, unsure what fate awaits me on the other side. My husband will be there, of course, magnificent and massive. And my enemies, so eager to be rid of me, may be there, too.

They'd love to dispatch me to the Tower. At the least, they want to silence me. They prefer their women to be as still as the lavish portraits on display in the palace gallery. The last thing they want is for me to speak.

I should have seen this coming. I should have remembered that in this kingdom, Queens are dispensable, discarded as easily as a maid dumps slops from a chamber pot onto a London street.

My breath catches in my throat; my palms feel cold and damp with sweat. I wipe them on my light pink kirtle. My sister and my friend have left. I listen until I can no longer hear the rustle of their skirts or the echoes of their careful footfalls.

I am alone.

Suddenly, the air stirs. I shiver, though I'm sure it's no more than the usual draught in these halls. Or is it?

For, somehow, I sense their presence—those dead wives, my fellow Queens. I have long imagined them, wandering together. In my imagination they are lost in a maze—an endless maze of death. Perhaps my desperation has brought them to me now.

There are four: first, Katharine of Aragon, loyal and desperate, followed by crafty Anne Boleyn, who so enticed Henry with her charms. Henry as he was then, vibrant and forceful, before he became swollen with fat, his wounded leg oozing sour, stinking pus.

Next comes plain Jane Seymour, prim and virginal on her wedding night, the perfect bride, full of love or perhaps just pretending—I cannot know. And finally, the fifth wife: lusty, foolhardy Catherine Howard. (There is no Anna of Cleves, of course. She lives still, and wouldn't lift a finger to help me even if she could.)

We have all been in Henry's magnificent bed. We have felt not just the imposing presence of the man, but the sense of being engulfed by the grandeur of the bedchamber itself—red-and-gold murals, spectacular paintings. It is hard not to be awed by such power.

Power. We were, each in her own way, powerless to change our fates. That is what I think of most now. Not the lovemaking of the other Queens—but their ends.

I imagine proud Katharine of Aragon, withering to death in a cold, forgotten house. I envision Anne Boleyn, herded onto a barge to the Tower to meet her death from that silver blade, her final sharp-edged gift from Henry. I see Jane Seymour, taken at her moment of triumph—the birth of the Prince. Oh, how she must have gasped and fought as the acrid stench of hot blood and sweat rose up to swallow her like fog on the River Thames. And then there is young Catherine Howard, whose spirit still lingers in these halls. It's not so long ago that she made her own way over that same river, its waters dark as the old blood clinging to her lovers' heads impaled above on London Bridge.

For a long time, I thought I was brighter, cleverer, more beloved than these other wives. But I was wrong. In the end, I made the same

errors. I forgot that in this kingdom no woman—not even a Queen—
can be ambitious; she can never let down her guard.

She can never show her own power, be her true self.

And yet, and yet . . .

The air stirs around me. Perhaps I can draw courage from Henry's
past wives still. I might have one more chance—if I am clever and
sharp enough. I take a breath to ready myself for the battle ahead.
Then the door opens and I step inside.

AT COURT

—◇·◇—

Winter 1542–1543

Now unto my lady
Promise to her I make:
From all other only
To her I me betake.
—from "Green Groweth the Holly"
Song by King Henry VIII

It began with a song.

All eyes turned towards the singer. He drank in the attention, savouring it like a fine wine. Even in that cluster of glittering courtiers, resplendent in rich shades of velvets and silks, he lit the centre like a brilliant candle. You couldn't take your gaze from him. At least I couldn't.

His lively dark eyes sought mine. I sensed that this promise was for me. I felt something unexpected stir inside, violent as a startling burst of rain. I was no stranger to the marriage bed. But this, well, I'd never felt like this.

The melody ended; he was at my side, speaking my name: "Lady Latimer." His lips brushed my cheek; I took in his scent of spices and woodsmoke. "I hope you're well. It's a pleasure to see you here again. Your brother suggested I should look for you." Those musical tones, almost a whisper now, for my ears only.

I curtseyed, willing the flush on my cheeks to subside. I knew when I looked up I'd see a reddish beard, a handsome face with high cheekbones, dancing eyes that held an invitation. When we'd met before on my occasional visits to court, he'd always put me in mind of a sleek, saucy fox.

"You do justice to the song, Sir Thomas. I believe His Majesty wrote it?"

"Yes, though I can't claim to sing as well as Henry." Thomas Seymour flashed a sly grin, wondering if I'd caught the joke.

I had, of course. The King's voice was comically high-pitched, as if God had given a great hound the peeping squeak of a little dog, like the one Anne Boleyn had loved so well. Poor Purkoy! My sister, Nan, who'd served all the Queens, said it was rumoured that one of Anne Boleyn's enemies had tossed the tiny creature out of a window. "How awful!" I'd exclaimed. "I'm glad no will ever hate me so much."

Oh, I was so innocent then.

"I'm sorry to hear of Lord Latimer's illness," Sir Thomas was saying.

"My husband complains I hover; he suggested I come to court to bring back gossip to distract him," I replied. "And since my mother, Maud Parr, served the first Queen, Princess Mary has kindly invited me to visit.

"Lady Mary, I mean to say." I corrected myself quickly. I glanced around, hoping no one had caught my mistake. *Princess or Lady? In the line of succession or not?* It was hard to know where things stood with regard to Henry's daughters, Mary and Elizabeth.

The same, I suppose, could be said for Henry's church. Nan had tried (more than once) to explain it to me. "Sometimes the King leans towards Protestant reforms, such as allowing people to read the Bible in English. But he doesn't want too much change; he is still attached to his strict Roman ways."

"It doesn't sound as though he knows what his church should be," I'd observed.

"There's truth in that. I think it may just depend on whom Henry has spoken to last—or who can manipulate him best."

"If you ask me," Nan concluded, "these struggles over religion are less about God and more about politics: influence, wealth, and most of all, power."

Another courtier began to sing. To listen better (and keep myself from stealing glances at Sir Thomas's handsome face), I closed my eyes. But I couldn't concentrate on the lilting notes of the lute. Instead, I thought of the other advice Nan had given me.

"You must always be on your guard at court," she'd said. "The fine ladies and gentlemen you meet may preen like glossy peacocks, as colourful as the glimmering gilt-thread tapestries on the walls, but they are raptors in disguise. Always ask yourself: 'With whom am I speaking? Who is listening? Who is spying for whom?'"

I brushed her words aside. "Nan, I am no more than a minor lady at court, nor is our family influential. I doubt anyone will ever have reason to spy on me."

"Just mind what I say, Kate. Your husband is near death; you'll soon be an eligible widow again. But you married John quickly after your brief first marriage. You've never been a single woman alone at court before."

"Well, as a twice-married woman, I don't think I have to worry too much about attracting a man's attention."

Nan had raised her eyebrows, a habit she'd picked up from our uncle William, who'd been like a father to us when our own had died.

"You're good at reading books, Kate. But at court you must learn to read people."

As the last, sweet notes of the lute faded away, I opened my eyes. To my surprise, King Henry was bearing down on me with all the force of a runaway cart on a London road. Sir Thomas was nowhere in sight.

All men must stand aside for the King, I thought.

"Lady Latimer, we are delighted to welcome you!" King Henry

boomed, beaming down from his great height and over his even greater girth. His face might be as broad and pale as a potato, but those blue eyes were still keen. Now they sparkled with pleasure, as if someone had just placed a delectable dessert before him.

"Thank you, Your Majesty," I managed, curtseying deeply and kissing the ring on the hand he extended to me.

I accepted the King's sympathies for my husband's illness, and breathed out in relief when he moved on. It was true what I'd heard: His leg did stink.

Poor old man, I thought.

In the six years since Jane Seymour's death, King Henry had become a lumbering, grumbling bear. People said it had to do with that old, festering wound. But I wondered: Was the King eating so much simply to make up for a hole in his heart that no other woman could ever hope to fill?

But then, with a little shrug, I forgot about Henry VIII and began to look around for Sir Thomas.

BLACK TAFFETA, RED STRAWBERRIES

◇·◇

Spring 1543

My Lady Latimer, Item. For making a kirtle, black taffeta.
—Tailor's bill, gift for Lady Latimer from King Henry VIII,
February 16, 1543

When the bitter, dreary cold began to lessen its grip, my husband at last found peace. I was only thirty years old, but for the second time in my life I was a widow.

Yet though I wore black, my spirits grew lighter each day. Spring was on its way. Winter jasmine would soon give way to forget-me-nots, tulips, and roses. We would dip red, luscious strawberries into fresh cream.

"Have you been flirting with courtiers while I've been away?" Nan teased one day. She'd been gone for several weeks, tending her little boy through an illness.

We were strolling in the gardens of Hampton Court, where the first spring blooms had already braved the cold. But it was the spectacular field of daffodils we had come to see, rippling before us in golden waves.

It was almost, I thought, as if King Henry could command Nature to put on a grand display, just as he could order the finest artists and craftsmen to transform each room of the palaces he owned into a spectacle of rich, vibrant colours from floor to ceiling.

"Well, a little," I admitted with a giggle, "especially with Thomas Seymour, who seems as eager to flirt as I am. But it's too soon to think of anything more than banter. Perhaps when I am out of mourning and stop wearing this black kirtle."

"By the way, that *is* a lovely gown, Kate."

"Isn't it? The midnight taffeta cloth was a gift from the King."

Nan turned wide eyes on me. "Truly?"

"Yes, the package arrived just before John died. I thought it a kind gesture, a sign that Henry had completely forgiven him for becoming entangled in that failed northern revolt a few years ago."

I shuddered, thinking of the night when an unruly mob had stormed our castle and taken me hostage, forcing my husband to take their side in that ill-fated rebellion called the Pilgrimage of Grace. We'd both been lucky to survive.

But Nan was frowning, a sceptical look on her pretty face. "Kate, while I was away, did you speak often with King Henry?"

"We've chatted several times when he has visited Lady Mary's rooms," I said. "Last week he was telling me all about his library at the Palace of Whitehall. Imagine! It has more than nine hundred books. I suppose reading is more important than ever to him. It must be hard for a man who had been so active to adjust to walking with a stick."

To my surprise, Nan grabbed my elbow and began whispering urgently. "Stop chattering, Kate."

"What's wrong?"

She steered me onto a side path. "Listen to me. King Henry doesn't just give presents to married women, even if their husbands are not long for this world. Nor did he used to visit Lady Mary often.

"I believe the King is singling you out. And there can be only one reason for his attention: He wants to marry you."

I felt suddenly light-headed and queasy. I took a long breath and willed myself to be calm. "You're wrong, Nan. You *must* be."

"Let's examine the evidence." Nan had a logical mind. If she'd been born a boy, she might have been a lawyer, like Thomas Cromwell. "Besides books, what else have you and Henry talked about?"

"Well, last week the King said he'd heard I was an excellent herb-alist," I replied. "He asked if I could suggest a tea to help him sleep at night because . . . because he was so lonely sleeping alone."

Sleeping alone.

Nan was silent. And in that silence the true implication of King Henry's words became clear, the way a candle reveals hidden forms in a dark room.

"But, Nan, this can't be. Why would King Henry choose me?"

"Kate, you are lovely, virtuous, and, it would seem, very sympathetic to him."

"It's true I've tried to cheer him," I said. "But that is *all*. Besides, everyone knows Henry wants another son. I . . . I've been married twice, and have never been able to conceive." My voice broke. "It . . . it must be God's will that I am barren."

Nan patted my hand. "Perhaps Henry believes he can succeed where your other husbands failed."

Now it was my turn to raise an eyebrow at her. "But look at the size of him. It hardly seems likely that—"

She cut me off. "Henry is still a king, and will always see it as his royal duty to beget male heirs. He certainly tried with Catherine Howard." She paused, looking deep in my eyes. "What would you do if the King asked you to marry him, Kate?"

I glanced away. My gaze fell on the sumptuous gold of the daffodils around us. "Oh, Nan, what *could* I do?"

That is what we said. The next day, more gifts from the King arrived.

O MY HEART!

◇·◇

Summer 1543

O my heart! and O my heart,
It is so sore!
Since I must needs from my Love depart;
And know no cause wherefore!
—"O My Heart"
Song by King Henry VIII

My bridegroom gave forth a hearty "Yea!" when Bishop Stephen Gardiner asked if he would take me for his wife. My own voice was steady, despite my pounding heart. And so on July 12, 1543, at Hampton Court Palace, I became the sixth wife of Henry VIII.

Afterwards, I retreated to a corner, trying to breathe in the stifling air of the Queen's Holy Day Closet, a small section within the Chapel Royal. I found myself staring up at the magnificent blue-and-gold ceiling, entranced by the detail and the brilliant colours. It made me wish I could look down at the scene from above, rather like one of the cherubs. Instead, I found myself the centre of attention and perhaps the object of ill will and envy.

Certainly, Henry's fourth wife, Anna of Cleves, had greeted me coolly. As she eyed me over her long, pointed nose, I could almost hear her thinking: *Henry would have been better off coming back to me.*

"I don't think Anna of Cleves likes me," I confided to my lively new lady-in-waiting, Cat Willoughby.

"Don't worry about *her*," Cat whispered. "But do watch out for those two over there, bending the King's ear as usual: Thomas

Wriothesley and Bishop Gardiner. They are suspicious of anyone who comes between Henry and them—especially a clever wife they fear they can't control. They want him under *their* influence alone."

She leaned closer, a mischievous expression on her face. "I've named my new spaniel Gardiner, just so I can have the pleasure of calling him to heel."

"Oh, Cat, I hope Bishop Gardiner doesn't find out!" I laughed.

Later, of course, I would come to realize that Gardiner had his ways of knowing everything that happened at court. At sumptuous dinners in the great hall, I'd sense his prying eyes on me. But when I turned to look, all I saw were the faces in one of Henry's tapestries, their golden threads shimmering in the candlelight. *Don't be foolish, Kate,* I'd tell myself. *Those embroidered men aren't watching you.* Still, I couldn't shake the feeling that Bishop Gardiner was always hovering just over my shoulder.

The smallest guest at my wedding turned out to be my favourite. Henry's youngest daughter was almost ten, with a surprising shock of red curls atop her thin face. But as Elizabeth made me a sweet, formal speech, I noticed her sharp brown eyes following her father longingly.

On an impulse, I bent down and took both her hands in mine. "Elizabeth, I hope I can be a true stepmother to you."

The girl looked at me blankly.

Poor thing, she hardly understands what a mother is, I thought. *She just wants to be loved.*

I'd known not to expect young Prince Edward, since Henry preferred to keep his five-year-old son away from court for fear of plague. But as I accepted Lady Mary's congratulations, I vowed to give all three of Henry's children as much of a family life as I could.

"If only Mother had lived to see this day," Nan said. "Look at Uncle William, strutting like a rooster back on his country estate. I heard him boast, 'My niece has been chosen because of her grace and virtue—not because of family scheming like some of the other Queens.'"

The other Queens. I'd felt the presence of Henry's dead wives all day. Lady Mary was a reminder of her mother, Katharine of Aragon; Princess Elizabeth of Anne Boleyn. And when I looked at Sir Thomas's brother, Edward Seymour, I thought of his sister Jane's brief marriage and early death.

But then, of course, part of Jane was even closer: Everyone knew Henry had ordered her heart buried beneath the stone altar of the Chapel Royal.

Despite the heat, I gave a little shiver. I couldn't help but wonder what else might lurk beneath the sumptuous, spectacular beauty of this place. It didn't take much imagination to sense the spirit of Catherine Howard. Less than two years ago, she'd run through the tapestry-lined halls, desperate to reach Henry to plead for her life. The guards had dragged her back; she never saw her husband again.

"Henry doesn't like good-byes of any kind. And once he turns against someone, he puts that person out of his mind completely," Nan once told me. "It's as if he's out riding. When he rounds a bend in the road, he never turns in the saddle to look behind him."

That won't happen to me, I resolved, eyeing the colossal figure of my new husband across the room. Anyone would have picked him out for a king. It wasn't just the erect posture, the greying beard, the ermine trim on his embroidered doublet. Henry projected power as mesmerizing as the shining gold on the ornate ceiling overhead.

Catherine Howard had been foolish to cross him. She'd flitted through life like a butterfly, heedless of the great wind that would tear her wings to pieces. I'd never behave so recklessly.

Or would I? I wondered. *Would I be just as tempted to let my heart rule my head if Thomas Seymour were here today?* Thomas wasn't even in London. Henry had sent him off to a post in the Netherlands.

Thomas and I had not dared to say good-bye; letters would have been too dangerous. There had been one long look across a room; he'd lifted his shoulders ever so slightly. I'd turned away.

All men must step aside for the King. And all women must bow to his will.

Just as I had done.

"Sire, you do the Parr family and me a great honour," I'd murmured when the King called me to his rooms and proposed. "May I have a few days to discuss this with my uncle William?"

Annoyance had shadowed the King's face. "Surely your uncle will not object! He fought loyally with me twenty years ago in France. Yet you hesitate, Lady Latimer?"

"It is a courtesy only, Your Majesty," I said, mustering my sweetest smile. "He has long been like a father to me."

Henry relaxed and pulled me towards him, planting a wet kiss on my lips. As he did, I caught a whiff of his vile wound. *God help me!* I thought, trying not to gag.

"Imagine the jewels you'll have," my sister consoled me later, when I shared the news. "Though I must warn you, Kate, it's quite likely that most of the gifts you receive will have once belonged to another of Henry's Queens."

I shrugged. "Well, at least I'll be able to order new clothes. I'll dress my minstrels in scarlet and provide my footmen with velvet cloaks of crimson. I shall keep brightly coloured parrots, too. You know how much I love paintings. I think I'll have my portrait painted wearing a red gown!" I smiled at the prospect. "Most of all, I'm excited about being able to buy books. I'll have them bound in leather and velvet and encrusted with sparkling stones."

"As Queen, you will be able to make your library as dazzling as the courtiers who surround you. But, Kate . . ."

"I can guess what you're about to say—that I must look beyond the rich exterior to read what is contained within." I reached over and took my sister's hands. "Nan, I know how to be a wife. But I don't know court as you do. I can make the King's eyes sparkle as he watches me dance a galliard with ease, but can I also make elegant conversation with diplomats? How can I suddenly learn to be Queen?"

Nan squeezed my hands to reassure me. "Do not fret, dear Kate. I promise to help you. And, remember, as Queen you can do much good for causes you care about—like education. You can be useful."

"Useful?" I repeated. "You've given me an idea! I'll propose this to Henry as my motto: 'To be useful in all I do.'"

TO FOLLOW HIS WILL

◇·◇

Summer and Fall 1543

God . . . made me renounce entirely mine own will,
and to follow His will most willingly . . .
—Kateryn Parr to Thomas Seymour, 1547

I knew the King would want me in his bed, or he would come to mine when the mood struck him. So one of my first acts as Queen was to order fine perfumes, as well as three pounds of sweet herb packets and flower sachets to place around my bed at Hampton Court.

"That's rather a lot," remarked Lady Jane Wriothesley. "Might there be a particular reason, Your Highness?"

I'd had to invite Lady Wriothesley to serve in my household because her husband was one of Henry's top advisors. But if this lady thought she could trick me into an indiscretion, she would be disappointed.

"Why, Lady Wriothesley, just this morning I heard you complain about the odour of roasting game from the kitchens below," I replied with a honeyed smile. "Surely no woman wants to greet her beloved husband smelling like a goose."

I was determined to perform my duty as a wife. If I did my best, I hoped I might yet conceive a child.

However, I soon discovered that Henry often had difficulty performing his duty as a husband, despite my most energetic and determined attempts to arouse him. Still, he never guessed that I feigned my pleasure or that my stomach roiled at the sight and smell of acrid, yellow pus on fine linen sheets. He never suspected that his grease-stained face and fingers robbed me of my appetite, or that his sour breath destroyed any desire to kiss his lips.

Henry never knew that when his heavy breathing turned to snores, I sometimes lay awake in the darkness and dreamt of Thomas Seymour.

Soon after we were married, plague broke out in London. The contagion consumed neighbourhoods like a rampaging fire. In one household after another, people broke out in tumours that soon turned into deadly black spots. Henry feared the Black Death and insisted on fleeing the city. And so we spent the rest of the summer and fall at his hunting manors in the countryside.

Away from the intrigues of court, we got a chance to know each other. And, rather to my surprise, a sweet affection began to grow between us. Often we spent evenings reading, enjoying the late-summer light. "Kate, there is a passage that intrigues me in this book," Henry would say. "Come sit on my lap and let me hear you read a little."

Though Henry could no longer hunt on horseback, he'd had stands built in the deer parks from which we could shoot, peering out into a dappled puzzle of green. We'd stroll through sweet-smelling meadows and spend long hours in the woods, speaking in whispers so as not to disturb any game. Henry seemed especially delighted with my talent as an archer.

"Good shot, sweetheart!" he exclaimed one day. "Your uncle William taught you well."

Henry turned to Bishop Gardiner, who'd come out from London with Thomas Wriothesley to consult him on royal business, especially England's disputes with Scotland and France. "You see, Bishop, I have found a wife who is intelligent and wise, and has the skill of Diana."

"Then you must be careful, Your Majesty, not to displease her lest she train her bow on you," Gardiner said.

I smiled, though his words sent a chill through me. "My bow will always be in service to my master, Bishop Gardiner, as I am sure yours is, too."

On our return to the manor, Wriothesley hung back to talk to Henry, while Gardiner fell into step beside me. "The King tells me you are quite a scholar, and interested in religious studies."

"I had a good education, Bishop, and am always seeking to improve my mind. I have just undertaken the study of Latin, to add to my knowledge of Greek."

I saw Gardiner frown; I doubted he would approve of any woman, even a queen, learning another language.

He was still frowning when I decided to shoot my own arrow. "And of course, I shall take a special interest in the education of my stepchildren," I said coolly. "I am sure Henry will welcome my advice, especially to ensure that Prince Edward receives a liberal education. Why, the Prince and I may even exchange letters in Latin as we learn together."

Bishop Gardiner shot me a dark glance under his lidded eyes. He had caught my hidden meaning. I would choose forward-thinking scholars who favoured reform.

Gardiner would, I knew, prefer to select conservative tutors for Prince Edward—teachers he could control. Though Gardiner had been instrumental in securing Henry's divorce and break with Rome, he was suspicious of taking reforms too far.

"Are you sure that is wise, Your Grace?"

Before I could respond, the King and Wriothesley joined us. Gardiner took his leave with a slight bow. "I look forward to hearing more of your ideas, Your Highness."

"Oh, yes, you will both be quite impressed. My Kate is brilliant!" Henry beamed. I leaned under my husband's protective arm and smiled at them serenely.

So long as I stood close to Henry, I knew Wriothesley and Gardiner could not touch me.

As we strolled to the manor in the glow of the late-afternoon sun, Henry reached for my hand to kiss it. "What an enjoyable day, Kate."

"Have I truly pleased you, sire? If so, I wonder if I may ask two favours."

"What? You don't have enough jewels, sweetheart?" Henry's blue eyes narrowed.

"It's nothing like that, husband!" I laughed and squeezed his arm. "No, it's simply that I hope you'll allow me to help guide the education of Edward, and Elizabeth, too. Perhaps we could discuss suitable tutors together."

"Why, yes, of course. And the second matter, Kate?"

I took a breath. "I . . . I wonder, Henry if we might have all three with us for the holidays for a family Christmas." I knew that while Mary had rooms at court, Edward and Elizabeth lived in separate households, under the care of others entrusted with their upbringing.

"A family Christmas," Henry repeated. "So you sincerely desire to be their stepmother, Kate?"

I nodded. "My fondest wish is to bear you a son someday. But I also pledge myself to being a loving mother to all three of the royal children."

"And so you shall be!" Henry squeezed my hand and teased, "And perhaps, wife, we can turn our attention tonight to the prospect of your becoming a mother."

I laughed—and, to my surprise, it was a genuine laugh.

By the time we returned to court in late fall, I'd lost my early fears of Henry—and of being Queen. I felt freer to share my opinions with my husband, and to speak my mind on the role of universities, foreign affairs, the education of his children—and, of course, religion.

I also began to make my own mark on Hampton Court. For the public reception room, I designed an elaborate mantel and six gorgeously painted panels incorporating my initials. And, rather than gossip, I established debate, learning, and discussion as the norm in my household.

"You look lovely tonight, Kate. Those milk baths you take certainly do seem to make your skin glow," said Nan, about six months after my marriage. Henry wasn't well and had left me in charge of entertaining a Spanish duke.

Nan arranged the folds of cloth behind me. "This gown of crimson satin and brocade becomes you. But be careful not to trip on the long train."

I looked at my sister and grinned. "I would have stumbled long before this without you, dearest Nan. How can I thank you?"

Nan reached over my elaborate costume to whisper in my ear. "Just keep the King happy, Kate. And stay alive."

A WELL-MANAGED BOLDNESS

◇ · ◇

Summer 1544

A well-managed boldness is the virtue of monarchical courts . . .
—William Parr, Lord Horton, Kateryn Parr's uncle

"Kate, I have something to ask you," said Henry one evening as we sat on a bench in the gardens of Hampton Court. "And I think it is something that will please you."

"You know my motto, sire: 'To be useful in all I do.'" I smiled and put my book in my lap. The scent of roses drifted on a light breeze. The daffodils were long past, but I realized we were not far from where Nan and I had been the previous spring. How much had changed!

My husband and I were alone, a rare occurrence of late. Whenever we were together, Wriothesley and Gardiner seemed to be underfoot. *Plotting,* I thought. *Those two are always plotting.*

In addition, Henry had been consumed by an escalation in conflicts between England and our neighbours. He was determined to control Scotland, and when France gave aid to the Scots, he had decided to retaliate and capture the French city of Boulogne. The prospect of riding off to battle again had energized him.

"Kate, I'd like you to be in charge—to serve as regent—while I am away in France this summer," Henry announced. His blue eyes twinkled: He knew this request would delight me.

I gasped and Henry grinned, showing me a glimpse of the young, vibrant leader he must once have been. "Now, sweetheart, don't get too excited. The campaign shouldn't take more than the summer, and I will want my throne back when I return," he teased. "But you have a sound head on your shoulders, and good men here to advise you. I won't worry at all."

"Husband, it is the highest honour you could have bestowed on me," I said. "And I promise to be worthy."

I admit I was excited by the prospect of being in charge of all England. Though it was also a serious responsibility, since part of my duties would be to keep the country free of invaders.

But my first act as regent had nothing to do with politics. While the younger children usually lived with their guardians and households away from court, I brought Elizabeth and Edward to Hampton Court Palace for the summer. I had a particular reason for doing so.

"Prince Edward has been trained to rule since birth," I told Nan and Cat one evening as we strolled through the gardens, with Gardiner sniffing at our heels. "But now that Parliament has passed a new Act of Succession, it's possible that Mary and Elizabeth could sit on the throne someday."

"Does Henry know you are bringing all three children here?" asked Nan.

"Yes, I told him I would watch over them while he is gone."

"But I expect you didn't tell him exactly why you're so keen to have the girls with you," said Cat. "And then there is Gardiner."

Her spaniel paused in his exploration of a hedge and barked at hearing his name.

"What about Gardiner?" I whispered.

"I heard that when the King proposed making you regent, Gardiner spoke against it. He does not like your growing influence with Henry. And I am sure he is troubled by the prospect that you might 'infect' the royal children with your reform-minded religious views."

"Let him stew." I shrugged. "Clearly, my husband trusts me in all things. And the fact is, Henry's daughters have never seen a woman at the helm before. I want them to see one now."

And so they would.

Mary and Elizabeth watched as I read dispatches, listened to advisors, and then made my own decisions. They saw me give orders—orders that sometimes seemed to anger the men around me—especially Thomas Wriothesley and Bishop Gardiner.

When Henry wrote asking for two thousand spades, shovels, and mattocks for use in digging trenches for the assault, I announced to my advisors that I would arrange for a man in my household, Sir Robert Tyrwhitt, to get the tools made and loaded onto vessels.

"Are you sure Your Majesty wishes to be troubled by this matter?" Gardiner asked, casting a glance at Wriothesley from his deeply hooded eyes.

"I would be happy to handle this for you," added Wriothesley.

"Gentlemen, the King entrusted me with this task, and I am quite capable of seeing that it is done to his satisfaction," I told them firmly.

"But—" began Gardiner.

"That is the end of the matter, Bishop," I reprimanded him. "Let us now take up the next piece of business."

Bishop Gardiner flushed with embarrassment.

Later, I mentioned the incident to Nan. "Perhaps you should have tried to flatter him," she said with a frown.

Just as I predicted, in September the King returned to England victorious. After he landed, I set out for Kent without the children. I wanted to meet him on his journey to London to assure him the realm was at peace.

As we parted, Elizabeth gave me a rare hug. She was just eleven, bright as an autumn day, with lively brown eyes and burnished red-gold hair. "Someday, I want to be a Queen like you, Mother," she whispered.

"We can't know the future, Elizabeth," I replied softly. "But if it's

God will that you sit on the throne, it won't be merely for a short time as regent. It will be your life's work."

After that, I signed no more letters as Kateryn the Queen Regent. But I didn't forget the thrill of action, the self-confidence I'd gained in my own abilities—and my conviction that in Henry's eyes, I could do no wrong.

It would prove to be a dangerous mistake.

SO FAR TO FALL

◇·◇

1545–1546

When we were girls, Nan and I often stayed with Uncle William's family. Our four girl cousins kept dogs, horses, pet birds, and cats. I especially recall a kitten named Ginger that loved climbing trees. Claws outstretched, she'd venture higher and higher, until suddenly she'd look down and wail piteously.

In the year after I served as regent, I became a bit like Ginger. I forgot how far I was from solid ground—and just how far I could fall. Instead, I climbed higher.

I convinced Henry to increase his support for universities, and continued to make my household a centre for learning and religious studies. My ladies and I read Scriptures aloud, debating their meaning and their role in our lives.

And, like the headstrong, overconfident Ginger, I sometimes forgot myself, chasing after ideas and enjoying the thrill of debate when I was with Henry and his advisors. I was full of my own power, secure in the knowledge that my husband loved me not just for my body, but also for my mind.

And then I climbed even higher still: I began to write.

Nan came upon me in my privy chamber on the very afternoon I'd ordered more parchment. Like a cat presented with a bowl of cream, I was almost purring with contentment.

She cocked her head and looked at me quizzically. "Whatever are you doing, Kate, with that foolish smile on your face?"

"I've begun a great project, Nan," I began, unable to contain my excitement. "Now that I am better at both Latin and Greek, I shall publish a book: my own translations of psalms and prayers into English.

All of Henry's people should be able to read the Word of God in their own language.

"And if this goes well, I just may write a book containing my own prayers and reflections on how to follow the Word of God."

"Translating Scripture may be acceptable, but publishing your own prayers?" Nan's face grew pale. "Does Henry know?"

I brushed her qualms aside. "No, but we often discuss Scriptures when we are together. I'm sure he will be proud to have such an accomplished and educated Queen."

I was trying not to think about a remark Bishop Gardiner had recently made. He and Wriothesley had been in Henry's rooms with me when the discussion turned to the importance of having the Bible available in English.

"I allowed it so that citizens might read the Word of God directly," Henry said. "But now I hear they are arguing about the meaning of Scriptures on the streets, and even in taverns."

"Surely, sire, that is a good thing!" I exclaimed. "For how are your people to understand religion if they do not debate and discuss its meaning?"

Gardiner admonished me in a stern voice. "The people should look to their King and bishops to understand religion, Your Highness."

"But—" I began, eager to engage in the argument.

And then Henry cut me off. "Exactly right, Bishop, exactly right," he declared in a loud, commanding tone. He glared at me and waved a swollen hand in my direction. "Kate, it is better if you leave us now. My leg pains me and I must rest."

Now I shook off the memory, assuring Nan, "Remember, Henry made me regent. I have his full trust and confidence."

* * *

Perhaps I was only reassuring myself. Perhaps I should have realized that there were limits to Henry's admiration and tolerance of
a strong, capable woman. And perhaps I should have also realized I
was always being compared to another Queen, an ideal wife who had
been gentle and self-effacing.

For soon after that incident, Henry invited me to see a new painting he'd commissioned. I loved art and smiled in anticipation as I entered the gallery on the King's arm.

"Isn't it marvellous?" he cried. "It's a good likeness of the Prince,
don't you agree?"

I managed to stammer, "It . . . it is a memorable portrait of your
dynasty, sire."

"Yes, indeed! You are transfixed, are you not?"

"Entirely." I was, though not for the reason he thought.

The large, magnificent painting depicted Henry seated under a
canopy rich with symbols of his reign, his arm draped across young
Edward's shoulders. Mary stood on the far right, Elizabeth on the
left. Both seemed barely in the picture.

And seated demurely at the King's side was his Queen.

But it wasn't me, his living wife, who had brought him closer to
his children. Not me, whom he had named regent. Not me, his intel-
lectual equal. Not me. Not me.

"Dear Jane. The artist has captured her well," Henry whispered
fondly with a sigh, placing a hand on his heart.

Dear Jane.

In November of 1545, I published my own translation into English
of Latin prayers, and hoped that Henry would be proud. To display
her own skill at languages, Princess Elizabeth translated my book
from English into Italian and French.

"I shall present it to Father for a New Year's gift," she told me, showing me her work. Her face had lost that haunted look I'd first perceived at my wedding. "Mother, do you think he will be pleased?"

"He'll be delighted," I told her, though I doubted Elizabeth would ever receive the love she craved from her father.

I felt sure Henry could never look at Elizabeth without recalling her mother, Anne Boleyn. He couldn't truly *see* that Elizabeth was already brilliant, driven, and ambitious—just like him.

Henry would never realize that Elizabeth was his true heir.

The truth is that Henry never commented on Elizabeth's gift—or, indeed, my own book. As the new year of 1546 turned to spring, Henry's leg grew worse than ever; he was often in pain. We were together less frequently, and rarely alone. His advisors and councillors clung to him like leeches.

One evening, the discussion in the King's room turned to a passage in the Bible. I listened for a while, and gave my opinion, which none of the men seemed to hear—not even my husband.

Henry spoke again. Frustrated at being ignored, I blurted out, "But, sire, if you read this Scripture more carefully, I think you will see that my interpretation is correct."

Henry's face turned red. I caught a gleam in Gardiner's hooded eyes.

Dr. Thomas Wendy, the king's physician, whom I counted as a friend, rose quickly. "I . . . I think it is time for His Majesty's medicine and for me to dress his leg. Perhaps, Your Highness, you should retire."

Hastily, I stood and planted a kiss on Henry's brow. "Of course. Sleep well, husband."

He did not reply. As I left the room, I felt his cold, pale eyes boring into my back, and I shivered under his stern gaze.

THEY LEAP AT ME LIKE DOGS

◇·◇

Summer 1546

They leap at me as it were so many dogs . . .
The companies of the wicked bark at me.
—Kateryn Parr

When the storm broke, it was violent. One afternoon, a few days later, while Nan, Cat, and I were reading by the window of my privy chamber, a young servant appeared in the doorway.

I beckoned the boy close. "You assist the court physician, Dr. Wendy, isn't that right?"

"Yes, my name is Gregory." He reached into his doublet.

For a moment I thought he might have found a wounded bird for me to care for, but instead, he pulled out a folded parchment. "Dr. Wendy asked me to show this to you."

"Such a mystery!" I said lightly, reaching for the paper. After scanning the words, I gave it back, hoping the boy didn't notice my shaking hand. "Please bid your master to come here."

"Kate, what is it?" Nan asked when he had gone.

"It's a warrant for my arrest," I said. "And it's been signed by the King."

We waited in shocked silence for Dr. Wendy. For some reason, my thoughts kept straying back to that wild, dark night when I had survived a mob of men who had threatened my life. *Steadiness saved me then, it will save me now*, I told myself.

My voice was calm when I greeted the doctor. "Let me be frank, sir. I believe my husband is playing at some game, though I don't understand it. What do you know about this business?"

Dr. Wendy cast a glance over his shoulder at Nan and Cat.

"You may speak openly," I assured him.

"Your Highness, it began the recent evening after . . . after you and the King had a heated debate."

I nodded. "Go on."

"Uh, yes . . . well, after you left, King Henry complained to Bishop Gardiner that it seemed to him you were becoming increasingly . . ."

"Outspoken and bold?" Nan suggested.

"Just so." Dr. Wendy nodded, looking relieved he hadn't had to speak the words himself. "The King grumbled that it was a fine thing to have his own wife trying to teach him and taking part in discussions so vigourously."

"We can imagine what happened next," put in Nan. "That one complaint was all Gardiner needed to take the next step. He must have convinced the King that you should be investigated. He wants to prove that you are taking reforms too far, beyond what is allowed." Nan began to pace, as her logical mind worked out the cause and effect. "And, of course, the timing is perfect. Gardiner wants to shore up his own power."

"What do you mean, sister?"

"Oh, Kate, take your eyes from your books and look around! The King's health has been declining—his leg is poisoning his entire body. Gardiner is looking ahead to what will happen after he dies. That snake wants to discredit you and other reformers now, to strengthen his conservative faction at court."

Cat nodded. "Nan has got it exactly, Kate. He doesn't want to take the chance that the King will put you in charge as regent if he dies while the Prince is still young. So Gardiner is trying to get rid of you. He has persuaded King Henry you must be stopped."

Dr. Wendy held up his hand. "Not *quite* persuaded, my dear

ladies. For while it's true that Gardiner and Wriothesley have a warrant, King Henry isn't entirely sure he wants to go down this path."

"What do you mean?" I asked.

"I suspect the King has become rather weary of ridding himself of wives and having to find new ones. Nor is he entirely sure he wants to retreat from all the reforms that have taken place in the break from Rome. In other words, the King doesn't trust Gardiner entirely, either. He has always excelled at playing off one faction against another.

"And so King Henry slipped me this arrest warrant, tucked inside a medical book he suggested I read," Dr. Wendy went on. "I shall return the book and the warrant without a word, but I have no doubt he meant for me to warn you, Your Highness. I believe your husband is challenging you, like a knight throwing down a gauntlet."

Despite my fear, I smiled a little. "Dr. Wendy, when my sister and I were girls in the country, we loved to play at being knights. I shall accept this challenge. But I cannot ride blindly into battle." Now it was my turn to pace. "Gardiner and Wriothesley are already mounted, lances at the ready. They want to run me down. We must act. But how?"

"Your Grace, you do wield one weapon rather well."

"And what would that be, Dr. Wendy?"

"Words!" exclaimed the doctor. "Your Highness, perhaps the right words can convince the King you are a loyal wife who follows his lead in all things—including what to think about religion."

Cat nodded thoughtfully. "Could you write the King a pleading letter begging his forgiveness?"

"No!" Nan cried sharply. "Remember Katharine of Aragon and Anne Boleyn: Henry didn't care a whit about their letters. And think about Catherine Howard: Henry may already have posted guards against you—just as he did her."

Suddenly, I thought of Henry's painting. There was only one Queen who could help me now.

"Queen Jane," I said. "I must become like dear, plain, faithful Jane. I must bring the King to me."

I looked at my sister. "Do you understand?"

" 'Bound to obey and serve': the motto of Queen Jane," Nan said softly, nodding.

"But . . . but how can I possibly be like Jane?" I asked desperately. "How can I . . . ?"

Cat turned to Nan and whispered in her ear. I could only make out her final words: "Now! It's the only thing."

The next instant, Nan rushed towards me in a swirl of skirts. Raising her hand, she slapped me—first on one cheek, then the other.

"What are you doing? Stop!" I stumbled back, my hand to my face.

But Nan didn't stop. She dug her fingers into my shoulders and shook me hard. I tried to break free, but she wouldn't let go. I felt a wave of terror rise up from inside. I cried out again, louder now, "Stop this!"

"No! You must scream to save yourself!" Nan's face was so close to mine I could make out gold flecks in her hazel eyes. "Scream so hard and for so long you make yourself sick, Kate—so ill and distraught that Dr. Wendy must send for your husband to comfort you—just as he would comfort his own dear Jane.

"Scream and cry, Kate, as if your life depends on it!"

Nan said more, but I didn't hear it. My own awful, wrenching screams filled the room. My steadiness had gone, and I felt only a deep, horrible terror. I did not want to die.

Dr. Wendy turned to flee, as though running from a madwoman. "I will fetch the King!"

* * *

"Sweetheart, what is this? Dr. Wendy insisted I come to see you. He tells me you are much distressed." Henry lowered himself painfully into a chair beside my bed, where I lay.

He looked annoyed, but at least he was here. Silently, I gave thanks to good Dr. Wendy. Now it was up to me, and, I thought, the spirit of Jane Seymour.

My heart still pounded. My cheeks still burned from Nan's slaps. Strands of hair had escaped my cap. But Cat had made sure that the silken pillows on my bed smelled as sweet as a summer meadow. Nan had perfumed my skin with fragrant rose water.

"Oh, thank you for coming, sire, especially given the pain that troubles you. Dr. Wendy is right. I do need you, as I have never done before," I whispered.

Nothing.

"I . . . I am overcome by a rumour that has reached my ears," I went on desperately. "I have heard . . . I fear you are unhappy with me; that I have displeased you." My lips trembled. I looked up into his broad face beseechingly, hoping for any sign that he still loved me.

His blue eyes stared coldly.

"Sire, I care only for your happiness. All that matters is being your obedient, humble wife and servant." I met his eyes, so cloudy with age and constant pain.

Henry was silent for another long moment, his face impassive. I lowered my eyes demurely. I was sure he could hear my pounding heart.

"Hmmmm," he said at last. "Well, Kate, rest tonight and we will talk again when you are more recovered."

That wasn't enough, I knew. *Meek. Obedient.* I must do more.

I slid off the bed and sank to the floor at his feet. Resting my hands on his good knee, I looked up from under my lashes, making my voice a hushed whisper. I bent forwards so that he could see the tops of my breasts peeking from my gown.

I caught a flicker of desire in those blue eyes.

"Sire, may I ... may I come to visit you tomorrow evening?" I pleaded. "Just knowing that I can see you on the morrow will, I am sure, help make me well."

Gently, Henry reached out to touch my cheek. His hand hesitated, then stroked the smooth skin above the top of my gown. I sighed.

All the while, I fought back a fear that threatened to choke me. *Gardiner or Wriothesley could be waiting outside this door with the warrant for my arrest.*

"Tears. These do seem to be real tears," Henry said, almost to himself. He kissed me gently on the lips. It was a tender kiss. Was it an honest kiss?

"All right then, Kate. Come to my bedchamber tomorrow and we'll see how we do together. I'll be sure you are admitted."

DANGEROUS SNARES

◇·◇

Summer 1546

*It [is] very unseemly and preposterous for the woman to take upon her
the office of instructor and teacher to her Lord and husband.*
—Kateryn Parr to Henry VIII,
quoted in John Foxe, *The Acts and Monuments*, 1583

"He'll try to entrap you, Kate. Be ready, and don't let yourself be
drawn into his snares."

Nan's warning echoed in my mind as we made our way along the
palace's torchlit halls the next evening. Nan walked a few steps behind me, Cat trailing last. I'd dressed carefully, perfuming my skin
with rose water again, and choosing a kirtle of soft, silky pink. I imagined Queen Jane had favoured gentle colours over the powerful red I
preferred.

When we reached Henry's rooms, I stopped. *What lies behind this
heavy, polished door?*

"Go back now," I said, keeping my voice low. "Return to your own
rooms."

Cat rolled her eyes and whispered to Nan. "Did she order you
about in this officious way even before she became Queen, Lady
Herbert?"

"She did, indeed, Lady Willoughby. She's the same annoying older
sister she's always been." Nan squeezed my hand. "We'll wait for you
in your bedchamber, Your Grace. *As usual.*"

As Cat leaned forwards to kiss me, she whispered in my ear. "And
don't worry. I've hidden your parchments and writing supplies some-
place Bishop Gardiner and his spies will never think to look."

"Where?"

"In Gardiner's bed!" Seeing my confusion, she grinned. "Gardiner my spaniel, that is. Everything is tucked safely under the cushions of his basket. And believe me, he's been trained to growl if the bishop comes near."

I watched my sister and dear friend walk away, then listened until I could no longer hear the rustle of their gowns or their soft footfalls. With a shaky breath, I turned around.

No one could help me now.

I stood facing the door alone. An attendant stepped forwards to open it. I took a breath and stepped through.

"Good evening, Majesty. I am much better thanks to your kind visit yesterday," I gushed, lowering my eyes and making my way to where Henry sat on a wide cushioned chair, his bad leg propped on a velvet-topped stool.

"Good evening, gentlemen," I added quietly, crossing the room to sit beside Henry. With one quick glance, I assessed my adversaries. Several of the king's advisors were present—but, to my surprise, Gardiner and Wriothesley weren't among them. Was this simply a coincidence—or by Henry's design?

After some pleasantries, our conversation turned to religion. Nan had been right: The King might not be able to hunt on horseback any longer, but he still knew how to lay a trap.

It happened almost casually. Henry asked for my opinion on a minor religious matter about which I did, indeed, have strong thoughts. If my husband intended to catch me out for my Reformist views, these men would be witnesses. I took a breath.

"Your Majesty, I cannot speak about this," I demurred, bowing my head. "Rather I would ask you to enlighten me. For, as you know, God has appointed a natural difference between men and women."

"What do you mean?"

"Husband, as a woman, I must always defer to your opinion. You are my anchor, my supreme head next to God on earth. I follow your lead on this point—and on all matters of religion."

Henry harrumphed. "Not so, for lately you are become like a teacher, seeking to instruct me instead of taking direction from me."

"Sire, you mistake me! If I have, at times, ventured to speak strongly or engage you in lively debate, it has been out of my deep love for you," I assured him, placing my hand on his good knee.

"Love?"

"Yes, my lord. I've only wanted to distract Your Majesty. When we are debating and arguing, you are not thinking about the pain in your leg, are you?" I smiled and leaned closer, to give him a good view of my cleavage.

I made my voice as sweet as honey. "Dearest husband, I've only tried to take your mind off your infirmity—as any helpmeet would do. Everything I do, I do for you and the benefit of your great kingdom."

I saw Henry study me, uncertainty shadowing his face. On an impulse I took his hand and kissed his ring.

There was only one more thing to say. "I seek only to obey and serve."

The moment stretched out, long and silent.

Afterwards, I wondered if conjuring Queen Jane's motto had brought her spirit into the room. For suddenly Henry's face cleared.

"And is it even so, sweetheart?" Henry grabbed both my hands. His broad face broke out in a smile. "Is this truly all you intended?"

"You know I live by the motto you graciously approved when I became your most fortunate Queen: 'To be useful in *all* I do,'" I reminded him. "That is my vow, just as I have pledged to be your wife in sickness and in health, till death do us part."

I saw relief spread over Henry's face like sunshine on the daffodils in the Hampton Court Gardens. Maybe that was all he'd needed: re-assurance that I was not plotting against him, as so many others had done.

I felt a sense of reprieve, but something else, too. For it seemed my husband could only be happy if I acted like a spaniel, lolling and looking up at him with doleful, begging eyes.

No, King Henry could only be happy with unconditional love from a woman, like Queen Jane, who was meek and obedient—or at least, who acted that way all the time. Jane had died early in their marriage. I wondered: Could she have kept her own spirit in check for a lifetime?

Henry was so entirely alone. He could only be a king—not a man who loved as other men do. He could never truly trust another human being: not me, not his advisors, not his own children.

No wonder he wants to be buried next to dear, plain Jane, I thought.

"Then, sweetheart, we are now perfect friends again. Come sit upon my lap." Henry stretched out his large hands to scoop me in.

"You are my anchor," I murmured. I let him fondle and kiss me. I giggled softly, pulling gently on his beard. "You need not doubt me, Your Majesty. I give you my word that I am true in all things."

Our eyes met. I might not be the delectable dessert he had first desired, but I fancied I saw a tiny glimmer of affection still lingering there. "I believe you speak the truth, Kate."

"I do, my love."

Then he waved his advisors out of the room.

Later, as I made my way, weary and drained, back to my rooms, I couldn't be sure whether I had succeeded. I still didn't know the answer to one question: Would my husband gain more pleasure from having me on his lap, or in the Tower, about to lose my head?

*   *   *

I remained uncertain the next afternoon, when Henry sent for me to come to the garden. Only Nan and Cat were with me. As we stood chatting by the roses, I caught movement out of the tail of my eye. I whirled to see Wriothesley striding towards us, forty men behind him. He was clutching a piece of parchment. He waved it triumphantly: It was the arrest warrant.

It's all been a trick, I thought. *Henry let me grovel. Yet all the while he intended to arrest me—and my ladies.*

I saw Nan go pale and Cat take her arm. Cat, like Nan, was already a young mother; I couldn't bear to have their deaths on my conscience.

I wanted to cry out, "Please, Henry!" But I bit my tongue. It was too late. Not even the ghost of Jane Seymour could help me now.

And then into the silence came my husband's booming voice. "What is this all about, Lord Chancellor?"

"Your Majesty . . . I . . . ," faltered Wriothesley.

"Over here," ordered Henry, drawing Wriothesley to one side.

Waves of confusion passed over Wriothesley's face. I held my breath as the two men talked. I saw Wriothesley's hand begin to shake; the parchment fluttered in the air. Grabbing it, Henry tore it with both hands.

"Knave! Beast and fool! Be off with you!" shouted the King. "And tell Bishop Gardiner to stop his meddling and poking at my wife."

Wriothesley retreated, looking as downcast as a dog rebuked by his master.

Henry returned to me, a satisfied smile on his face. He had, I suspected, made up his mind to spare me last night, but had not bothered to let Wriothesley and Gardiner know. He had let this charade play out for his own amusement.

I let out a shaky breath and linked my arm with my husband's. It was over.

* * *

"You're safe!" Nan exclaimed later.

I put my hand over hers. We were alone in my bedchamber. "No, I'll never really be safe, Nan. I never *have* been, though perhaps I never truly understood that before. But for now at least, the danger is past—thanks to you. I would never have feigned that terrible fit without your guidance."

"You must thank Cat for that." Nan grinned. "It was her idea that I hit you and make you lose control. She said she dare not, for fear that Dr. Wendy might have her arrested for attacking the Queen."

I smiled, remembering the doctor's shocked face.

Nan took my hand. "Kate, speaking of not being safe, there's something . . . a piece of news I've wanted to tell you. Sir Thomas Seymour is returning to England."

I nodded. "I know."

"There was such an attraction between you," Nan said, eyeing me sharply. "Kate, when he comes back to court you must—"

"Do not worry, sister," I assured her. "After what has just happened, I feel I can handle anything that comes my way."

I wrapped my hands around my knees. It was how we used to sit on our mother's bed, when she would return from court to tell us tales of gallant knights and lovely ladies, or sad stories about the poor dead babies of Katharine of Aragon. If one of those baby boys had lived, my own fate would have been far different.

"I have made a resolution, though, Nan," I said, thinking of her happy marriage, and the love match our own parents had enjoyed. "If I ever marry again, it will be for true love."

PERFECT FRIENDS

◇·◇

Fall and Winter 1846–1847

"We are now perfect friends again," Henry had said on the night I'd convinced him of my loyalty. And indeed we were, so long as I continued to obey him and follow his dictates.

Oh, there were rewards, I suppose. For the rest of that summer and into the fall, my husband showered me with gifts of rich fabric and sparkling jewels. Rather than take up my quill, I wrapped my fingers in perfumed gloves of crimson velvet, trimmed with buttons of diamond and ruby. I smiled sweetly, aiming to be a humble wife, a worthy Queen, the perfect consort.

I tried to make myself into Queen Jane.

But all the while, I hid the treasures I valued most—books and learning, prayers in English, my own writing.

As we had following our marriage three years earlier, we spent time in the countryside, where scented fruits bent the trees and sheep dotted hillsides like clusters of white flowers. Perhaps Henry realized it was the last time the glories of an English summer would be spread before him, more sumptuous than any palace feast. I think he knew.

I read to him often. I made sure to avoid religious texts, and never again offered my own opinion. Instead, I regaled him with the well-loved legends of King Arthur and the Knights of the Round Table. Sometimes, Henry would close his eyes and smile, a distant expression on his poor swollen face. I wondered then if he was seeing again the glorious days of his own youth as the golden king of the Tudor court.

Once, Henry had a fever, and as I bent over him with a cool cloth, he whispered, "Thank you, sweetheart. Thank you, Jane."

I did not correct him.

Then, in early December, Henry announced, "I am going to the Palace of Whitehall tomorrow, Kate."

"I shall have my things packed, husband, and accompany you."

Henry held up a swollen hand and shook his massive head. His eyes were bloodshot and clouded with pain. "No, dear Kate. I have the work of my kingdom to do, to assure Edward's ascension as my heir."

Suddenly, I understood. I would not see him again.

I knelt before my husband and felt his hand on my head as a blessing. We were silent. Four years before, this man had given me black taffeta. Within weeks, I would be a widow again, with the head of death staring up at me from a gold ring on my finger.

For me, it would be the end of a chapter. But, of course, it was much more: Henry's death would mark the end of an era. He had been king for thirty-eight years.

Henry did not plan to die as a normal man, surrounded by a sorrowing wife and children. He would die as he had lived, as a king.

Henry could no longer walk, but I stood in the doorway as a servant pushed his chair down the hallway.

I remembered what Nan had said, that Henry didn't like goodbyes. "It's as if he's out riding. When he rounds a bend in the road, he never turns in the saddle to look behind him." I knew he would not look back.

But then suddenly, to my astonishment, I saw Henry hold up his hand and order the servant to stop and turn him. I rushed forwards to close the distance between us.

"I just thought you'd like to know, Kate, that although I won't name you regent after I am gone, I am not letting Bishop Gardiner anywhere near Edward once he ascends the throne," Henry said quietly. "Neither he nor any of the conservatives will be allowed to advise him."

I nodded. I could have sworn I saw a twinkle in his eye.

"And so, sweetheart, don't despair. My people will still be able to read the Word of God in their own language," he went on. The King raised his shoulders, as if to acknowledge that reform and change—progress—were inevitable.

"Prince Edward has been taught well, Henry," I offered, hoping to reassure him. "He'll be a worthy successor to Your Majesty."

I stopped there, not daring to say my true thoughts aloud: *If anything should happen to Edward, his sisters are prepared to reign. Mary is dedicated. And Elizabeth—Elizabeth is much like her father.*

Henry reached out his hand. I knelt and kissed his ring one last time.

Then I watched until King Henry VIII was out of sight.

Back in my bedchamber, Nan and Cat were sorting through a pile of my garments. Just as she had when my John had been near death, Nan was choosing kirtles suitable for the mourning period we knew would soon come. *Women help one another survive much in this world,* I thought.

I sighed and straightened my shoulders, ready to meet the time of sorrow ahead. But I also couldn't help wondering if, as it had before, my path might take an unexpected turn. I might, I thought, renew an old acquaintance; I might make a new life for myself with a man I loved. I was even still young enough to bear a child.

There was something else, too. I noticed Cat's spaniel sleeping in a basket in the corner. "Gardiner, come!"

He padded over. I scratched his ears and smiled. "Cat, while Gardiner is up, I wonder if you could fetch my parchments and writing supplies from their hiding place under his cushions.

"I have a book to write."

HENRY VIII

Alone. Alone.

My throne is empty, but the courtiers who pass by it still must bow and bob before the seat. I am the King of England still.

Kateryn, I can trust, though some whisper, even now, that she betrays me and my God. We read together in the long afternoons. She is a good friend to my children: Mary, daughter of my pious and leaden Spanish wife; Elizabeth, the daughter of the first of the two whores; and blessed Edward, son of my beloved Jane.

Now this new Kateryn plays chess with them in the garden in the afternoons, and all the story is ended.

I know I cannot stay here long. "Bury me next to my beloved," I have said to Kateryn. When she did not understand, I said, "Jane. My sweet Jane." She frowned, but did not dare argue.

Everything I have done, I did for England. I never worried about the cost to me, though God knows I suffered for my country like none other.

This is what the doubters and intriguers don't understand: The wives—all of them—they were necessary. I needed them for heirs. Edward still is the only son, and if—God forbid it—a woman gains the throne: then, chaos. The great Anarchy. I have spent my life fighting for a clear succession.

But I gave the kingdom Edward. I have not failed. Never say that I failed. I cannot abide failure. I triumphed. My body might fail me now, but my loins never did.

Edward, you shall live long and rule wisely, with great age and might and manhood, and you shall be known as the greatest monarch England ever had. I see it in a vision.

God chose me as his instrument on Earth. He now smiles upon you, Edward, my hope, my heir, my boy, my darling son. Grasp the world with both hands, as your father did.

The pain is too great for me to move, and so I lie on my bed.

Kate, come suckle me. Render your teat. You alone are kind.

The minister who stands beside the bed in robes of black, I do not recognize.

I am the King. You must answer to me.

Will I be admired in the court of Heaven?

A short sleep. Wake me when the trumpets sound my fanfare.

QUEEN ELIZABETH I

"Always the Same"

TILBURY, 1588

◇·◇

She rides out towards the troops. There is news that her navy has clashed with the Spanish Armada off the coast. Tens of thousands of Spanish soldiers wait on the other side of the English Channel to cross over and invade. Watch fires burn up and down the beaches of Britain.

Elizabeth comes dressed not as a queen in silks, but as an armed hero, an Amazon, a warrior. Her silver breastplate shines beneath the sun; her arms flash with chased metal and gauntlets; and her hair, too, is red as metal and burns bright, just as her royal father's did, as her half sister's did and her half brother's.

All of them are gone now, dead. Edward died when merely a boy, his chest too weak for the world's thick air. Mary died a few years later, pregnant with ulcers and fantasies. Now it is Elizabeth, the Tudor Queen, who stands upon the field.

To the army assembled around her, she lifts her voice. It rings out over the ranks of the infantry in the chill morning air. To them all, she declares: "Let tyrants fear! I know I have the body of a woman, but I have the heart and stomach of a king, and of a King of England, too. I myself will be your general and judge. I have been your prince in peace; so will I be in war. The enemy perhaps may challenge my sex for that I am a woman—so may I likewise challenge them, for they are but men."

The Sword of State is carried unsheathed before her.

She raises her arm, and thousands of voices clamour together. Her subjects shout in triumph, and the bellows of defiance echo outwards from a tiny island across a startled globe.

TUDOR TIMELINE

1485   Katharine of Aragon is born.

1491   Prince Henry, second son of Henry VII, is born on June 28.

1501   Katharine of Aragon arrives in England and marries Prince Arthur, older brother of Henry, on November 14.

ca. 1501 Anne Boleyn is born.

1502   Prince Arthur dies on April 2.

ca. 1507 Jane Seymour is born.

1509   Henry VIII assumes the throne in April. In June he marries Katharine of Aragon.

1512   Kateryn Parr is born (probably in August), the eldest of three surviving children.

1513   Henry goes to war in France in June. He appoints Katharine of Aragon regent.

In August the Scots invade England. Two weeks later, Katharine and her troops defeat them, killing their king, James IV, and claiming a great victory.

1515   Anna of Cleves is born.

1516   Mary, the daughter of Henry VIII and Katharine of Aragon, is born.

1517   Kateryn Parr's father dies. Her mother, Lady Maud Parr, remains single and devotes herself to her children, hiring a tutor to teach them Latin, French, Italian, and arithmetic. She continues to serve as a lady-in-waiting at court.

1520   Henry meets with King Francis I of France on the Field of the Cloth of Gold.

ca. 1521 Catherine Howard is born.

1526   In February, Henry begins to court Anne Boleyn.

1529   Jane Seymour becomes maid of honor to Katharine of Aragon.

1530   Cardinal Thomas Wolsey dies.

1531   Henry separates from Katharine of Aragon and she is banished from court.

1533   Henry secretly marries Anne Boleyn around January 25.

In May, Archbishop of Canterbury Thomas Cranmer declares the marriage of Henry and Katharine of Aragon invalid. Five days later, he validates the king's marriage to Anne.

The coronation of Anne Boleyn takes place on June 1.

Princess Elizabeth is born on September 7.

1534   Parliament passes the Act of Succession, through which Anne Boleyn's children will succeed the king.

1535   Bishop John Fisher is beheaded on June 22 for refusing to accept Henry as the Supreme Head of the Church of England.

Sir Thomas More, who also refused to accept the Act of Supremacy, is beheaded on July 6.

Henry begins to court Jane Seymour in November.

1536   Katharine of Aragon dies on January 7.

On May 2, Anne Boleyn is arrested and taken to the Tower of London. She is beheaded on May 19.

On May 30, Henry marries Jane Seymour.

In June, Parliament passes the second Act of Succession, putting Jane Seymour's children ahead of Anne Boleyn's in line for the throne.

The Pilgrimage of Grace, a revolt against Henry's reign, takes place from September to March 1537.

1537　Prince Edward is born on October 12.

Jane Seymour dies on October 24.

1539　Henry is betrothed to Anna of Cleves on October 4. She arrives in Kent in England on December 27.

1540　Henry is married to Anna of Cleves on January 6. The marriage is annulled by a clerical convocation on July 9 and the annulment is confirmed by Parliament on July 12.

On July 28, the king's advisor Thomas Cromwell is beheaded, and the king marries Catherine Howard.

1542　Henry VIII's fifth wife, Catherine Howard, is beheaded on February 13.

1543　On July 12, Kateryn Parr marries Henry, becoming his sixth wife. The wedding is performed by Bishop Stephen Gardiner.

1544　In February, the king passes a new Act of Succession, ruling that Prince Edward is first in line for the throne, followed by any of Edward's children, then by Kateryn's children, then by the children of any other (potential) queens, then by Mary and Elizabeth.

1545　Kateryn Parr publishes *Prayers or Meditations*. This is the first work by a woman published in England in English.

1546 Kateryn Parr is nearly arrested for her outspoken Lutheran reformist ideas, as part of a plot to oust her led by the conservative Stephen Gardiner, Bishop of Winchester, among others.

1547 Henry VIII dies on January 28, and Edward becomes king at age nine.

1548 Kateryn dies of puerperal fever on September 5.

1549 Thomas Seymour is beheaded for high treason for plots against his brother, Edward Seymour, who served as young King Edward's Protector.

1553 Edward VI dies on July 6. Mary becomes queen.

1557 Anna of Cleves dies on July 16.

1558 Mary I dies; Elizabeth ascends the throne on November 17; she rules until her death in 1603.

WHO'S WHO IN THE COURT

Anna of Cleves, Queen of England (1515–1557)—Henry VIII's fourth wife, she was married just seven months before the English Parliament, at the king's request, passed an act declaring the union null and void.

Arthur, Prince of Wales (1486–1502)—Henry VIII's older brother and heir apparent to the Tudor throne. Six months after his marriage to Katharine of Aragon, he died of what many historians believe was tuberculosis.

Bessie (Elizabeth) Blount (1498–1540)—Henry's mistress from 1514 to 1522. She bore him an illegitimate son in June 1520.

Anne Boleyn, Queen of England (ca. 1501–1536)—The second wife of Henry VIII. Anne's refusal to be his mistress, along with his desperation for a male heir, led to Henry's abandonment of his marriage to Katharine of Aragon, and led as well to the English Reformation. The only living child from their three-year marriage, Princess Elizabeth, later became Elizabeth I. Anne was executed on false charges of incest and adultery in May 1536.

Elizabeth Boleyn (ca. 1480–ca. 1561)—Anne Boleyn's aunt through marriage, she was chosen to attend Anne in the Tower of London, largely because of her dislike for her niece.

George Boleyn, Lord Rochford (1503–1536)—In 1525, George Boleyn married Jane Parker, later known primarily as Lady Rochford. Close to his sister, Anne Boleyn, he became a member of Henry's privy chamber during her reign. George acquired a reputation for womanizing and was falsely convicted of committing adultery with his sister, along with courtiers William Brereton, Henry Norris, Mark Smeaton, and Francis Weston. On May 17, 1536, he was the first of the five men beheaded.

Thomas Boleyn, Earl of Wiltshire, Earl of Ormond, Viscount Rochford (1477–1539)—The ambitious father of Mary, George, and Anne Boleyn, he rose to great heights when his daughters caught the king's eye. Besides being showered with titles, he was also one of Henry's leading diplomats, and was Lord Privy Seal from 1530 until Anne and George were executed for treason six years later.

Catherine (Cat) Willoughby Brandon, Duchess of Suffolk (1519–1580)—Lady-in-waiting to Catherine Howard and close friend of Kateryn Parr, she was a proponent of the English Reformation and the wife of Charles Brandon.

Charles Brandon, First Duke of Suffolk (ca. 1484–1545)—Henry VIII's brother-in-law, he was also the king's longtime confidant and advisor, serving in several governmental positions.

William Brereton (1487–1536)—A groom of the privy chamber, Brereton was one of the servants who cared for Henry's person. He was the oldest of the five men wrongly convicted of having "illicit intercourse" with Anne Boleyn, and was the fourth man executed on May 17, 1536.

Francis Bryan (ca. 1490–1550)—An English courtier and a close friend of Henry's, as well as half cousin to Anne Boleyn and a second half cousin to Jane Seymour. Bryan worked behind the scenes to help bring about Anne's downfall and hasten Henry's marriage to Jane.

Joan Bulmer (1519–1590)—A Tudor noblewoman who lived in the Dowager Duchess of Norfolk's household with Catherine Howard. She later served in Catherine's court and testified against her.

Nicholas Carew (ca. 1496–1539)—Henry's courtier, he was entrusted with conveying the king's private messages to Jane Seymour before Anne Boleyn's death. In 1539, after falling out of Henry's favor, Carew was found guilty of high treason, and he was executed in March 1539.

Mary Boleyn Carey (ca. 1498–1543)—The sister of Anne Boleyn, Mary was Henry VIII's mistress from about 1521 to 1526, while she was married to William Carey, an influential courtier. Henry's passion for Mary quickly waned when he met her younger sister.

Nan Cobham (?)—History remains unclear about the specific details of her life, although it is known that she attended three of Henry VIII's wives: Katharine of Aragon, Anne Boleyn, and Kateryn Parr. Nan seemingly despised Anne Boleyn and gave testimony to Lord Cromwell that served to seal the fate of Henry's second wife.

Margaret Dymoke Coffin (1490–1545)—While attending Anne Boleyn during her time in the Tower, Margaret spied for the king's men. She went on to serve in Jane Seymour's household as a lady of the bedchamber.

Thomas Cranmer, Archbishop of Canterbury (1489–1556)—It was Cranmer, a reformist, who first suggested that the validity of Henry's marriage to Katharine of Aragon be decided in English courts rather than by the Pope. Cranmer remained in his position after Henry's death.

Thomas Cromwell, First Earl of Essex (ca. 1485–1540)—A lawyer and statesman who first served under Cardinal Wolsey, Cromwell eventually became Henry's chief minister. He helped further the English Reformation and worked toward the dissolution of Henry's marriage to Katharine of Aragon. Cromwell also brought about Anne Boleyn's downfall and execution, and engineered Henry's marriage to Jane Seymour. After Jane's death, Cromwell disastrously suggested that Henry marry Anna of Cleves, which led, in part, to his falling out of favor. Condemned to execution without trial, he was beheaded in July 1540.

Thomas Culpeper (ca. 1514–1541)—Courtier and Gentleman of the Privy Chamber under Henry VIII, he was the alleged lover of Catherine Howard and was executed for treason.

Francis Dereham (1513–1541)—A courtier in service to the Dowager Duchess of Norfolk, he was Catherine Howard's lover before her marriage to the king. He was later executed for treason.

Edward VI, King of England (1537–1553)—The son of Henry and his third wife, Jane Seymour, Edward was the king's only legitimate male heir to survive infancy. Crowned King of England and Ireland on February 20, 1547, he assumed the throne after his father's death in January. Just seven years later, he died at the age of fifteen, of what many historians believe was tuberculosis.

Elizabeth I, Queen of England (1533–1603)—The daughter of Henry VIII and Anne Boleyn, Elizabeth came to the throne in 1558 upon the death of her half sister, Mary, and ruled for almost forty-five years. Her reign is known as the Golden Age, an era that saw the birth of Shakespeare, the defeat of the Spanish Armada, and the emergence of England as a world power. Choosing to remain unwed and childless, Elizabeth was the last Tudor to sit on the throne.

Henry FitzRoy, First Duke of Richmond and Somerset (1519–1536)—The illegitimate son of Henry and Bessie Blount, he was publicly acknowledged as the king's child. Showered with honors and titles, he was treated as a prince until his death at age seventeen.

Margaret Foliot, Mrs. Stonor (died 1546)—Although much speculation surrounds her identification, most historians believe Margaret Foliot was the woman courtiers called Mrs. Stonor. She attended Anne Boleyn in the Tower and later became mistress, or "mother," of the maids of honors to Henry's next four queens.

Stephen Gardiner, Bishop of Winchester (ca. 1482–1555)—Although a conservative Roman Catholic, he went along with the increasing influence of Protestantism in the court. In 1533, he assisted Archbishop Cranmer in declaring the king's marriage to Katharine of Aragon null and void. Two years later, Gardiner wrote an influential treatise justifying the king's new title, Supreme Head of the Church of England. In 1555 he attempted to turn the king against his sixth wife, Kateryn Parr, but was unsuccessful.

Karl Harst (fl. 1540)—A German diplomat and one of the Duke of Cleves's ambassadors to England, he was advisor to Anna of Cleves during the dissolution of her marriage to Henry VIII.

Henry VII, King of England (1457–1509)—The first Tudor monarch and father of Arthur, Prince of Wales, and Henry VIII, he forged the alliance that brought Katharine of Aragon to England and eventually to the throne.

Henry VIII, King of England (1491–1547)—Ascending the throne on April 21, 1509, after his father, Henry VII, died, Henry VIII went on to rule England for almost thirty-six years. His desperation for a male heir resulted in six marriages, as well as the initiation of the English Reformation. Each of his three legitimate children, Edward, Mary, and Elizabeth, succeeded him.

Catherine Howard, Queen of England (ca. 1521–1542)—The fifth wife of Henry VIII, she was a teenager when she married the forty-nine-year-old king. Petite and vivacious, she was caught in an affair with one of the king's men, Thomas Culpeper, and beheaded for adultery just sixteen months later.

Thomas Howard, First Earl of Surrey and Second Duke of Norfolk (1443–1524)—A chief advisor to Henry, he joined with Katharine of Aragon to repel Scotland's attack on England in 1513.

Thomas Howard, Third Duke of Norfolk (1473–1554)—Uncle of both Anne Boleyn and Catherine Howard, he was a prominent nobleman who served Henry VIII as a military leader, as a judge, and on the Privy Council. He played a large role in the machinations behind both queens' marriages to the king.

Katharine of Aragon, Queen of England (1485–1536)—Henry VIII's first wife, she was married to him for nearly twenty-four years until a special court, convened at the king's behest, declared their union illegal in 1533. Despite banishment from the court and Henry's marriage to Anne Boleyn, Katharine refused to accept the court's verdict. Until her death, she insisted on calling Henry "my husband." Her only living child from the marriage, Princess Mary, became Queen Mary I of England.

William Kingston (1476–1540)—In charge of the Tower of London during Anne Boleyn's imprisonment, he passed information to Thomas Cromwell that was used against Anne at her trial.

Mary Lascelles (ca. 1515–?)—A chambermaid in the household of the Dowager Duchess of Norfolk, she gave evidence against Catherine Howard at the queen's trial.

Henry Manox (1515–?)—Music teacher in the Norfolk household, he was Catherine Howard's first paramour.

Maria, Duchess of Jülich-Berg (1491–1543)—The Catholic mother of Anna of Cleves. Her marriage to John III united the Rhine River territories of Cleves, Jülich, and Berg.

Mary I, Queen of England (1516–1558)—The only living child of Henry VIII and Katharine of Aragon, she ascended the throne in 1553 upon the death of her half brother, Edward VI. Seeking to convert England back to the Catholic Church, she repealed many of her father's religious laws and punished anyone who spoke out against the Pope. This resulted in the burning of over three hundred Protestants as heretics and earned her the moniker Bloody Mary. In 1554, she married the Catholic King Phillip II of Spain in hopes of producing an heir. Their union, however, remained childless. When Mary died after a five-year reign, her Protestant half sister, Elizabeth, assumed the throne.

John Neville, Lord Latimer (1493–1543)—Kateryn Parr's second husband, whom she married in 1534. When he was pressed into joining a northern revolt against Henry VIII, called the Pilgrimage of Grace in 1536, Kateryn was held hostage with her stepchildren at Snape Castle in Yorkshire.

Henry Norris (1482–1536)—A courtier who rose in the ranks to become Henry VIII's Groom of the Stool, responsible for assisting the king with his bodily functions. Renowned for his honesty and good character, he was a close friend of Henry's until he was accused of adultery with Anne Boleyn. He was the second of the five men beheaded on May 17, 1536.

Mary Orchard (died 1536)—The name Mary Orchard is used by historians for Anne Boleyn's childhood nurse, though her name may have been Mary Aucher. At Anne Boleyn's trial, when the Duke of Norfolk condemned Anne to death, Mary "shrieked out dreadfully" from the gallery. She was chosen as one of the ladies to attend Anne in the Tower.

Jane Parker, Lady Rochford (1505–1542)—Even though she was married to Anne Boleyn's brother, George, she testified against her sister-in-law, resulting in Anne's and George's deaths. She went on to serve in the courts of Jane Seymour, Anna of Cleves, and Catherine Howard. Her complicity in Catherine's extramarital affairs resulted in Lady Rochford's execution in 1542.

Matthew Parker, almoner (1504–1575)—Having begun his church career as an almoner, in charge of doling out alms (food and money) to the poor, Parker—who was a reformist—later helped write the thirty-nine articles of the Anglican Church. In 1537, he was appointed chaplain to Henry VIII, and ultimately served as the Archbishop of Canterbury from 1559 until his death in 1575.

Anne (Nan) Parr, Countess of Pembroke, Baroness Herbert of Cardiff (1515–1552)—The younger sister of Kateryn Parr, she came to court at age thirteen and served each of Henry's queens.

Kateryn Parr, Queen of England (1512–1548)—The last of Henry VIII's six wives, she was a fervent Protestant and a popular author of devotional works. For three and a half years, she was a dutiful wife and a kind stepmother to the royal children, managing to outwit and outlive the king.

Maud Parr (1492–1531)—Longtime lady-in-waiting to Katharine of Aragon, she was also the mother of Kateryn Parr.

William Parr, Lord Horton (1483–1547)—Uncle of Kateryn Parr who served with Henry VIII in France.

Eleanor Paston, Countess of Rutland (1495–1551)—Lady-in-waiting to four of Henry's wives: Anne Boleyn, Jane Seymour, Anna of Cleves, and Catherine Howard.

María de Salinas, Baroness Willoughby de Eresby (1490–1539)—Confidante and lady-in-waiting to Katharine of Aragon, she traveled with the young Katharine from Spain.

Mary Scrope, Lady Kingston (1476–1548)—One of Anne Boleyn's attending ladies in the Tower and wife of William Kingston, she spied on Anne on behalf of Thomas Cromwell. Later, at the christening of Jane Seymour and Henry's son, Prince Edward, she carried Princess Mary's train. Soon after, she was one of the twenty-nine women who walked in Jane Seymour's funeral procession.

Edward Seymour, First Duke of Somerset (ca. 1500–1552)—The brother of Jane Seymour, he became Viscount Beauchamp, Earl of Hertford, and Warden of the Scottish Marches after Henry's marriage to Jane. Later, when his young nephew Edward VI was crowned King of England, Seymour was appointed Lord Protector of England, effectively becoming ruler of the land until 1552, when he was beheaded on trumped-up charges of treason.

Elizabeth "Bess" Seymour (ca. 1518–1568)—Younger sister of Jane Seymour.

Jane Seymour, Queen of England (ca. 1507–1537)—The third wife of Henry VIII, she caught the king's eye while in the service of Queen Anne Boleyn. Henry and Jane wed just eleven days after Anne's execution. Seventeen months later, Jane died from complications of childbirth after delivering a son, Edward. She was mourned by Henry, who took to calling her his "true wife." Jane is the only one of his queens who was buried with him in the chapel at Windsor Castle.

John Seymour (1474–1536)—Father of Jane, Elizabeth (Bess), Edward, and Thomas Seymour, he brought disgrace to the family name after being caught in an affair with his eldest son's wife.

Margery Wentworth Seymour (ca. 1478–1550)—Mother of Jane Seymour and grandmother of Edward VI.

Thomas Seymour, First Baron Seymour of Sudeley (1508–1549)—The brother of Jane and Edward Seymour, he was an ambitious and dashing military man and courtier, as well as the fourth husband of Kateryn Parr.

Anne (Boleyn) Shelton (ca. 1476–1556)—During Anne Boleyn's reign, Lady Shelton and her husband, John, managed Princess Elizabeth's household. Unsympathetic to Anne's plight, Lady Shelton was chosen to attend her niece during Anne's imprisonment in the Tower.

John Skip, chaplain (died 1552)—A chaplain and almoner to Anne Boleyn for many years, both before and during her reign, Skip comforted her during her time in the Tower.

Mark Smeaton (1512–1536)—A court musician who got caught up in Anne Boleyn's adultery trial, he was tortured until he confessed to being her lover. He was the last of the five men executed on May 17, 1536.

Elizabeth Browne Somerset, Countess of Worcester (1502–1565)—Despite being a close friend and lady-in-waiting to Anne Boleyn, the countess likely betrayed her, providing Thomas Cromwell with information that was used at Anne's trial to seal her doom.

Lucy Somerset, Baroness Latimer (ca. 1524–1583)—A maid of honor to Catherine Howard.

Sibylle of Cleves (1512–1554)—Older sister of Anna of Cleves, she was married to Johann Friedrich of Saxony, who was a leader of Germany's Schmalkaldic League, a confederation of Protestant states.

Agnes Tilney, Dowager Duchess (1477–1545)—A Tudor noblewoman married to the Second Duke of Norfolk, she was stepgrandmother and guardian of Catherine Howard.

Thomas Wendy (ca. 1499–1560)—A physician who may have had Protestant sympathies, he became Henry's doctor in 1546 and attended him on his deathbed.

Francis Weston (1511–1536)—A minor courtier who was knighted at Anne Boleyn's coronation, he was accused of committing adultery with her. He was the third of the five men beheaded on May 17, 1536.

Wilhelm, Duke of Cleves (1516–1592)—The Protestant brother of Anna of Cleves.

Thomas Wolsey, cardinal (ca. 1475–1530)—A priest who rose rapidly through the ranks of the Catholic Church. The Pope made him a cardinal in 1515. Soon afterward, the king appointed him Lord Chancellor. Henry's most trusted and closest advisor, Wolsey fell from grace in 1529 when he was unable to get a papal annulment of Henry's marriage to Katharine of Aragon, which would have enabled the king to wed Anne Boleyn. Arrested in November 1530 for treason, Wolsey died that same month on his way to trial.

Thomas Wriothesley, First Earl of Southampton (1505–1550)—A ruthless politician, appointed Lord Chancellor in 1544, he plotted the downfall of Queen Kateryn Parr. His wife, Jane, served as one of Kateryn Parr's ladies-in-waiting.

ACKNOWLEDGMENTS

The authors would like to thank:

Two powerful quotations helped inspire my portrait of Anna of Cleves. Margaret Mead's beautiful words, *Never doubt that a small group of thoughtful, committed citizens can change the world; indeed, it's the only thing that ever has,* echo in Anna's plea to Dr. Edmonds. A quotation from "The Red Angel," an essay by G. K. Chesterton, *Fairy tales do not give the child his first idea of bogey. What fairy tales give the child is his first clear idea of the possible defeat of bogey,* reverberates in an observation Anna makes to Alice. A huge, heartfelt thank-you, as always, to Doug and Daisy, and to my agent, Steve Malk. To my fellow wives, Henry, and our fearless editor, Anne Schwartz—it has been a pleasure and an honor to work with you. —J.D.

To my generous, talented, and invincible court of honor—Tobin, Steph, Lisa, Jennifer, Linda Sue, and Deborah—thank you for your gorgeous stories as well as your friendship. Thanks also to my agent, Ethan Ellenberg, for taking the lead and taking charge, and to

Geovana Lopez for scrutinizing my Spanish. Thanks to Barbara Perris for her brilliant copyediting. And last, but never least, to my friend and editor Anne Schwartz—you deserve a crown. —C.F.

I could begin and end by thanking one person for bringing my dream of writing about Anne Boleyn to fruition—Candy Fleming. Thank you for guiding this project from an idea into a book and including me among writers I have so long admired. You are my one true Queen and dear friend. I also owe great thanks to the readers of the rough drafts, who give me encouragement when I need it most—Penny Blubaugh, Barb Rosenstock, Craig Martin, Mom, Dad, and always, Steven Malk. —S.H.

Thanks to Candy Fleming and Anne Schwartz for including me, to my fellow royals for their generosity and friendship, and to Steven Malk for his invaluable assistance. A special thanks to my family for putting up with my obsession with the Tudors. —D.H.

My thanks to Karen Cushman for her help and expertise; any errors that remain are my responsibility. Thanks also to the other five Queens and the King, from whom I learned so much; an extra shoutout to Candy Fleming, M. T. Anderson, Deborah Hopkinson, and Anne Schwartz. And always, love and gratitude to my personal court of honor, especially Ginger Knowlton, Julie Damerell, Anna Dobbin, Ben Dobbin, and all my family. —L.S.P.

I am eternally grateful to my dear friend Deborah Hopkinson, who, years ago, undertook the mission to keep me writing—I'll never stop saying thank you. Many thanks to Candy Fleming for the invitation to participate in this amazing endeavor—I am so deeply honored by your trust and vision. Thanks to Anne Schwartz, who edited brilliantly and bravely; I'm so glad to have met you! I must also thank my agent, Meredith Kaffel Simonoff, for her unending patience, wisest counsel, and constant encouragement. A million thanks to Aimee Friedman, for her loving friendship and support, and for reading the manuscript. And finally, all the gratitude and love in the world to my husband, Liel Leibovitz, who invaluably helped me to begin to understand Jane, and to my two darling kiddos, Lily and Hudson. I love you three so much. —L.A.S.

Additionally, we would like to thank our Random House family—Barbara Marcus, Lee Wade, Rachael Cole, Annie Kelley, Adrienne Waintraub, Noreen Herits, Barbara Perris, and Colleen Fellingham—for your time, your talents, and your constant support.

A BIBLIOGRAPHIC AFTERWORD

The novelist Norman Mailer once said that fiction writers who work with historical events and real people have a "unique opportunity—they can create superior histories out of an enhancement of the real, the unverified and the wholly fictional." We confess to enhancements of various kinds in this book. Not only have we occasionally invented characters, but also we have speculated about what might have happened in the many private, unrecorded moments of the Tudors' lives. Ours are fictional narratives. Still, we have chosen to stay close to the facts as we know them. These are documented in the multitudinous sources available in books and online. For readers who want to know more, we have listed some of these sources below.

BOOKS

Nonfiction

Ackroyd, Peter. *Tudors: The History of England from Henry VIII to Elizabeth I*. New York: Thomas Dunne Books, 2012.

Arnold, John H, ed. *The Oxford Handbook of Medieval Christianity*. Oxford, England: Oxford University Press, 2014.

Betteridge, Thomas, and Suzannah Lipscomb, eds. *Henry VIII and the Court: Art, Politics and Performance.* Farnham, England: Ashgate Publishing Limited, 2013.

Bordo, Susan. *The Creation of Anne Boleyn: A New Look at England's Most Notorious Queen.* New York: Houghton Mifflin Harcourt, 2013.

Borman, Tracy. *Elizabeth's Women: Friends, Rivals and Foes Who Shaped the Virgin Queen.* New York: Bantam Books, 2010.

———. *The Private Lives of the Tudors: Uncovering the Secrets of Britain's Greatest Dynasty.* London: Hodder & Stoughton, 2016.

Foister, Susan. *Holbein in England.* London: Tate Publishing, 2006.

Fraser, Antonia. *The Wives of Henry VIII.* New York: Knopf, 1993.

Froude, J. A. *The Divorce of Catherine of Aragon: The Story as Told by the Imperial Ambassadors Resident at the Court of Henry VIII.* New York: Charles Scribner's Sons, 1891.

Goodman, Ruth. *How to Be a Tudor: A Dawn-to-Dusk Guide to Tudor Life.* New York: Liveright Publishing Corporation, 2016.

Hunt, Alice. *The Drama of Coronation: Medieval Ceremony in Early Modern England.* Cambridge, England: Cambridge University Press, 2011.

Ives, Eric. *The Life and Death of Anne Boleyn.* Carlton, Victoria, Australia: Blackwell Publishing, 2004.

James, Susan. *Catherine Parr: Henry VIII's Last Love.* Stroud, Gloucestershire, England: Tempus Publishing, 2008.

Jones, Nigel. *Tower: An Epic History of the Tower of London.* New York: St. Martin's Press, 2012.

Lindsey, Karen. *Divorced, Beheaded, Survived: A Feminist Reinterpretation of the Wives of Henry VIII.* New York: De Capo Press, 1995.

Lipscomb, Suzannah. *A Journey through Tudor England.* New York: Pegasus Books, 2013.

Loades, David. *The Tudor Queens of England.* New York: Continuum, 2009.

Moorhouse, Geoffrey. *The Pilgrimage of Grace: The Rebellion that Shook Henry VIII's Throne.* London: Phoenix, 2003.

Mortimer, Ian. *The Time Traveler's Guide to Elizabethan England.* New York: Penguin Books, 2014.

Norton Elizabeth. *Anne Boleyn: Henry VIII's Obsession.* Gloucestershire, England: Amberley Publishing, 2009.

———. *The Anne Boleyn Papers.* Gloucestershire, England: Amberley Publishing, 2013.

———. *Anne of Cleves: Henry VIII's Discarded Bride.* Gloucestershire, England: Amberley Publishing, 2009.

———. *Catherine Parr.* Gloucestershire, England: Amberley Publishing, 2010.

Parr, Katherine. Edited by Janel Mueller. *Katherine Parr: Complete Works and Correspondence.* Chicago: University of Chicago Press, 2011.

Plowden, Alison. *Tudor Women: Queens & Commoners.* New York: Atheneum, 1979.

Porter, Linda. *Katherine the Queen: The Remarkable Life of Katherine Parr, the Last Wife of Henry VIII.* New York: St. Martin's Press, 2010.

Ridgway, Claire. *The Fall of Anne Boleyn: A Countdown.* Almeria, Spain: MadeGlobal Publishing, 2012.

Scarisbrick, J. J. *Henry VIII.* Los Angeles: University of California Press, 1968.

Seymour, William. *Ordeal by Ambition: An English Family in the Shadow of the Tudors.* London: Sidgwick & Jackson, 1972.

Smith, Lacey Baldwin. *Anne Boleyn: The Queen of Controversy*. Gloucestershire, England: Amberley Publishing, 2013.

———. *Catherine Howard*. Gloucestershire, England: Amberley Publishing, 2010.

Starkey, David. *The Reign of Henry VIII: Personalities and Politics*. New York: Vintage/Ebury, 2002.

———. *Six Wives: The Queens of Henry VIII*. London: Vintage, 2004.

Tremlett, Giles. *Catherine of Aragon: The Spanish Queen of Henry VIII*. New York: Walker & Company, 2010.

Vance, Marguerite. *Six Queens: The Wives of Henry VIII*. New York: Dutton, 1965.

Vasoli, Sandra. *Anne Boleyn's Letter from the Tower: A New Assessment*. Almeria, Spain: MadeGlobal Publishing, 2015.

Warnicke, Retha M. *The Marrying of Anne of Cleves: Royal Protocol in Tudor England*. New York: Cambridge University Press, 2010.

Weir, Alison. *Henry VIII: The King and His Court*. New York: Ballantine Books, 2001.

———. *The Lady in the Tower: The Fall of Anne Boleyn*. New York: Ballantine Books, 2009.

———. *The Six Wives of Henry VIII*. New York: Grove Press, 1991.

Williams, Patrick. *Katharine of Aragon: The Tragic Story of Henry VIII's First Unfortunate Wife*. Gloucestershire, England: Amberley Publishing, 2013.

Fiction

Byrd, Sandra. *The Secret Keeper: A Novel of Kateryn Parr*. New York: Howard Books, 2012.

Erickson, Carolly. *The Unfaithful Queen*. New York: St. Martin's Press, 2012.

Ford, Ford Madox. *The Fifth Queen.* New York: Vanguard Press, 1963.

Fremantle, Elizabeth. *Queen's Gambit.* New York: Thorndike Press, 2013.

Gregory, Philippa. *The Boleyn Inheritance.* New York: Touchstone, 2006.

———. *The Taming of the Queen.* New York: Touchstone, 2015.

Libby, Alisa M. *The King's Rose.* New York: Dutton Books for Young Readers, 2009.

Mantel, Hilary. *Bring Up the Bodies.* New York: Picador, 2013.

Plaidy, Jean. *Katharine of Aragon.* New York: Three Rivers Press, 2005.

———. *The Rose Without a Thorn.* New York: Putnam's Sons, 1994.

Weir, Alison. *Katherine of Aragon, The True Queen.* New York: Ballantine Books, 2016.

PERIODICALS

Borman, Tracy. "Anne of Cleves: Henry VIII's Most Successful Queen." *BBC History Magazine.* Vol. 16, No. 9, September 2015, pp. 34–38.

Hacker, Peter, and Candy Kuhl. "A Portrait of Anne of Cleves." *The Burlington Magazine.* Vol. 134, No. 1068, March 1992, pp. 172–175.

Travitsky, Betty S. "Reprinting Tudor History: The Case of Catharine of Aragon." *Renaissance Quarterly.* Vol. 50, No. 1, Spring 1997, pp. 164–172.

DVDS

Inside the Court of Henry VIII, produced by Peter Chinn and Jeremy Dear, PBS Distribution, 2015.

The Six Wives of Henry VIII, produced by Ronald Travers and Mark Shivas, BBC/Warner Home Video, 2006.

The Tudors, The Complete Series, Paramount, 2014.
Wolf Hall, PBS, 2015.

WEBSITES

Chalmers, C. R., and E. J. Chaloner. "500 Years Later: Henry VIII,
Leg Ulcers and the Course of History." *Journal of the Royal
Society of Medicine*, December 1, 2009. www.ncbi.nlm.gov/pmc
/articles/PMC2789029.

Dewhurst, Sir John. "The Alleged Miscarriages of Catharine of
Aragon and Anne Boleyn." ncbi.nlm.nih.gov/pmc/articles
/PMC1139382.

Foxe, John. *The Acts and Monuments*. 1583 Edition, Book 8,
Page 1266. johnfoxe.org/index.php?realm=text&gototype+
modern&edition=1583&pageid=1266.

Glanville, Stephen. "Canker." Tudor Blog: The Great Tale,
1485–1603, December 16, 2012. https://tudorblog.com/2012
/12/16/canker.

Hall, Edward. *Hall's Chronicle [1548/1550]*. London: Longman,
1809. https://archive.org/details/hallschroniclecoOOhalluoft.

Porter, Linda. *Lady Mary Seymour: An Unfit Traveller*. historytoday
.com/linda-porter/lady-mary-seymour-unfit-traveller.

Ridgway, Claire. theanneboleynfiles.com.

ABOUT THE AUTHORS

M. T. ANDERSON's books include the Astonishing Life of Octavian Nothing books: Volume I, *The Pox Party*, which won the National Book Award and the *Boston Globe–Horn Book* Award, and Volume II, *The Kingdom on the Waves*. Both were named Printz Honor Books and were *New York Times* bestsellers. Anderson is also the author of *Feed*, winner of the *LA Times* Book Prize. He lives in Cambridge, Massachusetts. Visit him on the Web at mt-anderson.com.

JENNIFER DONNELLY is the author of *Lost in a Book*, a *New York Times* bestseller; the Waterfire Saga, the first book of which, *Deep Blue*, won the Green Earth Book Award; *These Shallow Graves*, an ALA-YALSA Best Fiction for Young Adults book; *Revolution*, an ABA Young Adult Book of the Year; and *A Northern Light*, winner of the Carnegie Medal, the *LA Times* Book Prize, and a Printz Honor. She lives in New York's Hudson Valley. Visit Jennifer on the Web at jenniferdonnelly.com or on Facebook, Instagram, and Twitter at @jenwritesbooks.

CANDACE FLEMING is the author of *The Family Romanov*, winner of the *LA Times* Book Prize and the *Boston Globe–Horn Book* Award; *Amelia Lost*, a *New York Times* Notable Children's Book of the Year and a *Washington Post* Best Children's Book of the Year; and *The Lincolns*, also a winner of the *Boston Globe–Horn Book* Award, among many others. She lives in Oak Park, Illinois. Learn more about Candace and her books at candacefleming.com.

STEPHANIE HEMPHILL is the author of *Your Own, Sylvia*, a Printz Honor Book, which the *Horn Book Magazine* called "completely compelling: every word, every line, worth reading," and *Wicked Girls*, an *LA Times* Book Prize Finalist. She lives in Naperville, Illinois.

DEBORAH HOPKINSON is the author of many acclaimed books for children and teens, including *Titanic: Voices from the Disaster*, a Robert F. Sibert Honor Book and an ALA-YALSA Excellence in Nonfiction Finalist; *The Great Trouble*; *A Bandit's Tale*, a Charlotte Huck Award for Outstanding Fiction for Children recommended title, and many award-winning picture books. She lives near Portland, Oregon. Find her on the Web at deborahhopkinson.com.

LINDA SUE PARK's books for young readers include *A Single Shard*, winner of the Newbery Medal and an ALA-YALSA Best Book for Young Adults; *When My Name Was Keoko*, an ALA-YALSA Best Book for Young Adults; and the *New York Times* bestselling *A Long Walk to Water*, recipient of the Jane Addams Children's Book Award. She lives with her family in western New York. For more information on Linda Sue, visit lspark.com.

LISA ANN SANDELL is the author, most recently, of *A Map of the Known World*, which *Publishers Weekly* called "poetic" in a starred review; *Song of the Sparrow*; and *The Weight of the Sky,* called "lovely" and "poignant" by *Kirkus Reviews.* She is also an editor of children's books. She lives in New York City. Visit Lisa Ann on the Web at lisaannsandell.com.